PENGUIN CLASSIC   W9-BRZ-311

CLOTEL

WILLIAM WELLS BROWN was born a slave on a Kentucky plantation in 1814, the son of a slave woman, Elizabeth, and a white
man who was probably a relative of his owner. In 1833, he made
a first, unsuccessful attempt to escape slavery, bringing his mother
with him. A few months later, on January 1, 1834, Brown repeated the attempt by himself and succeeded in escaping to the
North. He was helped by Ohio Quaker Wells Brown, whose
name he adopted in gratitude. After his escape, Brown found
work as a steamboatman on Lake Erie, a position that enabled
him to help other fugitive slaves reach Canada. In 1843 he started
his career as an abolitionist lecturing agent and became known as
an eloquent orator. In 1847 he published his *Narrative of William
W. Brown, a Fugitive Slave. Written by Himself*, which went
through several American and British editions, earning Brown international success. During his prolific literary career, Brown was
a pioneer in several different genres, including travel writing, fiction, and drama. While spending a forced exile in Great Britain,
when the passage of the Fugitive Slave Law in 1850 made it dangerous for him to return to the United States, Brown published,
among other works, *Three Years in Europe; or, Places I Have
Seen and People I Have Met* (1852), which was the first known
travelogue by an African American, and *Clotel; or, The President's Daughter: A Narrative of Slave Life in the United States*
(1853), the first known novel of the African American literary
tradition. Brown's work is of great historical and artistic importance, as it introduced many of the formal and thematic concerns
that would characterize nineteenth-century African American fiction. After his return to the United States in 1854, Brown published three revised editions of *Clotel* (1860–1861, 1864, 1867)
as well as important works on African American history and culture (*St. Domingo: Its Revolution and Its Patriots*, 1855; *The
Black Man, His Antecedents, His Genius, and His Achievements*,
1863; *The Negro in the American Rebellion*, 1867; *The Rising
Son; or, The Antecedents and Advancement of the Colored Race*,
1874); autobiographical volumes (*Memoir of William Wells
Brown*, 1859; *My Southern Home: Or, The South and Its People*,

1880); and he also authored the first known plays by an African American ("Experience; or, How to Give a Northern Man a Backbone," written in 1856, and *The Escape; or, A Leap for Freedom: A Drama in Five Acts*, published in 1858). Brown died on November 6, 1884, at his home in Chelsea, Massachusetts.

M. GIULIA FABI is the author of *Passing and the Rise of the African American Novel* (2001) and a contributor to several other volumes, including *The Oxford Companion to African American Literature* (1997) and *The Cambridge Companion to the African American Novel*. She received her master's degree from the University of Wisconsin–Madison and her Ph.D. from the University of California, Berkeley. She now teaches American literature at the University of Ferrara, Italy. Professor Fabi has published an Italian-language concise history of African American literature and is the editor of a series of Italian translations of African American novels.

CHAPTER XXII
A RIDE IN A STAGE-COACH

We shall now return to Cincinnati, where we left Clotel preparing to go to Richmond in search of her daughter. Tired of the disguise in which she had escaped, she threw it off on her arrival at Cincinnati. But being assured that not a shadow of safety would attend her visit to a city in which she was well known, unless in some disguise, she again resumed men's apparel on leaving Cincinnati. This time she had more the appearance of an Italian or Spanish gentleman. In addition to the fine suit of black cloth, a splendid pair of dark false whiskers covered the sides of her face, while the curling moustache found its place upon the upper lip. From practice she had become accustomed to high-heeled boots, and could walk without creating any suspicion as regarded her sex. It was a cold evening that Clotel arrived at Wheeling, and took a seat in the coach going to Richmond. She was already in the state of Virginia, yet a long distance from the place of her destination.

A ride in a stage-coach, over an American road, is unpleasant under the most favourable circumstances. But now that it was winter, and the roads unusually bad, the journey was still more dreary. However, there were eight passengers in the coach, and I need scarcely say that such a number of genuine Americans could not be together without whiling away the time somewhat pleasantly. Besides Clotel, there was an elderly gentleman with his two daughters—one apparently under twenty years, the other a shade above. The pale, spectacled face of another slim, tall man, with a white neckerchief, pointed him out as a minister. The rough featured, dark countenance of a stout looking man, with a white hat on one side of his head, told that he was from the sunny South. There was nothing remarkable about the other two, who might pass for ordinary American gentlemen. It was on the eve of a presidential election, when every man is thought to be a politician. Clay, Van Buren, and Harrison were the men who expected the indorsement of the Baltimore Convention.[1]

"Who does this town go for?" asked the old gent. with the ladies, as the coach drove up to an inn, where groups of persons were waiting for the latest papers.

"We are divided," cried the rough voice of one of the outsiders.

"Well, who do you think will get the majority here?" continued the old gent.

"Can't tell very well; I go for 'Old Tip,'"[2] was the answer from without. This brought up the subject fairly before the passengers, and when the coach again started a general discussion commenced, in which all took a part except Clotel and the young ladies. Some were for Clay, some for Van Buren, and others for "Old Tip." The coach stopped to take in a real farmer-looking man, who no sooner entered than he was saluted with "Do you go for Clay?"

"No," was the answer.

"Do you go for Van Buren?"

"No."

"Well, then, of course you will go for Harrison."

"No."

"Why, don't you mean to work for any of them at the election?"

"No."

"Well, who will you work for?" asked one of the company.

"I work for Betsy and the children, and I have a hard job of it at that," replied the farmer, without a smile. This answer as a matter of course, set the new comer down as one upon whom the rest of the passengers could crack their jokes with the utmost impunity. "Are you an Odd Fellow?" asked one.

"No, sir, I've been married more than a month."

"I mean, do you belong to the order of Odd Fellows?"[3]

"No, no; I belong to the order of married men."

"Are you a mason?"

"No, I am a carpenter by trade."

"Are you a Son of Temperance?"

"Bother you, no; I am a son of Mr. John Gosling."

After a hearty laugh in which all joined, the subject of Temperance became the theme for discussion. In this the spectacled gent. was at home. He soon showed that he was a New Englander, and went the whole length of the "Maine Law."⁴ The minister was about having it all his own way, when the Southerner, in the white hat, took the opposite side of the question. "I don't bet a red cent on these teetotlars," said he, and at the same time looking round to see if he had the approbation of the rest of the company. "Why?" asked the minister. "Because they are a set who are afraid to spend a cent. They are a bad lot, the whole on 'em." It was evident that the white hat gent. was an uneducated man. The minister commenced in full earnest, and gave an interesting account of the progress of temperance in Connecticut, the state from which he came, proving, that a great portion of the prosperity of the state was attributable to the disuse of intoxicating drinks. Every one thought the white hat had got the worst of the argument, and that he was settled for the remainder of the night. But not he; he took fresh courage and began again. "Now," said he, "I have just been on a visit to my uncle's in Vermont, and I guess I knows a little about these here teetotlars. You see, I went up there to make a little stay of a fortnight. I got there at night, and they seemed glad to see me, but they didn't give me a bit of anything to drink. Well, thinks I to myself, the jig's up: I sha'n't get any more liquor till I get out of the state." We all sat up till twelve o'clock that night, and I heard nothing but talk about the 'Juvinal Temperence Army,' the 'Band of Hope,' the 'Rising Generation,' the 'Female Dorcas Temperance Society,' 'The None Such,' and I don't know how many other names they didn't have. As I had taken several pretty large 'Cock Tails' before I entered the state, I thought upon the whole that I would not spile for the want of liquor. The next morning, I commenced writing back to my friends, and telling them what's what. Aunt Polly said, 'Well, Johnny, I s'pose you are given 'em a pretty account of us all here.' 'Yes,' said I; I am tellin' 'em if they want anything to drink when they come up here, they had better bring it with 'em.' 'Oh,' said aunty, 'they would search their boxes; can't bring any spirits in the state.' Well, as I was saying, jist as I got my letters finished, and was going to the post office (for uncle's house was two miles from the town), aunty says, 'Johnny, I s'pose you'll try to get a little somethin' to drink in town won't you?' Says I, 'I s'pose it's no use.' 'No.' said she, 'you can't; it ain't to be had no how, for love nor money.' So jist as I was puttin' on my hat, 'Johnny,' cries out aunty, 'What,' says I. 'Now I'll tell you, I don't want you to say nothin' about it, but I keeps a little rum to rub my head with, for I am troubled with the headache; now I don't want you to mention it for the world, but I'll give you a little taste, the old man is such a teetotaller, that I should never hear the last of it, and I would not like for the boys to know it, they are members of the "Cold Water Army." '

"Aunty now brought out a black bottle and gave me a cup, and told me to help myself, which I assure you I did. I now felt ready to face the cold. As I was passing the barn I heard uncle thrashing oats, so I went to the door and spoke to him. 'Come in, John,' says he. 'No,' said I; 'I am goin' to post some letters,' for I was afraid that he would smell my breath if I went too near to him. 'Yes, yes, come in.' So I went in, and says he, 'It's now eleven o'clock; that's about the time you take your grog, I s'pose, when you are at home.' 'Yes,' said I. 'I am sorry for you, my lad; you can't get anything up here; you can't even get it at the chemist's, except as medicine, and then you must let them mix it and you take it in their presence.' 'This is indeed hard,' replied I; 'Well, it can't be helped,' continued he: 'and it ought not to be if it could. It's best for society; people's better off without drink. I recollect when your father and I, thirty years ago, used to go out on a spree and spend more than half a dollar in a night. Then here's the rising generation; there's nothing like settin' a good example. Look how healthy your cousins are—there's Benjamin, he never tasted spirits in his life. Oh, John, I would you were a teetotaller.' 'I suppose,' said I, 'I'll have to be one till I leave the state.' 'Now,' said he, 'John, I don't want you to mention it, for your aunt would go into hysterics if she thought there was a drop of intoxicating liquor about the place, and I would not have the boys to know it for anything, but I keep a little brandy to rub my joints for the rheumatics, and being it's you, I'll give you a little dust.' So the old man went to one corner of the barn, took out a brown jug and handed it to me, and I must say it was a little the best cogniac that I had tasted for many a day. Says I, 'Uncle, you are a good judge of brandy.' 'Yes,' said he, 'I learned when I was young.' So off I started for the post office. In returnin' I thought I'd jist go through the woods where the boys were chopping wood, and wait and go to the house with them when they went to dinner. I found them hard at work, but as merry as crickets. 'Well, cousin John, are you done writing?' 'Yes,' answered I. 'Have you posted them?' 'Yes.' 'Hope you didn't go to any place inquiring for grog.' 'No, I knowed it was no good to do that.' 'I suppose a cock-tail would taste good now.' 'Well, I guess it would,' says I. The three boys then joined in a hearty laugh. 'I suppose you have told 'em that we are a dry set up here?' 'Well, I aint told 'em anything else.' 'Now, cousin John,' said Edward, 'if you wont say anything, we will give you a small taste. For mercy's sake don't let father or mother know it; they are such rabid teetotallers, that they would not sleep a wink to-night if they thought there was any spirits about the place.' 'I am mum,' says I. And the boys took a jug out of a hollow stump, and gave me some first-rate peach brandy. And during the fortnight that I was in Vermont, with my teetotal relations, I was kept about as well corned as if I had been among my hot water friends in Tennessee."

This narrative, given by the white hat man, was received with unbounded applause by all except the pale gent. in spectacles, who showed, by the way in which he was running his fingers between his cravat and throat, that he did not intend to "give it up so." The white hat gent. was now the lion of the company.

"Oh, you did not get hold of the right kind of teetotallers," said the minister. "I can give you a tale worth a dozen of yours," continued he. "Look at society in the states where temperance views prevail, and you will there see real happiness. The people are taxed less, the poor houses are shut up for want of occupants, and extreme destitution is unknown. Every one who drinks at all is liable to become an habitual drunkard. Yes, I say boldly, that no man living who uses intoxicating drinks, is free from the danger of at least occasional, and if of occasional, ultimately of habitual excess. There seems to be no character, position, or circumstances that free men from the danger. *I have known* many young men of the finest promise, led by the drinking habit into vice, ruin, and early death. *I have known* many tradesmen whom it has made bankrupt. *I have known* Sunday scholars whom it has led to prison—teachers, and even superintendents, whom it has dragged down to profligacy. *I have known* ministers of high academic honours, of splendid eloquence, nay, of vast usefulness, whom it has fascinated, and hurried over the precipice of public infamy with their eyes open, and gazing with horror on their fate. *I have known* men of the strongest and clearest intellect and of vigorous resolution, whom it has made weaker than children and fools—gentlemen of refinement and taste whom it has debased into brutes—poets of high genius whom it has bound in a bondage worse than the galleys, and ultimately cut short their days. *I have known* statesmen, lawyers, and judges whom it has killed—kind husbands and fathers whom it has turned into monsters. *I have known* honest men whom it has made villains—elegant and Christian *ladies* whom it has *converted into bloated sots.*"

"But you talk too fast," replied the white hat man. "You don't give a feller a chance to say nothin'."

"I heard you," continued the minister, "and now you hear me out. It is indeed wonderful how people become lovers of strong drink. Some years since, before I became a teetotaller I kept spirits about the house, and I had a servant who was much addicted to strong drink. He used to say that he could not make my boots shine, without mixing the blacking with whiskey. So to satisfy myself that the whiskey was put in the blacking, one morning I made him bring the dish in which he kept the blacking, and poured in the whiskey myself. And now, sir, what do you think?"

"Why, I s'pose your boots shined better than before," replied the white hat.

"No," continued the minister. "He took the blacking out, and I watched him, and he drank down the whiskey, blacking, and all."

This turned the joke upon the advocate of strong drink, and he began to put his wits to work for arguments. "You are from Connecticut, are you?" asked the Southerner.

"Yes, and we are an orderly, pious, peaceable people. Our holy religion is respected, and we do more for the cause of Christ than the whole Southern States put together."

"I don't doubt it," said the white hat gent. "You sell wooden nutmegs and other spurious articles enough to do some good. You talk of your 'holy religion'; but your robes' righteousness are woven at Lowell and Manchester;[5] your paradise is high per centum on factory stocks; your palms of victory and crowns of rejoicing are triumphs over a rival party in politics, on the questions of banks and tariffs. If you could, you would turn heaven into Birmingham, make every angel a weaver, and with the eternal din of looms and spindles drown all the anthems of the morning stars. Ah! I know you Connecticut people like a book. No, no, all [old] hoss; you can't come it on me." This last speech of the rough featured man again put him in the ascendant, and the spectacled gent, once more ran his fingers between his cravat and throat.

"You live in Tennessee, I think," said the minister.

"Yes," replied the Southerner, "I used to live in Orleans, but now I claim to be a Tennessean."

"Your people of New Orleans are the most ungodly set in the United States," said the minister. Taking a New Orleans newspaper from his pocket he continued, "Just look here, there are not less than three advertisements of bull fights to take place on the Sabbath.[6] You people of the Slave States have no regard for the Sabbath, religion, morality or anything else intended to make mankind better."

Here Clotel could have borne ample testimony, had she

dared to have taken sides with the Connecticut man. Her residence in Vicksburgh had given her an opportunity of knowing something of the character of the inhabitants of the far South.

"Here is an account of a grand bull fight that took place in New Orleans a week ago last Sunday. I will read it to you." And the minister read aloud the following:

"Yesterday, pursuant to public notice, came off at Gretna, opposite the Fourth District, the long heralded fight between the famous grizzly bear, General Jackson (victor in fifty battles), and the Attakapas bull, Santa Anna.

"The fame of the coming conflict had gone forth to the four winds, and women and children, old men and boys, from all parts of the city, and from the breezy banks of Lake Pontchartrain and Borgne, brushed up their Sunday suit, and prepared to see the fun. Long before the published hour, the quiet streets of the rural Gretna were filled with crowds of anxious denizens, flocking to the arena, and before the fight commenced, such a crowd had collected as Gretna had not seen, nor will be likely to see again.

"The arena for the sports was a cage, twenty feet square, built upon the ground, and constructed of heavy timbers and iron bars. Around it were seats, circularly placed, and intended to accommodate many thousands. About four or five thousand persons assembled, covering the seats as with a cloud, and crowding down around the cage, were within reach of the bars.

"The bull selected to sustain the honour and verify the pluck of Attakapas on this trying occasion was a black animal from the Opelousas, lithe and sinewy as a four year old courser, and with eyes like burning coals. His horns bore the appearance of having been filed at the tips, and wanted that keen and slashing appearance so common with others of his kith and kin; otherwise it would have been 'all day' with Bruin at the first pass, and no mistake.

"The bear was an animal of note, and called General Jackson, from the fact of his licking up everything that came in his way, and taking 'the responsibility' on all occasions. He was a wicked looking beast, very lean and unamiable in aspect, with hair all standing the wrong way. He had fought some fifty bulls (so they said), always coming out victorious, but that neither one of the fifty had been an Attakapas bull, the bills of the performances did not say. Had he tackled Attakapas first it is likely his fifty battles would have remained unfought.

"About half past four o'clock the performances commenced.

"The bull was first seen, standing in the cage alone, with head erect, and looking a very monarch in his capacity. At an appointed signal, a cage containing the bear was placed alongside the arena, and an opening being made, bruin stalked into the battle ground—not, however, without sundry stirrings up with a ten foot pole, he being experienced in such matters, and backwards in raising a row.

"Once on the battle-field, both animals stood, like wary champions, eyeing each other, the bear cowering low, with head up-turned and fangs exposed, while Attakapas stood wondering, with his eye dilated, lashing his sides with his long and bushy tail, and pawing up the earth in very wrath.

"The bear seemed little inclined to begin the attack, and the bull, standing a moment, made steps first backward and then forward, as if measuring his antagonist, and meditating where to plant a blow. Bruin wouldn't come to the scratch no way, till one of the keepers, with an iron rod, tickled his ribs and made him move. Seeing this, Attakapas took it as a hostile demonstration, and, gathering his strength, dashed savagely at the enemy, catching him on the points of his horns, and doubling him up like a sack of bran against the bars. Bruin 'sung out' at this, 'and made a dash for his opponent's nose.'

"Missing this, the bull turned to the 'about face,' and the bear caught him by the ham, inflicting a ghastly wound. But Attakapas with a kick shook him off, and renewing the attack, went at him again, head on and with a rush. This time he was not so fortunate, for the bear caught him above the eye, burying his fangs in the tough hide, and holding him as in a vice. It was now the bull's turn to 'sing out,' and he did it, bellowing forth with a voice more hideous than that of all the bulls of Bashan.

Some minutes stood matters thus, and the cries of the bull, mingled with the hoarse growls of the bear, made hideous music, fit only for a dance of devils. Then came a pause (the bear having relinquished his hold), and for a few minutes it was doubtful whether the run was not up. But the magic wand of the keeper (the ten foot pole) again stirred up bruin, and at it they went, and with a rush.

"Bruin now tried to fasten on the bull's back, and drove his tusks in him in several places, making the red blood flow like wine from the vats of Luna. But Attakapas was pluck to the back bone, and, catching bruin on the tips of his horns, shuffled him up right merrily, making the fur fly like feathers in a gale of wind. Bruin cried 'Nuff' (in bear language), but the bull followed up his advantage, and, making one furious plunge full at the figure head of the enemy, struck a horn into his eye, burying it there, and dashing the tender organ into darkness and atoms. Blood followed the blow, and poor bruin, blinded, bleeding, and in mortal agony, turned with a howl to leave, but Attakapas caught him in the retreat, and rolled him over like a ball. Over and over again this rolling over was enacted, and finally, after more than an hour, bruin curled himself up on his back, bruised, bloody, and dead beat. The thing was up with California, and Attakapas was declared the victor amidst the applause of the multitude that made the heavens ring."[7]

"There," said he, "can you find anything against Connecticut equal to that?" The Southerner had to admit that he was beat by the Yankee. During all this time, it must not be supposed that the old gent. with the two daughters, and even the young ladies themselves, had been silent. Clotel and they had not only given their opinions as regarded the merits of the discussion, but that sly glance of the eye, which is ever given where the young of both sexes meet, had been freely at work. The American ladies are rather partial to foreigners, and Clotel had the appearance of a fine Italian. The old gentleman was now near his home, and a whisper from the eldest daughter, who was unmarried but marriageable, induced him to extend to "Mr. Johnson" an invitation to stop and spend a week with the young ladies at their family residence.[8] Clotel excused herself upon various grounds, and at last, to cut short the matter, promised that she would pay them a visit on her return. The arrival of the coach at Lynchburgh separated the young ladies from the Italian gent. and the coach again resumed its journey.

CHAPTER XXIII

TRUTH STRANGER
THAN FICTION

"Is the poor privilege to turn the key
Upon the captive, freedom? He's as far
From the enjoyment of the earth and air
Who watches o'er the chains, as they who wear."

—Byron.[1]

During certain seasons of the year, all tropical climates are subject to epidemics of a most destructive nature. The inhabitants of New Orleans look with as much certainty for the appearance of the yellow-fever, small-pox, or cholera, in the hot-season, as the Londoner does for fog in the month of November. In the summer of 1831, the people of New Orleans were visited with one of these epidemics. It appeared in a form unusually repulsive and deadly. It seized persons who were in health, without any premonition. Sometimes death was the immediate consequence. The disorder began in the brain, by an oppressive pain accompanied or followed by fever. The patient was devoured with burning thirst. The stomach, distracted by pains, in vain sought relief in efforts to disburden itself. Fiery veins streaked the eye; the face was inflamed, and dyed of a dark dull red colour; the ears from time to time rang painfully. Now mucous secretions surcharged the tongue, and took away the power of speech; now the sick one spoke, but in speaking had a foresight of death. When the violence of the disease approached the heart, the gums were blackened. The sleep, broken, troubled by convulsions, or by frightful visions, was worse than the waking hours; and when the reason sank under a delirium which had its seat in the brain, repose utterly forsook the patient's couch. The progress of the heat within was marked by yellowish spots, which spread over the surface of the body. If, then, a happy crisis came not, all hope was gone. Soon the breath infected the air with a fetid odour, the lips were glazed, despair painted itself in the eyes, and sobs, with long intervals of silence, formed the only language. From each side of the mouth spread foam, tinged with black and burnt blood. Blue streaks mingled with the yellow all over the frame. All remedies were useless. This was the Yellow Fever.[2] The disorder spread alarm and confusion throughout the city. On an average, more than 400 died daily. In the midst of disorder and confusion, death heaped victims on victims. Friend followed friend in quick succession. The sick were avoided from the fear of contagion, and for the same reason the dead were left unburied. Nearly 2000 dead bodies lay uncovered in the burial-ground, with only here and there a little lime thrown over them, to prevent the air becoming infected.

The Negro, whose home is in a hot climate, was not proof against the disease. Many plantations had to suspend their work for want of slaves to take the places of those carried off by the fever. Henry Morton and wife were among the thirteen thousand swept away by the raging disorder that year.[3] Like too many, Morton had been dealing extensively in lands and stocks; and though apparently in good circumstances was, in reality, deeply involved in debt. Althesa, although as white as most white women in a southern clime, was, as we already know, born a slave. By the laws of all the Southern States the children follow the condition of the mother. If the mother is free the children are free; if a slave, they are slaves. Morton was unacquainted with the laws of the land; and although he had married Althesa, it was a marriage which the law did not recognise; and therefore she whom he thought to be his wife was, in fact, nothing more than his slave. What would have been his feelings had he known this, and also known that his two daughters, Ellen and Jane, were his slaves? Yet such was the fact. After the disappearance of the disease with which Henry Morton had so suddenly been removed, his brother went to New Orleans to give what aid he could in settling up the affairs. James Morton, on his arrival in New Orleans, felt proud of his nieces, and promised them a home with his own family in Vermont; little dreaming that his brother had married a slave woman, and that his nieces were slaves. The girls themselves had never heard that their mother had been a slave, and therefore knew nothing of the danger hanging over their heads. An inventory of the property was made out by James Morton, and placed in the hands of the creditors; and the young ladies, with their uncle were about leaving the city to reside for a few days on the banks of Lake Pontchartrain, where they could enjoy a fresh air that the city could not afford. But just as they were about taking the train, an officer arrested the whole party; the young ladies as slaves, and the uncle upon the charge of attempting to conceal the property of his deceased brother. Morton was overwhelmed with horror at the idea of his nieces being claimed as slaves, and asked for time, that he might save them from such a fate. He even offered to mortgage his little farm in Vermont for the amount which young slave women of their ages would fetch. But the creditors pleaded that they were "an extra article," and would sell for more than common slaves; and must, therefore, be sold at auction. They were given up, but neither ate nor slept, nor separated from each other, till they were taken into the New Orleans slave market, where they were offered to the highest bidder. There they stood, trembling, blushing, and weeping; compelled to listen to the grossest language, and shrinking from the rude hands that examined the graceful proportions of their beautiful frames.

After a fierce contest between the bidders, the young ladies were sold, one for 2,300 dollars, and the other for 3,000 dollars. We need not add that had those young girls been sold for mere house servants or field hands, they would not have brought one half the sums they did. The fact that they were the grand-daughters of Thomas Jefferson, no doubt, increased their value in the market. Here were two of the softer sex, accustomed to the fondest indulgence, surrounded by all the refinements of life, and with all the timidity that such a life could produce, bartered away like cattle in Smithfield market.⁴ Ellen, the eldest, was sold to an old gentleman, who purchased her, as he said, for a housekeeper. The girl was taken to his residence, nine miles from the city. She soon, however, knew for what purpose she had been bought; and an educated and cultivated mind and taste, which made her see and understand how great was her degradation, now armed her hand with the ready means of death. The morning after her arrival, she was found in her chamber, a corpse. She had taken poison. Jane was purchased by a dashing young man, who had just come into the possession of a large fortune. The very appearance of the young Southerner pointed him out as an unprincipled profligate; and the young girl needed no one to tell her of her impending doom. The young maid of fifteen was immediately removed to his country seat, near the junction of the Mississippi river with the sea. This was a most singular spot, remote, in a dense forest spreading over the summit of a cliff that rose abruptly to a great height above the sea; but so grand in its situation, in the desolate sublimity which reigned around, in the reverential murmur of the waves that washed its base, that, though picturesque, it was a forest prison. Here the young lady saw no one, except an old Negress who acted as her servant. The smiles with which the young man met her were indignantly spurned. But she was the property of another, and could hope for justice and mercy only through him.

Jane, though only in her fifteenth year, had become strongly attached to Volney Lapuc, a young Frenchman,⁵ a student in her father's office. The poverty of the young man, and the youthful age of the girl, had caused their feelings to be kept from the young lady's parents. At the death of his master, Volney had returned to his widowed mother at Mobile, and knew nothing of the misfortune that had befallen his mistress, until he received a letter from her. But how could he ever obtain a sight of her, even if he wished, locked up as she was in her master's mansion. After several days of what her master termed "obstinacy" on her part, the young girl was placed in an upper chamber, and told that that would be her home, until she should yield to her master's wishes. There she remained more than a fortnight, and with the exception of a daily visit from her master, she saw no one but the old Negress who waited upon her. One bright moonlight evening as she was seated at the window, she perceived the figure of a man beneath her

window. At first, she thought it was her master; but the tall figure of the stranger soon convinced her that it was another. Yes,
it was Volney! He had no sooner received her letter, than he set
out for New Orleans; and finding on his arrival there, that his
mistress had been taken away, resolved to follow her. There he
was; but how could she communicate with him? She dared not
trust the old Negress with her secret, for fear that it might
reach her master. Jane wrote a hasty note and threw it out of
the window, which was eagerly picked up by the young man,
and he soon disappeared in the woods. Night passed away in
dreariness to her, and the next morning she viewed the spot beneath her window with the hope of seeing the footsteps of him
who had stood there the previous night. Evening returned, and
with it the hope of again seeing the man she loved. In this she
was not disappointed; for daylight had scarcely disappeared,
and the moon once more rising through the tops of the tall
trees, when the young man was seen in the same place as on the
previous night. He had in his hand a rope ladder. As soon as
Jane saw this, she took the sheets from her bed, tore them into
strings, tied them together, and let one end down the side of the
house. A moment more, and one end of the rope ladder was in
her hand, and she fastened it inside the room. Soon the young
maiden was seen descending, and the enthusiastic lover, with
his arms extended, waiting to receive his mistress. The planter
had been out on an hunting excursion, and returning home,
saw his victim as her lover was receiving her in his arms. At this
moment the sharp sound of a rifle was heard, and the young
man fell weltering in his blood, at the feet of his mistress. Jane
fell senseless by his side. For many days she had confused consciousness of some great agony, but knew not where she was,
or by whom surrounded. The slow recovery of her reason settled into the most intense melancholy, which gained at length
the compassion even of her cruel master. The beautiful bright
eyes, always pleading in expression, were now so heart-
piercing in their sadness, that he could not endure their gaze. In
a few days the poor girl died of a broken heart, and was buried
at night at the back of the garden by the Negroes; and no one

wept at the grave of her who had been so carefully cherished, and so tenderly beloved.

This, reader, is an unvarnished narrative of one doomed by the laws of the Southern States to be a slave. It tells not only its own story of grief, but speaks of a thousand wrongs and woes beside, which never see the light; all the more bitter and dreadful, because no help can relieve, no sympathy can mitigate, and no hope can cheer.[6]

CHAPTER XXIV
THE ARREST

"The fearful storm—it threatens lowering,
    Which God in mercy long delays;
Slaves yet may see their masters cowering,
    While whole plantations smoke and blaze!"
                                    —Carter.[1]

It was late in the evening when the coach arrived at Richmond, and Clotel once more alighted in her native city. She had intended to seek lodgings somewhere in the outskirts of the town, but the lateness of the hour compelled her to stop at one of the principal hotels for the night. She had scarcely entered the inn, when she recognised among the numerous black servants one to whom she was well known; and her only hope was, that her disguise would keep her from being discovered. The imperturbable calm and entire forgetfulness of self which induced Clotel to visit a place from which she could scarcely hope to escape, to attempt the rescue of a beloved child, demonstrate that over-willingness of woman to carry out the promptings of the finer feelings of her heart. True to woman's nature, she had risked her own liberty for another.

She remained in the hotel during the night, and the next morning, under the plea of illness, she took her breakfast alone. That day the fugitive slave paid a visit to the suburbs of the town, and once more beheld the cottage in which she had spent so many happy hours. It was winter, and the clematis and passion flower were not there; but there were the same walks she had so often pressed with her feet, and the same trees which had so often shaded her as she passed through the garden at the back of the house. Old remembrances rushed upon her memory, and caused her to shed tears freely. Clotel was now in her native town, and near her daughter; but how could she commu-

nicate with her? How could she see her? To have made herself
known, would have been a suicidal act; betrayal would have
followed, and she arrested. Three days had passed away, and
Clotel still remained in the hotel at which she had first put up;
and yet she had got no tidings of her child. Unfortunately for
Clotel, a disturbance had just broken out amongst the slave
population in the state of Virginia, and all strangers were eyed
with suspicion.

The evils consequent on slavery are not lessened by the in-
coming of one or two rays of light. If the slave only becomes
aware of his condition, and conscious of the injustice under
which he suffers, if he obtains but a faint idea of these things,
he will seize the first opportunity to possess himself of what he
conceives to belong to him.[2] The infusion of Anglo-Saxon with
African blood has created an insurrectionary feeling among the
slaves of America hitherto unknown. Aware of their blood
connection with their owners, these mulattoes labour under the
sense of their personal and social injuries; and tolerate, if they
do not encourage in themselves, low and vindictive passions.
On the other hand, the slave owners are aware of their critical
position, and are ever watchful, always fearing an outbreak
among the slaves.

True, the Free States are equally bound with the Slave States
to suppress any insurrectionary movement that may take place
among the slaves. The Northern freemen are bound by their
constitutional obligations to aid the slaveholder in keeping his
slaves in their chains. Yet there are, at the time we write, four
millions of bond slaves in the United States. The insurrection to
which we now refer was headed by a full-blooded Negro, who
had been born and brought up a slave. He had heard the twang
of the driver's whip, and saw the warm blood streaming from
the Negro's body; he had witnessed the separation of parents
and children, and was made aware, by too many proofs, that
the slave could expect no justice at the hand of the slave owner.
He went by the name of "Nat Turner."[3] He was a preacher
amongst the Negroes, and distinguished for his eloquence, respected by the whites, and loved and venerated by the Negroes.

On the discovery of the plan for the outbreak, Turner fled to the swamps, followed by those who had joined in the insurrection. Here the revolted Negroes numbered some hundreds, and for a time bade defiance to their oppressors. The Dismal Swamps cover many thousands of acres of wild land, and a dense forest, with wild animals and insects, such as are unknown in any other part of Virginia. Here runaway Negroes usually seek a hiding-place, and some have been known to reside here for years. The revolters were joined by one of these. He was a large, tall, full-blooded Negro, with a stern and savage countenance; the marks on his face showed that he was from one of the barbarous tribes in Africa, and claimed that country as his native land; his only covering was a girdle around his loins, made of skins of wild beasts which he had killed; his only token of authority among those that he led, was a pair of epaulettes made from the tail of a fox, and tied to his shoulder by a cord. Brought from the coast of Africa when only fifteen years of age to the island of Cuba, he was smuggled from thence into Virginia. He had been two years in the swamps, and considered it his future home. He had met a Negro woman who was also a runaway; and, after the fashion of his native land, had gone through the process of oiling her as the marriage ceremony. They had built a cave on a rising mound in the swamp; this was their home. His name was Picquilo.[4] His only weapon was a sword, made from the blade of a scythe, which he had stolen from a neighbouring plantation. His dress, his character, his manners, his mode of fighting, were all in keeping with the early training he had received in the land of his birth. He moved about with the activity of a cat, and neither the thickness of the trees, nor the depth of the water could stop him. He was a bold, turbulent spirit; and from revenge imbrued his hands in the blood of all the whites he could meet. Hunger, thirst, fatigue, and loss of sleep he seemed made to endure as if by peculiarity of constitution. His air was fierce, his step oblique, his look sanguinary. Such was the character of one of the leaders in the Southampton insurrection. All Negroes were arrested who were found beyond their master's threshold, and all strange whites watched with a great degree of alacrity.

Such was the position in which Clotel found affairs when she returned to Virginia in search of her Mary. Had not the slave-owners been watchful of strangers, owing to the outbreak, the fugitive could not have escaped the vigilance of the police; for advertisements, announcing her escape and offering a large reward for her arrest, had been received in the city previous to her arrival, and the officers were therefore on the look-out for the runaway slave. It was on the third day, as the quadroon was seated in her room at the inn, still in the disguise of a gentleman, that two of the city officers entered the room, and informed her that they were authorised to examine all strangers, to assure the authorities that they were not in league with the revolted Negroes. With trembling heart the fugitive handed the key of her trunk to the officers. To their surprise, they found nothing but woman's apparel in the box, which raised their curiosity, and caused a further investigation that resulted in the arrest of Clotel as a fugitive slave. She was immediately conveyed to prison, there to await the orders of her master. For many days, uncheered by the voice of kindness, alone, hopeless, desolate, she waited for the time to arrive when the chains were to be placed on her limbs, and she returned to her inhuman and unfeeling owner.

The arrest of the fugitive was announced in all the newspapers, but created little or no sensation. The inhabitants were too much engaged in putting down the revolt among the slaves; and although all the odds were against the insurgents, the whites found it no easy matter, with all their caution. Every day brought news of fresh outbreaks. Without scruple and without pity, the whites massacred all blacks found beyond their owners' plantations: the Negroes, in return, set fire to houses, and put those to death who attempted to escape from the flames. Thus carnage was added to carnage, and the blood of the whites flowed to avenge the blood of the blacks. These were the ravages of slavery. No graves were dug for the Negroes; their dead bodies became food for dogs and vultures,

and their bones, partly calcined by the sun, remained scattered
about, as if to mark the mournful fury of servitude and lust of
power. When the slaves were subdued, except a few in the
swamps, bloodhounds were put in this dismal place to hunt out
the remaining revolters. Among the captured Negroes was one
of whom we shall hereafter make mention.

CHAPTER XXV

DEATH IS FREEDOM

"I asked but freedom, and ye gave
Chains, and the freedom of the grave."
—Snelling.[1]

There are, in the district of Columbia, several slave prisons, or "Negro pens," as they are termed. These prisons are mostly occupied by persons to keep their slaves in, when collecting their gangs together for the New Orleans market. Some of them belong to the government, and one, in particular, is noted for having been the place where a number of free coloured persons have been incarcerated from time to time. In this district is situated the capital of the United States. Any free coloured persons visiting Washington, if not provided with papers asserting and proving their right to be free, may be arrested and placed in one of these dens. If they succeed in showing that they are free, they are set at liberty, provided they are able to pay the expenses of their arrest and imprisonment; if they cannot pay these expenses, they are sold out. Through this unjust and oppressive law, many persons born in the Free States have been consigned to a life of slavery on the cotton, sugar, or rice plantations of the Southern States. By order of her master, Clotel was removed from Richmond and placed in one of these prisons, to await the sailing of a vessel for New Orleans. The prison in which she was put stands midway between the capitol at Washington and the President's house. Here the fugitive saw nothing but slaves brought in and taken out, to be placed in ships and sent away to the same part of the country to which she herself would soon be compelled to go. She had seen or heard nothing of her daughter while in Richmond, and all hope of seeing her now had fled. If she was carried back to New Orleans, she could expect no mercy from her master.

At the dusk of the evening previous to the day when she was

to be sent off, as the old prison was being closed for the night, she suddenly darted past her keeper, and ran for her life. It is not a great distance from the prison to the Long Bridge,² which passes from the lower part of the city across the Potomac, to the extensive forests and woodlands of the celebrated Arlington Place, occupied by that distinguished relative and descendant of the immortal Washington, Mr. George W. Custis.³ Thither the poor fugitive directed her flight. So unexpected was her escape, that she had quite a number of rods the start before the keeper had secured the other prisoners, and rallied his assistants in pursuit. It was at an hour when, and in a part of the city where, horses could not be readily obtained for the chase; no blood-hounds were at hand to run down the flying woman; and for once it seemed as though there was to be a fair trial of speed and endurance between the slave and the slave-catchers. The keeper and his forces raised the hue and cry on her pathway close behind; but so rapid was the flight along the wide avenue, that the astonished citizens, as they poured forth from their dwellings to learn the cause of alarm, were only able to comprehend the nature of the case in time to fall in with the motley mass in pursuit, (as many a one did that night,) to raise an anxious prayer to heaven, as they refused to join in the pursuit, that the panting fugitive might escape, and the merciless soul dealer for once be disappointed of his prey. And now with the speed of an arrow—having passed the avenue—with the distance between her and her pursuers constantly increasing, this poor hunted female gained the *"Long Bridge,"* as it is called, where interruption seemed improbable, and already did her heart begin to beat high with the hope of success. She had only to pass three-fourths of a mile across the bridge, and she could bury herself in a vast forest, just at the time when the curtain of night would close around her, and protect her from the pursuit of her enemies.

But God by his Providence had otherwise determined. He had determined that an appalling tragedy should be enacted that night, within plain sight of the President's house and the capitol of the Union, which should be an evidence wherever it should be known, of the unconquerable love of liberty the heart may inherit; as well as a fresh admonition to the slave dealer, of the cruelty and enormity of his crimes. Just as the pursuers crossed the high draw for the passage of sloops, soon after entering upon the bridge, they beheld three men slowly approaching from the Virginia side. They immediately called to them to arrest the fugitive, whom they proclaimed a runaway slave. True to their Virginian instincts as she came near, they formed in line across the narrow bridge, and prepared to seize her. Seeing escape impossible in that quarter, she stopped suddenly, and turned upon her pursuers. On came the profane and ribald crew, faster than ever, already exulting in her capture, and threatening punishment for her flight. For a moment she looked wildly and anxiously around to see if there was no hope of escape. On either hand, far down below, rolled the deep foamy waters of the Potomac, and before and behind the rapidly approaching step and noisy voices of pursuers, showing how vain would be any further effort for freedom. Her resolution was taken. She clasped her *hands* convulsively, and raised *them*, as she at the same time raised her *eyes* towards heaven, and begged for that mercy and compassion *there*, which had been denied her on earth; and then, with a single bound, she vaulted over the railings of the bridge, and sunk for ever beneath the waves of the river!

Thus died Clotel, the daughter of Thomas Jefferson, a president of the United States; a man distinguished as the author of the Declaration of American Independence, and one of the first statesmen of that country.

Had Clotel escaped from oppression in any other land, in the disguise in which she fled from the Mississippi to Richmond, and reached the United States, no honour within the gift of the American people would have been too good to have been heaped upon the heroic woman. But she was a slave, and therefore out of the pale of their sympathy. They have tears to shed over Greece and Poland; they have an abundance of sympathy for "poor Ireland"; they can furnish a ship of war to convey the Hungarian refugees from a Turkish prison to the "land of the free and home of the brave."⁴ They boast that America is the "cradle of liberty"; if it is, I fear they have rocked the

child to death. The body of Clotel was picked up from the
bank of the river, where it had been washed by the strong cur-
rent, a hole dug in the sand, and there deposited, without either
inquest being held over it, or religious service being performed.
Such was the life and such the death of a woman whose virtues
and goodness of heart would have done honour to one in a
higher station of life, and who, if she had been born in any
other land but that of slavery, would have been honoured and
loved. A few days after the death of Clotel, the following poem
appeared in one of the newspapers.

> "Now, rest for the wretched! the long day is past,
> And night on yon prison descendeth at last.
> Now lock up and bolt! Ha, jailor, look there!
> Who flies like a wild bird escaped from the snare?
>   A woman, a slave—up, out in pursuit,
>   While linger some gleams of day!
>   Let thy call ring out!—now a rabble rout
>   Is at thy heels—speed away!
>
> "A bold race for freedom!—On, fugitive, on!
> Heaven help but the right, and thy freedom is won.
> How eager she drinks the free air of the plains;
> Every limb, every nerve, every fibre she strains;
>   From Columbia's glorious capitol,
>   Columbia's daughter flees
>   To the sanctuary God has given—
>   The sheltering forest trees.
>
> "Now she treads the Long Bridge—joy lighteth her eye—
> Beyond her the dense wood and darkening sky—
> Wild hopes thrill her heart as she neareth the shore:
> O, despair! there are *men* fast advancing before!
>   Shame, shame on their manhood! they hear, they heed
>   The cry, her flight to stay,
>   And like demon forms with their outstretched arms,
>   They wait to seize their prey!

"She pauses, she turns! Ah, will she flee back?
Like wolves, her pursuers howl loud on their track;
She lifteth to Heaven one look of despair—
Her anguish breaks forth in one hurried prayer—
    Hark! her jailor's yell! like a bloodhound's bay
        On the low night wind it sweeps!
    Now, death or the chain! to the stream she turns,
        And she leaps! O God, she leaps!

"The dark and the cold, yet merciful wave,
Receives to its bosom the form of the slave:
She rises—earth's scenes on her dim vision gleam,
Yet she struggleth not with the strong rushing stream:
    And low are the death-cries her woman's heart gives,
        As she floats adown the river,
    Faint and more faint grows the drowning voice,
        And her cries have ceased for ever!

"Now back, jailor, back to thy dungeons, again,
To swing the red lash and rivet the chain!
The form thou would'st fetter—returned to its God;
The universe holdeth no realm of night
    More drear than her slavery—
    More merciless fiends than here stayed her flight—
        Joy! the hunted slave is free!

"That bond-woman's corse—let Potomac's proud wave
Go bear it along *by our Washington's grave*,
And heave it high up on that hallowed strand,
To tell of the freedom he won for our land.
    A week woman's corse, by freemen chased down;
        Hurrah for our country! hurrah!
    To freedom she leaped, through drowning and death—
        Hurrah for our country! hurrah!"⁵

CHAPTER XXVI
THE ESCAPE

"No refuge is found on our unhallowed ground,
   For the wretched in Slavery's manacles bound;
   While our star-spangled banner in vain boasts to wave
   O'er the land of the free and the home of the brave!"[1]

We left Mary, the daughter of Clotel, in the capacity of a servant in her own father's house, where she had been taken by her mistress for the ostensible purpose of plunging her husband into the depths of humiliation.[2] At first the young girl was treated with great severity; but after finding that Horatio Green had lost all feeling for his child, Mrs. Green's own heart became touched for the offspring of her husband, and she became its friend. Mary had grown still more beautiful, and, like most of her sex in that country, was fast coming to maturity.

The arrest of Clotel, while trying to rescue her daughter, did not reach the ears of the latter till her mother had been removed from Richmond to Washington. The mother had passed from time to eternity before the daughter knew that she had been in the neighbourhood. Horatio Green was not in Richmond at the time of Clotel's arrest; had he been there, it is not probable but he would have made an effort to save her. She was not his slave, and therefore was beyond his power, even had he been there and inclined to aid her. The revolt amongst the slaves had been brought to an end, and most of the insurgents either put to death or sent out of the state. One, however, remained in prison. He was the slave of Horatio Green, and had been a servant in his master's dwelling. He, too, could boast that his father was an American statesman. His name was George. His mother had been employed as a servant in one of the principal hotels in Washington, where members of Congress usually put up. After George's birth his mother was sold to a slave trader, and he to an agent of Mr. Green, the father of

Horatio. George was as white as most white persons.[3] No one would suppose that any African blood coursed through his veins. His hair was straight, soft, fine, and light; his eyes blue, nose prominent, lips thin, his head well formed, forehead high and prominent; and he was often taken for a free white person by those who did know him. This made his condition still more intolerable; for one so white seldom ever receives fair treatment at the hands of his fellow slaves; and the whites usually regard such slaves as persons who, if not often flogged, and otherwise ill treated, to remind them of their condition, would soon "forget" that they were slaves, and "think themselves as good as white folks." George's opportunities were far greater than most slaves. Being in his master's house, and waiting on educated white people, he had become very familiar with the English language. He had heard his master and visitors speak of the down-trodden and oppressed Poles; he heard them talk of going to Greece to fight for Grecian liberty, and against the oppressors of that ill-fated people. George, fired with the love of freedom, and zeal for the cause of his enslaved countrymen, joined the insurgents, and with them had been defeated and captured. He was the only one remaining of these unfortunate people, and he would have been put to death with them but for a circumstance that occurred some weeks before the outbreak. The court house had, by accident, taken fire, and was fast consuming. The engines could not be made to work, and all hope of saving the building seemed at an end. In one of the upper chambers there was a small box containing some valuable deeds belonging to the city; a ladder was placed against the house, leading from the street to the window of the room in which the box stood. The wind blew strong, and swept the flames in that direction. Broad sheets of fire were blown again and again over that part of the building, and then the wind would lift the pall of smoke, which showed that the work of destruction was not yet accomplished. While the doomed building was thus exposed, and before the destroying element had made its final visit, as it did soon after, George was standing by, and hearing that much depended on the contents of the box, and seeing no one disposed to venture through the fiery element to save the treasure, mounted the ladder and made his way to the window, entered the room, and was soon seen descending with the much valued box. Three cheers rent the air as the young slave fell from the ladder when near the ground; the white men took him up in their arms, to see if he had sustained any injury. His hair was burnt, eyebrows closely singed, and his clothes smelt strongly of smoke; but the heroic young slave was unhurt. The city authorities, at their next meeting, passed a vote of thanks to George's master for the lasting benefit that the slave had rendered the public, and commended the poor boy to the special favour of his owner. When George was on trial for participating in the revolt, this "meritorious act," as they were pleased to term it, was brought up in his favour. His trial was put off from session to session, till he had been in prison more than a year. At last, however, he was convicted of high treason, and sentenced to be hanged within ten days of that time. The judge asked the slave if he had anything to say why sentence of death should not be passed on him. George stood for a moment in silence, and then said, "As I cannot speak as I should wish, I will say nothing."

"You may say what you please," said the judge. "You had a good master," continued he, "and still you were dissatisfied; you left your master and joined the Negroes who were burning our houses and killing our wives."

"As you have given me permission to speak," remarked George, "I will tell you why I joined the revolted Negroes. I have heard my master read in the Declaration of Independence 'that all men are created free and equal,' and this caused me to inquire of myself why I was a slave. I also heard him talking with some of his visitors about the war with England, and he said, all wars and fightings for freedom were just and right. If so, in what am I wrong? The grievances of which your fathers complained, and which caused the Revolutionary War, were trifling in comparison with the wrongs and sufferings of those who were engaged in the late revolt. Your fathers were never slaves, ours are; your fathers were never bought and sold like cattle, never shut out from the light of knowledge and religion, never subjected to the lash of brutal task-masters. For the crime of having a dark skin, my people suffer the pangs of hunger, the infliction of stripes, and the ignominy of brutal servitude. We are kept in heathenish darkness by laws expressly enacted to make our instruction a criminal offence. What right has one man to the bones, sinews, blood, and nerves of another? Did not one God make us all? You say your fathers fought for freedom—so did we. You tell me that I am to be put to death for violating the laws of the land. Did not the American revolutionists violate the laws when they struck for liberty? They were revolters, but their success made them patriots—we were revolters, and our failure makes us rebels. Had we succeeded, we would have been patriots too. Success makes all the difference. You make merry on the 4th of July; the thunder of cannon and ringing of bells announce it as the birthday of American independence.⁴ Yet while these cannons are roaring and bells ringing, one-sixth of the people of this land are in chains and slavery. You boast that this is the 'Land of the Free'; but a traditionary freedom will not save you. It will not do to praise your fathers and build their sepulchres. Worse for you that you have such an inheritance, if you spend it foolishly and are unable to appreciate its worth. Sad if the genius of a true humanity, beholding you with tearful eyes from the mount of vision, shall fold his wings in sorrowing pity, and repeat the strain, 'O land of Washington, how often would I have gathered thy children together, as a hen doth gather her brood under her wings, and ye would not; behold your house is left unto you desolate.' This is all I have to say; I have done."⁵

Nearly every one present was melted to tears; even the judge seemed taken by surprise at the intelligence of the young slave. But George was a slave, and an example must be made of him, and therefore he was sentenced. Being employed in the same house with Mary, the daughter of Clotel, George had become attached to her, and the young lovers fondly looked forward to the time when they should be husband and wife.

After George had been sentenced to death, Mary was still more attentive to him, and begged and obtained leave of her mistress to visit him in his cell. The poor girl paid a daily visit

to him to whom she had pledged her heart and hand. At one of
these meetings, and only four days from the time fixed for the
execution, while Mary was seated in George's cell, it occurred
to her that she might yet save him from a felon's doom. She revealed to him the secret that was then occupying her thoughts,
viz. that George should exchange clothes with her, and thus attempt his escape in disguise. But he would not for a single moment listen to the proposition. Not that he feared detection;
but he would not consent to place an innocent and affectionate
girl in a position where she might have to suffer for him. Mary
pleaded, but in vain—George was inflexible. The poor girl left
her lover with a heavy heart, regretting that her scheme had
proved unsuccessful.

Towards the close of the next day, Mary again appeared at
the prison door for admission, and was soon by the side of him
whom she so ardently loved. While there the clouds which had
overhung the city for some hours broke, and the rain fell in torrents amid the most terrific thunder and lightning. In the most
persuasive manner possible, Mary again importuned George to
avail himself of her assistance to escape from an ignominious
death. After assuring him that she, not being the person condemned, would not receive any injury, he at last consented, and
they began to exchange apparel. As George was of small
stature, and both were white, there was no difficulty in his
passing out without detection; and as she usually left the cell
weeping, with handkerchief in hand, and sometimes at her
face, he had only to adopt this mode and his escape was safe.
They had kissed each other, and Mary had told George where
he would find a small parcel of provisions which she had
placed in a secluded spot, when the prison-keeper opened the
door and said, "Come, girl, it is time for you to go." George
again embraced Mary, and passed out of the jail. It was already
dark, and the street lamps were lighted, so that our hero in his
new dress had no dread of detection. The provisions were
sought out and found, and poor George was soon on the road
towards Canada. But neither of them had once thought of a
change of dress for George when he should have escaped, and

he had walked but a short distance before he felt that a change
of his apparel would facilitate his progress. But he dared not go
amongst even his coloured associates for fear of being betrayed. However, he made the best of his way on towards
Canada, hiding in the woods during the day, and travelling by
the guidance of the North Star at night.

With the poet he could truly say,

> "Star of the North! while blazing day
> Pours round me its full tide of light,
> And hides thy pale but faithful ray,
> I, too, lie hid, and long for night."[6]

One morning, George arrived on the banks of the Ohio river
and found his journey had terminated, unless he could get some
one to take him across the river in a secret manner, for he
would not be permitted to cross in any of the ferry boats, it
being a penalty for crossing a slave, besides the value of the
slave. He concealed himself in the tall grass and weeds near the
river, to see if he could embrace an opportunity to cross. He
had been in his hiding place but a short time, when he observed
a man in a small boat, floating near the shore, evidently fishing.
His first impulse was to call out to the man and ask him to take
him over to the Ohio side, but the fear that the man was a
slaveholder, or one who might possibly arrest him, deterred
him from it. The man after rowing and floating about for some
time fastened the boat to the root of a tree, and started to a
neighbouring farmhouse.

This was George's moment, and he seized it. Running down
the bank, he unfastened the boat, jumped in, and with all the
expertness of one accustomed to a boat, rowed across the river
and landed on the Ohio side.

Being now in a Free State, he thought he might with perfect
safety travel on towards Canada. He had, however, gone but a
very few miles when he discovered two men on horseback coming behind him. He felt sure that they could not be in pursuit of
him, yet he did not wish to be seen by them, so he turned into

another road leading to a house near by. The men followed, and were but a short distance from George, when he ran up to a farmhouse, before which was standing a farmer-looking man, in a broad-brimmed hat and straight-collared coat, whom he implored to save him from the "slave-catchers." The farmer told him to go into the barn near by; he entered by the front door, the farmer following, and closing the door behind George, but remaining outside, and gave directions to his hired man as to what should be done with George. The slaveholders by this time had dismounted, and were in front of the barn demanding admittance, and charging the farmer with secreting their slave woman, for George was still in the dress of a woman. The Friend, for the farmer proved to be a member of the Society of Friends,[7] told the slave-owners that if they wished to search his barn, they must first get an officer and a search warrant. While the parties were disputing, the farmer began nailing up the front door, and the hired man served the back door in the same way. The slaveholders, finding that they could not prevail on the Friend to allow them to get the slave, determined to go in search of an officer. One was left to see that the slave did not escape from the barn, while the other went off at full speed to Mount Pleasant, the nearest town. George was not the slave of either of these men, nor were they in pursuit of him, but they had lost a woman who had been seen in that vicinity, and when they saw poor George in the disguise of a female, and attempting to elude pursuit, they felt sure they were close upon their victim. However, if they had caught him, although he was not their slave, they would have taken him back and placed him in jail, and there he would have remained until his owner arrived.

After an absence of nearly two hours, the slave-owner returned with an officer and found the Friend still driving large nails into the door. In a triumphant tone and with a corresponding gesture, he handed the search-warrant to the Friend, and said, "There, sir, now I will see if I can't get my nigger."

"Well," said the Friend, "thou hast gone to work according to law, and thou canst now go into my barn."

"Lend me your hammer that I may get the door open," said the slaveholder.

"Let me see the warrant again." And after reading it over once more, he said, "I see nothing in this paper which says I must supply thee with tools to open my door; if thou wishest to go in, thou must get a hammer elsewhere."

The sheriff said, "I will go to a neighbouring farm and borrow something which will introduce us to Miss Dinah;" and he immediately went in search of tools. In a short time the officer returned, and they commenced an assault and battery upon the barn door, which soon yielded; and in went the slaveholder and officer, and began turning up the hay and using all other means to find the lost property; but, to their astonishment, the slave was not there. After all hope of getting Dinah was gone, the slave-owner in a rage said to the Friend, "My nigger is not here."

"I did not tell thee there was any one here."

"Yes, but I saw her go in, and you shut the door behind her, and if she was not in the barn, what did you nail the door for?"

"Can't I do what I please with my own barn door? Now I will tell thee; thou need trouble thyself no more, for the person thou art after entered the front door and went out at the back door, and is a long way from here by this time. Thou and thy friend must be somewhat fatigued by this time; wont thou go in and take a little dinner with me?"

We need not say that this cool invitation of the good Quaker was not accepted by the slaveholders. George in the meantime had been taken to a friend's dwelling some miles away, where, after laying aside his female attire, and being snugly dressed up in a straight collared coat, and pantaloons to match, was again put on the right road towards Canada.

The fugitive now travelled by day, and laid by during night. After a fatiguing and dreary journey of two weeks, the fugitive arrived in Canada, and took up his abode in the little town of St. Catherine's, and obtained work on the farm of Colonel Street. Here he attended a night-school, and laboured for his employer during the day. The climate was cold, and wages small, yet he was in a land where he was free, and this the young slave prized more than all the gold that could be given to him. Besides doing his best to obtain education for himself, he imparted what he could to those of his fellow-fugitives about him, of whom there were many.

CHAPTER XXVII

THE MYSTERY

George, however, did not forget his promise to use all the means in his power to get Mary out of slavery. He, therefore, laboured with all his might to obtain money with which to employ some one to go back to Virginia for Mary. After nearly six months' labour at St. Catherine's, he employed an English missionary to go and see if the girl could be purchased, and at what price. The missionary went accordingly, but returned with the sad intelligence that, on account of Mary's aiding George to escape, the court had compelled Mr. Green to sell her out of the state, and she had been sold to a Negro trader, and taken to the New Orleans market. As all hope of getting the girl was now gone, George resolved to quit the American continent for ever. He immediately took passage in a vessel laden with timber, bound for Liverpool, and in five weeks from that time he was standing on the quay of the great English seaport. With little or no education, he found many difficulties in the way of getting a respectable living. However he obtained a situation as porter in a large house in Manchester, where he worked during the day, and took private lessons at night. In this way he laboured for three years, and was then raised to the situation of clerk. George was so white as easily to pass for a white man, and being somewhat ashamed of his African descent, he never once mentioned the fact of his having been a slave.[1] He soon became a partner in the firm that employed him, and was now on the road to wealth.

In the year 1842, just ten years[2] after George Green (for he adopted his master's name)[3] arrived in England, he visited France, and spent some days at Dunkirk.[4] It was towards sunset, on a warm day in the month of October, that Mr. Green, after strolling some distance from the Hotel de Leon, entered a burial ground, and wandered long alone among the silent dead, gazing upon the many green graves and marble tombstones of those who once moved on the theatre of busy life, and whose sounds of gaiety once fell upon the ear of man. All nature around was hushed in silence, and seemed to partake of the general melancholy which hung over the quiet resting-place of departed mortals. After tracing the varied inscriptions which told the characters or conditions of the departed, and viewing the mounds beneath which the dust of mortality slumbered, he had now reached a secluded spot, near to where an aged weeping willow bowed its thick foliage to the ground, as though anxious to hide from the scrutinising gaze of curiosity the grave beneath it. Mr. Green seated himself upon a marble tomb, and began to read Roscoe's *Leo X.*,[5] a copy of which he had under his arm. It was then about twilight, and he had scarcely gone through half a page, when he observed a lady in black, leading a boy, some five years old, up one of the paths; and as the lady's black veil was over her face, he felt somewhat at liberty to eye her more closely. While looking at her, the lady gave a scream, and appeared to be in a fainting position, when Mr. Green sprang from his seat in time to save her from falling to the ground. At this moment, an elderly gentleman was seen approaching with a rapid step, who, from his appearance, was evidently the lady's father, or one intimately connected with her. He came up, and, in a confused manner, asked what was the matter. Mr. Green explained as well as he could. After taking up the smelling bottle which had fallen from her hand, and holding it a short time to her face, she soon began to revive. During all this time the lady's veil had so covered her face, that Mr. Green had not seen it. When she had so far recovered as to be able to raise her head, she again screamed, and fell back into the arms of the old man. It now appeared quite certain, that either the countenance of George Green, or some other object, was the cause of these fits of fainting; and the old gentleman, thinking it was the former, in rather a petulant tone said, "I will thank you, sir, if you will leave us alone." The child whom the lady was leading, had now set up a squall; and amid the death-like appearance of the lady, the harsh look of the old man, and the cries of the boy, Mr. Green left the grounds, and returned to his hotel.

Whilst seated by the window, and looking out upon the crowded street, with every now and then the strange scene in the grave-yard vividly before him, Mr. Green thought of the book he had been reading, and, remembering that he had left it on the tomb, where he had suddenly dropped it when called to the assistance of the lady, he immediately determined to return in search of it. After a walk of some twenty minutes, he was again over the spot where he had been an hour before, and from which he had been so unceremoniously expelled by the old man. He looked in vain for the book; it was nowhere to be found: nothing save the bouquet which the lady had dropped, and which lay half-buried in the grass from having been trodden upon, indicated that any one had been there that evening. Mr. Green took up the bunch of flowers, and again returned to the hotel.

After passing a sleepless night, and hearing the clock strike six, he dropped into a sweet sleep, from which he did not awaken until roused by the rap of a servant, who, entering his room, handed him a note which ran as follows:—"Sir,—I owe you an apology for the inconvenience to which you were subjected last evening, and if you will honour us with your presence to dinner to-day at four o'clock, I shall be most happy to give you due satisfaction. My servant will be in waiting for you at half-past three. I am, sir, your obedient servant, J. Devenant. October 23. To George Green, Esq."

The servant who handed this note to Mr. Green, informed him that the bearer was waiting for a reply. He immediately resolved to accept the invitation, and replied accordingly. Who this person was, and how his name and the hotel where he was stopping had been found out, was indeed a mystery. However, he waited impatiently for the hour when he was to see this new acquaintance, and get the mysterious meeting in the grave-yard solved.

CHAPTER XXVIII
THE HAPPY MEETING

"Man's love is of man's life, a thing apart;
'Tis woman's whole existence."
—*Byron.*[1]

The clock on a neighbouring church had scarcely ceased striking three, when the servant announced that a carriage had called for Mr. Green. In less than half an hour he was seated in a most sumptuous barouche, drawn by two beautiful iron greys, and rolling along over a splendid gravel road completely shaded by large trees, which appeared to have been the accumulating growth of many centuries. The carriage soon stopped in front of a low villa, and this too was embedded in magnificent trees covered with moss. Mr. Green alighted and was shown into a superb drawing room, the walls of which were hung with fine specimens from the hands of the great Italian painters, and one by a German artist representing a beautiful monkish legend connected with "The Holy Catherine," an illustrious lady of Alexandria. The furniture had an antique and dignified appearance. High backed chairs stood around the room; a venerable mirror stood on the mantle shelf; rich curtains of crimson damask hung in folds at either side of the large windows; and a rich Turkey carpet covered the floor. In the centre stood a table covered with books, in the midst of which was an old-fashioned vase filled with fresh flowers, whose fragrance was exceedingly pleasant. A faint light, together with the quietness of the hour, gave beauty beyond description to the whole scene.

Mr. Green had scarcely seated himself upon the sofa, when the elderly gentleman whom he had met the previous evening made his appearance, followed by the little boy, and introduced himself as Mr. Devenant. A moment more, and a lady—a beautiful brunette—dressed in black, with long curls of a chestnut colour hanging down her cheeks, entered the room. Her eyes were of a dark hazel, and her whole appearance indicated that she was a native of a southern clime. The door at which she entered was opposite to where the two gentlemen were seated. They immediately rose; and Mr. Devenant was in the act of introducing her to Mr. Green, when he observed that the latter had sunk back upon the sofa, and the last word that he remembered to have heard was, "It is her." After this, all was dark and dreamy: how long he remained in this condition it was for another to tell. When he awoke, he found himself stretched upon the sofa, with his boots off, his neckerchief removed, shirt collar unbuttoned, and his head resting upon a pillow. By his side sat the old man, with the smelling bottle in the one hand, and a glass of water in the other, and the little boy standing at the foot of the sofa. As soon as Mr. Green had so far recovered as to be able to speak, he said, "Where am I, and what does this mean?"

"Wait a while," replied the old man, "and I will tell you all."

After a lapse of some ten minutes he rose from the sofa, adjusted his apparel, and said, "I am now ready to hear anything you have to say."

"You were born in America?" said the old man.

"Yes," he replied.

"And you were acquainted with a girl named Mary?" continued the old man.

"Yes, and I loved her as I can love none other."

"The lady whom you met so mysteriously last evening is Mary," replied Mr. Devenant.

George Green was silent, but the fountains of mingled grief and joy stole out from beneath his eyelashes, and glistened like pearls upon his pale and marble-like cheeks. At this juncture the lady again entered the room. Mr. Green sprang from the sofa, and they fell into each other's arms, to the surprise of the old man and little George, and to the amusement of the servants who had crept up one by one, and were hid behind the doors, or loitering in the hall. When they had given vent to their feelings, they resumed their seats, and each in turn related the adventures through which they had passed.

"How did you find out my name and address?" asked Mr. Green.

"After you had left us in the grave-yard, our little George said, 'O, mamma, if there aint a book!' and picked it up and brought it to us. Papa opened it, and said, 'The gentleman's name is written in it, and here is a card of the Hotel de Leon, where I suppose he is stopping.' Papa wished to leave the book, and said it was all a fancy of mine that I had ever seen you before, but I was perfectly convinced that you were my own George Green. Are you married?"

"No, I am not."

"Then, thank God!" exclaimed Mrs. Devenant.

"And are you single now?" inquired Mr. Green.

"Yes," she replied.

"This is indeed the Lord's doings," said Mr. Green, at the same time bursting into a flood of tears. Mr. Devenant was past the age when men should think upon matrimonial subjects, yet the scene brought vividly before his eyes the days when he was a young man, and had a wife living. After a short interview, the old man called their attention to the dinner, which was then waiting. We need scarcely add, that Mr. Green and Mrs. Devenant did very little towards diminishing the dinner that day.

After dinner the lovers (for such we have to call them) gave their experience from the time that George left the jail dressed in Mary's clothes. Up to that time Mr. Green's was substantially as we have related it. Mrs. Devenant's was as follows:—
"The night after you left the prison," said she, "I did not shut my eyes in sleep. The next morning, about eight o'clock, Peter the gardener came to the jail to see if I had been there the night before, and was informed that I had, and that I had left a little after dark. About an hour after, Mr. Green came himself, and I need not say that he was much surprised on finding me there, dressed in your clothes. This was the first tidings they had of your escape."

"What did Mr. Green say when he found that I had fled?"

"Oh!" continued Mrs. Devenant, "he said to me when no one was near, I hope George will get off, but I fear you will have to suffer in his stead. I told him that if it must be so I was willing to die if you could live." At this moment George Green burst into tears, threw his arms around her neck, and exclaimed, "I am glad I have waited so long, with the hope of meeting you again."

Mrs. Devenant again resumed her story:—"I was kept in jail three days, during which time I was visited by the magistrates, and two of the judges. On the third day I was taken out, and master told me that I was liberated, upon condition that I should be immediately sent out of the state.² There happened to be just at the time in the neighbourhood a Negro-trader, and he purchased me, and I was taken to New Orleans. On the steamboat we were kept in a close room, where slaves are usually confined, so that I saw nothing of the passengers on board, or the towns we passed. We arrived at New Orleans, and were all put into the slave-market for sale. I was examined by many persons, but none seemed willing to purchase me, as all thought me too white, and said I would run away and pass as a free white woman. On the second day, while in the slave-market, and while planters and others were examining slaves and making their purchases, I observed a tall young man, with long black hair, eyeing me very closely, and then talking to the trader. I felt sure that my time had now come, but the day closed without my being sold. I did not regret this, for I had heard that foreigners made the worst of masters, and I felt confident that the man who eyed me so closely was not an American.

"The next day was the Sabbath. The bells called the people to the different places of worship. Methodists sang, and Baptists immersed, and Presbyterians sprinkled, and Episcopalians read their prayers, while the ministers of the various sects preached that Christ died for all; yet there were some twenty-five or thirty of us poor creatures confined in the 'Negro Pen,' awaiting the close of the holy Sabbath, and the dawn of another day, to be again taken into the market, there to be examined like so many beasts of burden. I need not tell you with what anxiety we waited for the advent of another day. On Monday we were again brought out and placed in rows to be inspected; and, fortunately for me, I was sold before we had been on the stand an hour. I was purchased by a gentleman residing in the city, for a waiting-maid for his wife, who was just on the eve of starting for Mobile, to pay a visit to a near relation. I was then dressed to suit the situation of a maid-servant; and upon the whole, I thought that, in my new dress, I looked as much the lady as my mistress.

"On the passage to Mobile,³ who should I see among the passengers but the tall, long-haired man that had eyed me so closely in the slave-market a few days before. His eyes were again on me, and he appeared anxious to speak to me, and I as reluctant to be spoken to. The first evening after leaving New Orleans, soon after twilight had let her curtain down, and pinned it with a star, and while I was seated on the deck of the boat near the ladies' cabin, looking upon the rippled waves, and the reflection of the moon upon the sea, all at once I saw the tall young man standing by my side. I immediately rose from my seat, and was in the act of returning to the cabin, when he in a broken accent said, 'Stop a moment; I wish to have a word with you. I am your friend.' I stopped and looked him full in the face, and he said, 'I saw you some days since in the slave-market, and I intended to have purchased you to save you from the condition of a slave. I called on Monday, but you had been sold and had left the market. I inquired and learned who the purchaser was, and that you had to go to Mobile, so I resolved to follow you. If you are willing I will try and buy you from your present owner, and you shall be free.' Although this was said in an honest and off-hand manner, I could not believe the man to be sincere in what he said. 'Why should you wish to set *me* free?' I asked. 'I had an only sister,' he replied, 'who died three years ago in France, and you are so much like her that had I not known of her death, I would most certainly have taken you for her.' 'However much I may resemble your sister, you are aware that I am not her, and why take so much interest in one whom you never saw before?' 'The love,' said he, 'which I had for my sister is transferred to you.' I had all along suspected that the man was a knave, and this profession of love confirmed me in my former belief, and I turned away and left him.

"The next day, while standing in the cabin and looking

through the window, the French gentleman (for such he was) came to the window while walking on the guards, and again commenced as on the previous evening. He took from his pocket a bit of paper and put it into my hand, at the same time saying, 'Take this, it may some day be of service to you; remember it is from a friend,' and left me instantly. I unfolded the paper, and found it to be a 100 dollars bank note, on the United States Branch Bank, at Philadelphia. My first impulse was to give it to my mistress, but, upon a second thought, I resolved to seek an opportunity, and to return the hundred dollars to the stranger.

"Therefore I looked for him, but in vain; and had almost given up the idea of seeing him again, when he passed me on the guards of the boat and walked towards the stem of the vessel. It being now dark, I approached him and offered the money to him. He declined, saying at the same time, 'I gave it to you—keep it.' 'I do not want it,' I said. 'Now,' said he, 'you had better give your consent for me to purchase you, and you shall go with me to France.' 'But you cannot buy me now,' I replied, 'for my master is in New Orleans, and he purchased me not to sell, but to retain in his own family.' 'Would you rather remain with your present mistress than be free?' 'No,' said I. 'Then fly with me tonight; we shall be in Mobile in two hours from this, and when the passengers are going on shore, you can take my arm, and you can escape unobserved. The trader who brought you to New Orleans exhibited to me a certificate of your good character, and one from the minister of the church to which you were attached in Virginia; and upon the faith of these assurances, and the love I bear you, I promise before high heaven that I will marry you as soon as it can be done.' This solemn promise, coupled with what had already transpired, gave me confidence in the man; and rash as the act may seem, I determined in an instant to go with him. My mistress had been put under the charge of the captain; and as it would be past ten o'clock when the steamer would land, she accepted an invitation of the captain to remain on board with several other ladies till morning. I dressed myself in my best clothes, and put a veil over my face, and was ready on the landing of the boat. Surrounded by a number of passengers, we descended the stage leading to the wharf, and were soon lost in the crowd that thronged the quay. As we went on shore we encountered several persons announcing the names of hotels, the starting of boats for the interior, and vessels bound for Europe. Among these was the ship Utica, Captain Pell, bound for Havre.⁴ 'Now,' said Mr. Devenant, 'this is our chance.' The ship was to sail at twelve o'clock that night, at high tide; and following the men who were seeking passengers, we went immediately on board. Devenant told the captain of the ship that I was his sister, and for such we passed during the voyage. At the hour of twelve the Utica set sail, and we were soon out at sea.

"The morning after we left Mobile, Devenant met me as I came from my state-room, and embraced me for the first time. I loved him, but it was only that affection which we have for one who has done us a lasting favour: it was the love of gratitude rather than that of the heart. We were five weeks on the sea, and yet the passage did not seem long, for Devenant was so kind. On our arrival at Havre we were married and came to Dunkirk, and I have resided here ever since."

At the close of this narrative, the clock struck ten, when the old man, who was accustomed to retire at an early hour, rose to take leave, saying at the same time, "I hope you will remain with us to-night." Mr. Green would fain have excused himself, on the ground that they would expect him and wait at the hotel, but a look from the lady told him to accept the invitation. The old man was the father of Mrs. Devenant's deceased husband, as you will no doubt long since have supposed. A fortnight from the day on which they met in the grave-yard, Mr. Green and Mrs. Devenant were joined in holy wedlock; so that George and Mary, who had loved each other so ardently in their younger days, were now husband and wife.

A celebrated writer has justly said of woman, "A woman's whole life is a history of the affections. The heart is her world; it is there her ambition strives for empire; it is there her avarice seeks for hidden treasures. She sends forth her sympathies on adventure; she embarks her whole soul in the traffic of affection: and, if shipwrecked, her case is hopeless, for it is a bankruptcy of the heart."[5]

Mary had every reason to believe that she would never see George again; and although she confesses that the love she bore him was never transferred to her first husband, we can scarcely find fault with her for marrying Mr. Devenant. But the adherence of George Green to the resolution never to marry, unless to his Mary, is, indeed, a rare instance of the fidelity of man in the matter of love. We can but blush for our country's shame when we recall to mind the fact, that while George and Mary Green, and numbers of other fugitives from American slavery, can receive protection from any of the governments of Europe, they cannot return to their native land without becoming slaves.[6]

CHAPTER XXIX
CONCLUSION

My narrative has now come to a close. I [1] may be asked, and no doubt shall, Are the various incidents and scenes related founded in truth? I answer, Yes. I have personally participated in many of those scenes. Some of the narratives I have derived from other sources; many from the lips of those who, like myself, have run away from the land of bondage. Having been for nearly nine years employed on Lake Erie, I had many opportunities for helping the escape of fugitives, who, in return for the assistance they received, made me the depositary of their sufferings and wrongs. Of their relations I have made free use. To Mrs. Child, of New York, I am indebted for part of a short story. American Abolitionist journals are another source from whence some of the characters appearing in my narrative are taken. All these combined have made up my story. [2] Having thus acknowledged my resources, I invite the attention of my readers to the following statement, from which I leave them to draw their own conclusions:—"It is estimated that in the United States, members of the Methodist church own 219,363 slaves; members of the Baptist church own 226,000 slaves; members of the Episcopalian church own 88,000 slaves; members of the Presbyterian church own 77,000 slaves; members of all other churches own 50,000 slaves; in all, 660,563 slaves owned by members of the Christian church in this pious democratic republic!" [3]

May these facts be pondered over by British Christians, and at the next anniversaries of the various religious denominations in London may their influence be seen and felt! The religious bodies of American Christians will send their delegates to these meetings. Let British feeling be publicly manifested. Let British sympathy express itself in tender sorrow for the condition of my unhappy race. Let it be understood, unequivocally understood, that no fellowship can be held with slaveholders professing the same common Christianity as yourselves. And until this stain from America's otherwise fair escutcheon be wiped away, let no Christian association be maintained with those who traffic in the blood and bones of those whom God has made of one flesh as yourselves. Finally, let the voice of the whole British nation be heard across the Atlantic, and throughout the length and breadth of the land of the Pilgrim Fathers, beseeching their descendants, as they value *the* common salvation, which knows no distinction between the bond and the free, to proclaim the Year of Jubilee.[4] Then shall the "earth indeed yield her increase, and God, even our own God, shall bless us; and all the ends of the earth shall fear Him."[5]

Appendix A

FROM *MIRALDA; OR, THE BEAUTIFUL QUADROON. A ROMANCE OF AMERICAN SLAVERY, FOUNDED ON FACT.*
(1860–1861)

CHAPTER XXXIII
THE HAPPY DAY[1]

> "Well hast thou played the lover's part,
> And all thy threads, with magic art,
> Have wound themselves about my heart."
> —Cowper[2]

It was a bright day in the latter part of October that Jerome and Miralda set out for the church, where the marriage ceremony was to be performed.[3] The clear, bracing air added buoyancy to every movement, and the sun poured its brilliant rays through the deeply-stained windows as the happy couple entered the sanctuary, followed by old Mr. Devenant, whose form, bowed down with age, attracted almost as much attention from the assembly as did the couple more particularly interested.

As the ceremonies were finished and the priest pronounced

the benediction on the newly married pair, Miralda whispered
in the ear of Jerome:

"No power in death shall tear our names apart,
    As none in life could rend thee from my heart."

A smile beamed on every face as the wedding party left the
church and entered their carriage. What a happy day, after ten
years' separation, when both hearts have been blighted for a
time, they are brought together by the hand of a beneficent and
kind Providence, and united in holy wedlock.

Everything being arranged for a wedding tour extending up
the Rhine,[4] the party set out the same day for Antwerp.[5] There
are many rivers of greater length and width than the Rhine. Our
Mississippi would swallow up half-a-dozen Rhines. The Hudson is grander, the Tiber, the Po and the Mincio more classic;
the Thames and Seine bear upon their waters greater amounts
of wealth and commerce, the Nile and the Euphrates have a
greater antiquity; but for a combination of interesting historical
incidents and natural scenery, the Rhine surpasses them all.[6]
Nature has so ordained it that those who travel in the valley of
the Rhine shall see the river, for there never will be a railroad
upon its banks. So mountainous is the land that it would have
to be one series of tunnels. Every three or four miles from the
time you enter this glorious river, hills, dales, castles, and crags
present themselves as the steamer glides onward.

It was a beautiful night, the bright moonbeams dancing on
the gleaning waters, the glistening stars seeming suspended in
the air like globes of liquid light, with fresh, balmy breezes
bearing sweet odors from the shores, when Jerome and Miralda
ascended the river in the steamer. During the evening, Jerome
read, at his wife's request, that portion of the third canto of
"Childe Harold" which describes in such a graphic manner the
stream they were then ascending:[7]

"The castled crag of Drachenfels
    Frowns o'er the wide and winding Rhine,
    Whose breast of waters proudly swells

Between the banks which bear the vine,
And hills all rich with blossom'd trees,
And fields which promise corn and wine,
And scattered cities crowning these,
Whose far white walls along them shine,
Have strewed a scene which I should see
With double joy wert thou with me.

"And peasant girls with deep blue eyes,
And hands which offer early flowers,
Walk smiling o'er this paradise;
Alone the frequent feudal towers
Through green leaves lift their walls of gray,
And many a rock which steeply lowers,
And noble arch in proud decay,
Look o'er this vale of vintage bowers,
But one thing wants these banks of Rhine—
Thy gentle hand to clasp in mine.

"The river nobly foams and flows,
The charm of this enchanted ground,
And all its thousand turns disclose
Some fresher beauties varying round;
The haughtiest breast its wish might bound
Through life to dwell delighted here;
Nor could on earth a spot be found
To nature and to me so dear,
Could thy dear eyes, in following mine,
Still sweeten more these banks of Rhine."

Their first resting place for any length of time was at Coblentz,[8] at the month of the "Blue Moselle," the most interesting place on the river. From Coblentz they went to Brussels,[9] where they had the greatest attention paid them. Besides being provided with letters of introduction, Jerome's complexion secured for him more deference than is usually awarded to travelers. In his native country his dark complexion would have gained for him mistreatment in a majority of the States.[10] Here, however, the royal palaces, parks, gardens, and saloons were thrown open to them by order of the King. Having letters of introduction to M. Deceptiax, the great lace manufacturer, that gentleman received them with distinguished honors and gave them a splendid *soiree* at which the *elite* of the city were assembled. The sumptuously furnished mansion was lavishly decorated for the occasion, and every preparation made that could add to the novelty or interest of the event.

Jerome, with his beautiful bride, next visited Cologne,[11] the largest and wealthiest city on the banks of the Rhine. The cathedral of Cologne is the most splendid structure of the kind in Europe, and Jerome and Miralda viewed with interest the beautiful arches and columns of this stupendous building, which strikes with awe the beholder, as he gazes at its unequalled splendor, surrounded as it is by villas, cottages, and palace-like mansions, with the enchanting Rhine winding through the vine-covered hills.

After strolling over miles and miles of classic ground, and visiting castles whose legends and traditions have given them an enduring fame, our delighted travelers started for Geneva,[12] bidding the picturesque banks of the Rhine a regretful farewell. Being much interested in literature, and aware that Geneva was noted for having been the city of refuge to the victims of religious and political persecution, Jerome arranged to stay here for some days. He was provided with a letter of introduction to M. de Stee, who had been a fellow soldier of Mr. Devenant in the East India wars, and they were invited to make his house their home during their sojourn. On the side of a noble mountain whose base is kissed by the waves of Lake Geneva, and whose slopes are decked with verdure to the utmost peak of its rocky crown, is situated the delightful country residence of this wealthy retired French officer. A winding road, with frequent climbs and brakes, leads from the valley to this enchanting spot, the air and scenery of which cannot be surpassed in the world.

The first Sunday of their stay at Geneva Jerome and Miralda attended worship at the cathedral, a building which has the name of Calvin [13] so intimately associated with it that it is regarded by all strangers as one of the first places to be seen. Here the great preacher for many years exercised almost unlimited sway over the people, and here he promulgated those doctrines which are still the rule of faith to the strictest sect of the religious world. Jerome felt the more freedom in visiting these places from the fact that the hatred against his color which had pursued him wherever he went in America was unknown and unfelt here, whether in hotels on the banks of the Rhine or in the streets of the towns through which he passed. In *fêtes* that were given in his honour he was treated according to his intellectual worth, and not with reference to the complexion of his face. It was a pleasure to move about when he could do so without being insulted, as would have been the case had he been a pleasure-seeking traveler in democratic, Christian America. What a shame and what a comment upon our institutions and the civilization of the nineteenth century![14]

CHAPTER XXXIV

MIRALDA MEETS HER FATHER

"Hath thee ought for me to fear,
When death is on thy brow?
The world! what means it?
I will not leave thee now."

—Mrs. Hemans.[1]

The clouds that had skirted the sky during the day broke at last, and the rain fell in torrents, as Jerome and Miralda retired for the night in the little town of Ferney,[2] on the borders of Lake Lemon.[3] The peals of thunder and flashes of vivid lightning, which seemed to leap from mountain to mountain and from crag to crag, reverberating among the surrounding hills, foretold a heavy storm.

"I would we were back at Geneva," said Miralda, as she heard groans issuing from an adjoining room. The sounds, at first faint, grew louder and louder, plainly indicating that some person was suffering extreme pain.

"I did not like this hotel much when we came in," said Jerome," re-lighting the lamp, which had been accidentally extinguished.

"Nor I," returned Miralda.

The shrieks increased, and an occasional "She's dead!" "I killed her!" "No, she is not dead!" and such like expressions, would be heard from the person, who seemed to be deranged.

The thunder grew louder and the flashes of lightning more vivid, while the noise from the sick room seemed to increase. As Jerome opened the door, to learn, if possible, the cause of the cries and groans, he could distinguish the words—"She's dead—yes, she's dead; but I did not kill her. She was my child— my own daughter, I loved her, and yet I did not protect her."

"Whoever he is," said Jerome, "he's crack-brained; some robber, probably, from the mountains."

The storm continued to rage, and the loud peals of thunder and sharp flashes of lightning, together with the shrieks and moans of the maniac in the adjoining room, made the night a fearful one. The long hours wore slowly away, but neither Jerome nor his wife could sleep, and they arose at an early hour in the morning, ordered breakfast, and resolved to return to Geneva.

"I am sorry, sir, that you were so much disturbed by the sick man last night," said the landlord, as he handed Jerome his bill. "I should be glad if he would get able to go away or die, for he's a deal of trouble to me. Several persons have left my house on his account."

"Where is he from?" inquired Jerome.

"He's from the United States, and has been here a week to-day, and has been crazy ever since."

"Has he no friends with him?" asked the guest.

"No, he is alone," was the reply.

Jerome related to his wife what he had learned from the landlord respecting the sick man, and the intelligence impressed her so strongly that she requested him to make further inquiries concerning the stranger. He therefore consulted the book in which guests usually register their names, and to his great surprise found that the American's name was Henry Linwood, and that he was from Richmond, Va.⁴

It was with feelings of trepidation that Miralda heard these particulars from the lips of her husband. "We must see this poor man, whoever he is," said she, as Jerome finished the sentence.

The landlord was glad to hear that his guests felt some interest in the sick man, and promised that the invalid's room should be got ready for their reception.

The clock in the hall was just striking ten as Jerome passed through and entered the sick man's chamber. Stretched upon a mattress, with both hands tightly bound to the bedstead, the friendless stranger was indeed a pitiful sight. His dark, dishevelled hair, prematurely grey—his long, unshaven beard, and the wildness of the eyes which glanced upon them as they opened the door and entered, caused the faint hope which had so suddenly risen in Miralda's heart to sink, and she felt that this man could claim no kindred with her. Certainly he bore no resemblance to the man whom she had called her father, and who had fondly dandled her on his knee in those happy days of childhood.

"Help!" cried the poor man, as Jerome and his wife walked into the room. His eyes glared, and shriek after shriek broke forth from his parched and fevered lips.

"No, I did not kill my daughter—I did not!—she is not dead! Yes, she is dead, but I did not kill her, poor girl! Look! that is her! No, it cannot be! She cannot come here—it cannot be my poor Miralda!"

At the sound of her own name coming from the maniac's lips, Miralda gasped for breath, and her husband saw that she had grown deadly pale. It seemed evident to him that the man was either guilty of some terrible act, or imagined himself to be. His eyeballs rolled in their sockets, and his features showed that he was undergoing "the tortures of that inward hell,"⁵ which seemed to set his whole brain on fire.

After recovering her self-possession and strength, Miralda approached the bedside, and laid her soft hand upon the stranger's hot and fevered brow. One long loud shriek rang out on the air, and a piercing cry, "It is her!—yes, it is her! I see, I see. Ah! no—it is not my daughter!—she would not come to me if she could," broke forth from him.

"I am your daughter," said Miralda, as she pressed her handkerchief to her face, and sobbed aloud.

Like balls of fire the poor man's eyes rolled and glared upon the company, while large drops of perspiration ran down his pale and emaciated face. Strange as the scene appeared, all present saw that it was indeed a meeting between a father and his long lost daughter. Jerome now ordered all present to leave the room except the nurse, and every effort was at once made to quiet the sufferer. When a calm, a joyous smile would illuminate the sick man's face, and a strange light beam in his eyes, as he seemed to realize that she who stood before him was indeed his child.

For two long days and nights did Miralda watch at the bedside of her father before he could speak to her intelligently. Sometimes, in his insane fits, he would rave in the most frightful manner, and then, in a few moments, would be as easily governed as a child. At last, however after a long and apparently refreshing sleep, he awoke suddenly to a full consciousness that it was indeed his daughter who was watching so patiently by his side.

The presence of his long absent child had a soothing effect upon Mr. Lindwood and he now recovered rapidly from the sad and almost hopeless condition in which she had found him. When able to converse without danger of a relapse, he told Miralda of his fruitless efforts to obtain a clue to her whereabouts after old Mrs. Miller had sold her to the slave-trader.[6] In answer to his daughter's inquiries about his family affairs up to the time that he left America, he said:

"I blamed my wife for your being sold and sent away, for I thought she and her mother were acting in collusion; but I afterwards found that I had blamed her wrongfully. Poor woman! she knew that I loved your mother, and feeling herself forsaken, she grew melancholy, and died in a decline three years ago."

Here both father and daughter wept at the thought of other days. When they had somewhat recovered their composure Mr. Linwood went on again:

"Old Mrs. Miller," said he, "after the death of Gertrude, aware that she had contributed much towards her unhappiness, took to the free use of intoxicating drinks, and became the most brutal creature that ever lived. She whipped her slaves without the slightest provocation, and seemed to take delight in inventing new tortures with which to punish them. One night last winter, after having flogged one of her slaves nearly to death, she returned to her room, and by some means the bedding took fire, and the house was in flames before anyone was awakened. There was no one in the building at the time but the old woman and the slaves, and although the latter might have saved their mistress, they made no attempts to do so. Thus, after a frightful career of many years, this hard-hearted woman died a most miserable death, unlamented by a single person."

Miralda wiped the tears from her eyes as her father finished this story, for although Mrs. Miller had been her greatest enemy, she regretted to learn that her end had been such a sad one.

"My peace of mind destroyed," resumed the father, "and broken down in health, my physician advised me to travel, with the hope of recruiting myself, and I sailed from New York two months ago."

Being brought up in America, and having all the prejudice against color which characterizes his white fellow-countrymen, Mr. Linwood very much regretted that his daughter, although herself tinctured with African blood, should have married a black man, and he did not fail to express to her his dislike of her husband's complexion.

"I married him," said Miralda, "because I loved him. Why should the white man be esteemed as better than the black? I find no difference in men on account of their complexion. One of the cardinal principles of Christianity and freedom is the equality and brotherhood of man. In the sight of God and all just institutions, the whites can claim no precedence or privilege on account of their being white, and if colored men are not treated as they should be in America, it is a pleasure to know there is no distinction in any of the European countries."[7]

Every day Mr. Linwood became more and more familiar with Jerome, and eventually they were on the most intimate terms.

Fifteen days from the time that Miralda was introduced into her father's room, they left Ferney for Geneva. Many were the excursions Miralda made under the shadows of Mont Blanc,[8] and with her husband and father for companions, she was now in the enjoyment of pleasures hitherto unknown.

CHAPTER XXXV
THE FATHER'S RESOLVE

"Remember free-born father!
Forget not, faithful wife!
Contribute still for freedom,
The worth and joy of life.
Oh! child and Happy mother!
Forget the slave no more,
But each as God hath prospered,
Lay by his claims in store."

—Maria Weston Chapman.[1]

Aware that her father was still a slaveowner, Miralda determined to use all her persuasive power to induce him to set them free, and in this effort she found a substantial supporter in her husband.

"I have always treated my slaves well," said Mr. Linwood to Jerome, as the latter expressed his abhorrence to the system; "and my neighbors, too, are generally good men, for slavery in Virginia, is not like slavery in the other States," continued the proud son of the "Old Dominion."

"Their right to be free, Mr. Linwood," said Jerome, "is taken from them, and they have no security for their comfort, but the humanity and generosity of men who have been trained to regard them not as brethren, but as mere property. Humanity and generosity are, at best, but poor guarantees from [sic] the protection of those who cannot assert their rights, and over whom, law throws no protection.

"Our own conditions we would feel to be wretched indeed, if no law secured us from the insults, and maltreatment, even of our equals. But superiority, naturally begets contempt; and contempt generates maltreatment; for checking which, we can rely, not on virtue, but only on law.[2]

"There are in America, hundreds of thousands clothed with arbitrary power whom they are educated to regard as their property, as the instruments of their will, as creatures beneath their sympathy, devoid of all feeling which dignifies humanity, and but one remove above cattle. Is it not certain that many of these hundreds of thousands will inflict outrages on their despised dependants?

"Not only has the slave no right to his wife and children, he has no right even to himself. His very body, his muscles, his bones, his flesh, are all the property of another. The movements of his limbs are regulated by the will of a master. He may be sold like the beast of the field; he may be transported in chains like a felon. Was the blood of our revolution shed to establish a false principle, when it was poured out in defence of the assertion, that 'all men are created equal,' that 'they are endowed by their Creator with certain inalienable rights; that among these are life, liberty, and the pursuit of happiness?'

"If it be a violation of the rights of nature to deprive them of their political freedom, the injustice is surely much more flagrant when we rob them of personal liberty. The condition of a subject is enviable compared to the position of a slave."

Mr. Linwood felt the force of Jerome's reasoning, and saw very clearly his false position. It was long before Miralda's father could eradicate from his mind, the belief of the inferiority of the negro race.

"My husband," said Miralda, "is possessed of as true feelings as the whitest person in existence. The breast that glows with indignation at the unmerited oppression of a forlorn, and helpless fellow-creature, that melts with sorrow at the hapless tale of woe, that spontaneously prompts the vindication of the violated rights of humanity, in whatever form or comparison, or under whatever plea or pretext they may have been invaded—that breast is the hallowed abode of all the best affections of our fallen nature, and requires no argument to show that feelings thus radiated and diffused, like the genial rays of the sun, when once conveyed or concentrated, become, if possible, infinitely more fervent and powerful in their influence.

"This feeling is not confined to sect or color; but is shared by black as well as white."

It was with pleasure that Miralda obtained from her father, a promise that he would liberate all his slaves on his return to Richmond. In a beautiful little villa, situated in a pleasant spot fringed with hoary rocks and thick dark woods, within sight of the deep blue waters of Lake Lemon, Mr. Linwood, his daughter and her husband, took up their residence for a short time. For more than three weeks, this little party spent their time in visiting the birth-place on Rousseau, and the former abodes of Byron, Gibbon, Voltaire, De Stael, Shelley, and other literary characters.[3]

We can scarcely contemplate a visit to a more historic and interesting place than Geneva and its vicinity. Here, Calvin that great luminary in the Church, lived and ruled for years; here, Voltaire, the mighty genius, who laid the foundation of the French Revolution, and who boasted "When I shake my wig, I powder the whole republic," governed in the higher walks of life.

Fame is the recompense, not of the living, but of the dead—not always do they reap and gather in the harvest who sow the seed, the flame of its altar is too often kindled from the ashes of the great. A distinguished critic has beautifully said, "The sound which the stream of high thought, carried down to future ages, makes as it flows—deep, distant, murmuring ever more, like the waters of the mighty ocean." No reputation can be called great, that will not endure this test. The distinguished men who had lived in Geneva, transfused their spirit by their writings, into the spirit of other lovers of literature and everything that treated of great authors. Jerome and Miralda lingered long in, and about the haunts of Geneva and Lake Lemon.

An autumn sun sent down her bright rays, and bathed every object in her glorious light, as Miralda, accompanied by husband and father, set out one fine morning on her return home to France. Throughout the whole route, Mr. Linwood, saw by the deference paid to Jerome, whose black complexion excited astonishment in those who met him, that there was no hatred to the man in Europe, on account of his color; that what is called prejudice against color, is the offspring of the institution of slavery; and he felt ashamed of his own countrymen, when he thought of the complexion as distinctions, made in the United States, and resolved to dedicate the remainder of his life to the eradication of this irrepublican and unchristian feeling from the land of his birth, on his return home.

CHAPTER XXXVI

CONCLUSION[1]

"The world is bright before thee,
The summer flowers are thine.
It's calm blue sky is o'er thee,
Thy bosoms pleasures shine.

—Halleck.[2]

Unless it be those slaves who adopt their master's name, the negroes of the South seldom have more than one. Jim, Peter, Tom, Henry, is generally the call for the slave, and even the one name that the slave bears frequently, is denied him by the master's calling him "boy." As a general thing, the slave is called "boy" or "gal," until fifty or sixty years of age, and then it is "uncle" or "aunt." Jerome had but one name when he escaped from slavery, and having an inveterate hatred to his master, he early determined not to take the name of his late boss. However, on arriving in Canada, he felt that he ought to have two names, and therefore called himself Jerome Fletcher.[3] Thus, the system of oppression that exists in the Southern States, robs its victim of even so poor a thing as a name. It is indeed strange, passing strange, that so many milk and water or honied [sic] phrases, have been coined to apply to this most atrocious, and unparalleled evil. For say what we may, chattel slavery is a crime that has no equal in the great catalogue of outrages. It is that evil which casts man down from that exaltation where God has placed him, "a little lower than the angels,"[4] and sinks him level with the beasts of the field. This intelligent and immortal being, is confounded with the brutes that perish. He, whose spirit was formed to rise in aspirations of gratitude and praise, whilst here, and to spend an eternity with God in heaven, is horded with beasts, whose spirits go downwards with their bodies of clay to the dust of which they were made.

Slavery, is that crime by which man is robbed of his inalienable right to liberty, and the pursuit of happiness, the diadem of glory and honor with which he was crowned, and that sceptre of dominion which was placed in his hand when he was ushered upon the theatre of creation, and was divinely commissioned to "have dominion over the fish of the sea, and over the fowls of the air, and over the cattle, and over all the earth, and every creeping thing that creepeth upon the earth."[5]

Slavery, throws confusion into the arrangements of Infinite wisdom, breaks up the divine harmony, and tears up the very foundations of human society. It produces a state of things at war with nature, and hence those natural expedients to preserve this system from distinction; hence, the severity of those laws, which disgrace the statute books of our Southern States as well as the Congressional enactments to stay up and protect the foul system.

We have well nigh lost our national reputation, by keeping within our embrace the foul institution which degrades man, as no other kind of vassalage ever did. In all his travels in Europe, Mr. Linwood saw that liberty at home, was more a name than reality, and felt that our country ought to be redeemed from the dark stain. On their return from Geneva, the party stopped a few days at Lyons,[6] and remained a week at Paris,[7] where

Jerome's letters of introduction gained them admission into the best society of which the French metropolis could boast.

After a stay of four weeks at Dunkirk,[8] the home of the Fletchers's, Mr. Linwood set out for America, with the full determination of freeing his slaves, and settling them in one of the Northern States, and then to return to France to end his days in the society of his beloved daughter.[9]

Thus reader, I have given you an unvarnished and true tale of American slavery. If I have sometimes seemed to favor the slaveholder, I may be pardoned upon the ground of my connection with men and women, who are extensive owners in the staple product of my native State, yet I have tried to do justice to both master and slave, knowing I must meet both in the world to come.[10]

Appendix B

FROM *CLOTELLE: A TALE OF THE SOUTHERN STATES* (1864)

CHAPTER XXXIII
THE HAPPY DAY

It was a bright day in the latter part of October that Jerome and Clotelle set out for the church, where the marriage ceremony was to be performed. The clear, bracing air added buoyancy to every movement, and the sun poured its brilliant rays through the deeply-stained windows, as the happy couple entered the sanctuary, followed by old Mr. Devenant, whose form, bowed down with age, attracted almost as much attention from the assembly as did the couple more particularly interested.

As the ceremonies were finished and the priest pronounced the benediction on the newly-married pair, Clotelle whispered in the ear of Jerome,—

> " 'No power in death shall tear our names apart,
> As none in life could rend thee from my heart.' "

A smile beamed on every face as the wedding-party left the church and entered their carriage. What a happy day, after ten years' separation, when, both hearts having been blighted for a time, they are brought together by the hand of a beneficent and kind Providence, and united in holy wedlock.

Everything being arranged for a wedding tour extending up the Rhine, the party set out the same day for Antwerp. There are many rivers of greater length and width than the Rhine. Our Mississippi would swallow up half a dozen Rhines. The Hudson is grander, the Tiber, the Po, and the Mincio more classic; the Thames and Seine bear upon their waters greater amounts of wealth and commerce; the Nile and the Euphrates have a greater antiquity; but for a combination of interesting historical incidents and natural scenery, the Rhine surpasses them all. Nature has so ordained it that those who travel in the valley of the Rhine shall see the river, for there never will be a railroad upon its banks. So mountainous is the land that it would have to be one series of tunnels. Every three or four miles from the time you enter this glorious river, hills, dales, castles, and crags present themselves as the steamer glides onward.

Their first resting-place for any length of time was at Coblentz, at the mouth of the "Blue Moselle," the most interesting place on the river. From Coblentz they went to Brussels, where they had the greatest attention paid them. Besides being provided with letters of introduction, Jerome's complexion secured for him more deference than is usually awarded to travellers.

Having letters of introduction to M. Deceptiax, the great lace manufacturer, that gentleman received them with distinguished honors, and gave them a splendid *soiree*, at which the *elite* of the city were assembled. The sumptuously-furnished mansion was lavishly decorated for the occasion, and every preparation made that could add to the novelty or interest of the event.

Jerome, with his beautiful bride, next visited Cologne, the largest and wealthiest city on the banks of the Rhine. The Cathedral of Cologne is the most splendid structure of the kind in Europe, and Jerome and Clotelle viewed with interest the beautiful arches and columns of this stupendous building, which strikes with awe the beholder, as he gazes at its unequalled splendor, surrounded, as it is, by villas, cottages, and palace-like mansions, with the enchanting Rhine winding through the vine-covered hills.

After strolling over miles and miles of classic ground, and visiting castles, whose legends and tradions have given them an enduring fame, our delighted travellers started for Geneva, bidding the picturesque banks of the Rhine a regretful farewell. Being much interested in literature, and aware that Geneva was noted for having been the city of refuge to the victims of religious and political persecution, Jerome arranged to stay here for some days. He was provided with a letter of introduction to M. de Stee, who had been a fellow-soldier of Mr. Devenant in the East India wars, and they were invited to make his house their home during their sojourn. On the side of a noble mountain, whose base is kissed by the waves of Lake Geneva, and whose slopes are decked with verdure to the utmost peak of its rocky crown, is situated the delightful country residence of this wealthy, retired French officer. A winding road, with frequent climbs and brakes, leads from the valley to this enchanting spot, the air and scenery of which cannot be surpassed in the world.

CHAPTER XXXIV

CLOTELLE MEETS HER FATHER

The clouds that had skirted the sky during the day broke at last, and the rain fell in torrents, as Jerome and Clotelle retired for the night, in the little town of Ferney, on the borders of Lake Leman. The peals of thunder, and flashes of vivid lightening, which seemed to leap from mountain to mountain and from crag to crag, reverberating among the surrounding hills, foretold a heavy storm.

"I would we were back at Geneva," said Clotelle, as she heard groans issuing from an adjoining room. The sounds, at first faint, grew louder and louder, plainly indicating that some person was suffering extreme pain.

"I did not like this hotel, much, when we came in," said Jerome, relighting the lamp, which had been accidentally extinguished.

"Nor I," returned Clotelle.

The shrieks increased, and an occasional "She's dead!" "I killed her!" "No, she is not dead!" and such-like expressions, would be heard from the person, who seemed to be deranged.

The thunder grew louder, and the flashes of lightening more vivid, while the noise from the sick-room seemed to increase.

As Jerome opened the door, to learn, if possible, the cause of the cries and groans, he could distinguish the words, "She's dead! yes, she's dead! but I did not kill her. She was my child! my own daughter. I loved her, and yet I did not protect her."

"Whoever he is," said Jerome, "he's crack-brained; some robber, probably, from the mountains."

The storm continued to rage, and the loud peals of thunder and sharp flashes of lightening, together with the shrieks and moans of the maniac in the adjoining room, made the night a fearful one. The long hours wore slowly away, but neither Jerome nor his wife could sleep, and they arose at an early hour in the morning, ordered breakfast, and resolved to return to Geneva.

"I am sorry, sir, that you were so much disturbed by the sick man last night," said the landlord, as he handed Jerome his bill. "I should be glad if he would get able to go away, or die, for he's a deal of trouble to me. Several persons have left my house on his account."

"Where is he from?" inquired Jerome.

"He's from the United States, and has been here a week to-day, and has been crazy ever since."

"Has he no friends with him?" asked the guest.

"No, he is alone," was the reply.

Jerome related to his wife what he had learned from the landlord, respecting the sick man, and the intelligence impressed her so strongly, that she requested him to make further inquiries concerning the stranger.

He therefore consulted the book in which guests usually register their names, and, to his great surprise, found that the American's name was Henry Linwood, and that he was from Richmond, Va.

It was with feelings of trepidation that Clotelle heard these particulars from the lips of her husband.

"We must see this poor man, whoever he is," said she, as Jerome finished the sentence.

The landlord was glad to hear that his guests felt some interest in the sick man, and promised that the invalid's room should be got ready for their reception.

The clock in the hall was just striking ten, as Jerome passed through and entered the sick man's chamber. Stretched upon a mattress, with both hands tightly bound to the bedstead, the friendless stranger was indeed a pitiful sight. His dark, dishevelled hair prematurely gray, his long, unshaven beard, and the wildness of the eyes which glanced upon them as they opened the door and entered, caused the faint hope which had so suddenly risen in Clotelle's heart, to sink, and she felt that this man could claim no kindred with her. Certainly, he bore no resemblance to the man whom she had called her father, and who had fondly dandled her on his knee in those happy days of childhood.

"Help!" cried the poor man, as Jerome and his wife walked into the room. His eyes glared, and shriek after shriek broke forth from his parched and fevered lips.

"No, I did not kill my daughter!—I did not! she is not dead! Yes, she is dead! but I did not kill her—poor girl! Look! that is she! No, it cannot be! she cannot come here! it cannot be my poor Clotelle."

At the sound of her own name, coming from the maniac's lips, Clotelle gasped for breath, and her husband saw that she had grown deadly pale. It seemed evident to him that the man was either guilty of some terrible act, or imagined himself to be. His eyeballs rolled in their sockets, and his features showed that he was undergoing "the tortures of that inward hell," which seemed to set his whole brain on fire.

After recovering her self-possession and strength, Clotelle

approached the bedside, and laid her soft hand upon the stranger's hot and fevered brow.

One long, loud shriek rang out on the air, and a piercing cry, "It is she!—Yes, it is she! I see, I see! Ah! no, it is not my daughter! She would not come to me if she could!" broke forth from him.

"I am your daughter," said Clotelle, as she pressed her handkerchief to her face, and sobbed aloud.

Like balls of fire, the poor man's eyes rolled and glared upon the company, while large drops of perspiration ran down his pale and emaciated face. Strange as the scene appeared, all present saw that it was indeed a meeting between a father and his long-lost daughter. Jerome now ordered all present to leave the room, except the nurse, and every effort was at once made to quiet the sufferer. When calm, a joyous smile would illuminate the sick man's face, and a strange light beam in his eyes, as he seemed to realize that she who stood before him was indeed his child.

For two long days and nights did Clotelle watch at the bedside of her father before he could speak to her intelligently. Sometimes, in his insane fits, he would rave in the most frightful manner, and then, in a few moments, would be as easily governed as a child. At last, however, after a long and apparently refreshing sleep, he awoke suddenly to a full consciousness that it was indeed his daughter who was watching so patiently by his side.

The presence of his long absent child had a soothing effect upon Mr. Linwood, and he now recovered rapidly from the sad and almost hopeless condition in which she had found him. When able to converse, without danger of a relapse, he told Clotelle of his fruitless efforts to obtain a clew to her whereabouts after old Mrs. Miller had sold her to the slave-trader. In answer to his daughter's inquiries about his family affairs up to the time that he left America, he said,—

"I blamed my wife for your being sold and sent away, for I thought she and her mother were acting in collusion; But I afterwards found that I had blamed her wrongfully. Poor woman!

she knew that I loved your mother, and feeling herself forsaken, she grew melancholy and died in a decline three years ago."

Here both father and daughter wept at the thought of other days. When they had recovered their composure, Mr. Linwood went on again:

"Old Mrs. Miller," said he, "after the death of Gertrude, aware that she had contributed much toward her unhappiness, took to the free use of intoxicating drinks, and became the most brutal creature that ever lived. She whipped her slaves without the slightest provocation, and seemed to take delight in inventing new tortures with which to punish them. One night last winter, after having flogged one of her slaves nearly to death, she returned to her room, and by some means the bedding took fire, and the house was in flames before any one was awakened. There was no one in the building at the time but the old woman and the slaves, and although the latter might have saved their mistress, they made no attempt to do so. Thus, after a frightful career of many years, this hard-hearted woman died a most miserable death, unlamented by a single person."

Clotelle wiped the tears from her eyes, as her father finished this story, for, although Mrs. Miller had been her greatest enemy, she regretted to learn that her end had been such a sad one.

"My peace of mind destroyed," resumed the father, "and broke down in health, my physician advised me to travel, with the hope of recruiting myself, and I sailed from New York two months ago."

Being brought up in America, and having all the prejudice against color which characterizes his white fellow-countrymen, Mr. Linwood very much regretted that his daughter, although herself tinctured with African blood, should have married a black man, and he did not fail to express to her his dislike of her husband's complexion.

"I married him," said Clotelle, "because I loved him. Why should the white man be esteemed as better than the black? I find no difference in men on account of their complexion. One

WILLIAM WELLS BROWN

Clotel;

or,

The President's Daughter

Edited with an Introduction and Notes by
M. Giulia Fabi

PENGUIN BOOKS

PENGUIN BOOKS
Published by the Penguin Group
Penguin Group (USA) Inc., 375 Hudson Street, New York, New York 10014, U.S.A.
Penguin Group (Canada), 90 Eglinton Avenue East, Suite 700, Toronto, Ontario,
Canada M4P 2Y3 (a division of Pearson Penguin Canada Inc.)
Penguin Books Ltd, 80 Strand, London WC2R 0RL, England
Penguin Ireland, 25 St Stephen's Green, Dublin 2, Ireland
(a division of Penguin Books Ltd)
Penguin Group (Australia), 250 Camberwell Road, Camberwell, Victoria 3124,
Australia (a division of Pearson Australia Group Pty Ltd)
Penguin Books India Pvt Ltd, 11 Community Centre, Panchsheel Park,
New Delhi – 110 017, India
Penguin Group (NZ), 67 Apollo Drive, Rosedale, North Shore 0632, New Zealand
(a division of Pearson New Zealand Ltd)
Penguin Books (South Africa) (Pty) Ltd, 24 Sturdee Avenue,
Rosebank, Johannesburg 2196, South Africa

Penguin Books Ltd, Registered Offices: 80 Strand, London WC2R 0RL, England

First published in Great Britain by Partridge & Oakey 1853
First published in the United States of America by James Redpath 1864
This edition with an introduction and notes by Maria Giulia Fabi published in Penguin Books 2004,

7 9 10 8 6

Introduction and notes copyright © Maria Giulia Fabi, 2004
All rights reserved

LIBRARY OF CONGRESS CATALOGING IN PUBLICATION DATA
Brown, William Wells, 1815–1884.
Clotel, or, The president's daughter / William Wells Brown ;
edited with an introduction
and notes by M. Giulia Fabi.
p. cm.
Includes bibliographical references.
ISBN 978-0-14-243772-8
1. Jefferson, Thomas, 1743–1826—Relations with women—Fiction. 2. African American
families—Fiction 3. Children of presidents—Fiction. 4. African American women—Fiction.
5. Racially mixed people—Fiction. 6. Women slaves—Fiction. I. Title: Clotel. II. Title:
President's daughter. III. Fabi, M. Giulia (Maria Giulia) IV. Title.
PS1139.B9C53 2004
813'.4—dc22   2003053661

Printed in the United States of America
Set in Adobe Sabon

Except in the United States of America, this book is sold subject to the condition that it shall not, by
way of trade or otherwise, be lent, resold, hired out, or otherwise circulated without the publisher's
prior consent in any form of binding or cover other than that in which it is published and without
a similar condition including this condition being imposed on the subsequent purchaser.

The scanning, uploading and distribution of this book via the Internet or via any other means
without the permission of the publisher is illegal and punishable by law. Please purchase
only authorized electronic editions, and do not participate in or encourage electronic
piracy of copyrighted materials. Your support of the author's rights is appreciated.

Contents

CLOTEL;
OR, THE PRESIDENT'S DAUGHTER

Introduction

DNA research has finally, conclusively proven that Thomas Jefferson (1743–1826), author of the Declaration of Independence (1776) and third president of the United States, fathered children with one of his female slaves, Sally Hemings.[1] Scientific evidence has thus substantiated the historical accuracy of a central element of the plot of the first known African American novel, William Wells Brown's *Clotel; or, The President's Daughter: A Narrative of Slave Life in the United States* (1853).[2] Previously, scholars and historians had underplayed this aspect of Brown's novel as a sensationalistic rumor on which the author had capitalized to advance his antislavery argument. Over the last three decades of the twentieth century, however, as part of a broader scholarly process of recovery and reinterpretation of early African American literary texts, critics also started reevaluating Brown's novel's literary artistry. They now have moved beyond traditionally ambivalent evaluations of *Clotel* that emphasized its historical importance as the founding text of the African American novelistic tradition but lamented it as "not so much an artistic novel as a loosely structured skeleton of a plot."[3]

Brown's *Clotel* is a brilliantly constructed work of fiction that exemplifies well that extraordinary mid-nineteenth-century artistic flowering critics have called the "American Renaissance."[4] Its complex exploration of human relations in the New World and of the cultural identity of the American nation is compounded by a sophisticated experimentation with literary form, which aimed to introduce a new protagonist in the American novel: the slave community.

Brown possessed a profound understanding of slavery, having "had opportunities," as he wrote, "far greater than most slaves, of acquiring knowledge of the different phases of the '*peculiar institution*.' " He was born a slave on a Kentucky plantation in 1814, the son of a slave woman, Elizabeth, and a white man who was probably a relative of his owner. He had several masters who made him serve in a variety of occupations: at a hotel, in a printing office, for a slave trader, on steamboats, and as a carriage driver. In 1833, he made a first attempt to escape from slavery, taking his mother with him, but the fugitives were captured, separated, and sold to different masters. A few months later, on January 1, 1834, Brown repeated the attempt by himself and succeeded, with the help of Mr. and Mrs. Wells Brown, Quakers from Ohio who gave shelter, food, and clothes to the fugitive, who had become ill "through cold and hunger." In gratitude, Brown, who, like most slaves, had been given only a first name, added his benefactor's to create his full name.

After his escape, Brown found work as a steamboatman on Lake Erie, a position he would hold for the following nine years, enabling him to help other fugitive slaves reach Canada. In 1843 he started his career as a lecturer, initially for the Western New York Anti-Slavery Society. In that same year, his first published piece of writing, a letter, appeared in *The National Anti-Slavery Standard*. In 1847 he moved to Boston, where the Boston Anti-Slavery Office published his *Narrative of William W. Brown, a Fugitive Slave. Written by Himself* (1847). The *Narrative* went through four American editions, selling ten thousand copies, and through five British editions, earning Brown an international reputation.

The publication of Brown's autobiography was only the beginning of his fast-paced, prolific, pioneering, and varied literary career. Besides revising and expanding the subsequent editions of his *Narrative*, Brown published in 1848 *The Anti-Slavery Harp: A Collection of Songs for Anti-Slavery Meetings* (which went through several editions), in 1850 *A Description of William Wells Brown's Original Panoramic Views of the Scenes in the Life of an American Slave, from His Birth in*

Slavery to His Death or His Escape to His First Home of Freedom on British Soil (a series of sketches and stories accompanying twenty-four antislavery drawings), and in 1852 *Three Years in Europe; or, Places I Have Seen and People I Have Met.* This is the first known travel book by an African American author. It is based on Brown's experiences in Europe, where he had been sent in 1849 as a delegate to the International Peace Congress in Paris, and where he eventually stayed for five years because the passage in the United States of the Fugitive Slave Law in 1850 made it dangerous for him to return to his home country.[5] In London in 1853, Brown published *Clotel; or, The President's Daughter: A Narrative of Slave Life in the United States*, his first novel and the first known novel of the African American literary tradition.[6]

Brown's prolific career as a writer continued after his return to the United States in 1854, when his friends bought his freedom from his last owner, until his death in 1884. He published three revised editions of his novel, important volumes on African American history and culture (*St. Domingo: Its Revolution and Its Patriots*, 1855; *The Black Man, His Antecedents, His Genius, and His Achievements*, 1863; *The Negro in the American Rebellion: His Heroism and His Fidelity*, 1867; *The Rising Son; or, The Antecedents and Advancement of the Colored Race*, 1874), other autobiographical volumes (*Memoir of William Wells Brown*, 1859; *My Southern Home: Or, The South and Its People*, 1880), and the first known plays by an African American ("Experience, or, How to Give a Northern Man a Backbone," written in 1856; *The Escape; or, A Leap for Freedom. A Drama in Five Acts*, published in 1858).

Clotel is a harrowing tale of slavery and freedom that in many ways represents the conscious flowering of Brown's previous literary work. He borrowed and rewrote material from his own earlier works as well as from a wide variety of other sources, but he put that material to new, explicitly fictional use.[7] In *Clotel*, Brown orchestrates very carefully his unprecedented (for an African American author) entrance into the realm of novel writing. Well aware that contemporary expectations (widespread even among antislavery activists and sympathizers) confined ex-slaves to the role of witness rather than commentator, and their literary contributions to personal narratives, Brown intends from the beginning to take control of his fictional text and assert his authority as a writer and as an interpreter not only of his own life but also of the lives of his community and his nation.

Defying nineteenth-century assumptions of black inferiority and the related literary convention that saw white abolitionists write prefatory materials for works by black authors in order to authenticate their authorship and their reliability, Brown wrote his own preface to his novel. In it, he does not mention his own personal experience of slavery,[8] but rather maintains a scholarly, professional tone: he provides a brief history of the origins and the present situation of slavery in America both to instruct his British readers and to demonstrate his own authoritativeness and greater knowledge. Brown solicits his readers in Britain (where slavery had been abolished in 1838) to put pressure on America (where slavery was still a reality), but he also quells any unexamined tendency to self-complacency. He reminds them, with a matter-of-fact tone that diplomatically underemphasizes the polemical import of his statement, that "The fact that slavery was introduced in the American colonies, while they were under the control of the British crown, is a sufficient reason why Englishmen should feel a lively interest in its abolition."

In the preface, Brown also anticipates, albeit obliquely, the most explicitly controversial and sensationalistic element of his novel. He notes that "Were it not for persons in high places owning slaves and thereby giving the system a reputation, . . . slavery would long since have been abolished" and maintains that "to fasten the guilt on those who move in a higher circle" is an effective abolitionist strategy. These words reverberate with more specific meaning when connected with those on the preceding title page. There, Brown juxtaposes the title reference to Clotel as "The President's Daughter," with a closing quote from the Declaration of Independence, thus pointing indirectly, but effectively, to Thomas Jefferson as one of those "persons in high places" whom he deems it important to expose in order to "lay bare the institution . . . and cause the wise, the prudent, and the pious to withdraw their support from it."

Brown's preface, which eases the reader into trusting in the objectivity of his authorial voice, is reinforced by the autobiographical sketch that precedes the novel proper. Entitled "Narrative of the Life and Escape of William Wells Brown," it presents a revised and shorter version of his 1847 Narrative. However, in this version, Brown, with a brilliant stroke of rhetorical skill, talks about himself not in the first person but in the third. Determined to distance his authorial persona from his autobiographical self, Brown emerges as the third-person "editor" of his first-person deeds.[9] He cites, using quotation marks, his own memoir, speeches, and other published works, including reviews of his books, treating his own life as a primary source upon which he can elaborate from a detached, self-consciously writerly standpoint. At the same time, in contrast to his 1847 autobiography, the shorter "Narrative" eliminates episodes that showed his cunning and ability to deceive. His remarkable skill as a trickster and his autobiographical stance as "a Negro antihero who defies all the norms of respectability which the fictive reader would presumably hold dear"[10] was an aspect of his self-presentation that played an important part in his 1847 autobiography but which he chooses to minimize here in order to, once again, strengthen the reader's trust.

The careful, deliberately smooth transition from the nonfictional prose of the preface and the "Narrative" to the fictional story of Clotel continues in the first chapter of the novel itself. Brown devotes the first half of the opening chapter, entitled "The Negro Sale," to discussing "the fearful increase of half whites" and the legal impossibility of slave marriages in the Southern states as proof of the immorality of slavery as an institution, quoting famous politicians, laws, and other sources.[11] It is only halfway through the first chapter of Clotel that Brown finally leads the readers into his fictive world with the following words: "We have thought it advisable to show that the present system of chattel slavery in America undermines the entire social condition of man, so as to prepare the reader for the following narrative of slave life, in that otherwise happy and prosperous country."

Those readers who, in this slow transition from autobiography and history to a fiction "founded in truth," have allowed themselves to be "prepare[d]" by Brown's professional, earnest, scholarly tone are in for a big surprise. Right after the first chapter, the novel plunges them into a fast-paced series of adventures, into a proliferation of characters and situations, into a "stunning . . . literary pastiche" that thrusts the reader into the enormous and intricate maze of the world of slavery.[12]

The most immediately visible, because more familiar, Ariadne's thread that Brown uses to guide readers through this maze concerns the adventures and peregrinations of two generations of Jefferson's all-but-white mulatta offspring. By the time Brown wrote *Clotel*, mulattas were established, even stock figures in American literature, very popular among white writers.[13] Trapped in a racial limbo because she was neither black nor white, the stereotypical tragic mulatta suffered from a supposedly inherent and fatal condition of "in-betweenness" that inexorably led to her death, a tragic ending that ultimately reinforced the viability of the separation between blacks and whites that the mulatta's existence had temporarily called into question. Brown, like other early African American writers, has been criticized for his choice to portray "white Negroes," as they were called, a choice that later critics have often read as a capitulation to dominant notions of white superiority.[14]

However, in depicting his all-but-white characters, Brown employs several crucial revisions which, contrary to first impressions, reveal his subversive stance and literary goals. First, in the very first chapter of the novel, Brown's emphasis on the "fearful increase of half whites" in the Southern states points to the structural, endemic immorality fostered by slavery. At the same time, his controversial choice of Thomas Jefferson as father takes the issue of the sexual exploitation of slave women out of the private homes of individually immoral slaveholders and effectively exposes it as a national practice with national consequences for the very credibility of those revolutionary

democratic principles that had justified the war for the creation
of an American nation. The hypocrisy of individual slaveholders,
of which Brown provides a wealth of examples in his novel,
thus reverberates on and foregrounds the larger contradictions
of the American nation as a whole (South *and* North), as
Brown connects the existence of slavery in the South with the
racism and discrimination that made free blacks second-class
citizens even in the "free" North: "In most of the Free States,"
he notes in *Clotel*, "the coloured people are disfranchised on
account of their colour."

Second, Brown's female protagonists are not simply traditional light-skinned mulattas. Rather, they are *so* light-skinned
as to be able to pass for white, an option of which they do take
advantage at different moments in the attempt to achieve freedom for themselves or their loved ones. Foreshadowing late-
twentieth-century deconstructionist discourses on "race" as a
cultural construct and a social fiction rather than a biological
fact, Brown shows the permeability of racial boundaries, the
unreadability of "race" (and gender, for that matter)[15], and the
precariousness and contingency of those very definitions of
blackness and whiteness in which social institutions like slavery
(as well as the right to first-class citizenship in the American nation as a whole) found their supposed legitimation.

In Brown's novel, people who are legally considered black
can pass for white, but also whites can pass for black. The author provides the examples of Salome, the German immigrant
who has been reduced to slavery (chapter XIV) and, more sen-
sationalistically, of the famous senator Daniel Webster, whom
Brown shows to be denied service at a hotel because the landlord "seemed woefully to mistake the dark features of the traveller as he sat back in the corner of the carriage, and to suppose
him a *coloured man*, particularly as there were two coloured
servants of Mr. W. outside." In *Clotel*, even people who are
legally white may be passing after all, as Brown remarks that
"Thomas Corwin, a member of the American Congress, is one
of the blackest white men in the United States." In all of these
cases, the difficulties, contradictions, and paradoxes involved
in racial classification demonstrate how "race" is not self-

explanatory, but rather rests on social conventions, a knowledge of someone's ancestry, and the legal interpretation of the meaning of that ancestry. In his indictment of the absurdities of "the prejudice of looks," Brown subversively hints that "whiteness," after all, may indicate nothing more than ignorance of one's mixed ancestry.

By emphasizing the instability of supposedly "natural" racial categories, Brown also radically enhances and transforms the narrative role of his all-but-white heroines, moving beyond the stereotype of the "tragic mulatta." His heroines use their liminality strategically to escape and to help others escape from slavery. Their rebellion, moreover, is often successful, and even in those cases when it is not, their deaths, far from being the inevitable result of their personal mixed-race status, are, on the contrary, clearly connected with their search for freedom and take on explicitly political connotations. The title character is a case in point. Like the real-life fugitive Ellen Craft, Clotel succeeds in escaping from slavery by passing for a white man.[16] It is only when she returns to the South to liberate her daughter that she is discovered and arrested, but she fights to the end. Brown emphasizes her final moments not so much for their pathos, but more aggressively as "an evidence . . . of the unconquerable love of liberty the heart may inherit; as well as a fresh admonition to the slave dealer, of the cruelty and enormity of his crimes."[17]

Brown's recasting of a stock figure and literary icon like the tragic mulatta in new and combative terms opens the way for post–Civil War representations of heroic black womanhood in the works of Frances Ellen Watkins Harper (1825–1911) and Pauline E. Hopkins (1859–1930) and also exemplifies his concern, which he expressed in all his writings, for reinterpreting dominant modes of representation of blackness. He was profoundly aware of the close interaction between popular cultural images, social hierarchies, and the political workings of American democracy. As critics have pointed out, Brown's revision of prevalent, and characteristically demeaning, figurations of blackness "is a means by which he challenges stereotypes, not only by arguing against them but also by turning them to other purposes."[18] As has already been noted in the case of the mulatta, Brown evokes elements from the popular culture of his time only to refill them with new meaning. He infuses them with the intimate knowledge of slavery and racism, and the ethos of resistance of the black community itself, to involve the reader actively in thinking through the contrast between the superficial recognizability of the type and the puzzling new depth it possesses.

Brown's literary strategy is particularly clear in the case of Sam. Initially presented as a contented house slave who, despite being "one of the blackest of his race," harbors prejudices against blackness and aggrandizes himself by imitating his owner (chapter XII), Sam exceeds the comic boundaries of a minstrel caricature when at a secret meeting he leads his fellow slaves in a song that expresses joy at the death of their master, Mr. Peck, a parson (chapter XVI). The unexpectedness of this scene enhances the shock effect of Brown's ongoing disclosure of the slave community's opposition to slavery.

Fully aware of the strength of the cultural images he means to reshape, and clearly reluctant to rely too much on the interpretive skills of his British readers, Brown not only presents such "unguarded expressions of the feelings of the Negroes," but also makes sure to provide his intended audience with adequate tools to interpret them. For this purpose, he dramatizes the reception of his revisionary portrayal of Sam in the discussion between the two white people who have overheard Sam's song: the deceased parson's daughter, Georgiana, and her suitor, Mr. Carlton. While Mr. Carlton, though a Northerner and a believer in natural rights, indignantly reads Sam's behavior according to conventional, stereotypical views of the slave's inherent deceitfulness, Georgiana undermines her suitor's right to assume a position of moral superiority by explaining the "lesson" to be learned from Sam's behavior. She invokes the inalienable right of all human beings to be free and the causal relationship between the larger social context of the United States' institutionalized inconsistency with its democratic principles and Sam's deceitfulness: "Our system of slavery is one of deception; and Sam . . . has only been a good scholar. However, he is as honest a fellow as you will find among the slave population here. If we would have them more honest, we should give them their liberty, and then the inducement to be dishonest would be gone."[19]

As Sam's episode makes clear, and while it is important to appreciate the radical novelty of Brown's subversive mulattas, to analyze *Clotel* following only the story of Jefferson's all-but-white offspring would not do justice to the originality and brilliance of Brown's novel. In fact, the second, less familiar but more powerful Ariadne's thread Brown uses to guide readers through the horrifying maze of slavery is represented by his unprecedented insertion of a vocal protagonist new to the American novel: the slave community. Surrounding, interrupting, criss-crossing, expanding the story of the all-but-white protagonists are myriad slave characters. These characters are most often visibly black and male, while visibly black women are more marginalized. While the individual adventures of this chorus of slave figures remain secondary to those of Jefferson's offspring, their collective importance in the novel builds by accretion. And while this proliferation of characters, episodes, and subplots threatens to collapse the structure of the novel by consistently thwarting traditional readerly expectations of narrative order and coherence, the novel does not implode. Rather, it allows our "entrance into a world in which the work's apparent lack of unity and overabundance of materials are entirely appropriate."[20] The unsettling effect of Brown's formal experimentalism is enhanced by the plot of the novel, as the ever-proliferating secondary black characters pose a threat to the institution of slavery through the multiple forms of resistance they engage in, as well as through the radically different value system they give voice to. Their ethos of resistance, knowledge of American political, religious, and institutional hypocrisy, and sense of belonging to a community (not only because they are communally oppressed, but because they are united by a common history and shared cultural values) effectively qualify them as a veritable nation within the nation, as another African American author, Sutton Griggs, would put it a few years later in his novel *Imperium in Imperio* (1890).

Critics have traditionally reacted with ambivalence to the structure of *Clotel*, noticing, for instance, with some dismay that "enough material for a dozen novels is crowded into its two hundred and forty-five pages."[21] This comment is accurate in stating, hyperbolically, the richness of the novel, but its negative connotations need to be reinterpreted. Rather than a shortcoming, this wealth of material is in fact a crucial, deliberate element of Brown's aesthetic, of his fictional re-creation of his intimate knowledge of slavery, and of his awareness of the almost inexpressible magnitude of that experience and of the far from monolithic quality even of a condition of such extreme oppression. Brown's narrative strategy is a finely tuned literary tool to re-create on the page—and to make readers experience, albeit mildly—the overwhelming, absurd, brutal, uncertain qualities of the "peculiar institution," as slavery was euphemistically called. Brown mirrors in the very structure of the novel the uncertainty and limited control that were characteristic of slave life. For instance, in having characters appear and disappear without previous notice from the text (for example, the sudden elimination of Currer from the novel in chapter XVIII, or the swift appearance and disappearance of Althesa's daughters in chapter XXIII), he gives his audience a readerly experience of the familial disruption caused by slavery. Brown's is a bold experiment with literary form that critics have recently re-read in connection with other later, sophisticated works like Mark Twain's *Life on the Mississippi* (1883), Herman Melville's *The Confidence-Man* (1857), and Ishmael Reed's *Flight to Canada* (1976).[22]

In other words, the violent disruption of black lives caused by slavery is translated by Brown into a disruption of narrative expectations. The ambivalent and somewhat disconcerted reactions of critics who lament that Brown "never attempts to signal who is important and who is not, where we are ultimately going and where we are not" prove that the message has been received, though not necessarily appreciated or enjoyed.[23] The fact that some critics continue to search for a "unifying principle" is a telling attempt to resist the condition of uncertainty of slave life as Brown re-creates it on a fictional level, and it can be read as an effort by such critics to recover some control in a situation of powerlessness and frustrated expectations.[24] This effort at readerly resistance, as one might call it, lends indirect insight both into the enormous struggle for self-preservation of the slaves in conditions of incommensurably greater powerlessness and oppression, and into the efficacy of Brown's literary mastery in managing an enormous amount of material to provide new interpretive and cognitive tools to understand slavery. Brown moves beyond the simple effects of horror and pity, which distance the readers from the "other" in the very process of stimulating their sympathy.[25] He attempts to involve the reader actively in a new, more complex, more self-questioning understanding—of the interdependence between definitions of freedom and bondage; of the centrality of slavery in the American nation as a whole (North and South); and of the ideological continuum between social institutions such as slavery in the South and systems of thought such as racism that dominate in the North as well: "The slaves of America . . . lie under the most absolute and grinding despotism the world ever saw. But who are the despots? The rulers of the country—the sovereign people! Not merely the slaveholder who cracks the lash. He is but the instrument in the hands of despotism. That despotism is the government of the Slave States, and the United States, consisting of all its rulers—all the free citizens."

If the disruption of narrative expectations serves, on the one hand, to put the reader in a position of powerlessness, the wealth of material Brown includes in his novel emphasizes, on the other hand, the chaos engendered by slavery and its ultimate unmanageability as it emerges from the many episodes of slave resistance that Brown recounts. The strategies of resistance range from insurrections (such as the historical references to the slave revolt led by Nat Turner in 1831), to the passing of the heroines, to the actions of the all-but-white male hero George (who engages in both overt and covert resistance by participating in Turner's revolt and later cross-dressing as a woman in order to escape from the prison where he is waiting to be executed), to the multifarious strategies of everyday resistance adopted by a host of secondary, often anonymous, and mostly male figures who devise plans that testify to their cunning, intelligence, self-respect, and love for their family as well as for freedom (see chapters III, VI, VII, XIII, XIX). Within the economy of Brown's novel, these instances of individual resistance, seemingly insignificant compared to the grander scope and heroism of slave insurrections, accumulate a sense that the slaves share a communal ethos. This ethos is no simple reaction to oppression but the expression of a complex worldview and of how the slaves opposed "their own angle of vision to that of their oppressor," as historian Sterling Stuckey would argue again more than a century after the publication of *Clotel*.[16] This worldview is the basis of the culture that they have been able to develop despite conditions of extreme and brutal captivity, a culture Brown would continue to document, celebrate, and popularize in the historical and encyclopedic volumes he wrote after the abolition of slavery.

With this insight into slave culture, Brown anticipates twentieth-century historical debates on slavery and provides a clear sense of the cultural specificity that flowered in the distinctively African American literary tradition of which he was a major protagonist. It is an insight into slave life that Brown does not present to his British readers as exclusive or "natural" racial property, but rather as important knowledge that is hard to acquire. The ethos of resistance of the slaves can be understood by outsiders who have dared to become aware of the interpretive blinders of race prejudice, who have penetrated the oxymoron of a slaveholding democracy, who have questioned the source of their own privilege, and who have emerged with new interpretive tools to reread American reality from a point of view that includes the perspective of the subaltern. As we have seen, Brown dramatizes this possibility in Georgiana, the parson's daughter, who understands her slaves' love for and right to freedom and consequently devises a plan for their emancipation in which the ex-contented house slave Sam will play an important role. She is paradigmatic of the process of interpretive retraining that Brown tries to ignite in his readers through his novel.

Brown attributed considerable importance to *Clotel*, as is testified to by his publication of three subsequent editions, which appeared in the United States. In the three American editions, the novel is not preceded by any ancillary autobiographical narrative, a fact that may indicate both Brown's increased fame as an author, which dispensed him from the need to provide his "résumé," and his awareness of having accomplished the transition from autobiography to fiction.[27] In the American editions, Brown profoundly revised the original text of his novel in ways that show both his determination to continue to comment on contemporary affairs as well as the negotiations and limitations imposed on early black writers by American racial ideology, the American literary market, and the internally divided audience of black and white readers with often diametrically different interests and points of view.

In the months preceding the outbreak of the Civil War, from December 1, 1860, to March 16, 1861, Brown serialized his novel in an African American newspaper, *The Weekly Anglo-African*, under a different title: *Miralda; or, The Beautiful Quadroon. A Romance of American Slavery, Founded on Fact*. It was upon this shortened and deeply reconceived version of the original *Clotel* that the two subsequent editions of Brown's novel, published in the United States in 1864 and 1867, were based. In *Miralda*, an important but lesser-read work, Brown revises the plot and narrative structure of the British edition in ways that reveal a less pronounced "preoccupation with documenting the facts"[28] (since he edits out most of the documentary evidence he had quoted in *Clotel*) and a greater authorial self-assuredness in handling the explicit fictionality of his text. He organizes the plot more consistently around the central all-but-white female characters and individual figures of heroic black manhood. He enhances the proud, confrontational individualism of his hero, now renamed Jerome, who becomes more representative of the slave community. In contrast with the British edition of *Clotel*, in which George is said to be "as white as most white persons," in *Miralda* and in the other American editions, Jerome is "of pure African origin" and "perfectly black." The title heroine herself, though still able to pass for white, is now described as "olive-tinted." Brown also recounts Jerome's escape from slavery in greater detail, including instances of tricksterism and bravery previously connected with secondary characters. In addressing the readers of the *Weekly Anglo-African*, whose front-page motto was "Man must be Free!—If not through Law, why then above the Law," Brown retains the sensationalism of the reference to the sale of Jefferson's slave children (which would be eliminated from the two subsequent book editions), and gives his black and white characters longer speeches that sharply denounce Southern slavery, American religious hypocrisy, and the "revolting prejudice against the negro" prevalent even in the North. However, as Brown reduces his emphasis on documentary evidence in these editions, he also curtails the proliferation of characters and subplots that characterized his strategy of representation of slave life in *Clotel*, thereby softening the formal experimentalism of his novel.

In *Miralda*, Brown contemplates for the first time the possibility of sectional reconciliation, though it is contingent upon the elimination of slavery. On the one hand, he strikes a hopeful note of survival by renaming the protagonists. Isabella is the new name of the brave heroine who returns to the South to save her daughter but dies in the attempt, while the title heroine is her daughter, who eventually succeeds in escaping to France. On the other hand, the closing reunion in France includes not only the heroine's long-lost lover Jerome, but also her slaveholding father. The father's newfound affection for the daughter he had previously deserted and the heroine's own "persuasive power" lead him to convert to abolitionism, though Brown makes clear that "It was long before Miralda's father could eradicate from his mind, the belief of the inferiority of the negro race." The ending of *Miralda* (see Appendix A) sees the heroine's father go back to America "with the full determination of freeing his slaves, and settling them in one of the Northern States, and then to return to France to end his days in the society of his beloved daughter." However, the optimism of this ending is qualified in *Miralda* by the author's tirade against slavery ("that crime by which man is robbed of his inalienable right to liberty, and the pursuit of happiness") that dominates the last chapter.

Much of the sensationalism of *Miralda* disappears in the 1864 book-form edition of Brown's novel, now titled *Clotelle: A Tale of the Southern States*. As the Civil War raged, *Clotelle* appeared in abolitionist editor James Redpath's series of *Books for the Camp Fires*, whose aim was "to relieve the monotony of camp-life to the soldiers of the Union, and therefore of Liberty, and at the same time [kindle] their zeal in the cause of universal emancipation."[29] In his effort to inspire Union soldiers at war, Brown retains his characterization of slavery as immoral, though he reduces the long antislavery speeches present in *Miralda* and underplays the representation of Southern violence and brutality. On the other hand, faced with a dual audience of black and white Union soldiers, and unwilling to overestimate the latter's desire for critical self-examination, he softens his denunciation of Northern prejudice. Dark-skinned Jerome remains the primary figure of confrontational black heroism, but, striking a patriotic note absent in the previous editions and now justified in a country waging a war against slavery, Brown eliminates all controversial references to Jefferson and substitutes for him a nameless senator. Similarly, the novel's closure (see Appendix B), which is characterized by a much speedier conversion of Clotelle's father to abolitionism and by the absence of the final tirade against slavery seen in *Miralda*, emphasizes more strongly the possibility of sectional reconciliation after the end of the war. Clotelle's father's resolve to free his slaves suggests the more just social order that will follow the elimination of slavery and the beneficial effect abolition will have not only on former slaves but also on former slaveholders.

The optimism of this closure is at once enhanced and qualified in the third and last edition of Brown's novel. Published in 1867 after the end of the Civil War, at a time when the Thirteenth Amendment to the Constitution (1865) had officially abolished slavery, *Clotelle; or, The Colored Heroine. A Tale of the Southern States* differs from the previous 1864 American edition most significantly in the addition of four closing chapters that update the story to "June 1867" (see Appendix C).

These four new chapters take place after "Twenty-two years had passed" and see Clotelle and Jerome leave France and return to the United States to take part in the Civil War. Jerome enrolls in the Union army and dies heroically in the South. After his death, Clotelle passes as a "rebel lady" to gain access to confederate prisons, where she helps Union soldiers and "secretly aid[s] prisoners in their escape." In this new ending, written during Reconstruction, Brown underscores the "fiendish and heartless conduct of a large number of the people of the South towards Union men during the war." Their brutality is shown to be on a continuum with their prewar violence against the slaves, as well as with their violence against the freedmen that Brown knew to be rampant in the postwar South. The author also introduces new folk figures of great depth. Clotelle is helped in her efforts, which lead to the successful escape of ninety-three prisoners, by "a negro man named Pete," who "was employed about the prison, and, having the entire confidence of the commandant, was in a position to do much good without being suspected." Pete exhibits the cunning and tricksterism that characterized folk figures like Sam in the first edition of the novel. As in Sam's case, Pete's strategic duplicity and subversiveness are signalled by a bold and explicitly pro-Union song he sings when "away from the whites, and among his own class." The new ending of the 1867 *Clotelle* allows some room also for the representation of the antislavery activism of visibly black women, characters who had not gained center stage in any of the previous editions. The greater importance of Aggy and Dinah, who help Clotelle escape before she is taken to prison, is short-lived but significant. However, visibly black female characters do not fully escape their subordinate role even in the last edition of the novel, as becomes clear in the closing comic scene where Dinah's husband "govern[s] the tongue" of his wife who, "like many of her sex, was an inveterate scold," by threatening to sell her. Brown does not seem interested in questioning gender roles within the black community, an issue which would become central in the work of postwar African American women novelists.

The final description of Clotelle's postwar life underscores the sense of change brought about by the Civil War, but the overall tone of the ending is nevertheless strikingly far from triumphant. Clotelle buys Poplar Farm, where she had lived as a slave and where, having relinquished passing, she decides to open a school for the freedmen, thus foreshadowing the life choice of so many heroines of post-Reconstruction African American novels. However, while Clotelle's personal privilege, which is based on the wealth inherited from her deceased French husband, is put to the service of her community, Brown emphasizes that the economic and social conditions of the freedmen was still extremely precarious and "attracted the attention of the friends of humanity." What filters clearly through the sobering, willful optimism of the ending is Brown's strong suggestion that the Civil War should be seen as only the beginning, rather than the culmination, of the process of social change to which the nation as a whole ought to be committed.

From this vantage point, the ending of the 1867 edition of *Clotelle* echoes the even more cautious tone of another novel published during Reconstruction, Frances E. W. Harper's *Minnie's Sacrifice* (1869). This novel, which Harper serialized in the African American newspaper *The Christian Recorder*, is dominated by the admonitory sense that the promise and the hope raised by the Civil War may already be in peril of being betrayed, as in fact they would be with the institutionalization of segregation, which the 1896 Supreme Court ruling in the Plessy vs. Ferguson case would make constitutional. The sobering tone of Brown's ending harkens back to the foreground his earlier insistence on the need to fight not only against the institution of slavery but also against the underlying, widespread racist ideology, and anticipates other unfulfilled commitments to enforcing racial equality, including the steady process of erosion of the progress made during the Civil Rights movement that has characterized the end of the twentieth century.

Notwithstanding his earlier contention that "Slavery has never been represented; Slavery never can be represented,"[30] in *Clotel*, Brown succeeded in giving literary expression not only to the institution of slavery but also to the worldview of the slaves. More than one hundred and fifty years after its original publication, the contemporary relevance and stunning modernity of this

novel rests in the author's brilliant experimentation with literary
form that enabled him to break through the veil of slavery, repre-
sent the "prodigious magnitude" of its oppressiveness, and un-
mask its deep-seated and long-lasting ideological ramifications in
ways that change radically our understanding of American history, literature, and culture.[31] *Clotel* catapults us into a new relationship with that foundational part of the nation's past,
ultimately exceeding the boundaries of time and fiction to provide us with interpretive tools to reread critically and, as Brown
would have hoped, intervene actively in the politics of literary
and cultural representation of race in our twenty-first century.

NOTES

1. See Eugene A. Foster, et al., "Jefferson Fathers Slave's Last Child,"
   Nature, 5 November 1998, 27–28. The fact became a major news
   item. See Barbra Murray and Brian Duffy, "Jefferson's Secret
   Life," *U.S. News & World Report* 125.19, 9 November 1998,
   58–63.
2. Rumors about Jefferson's slave children were already circulating in
   the early 1800s. Later, the antislavery press published several articles on the sale of one of Jefferson's daughters in the 1830s and
   1840s. In 1848, Brown included a sensationalistic poem in *The
   Anti-Slavery Harp* entitled "Jefferson's Daughter." This poem,
   which had originally been published in *Tait's Edinburgh Magazine*
   in 1839, was apparently not included in other antislavery song-
   books of the period. See William Edward Farrison, *William Wells
   Brown: Author and Reformer* (Chicago: University of Chicago
   Press, 1969), 125.
3. J. Noel Heermance, *William Wells Brown and Clotelle: A Portrait
   of the Artist in the First Negro Novel* (n.p.: Archon, 1969), 164.
4. See F. O. Matthiessen, *American Renaissance: Art and Expression
   in the Age of Emerson and Whitman* (London: Oxford University
   Press, 1941).
5. The Fugitive Slave Law of 1850 made it easier for slaveholders to
   capture slaves who had escaped to the North, because protecting
   or helping fugitive slaves became a federal crime that could be punished by fines or imprisonment.

6. It is important to underline that Brown's *Clotel* is the first *known* African American novel, because critics continue to discover new and previously unknown texts belonging to the African American literary tradition. See, for instance, Henry Louis Gates's recent publication of the manuscript of Hannah Craft's *The Bondwoman's Narrative* (New York: Warner Books, 2002), a novel written in the late 1850s or early 1860s.

7. On Brown's use of his sources, see William Edward Farrison's excellent biography, *William Wells Brown: Author and Reformer* (Chicago: University of Chicago Press, 1969); Robert S. Levine's introduction to *Clotel; or, The President's Daughter* (Boston: Bedford/St. Martin's, 2000); and John Ernest's *Resistance and Reformation in Nineteenth-Century African-American Literature* (Jackson: University Press of Mississippi, 1995).

8. Brown's own ex-slave status features in the title page of *Clotel*, where he describes himself as "a fugitive slave." Even there, he balances that autobiographical statement with a description of himself as "author," not of his slave narrative, but rather of *Three Years in Europe*.

9. Robert B. Stepto, *From Behind the Veil: A Study of Afro-American Narrative* (Urbana: University of Illinois Press, 1979), 29.

10. William L. Andrews, *To Tell a Free Story: The First Century of Afro-American Autobiography, 1760–1865* (Urbana: University of Illinois Press, 1986), 145.

11. On Brown's use of the marriage plot and his influence on later African American writers, see Ann duCille, *The Coupling Convention: Sex, Text, and Tradition in Black Women's Fiction* (New York: Oxford University Press, 1993).

12. Robert S. Levine, ed., *Clotel; or, The President's Daughter: A Narrative of Slave Life in the United States* (Boston: Bedford/St. Martin's, 2000), 7.

13. On the trope of the tragic female mulatta, see Sterling Brown, *The Negro in American Fiction* (1937; New York: Argosy, 1969), Judith R. Berzon, *Neither White Nor Black: The Mulatto Character in American Fiction* (New York: New York University Press, 1978), and Jean Fagan Yellin, *The Intricate Knot: Black Figures in American Literature, 1776–1863* (New York: New York University Press, 1972).

14. On the critical reception of African American novels of passing, see M. Giulia Fabi, *Passing and the Rise of the African American Novel* (Urbana: University of Illinois Press, 2001).

15. Many of Brown's all-but-white characters not only pass, but also

cross-dress. Defying prevalent pseudobiological notions of race, Brown ultimately presents passing as another form of cross-dressing that relies on how physical appearance is socially interpreted.

16. William and Ellen Craft escaped from slavery in Georgia in 1848. She was light enough to pass as white and disguised herself as a man, while William posed as her servant. William later published their story in an autobiography, *Running a Thousand Miles for Freedom* (1860).

17. As will be underlined in the explanatory notes for chapter XXIII, Brown revises the portrayal also of a secondary character like Althesa's daughter Jane, who would seem to reproduce the tragic mulatta trope.

18. See "Introduction" in *The Escape; or, A Leap for Freedom. A Drama in Five Acts*, ed. John Ernest (Knoxville: University of Tennessee Press, 2001), xxxv.

19. This "lesson in interpretive method" (John Ernest, *Resistance*, 47) is brilliantly reinforced by Brown's decision to intertwine the reshaping of a minstrel type like Sam with that of a white Southern lady like Georgiana. Delicate, eventually doomed to die of consumption, "timid" but also "sanguine" in defending what is right, Georgiana represents Brown's characteristically combative response to a central character of Harriet Beecher Stowe's immensely popular *Uncle Tom's Cabin; or, Life among the Lowly* (1852; New York: Penguin, 1986): Little Eva. Whereas Little Eva's abolitionist plea to her father is submerged under the pathos of her death and eventually leaves the slaves' condition unchanged, Brown endows Georgiana with the determination to achieve the means to act on her abolitionist principles and free her slaves.

20. John Ernest, *Resistance*, 21.

21. Vernon Loggins, *The Negro Author: His Development in America* (New York: Columbia University Press, 1931), 166.

22. See M. Giulia Fabi, *Passing*, 148, and John Ernest, *Resistance*, 16, 21.

23. J. Noel Heermance, *William Wells Brown*, 181.

24. Charles J. Heglar, *Rethinking the Slave Narrative: Slave Marriage and the Narratives of Henry Bibb and William and Ellen Craft* (Westport: Connecticut: Greenwood Press, 2001), 128.

25. Brown shows this process of change in Carlton, who "had looked upon the Negro as an ill-treated distant link of the human family" and learns to regard them "as a part of God's children." Similarly, forty years later, the title heroine of another African American novel, Frances E. W. Harper's *Iola Leroy; or, Shadows*

Uplifted (1892; Boston: Beacon, 1987), will argue: "But there is a difference between looking on a man as an object of pity and protecting him as such, and being identified with him and forced to share his lot" (126). Brown and Harper knew each other, having lectured together for both the Massachusetts and the American Anti-Slavery Societies in 1857.

26. Sterling Stuckey, "Through the Prism of Folklore: The Black Ethos in Slavery," in *Going Through the Storm: The Influence of African American Art in History* (New York: Oxford University Press, 1994), 17.

27. Robert B. Stepto, *From Behind the Veil*, 29. In this regard, it is also significant that the American editions of *Clotel* present a shorter and more clearly fictional first chapter and that they do not include a closing list of sources.

28. William L. Andrews, "The 1850's: The First Afro-American Literary Renaissance," in *Literary Romanticism in America*, ed. William L. Andrews (Baton Rouge: Louisiana State University Press, 1981), 43.

29. William Wells Brown, *Clotelle: A Tale of the Southern States* (1864), in J. Noel Heermance, *William Wells Brown and Clotelle: A Portrait of the Artist in the First Negro Novel* (n.p.: Archon, 1969), 104.

30. William Wells Brown, "A Lecture Delivered before the Female Anti-Slavery Society of Salem" (1847), in *The Narrative of William Wells Brown, a Fugitive Slave, Written by Himself* (1848), ed. Larry Gara (Reading, Massachusetts: Addison-Wesley Publishing Company, 1969), 82.

31. William Wells Brown, *The Narrative of William Wells Brown, a Fugitive Slave, Written by Himself* (1848), in *From Fugitive Slave to Free Man: The Autobiographies of William Wells Brown*, ed. William L. Andrews (New York: Mentor, 1993), 83.

Suggestions for Further Reading

Andrews, William L. "The 1850s: The First Afro-American Literary Renaissance." In *Literary Romanticism in America*. William L. Andrews, ed. Baton Rouge: Louisiana State University Press, 1981.

———. *From Fugitive Slave to Free Man: The Autobiographies of William Wells Brown*. New York: Mentor, 1993.

———. "Mark Twain, William Wells Brown, and the Problem of Authority in New Southern Writing." In *Southern Literature and Literary Theory*. Jefferson Humphries, ed. Athens: University of Georgia Press, 1990.

———. "The Novelization of Voice in Early African American Narrative." *Proceedings of the Modern Language Association* 105, no. 1 (1990).

———. *To Tell a Free Story: The First Century of Afro-American Autobiography, 1760–1865*. Urbana: University of Illinois Press, 1986.

Berzon, Judith R. *Neither White Nor Black: The Mulatto Character in American Fiction*. New York: New York University Press, 1978.

Brown, Josephine. *Biography of an American Bondman*. 1856. In *Two Biographies by Afro-American Women*. William L. Andrews, ed. New York: Oxford University Press, 1991.

Brown, William Wells. *The Black Man, His Antecedents, His Genius, and His Achievements*. New York: Thomas Hamilton, 1863.

———. *Clotel; or, The President's Daughter: A Narrative of Slave Life in the United States*. 1853. New York: Carol Publishing, 1989.

————. *Clotelle: A Tale of the Southern States.* 1864. In *William Wells Brown and Clotelle. A Portrait of the Artist in the First Negro Novel.* J. Noel Heermance, ed. N.p.: Archon Books, 1969.

————. *Clotelle; or, The Colored Heroine. A Tale of the Southern States.* 1867. Miami: Mnemosyne, 1969.

————. *A Description of William Wells Brown's Original Panoramic Views of the Scenes in the Life of an American Slave, from His Birth in Slavery to His Death or His Escape to His First Home of Freedom on British Soil.* London: Charles Gilpin, 1850.

————. *The Escape; or, A Leap for Freedom. A Drama in Five Acts.* John Ernest ed. Knoxville: University of Tennessee Press, 2001.

————. *Memoir of William Wells Brown, an American Bondman, Written by Himself.* Boston: Boston Anti-Slavery Office, 1859.

————. *Miralda; or, The Beautiful Quadroon. A Romance of American Slavery, Founded on Fact.* In *Weekly Anglo-African,* December 1, 1860–March 16, 1861.

————. *My Southern Home: Or, The South and Its People.* Boston: A. G. Brown, 1880.

————. *Narrative of William W. Brown, a Fugitive Slave. Written by Himself.* 1847. In *Puttin' On Ole Massa.* Gilbert Osofsky, ed. New York: Harper & Row, 1969.

————. *The Negro in the American Rebellion: His Heroism and His Fidelity.* Boston: Lee & Shephard, 1867.

————. *The Rising Son; or, The Antecedents and Advancement of the Colored Race.* Boston: A. G. Brown, 1874.

————. *St. Domingo: Its Revolution and Its Patriots. A lecture.* Boston: Bela Marsh, 1855.

————. *Three Years in Europe; or, Places I Have Seen and People I Have Met.* London: Charles Gilpin, 1852.

Brown, William Wells, ed. *The Anti-Slavery Harp: A Collection of Songs for Anti-Slavery Meetings Compiled by William W. Brown, A Fugitive Slave.* Boston: Bela Marsh, 1848.

duCille, Ann. *The Coupling Convention: Sex, Text, and Tradi-

tion in Black Women's Fiction. New York: Oxford University Press, 1993.

Ernest, John. *Resistance and Reformation in Nineteenth-Century African-American Literature: Brown, Wilson, Jacobs, Delany, Douglass, and Harper*. Jackson: University Press of Mississippi, 1995.

Fabi, M. Giulia. *Passing and the Rise of the African American Novel*. Urbana: University of Illinois Press, 2001.

Farrison, William Edward. *William Wells Brown, Author and Reformer*. Chicago: University of Chicago Press, 1969.

———. *Clotel; or, The President's Daughter: A Narrative of Slave Life in the United States*. William Edward Farrison, ed. New York: Carol Publishing, 1989.

Foreman, P. Gabrielle. " 'Who's Your Mama?' White Mulatta Genealogies, Early Photography, and Anti-Passing Narratives of Slavery and Freedom." *American Literary History* 14, no. 3 (Fall 2002).

Gilmore, Paul. *The Genuine Article: Race, Mass Culture, and American Literary Manhood*. Durham, N.C.: Duke University Press, 2001.

Heermance, J. Noel. *William Wells Brown and Clotelle: A Portrait of the Artist in the First Negro Novel*. N.p.: Archon Books, 1969.

Heglar, Charles J. *Rethinking the Slave Narrative: Slave Marriage and the Narratives of Henry Bibb and William and Ellen Craft*. Westport, Connecticut: Greenwood Press, 2001.

Levine, Robert S. " 'Whiskey, Blacking, and All': Temperance and Race in William Wells Brown's *Clotel*." In *The Serpent and the Cup: Temperance in American Literature*. David S. Reynolds and Debra J. Rosenthal, eds. Amherst: University of Massachusetts Press, 1997.

———. *Clotel; or, The President's Daughter: A Narrative of Slave Life in the United States*. Robert S. Levine, ed. Boston: Bedford/St. Martin's, 2000.

Lewis, Richard O. "Literary Conventions in the Novels of William Wells Brown." *CLA Journal* 29, no. 2 (1985).

Mulvey, Christopher, ed. *Clotel by William Wells Brown: An*

Electronic Scholarly Edition. Adam Matthews Publications Ltd., http://www.adam-matthew-publications.co.uk, 2003.

———. "The Fugitive Self and the New World of the North: William Wells Brown's Discovery of America." In *The Black Columbiad: Defining Moments in African American Literature and Culture*. Werner Sollors and Maria Diedrich, eds. Cambridge: Harvard University Press, 1994.

Peterson, Carla L. "Capitalism, Black (Under)development, and the Production of the African American Novel in the 1850s." *American Literary History* 4, no. 4 (Winter 1992).

Reid-Pharr, Robert F. *Conjugal Union: The Body, the House, and the Black American*. New York: Oxford University Press, 1999.

Stepto, Robert B. *From Behind the Veil. A Study of Afro-American Narrative*. Urbana: University of Illinois Press, 1979.

Stuckey, Sterling. *Going Through the Storm: The Influence of African American Art in History*. New York: Oxford University Press, 1994.

Yellin, Jean Fagan. *The Intricate Knot: Black Figures in American Literature, 1776–1863*. New York: New York University Press, 1972.

A Note on the Texts

The present text of *Clotel; or, The President's Daughter* is based on the first published edition of 1853, published in London by Partridge & Oakey. The appendices contain the endings of the novel's subsequent three American editions, all of which were revised. Appendix A, the final four chapters of *Miralda; or, The Beautiful Quadroon*, is taken from the *Weekly Anglo-African*, which serialized the novel from December 1, 1860, through March 16, 1861. Appendix B consists of the last three chapters of *Clotelle: A Tale of the Southern States*, the first American book edition of the novel, which was published in 1864 by Boston publisher James Redpath. Appendix C contains the last four chapters of the 1867 book edition of *Clotelle; or, The Colored Heroine*, published by Lee & Shephard.

A Note on the Texts

CLOTEL;

OR,

THE PRESIDENT'S DAUGHTER:

A Narrative of Slave Life

IN

THE UNITED STATES.

BY

WILLIAM WELLS BROWN,

A FUGITIVE SLAVE, AUTHOR OF "THREE YEARS IN EUROPE."

With a Sketch of the Author's Life.

"We hold these truths to be self-evident: that all men are created
equal; that they are endowed by their Creator with certain inalienable
rights, and that among these are LIFE, LIBERTY, and the PURSUIT OF
HAPPINESS."—*Declaration of American Independence.*

LONDON:
PARTRIDGE & OAKEY, PATERNOSTER ROW;
AND 70, EDGWARE ROAD.

1853

Preface

More than two hundred years have elapsed since the first cargo of slaves was landed on the banks of the James River, in the colony of Virginia, from the West coast of Africa. From the introduction of slaves in 1620[1] down to the period of the separation of the Colonies from the British Crown, the number had increased to five hundred thousand; now there are nearly four million. In fifteen of the thirty-one States, Slavery is made lawful by the Constitution, which binds the several States into one confederacy.

On every foot of soil, over which *Stars and Stripes* wave, the Negro is considered common property, on which any white man may lay his hand with perfect impunity. The entire white population of the United States, North and South, are bound by their oath to the constitution, and their adhesion to the Fugitive Slave Law[2] to hunt down the runaway slave and return him to his claimant, and to suppress any effort that may be made by the slaves to gain their freedom by physical force. Twenty-five millions of whites have banded themselves in solemn conclave to keep four millions of blacks in their chains. In all grades of society are to be found men who either hold, buy, or sell slaves, from the statesmen and doctors of divinity, who can own their hundreds, down to the person who can purchase but one.

Were it not for persons in high places owning slaves, and thereby giving the system a reputation, and especially professed Christians, Slavery would long since have been abolished. The influence of the great "honours the corruption, and chastisement doth therefore hide his head."[3] The great aim of the true friends of the slave should be to lay bare the institution, so that the gaze of the world may be upon it, and cause the wise, the prudent, and the pious to withdraw their support from it, and leave it to its own fate. It does the cause of emancipation but little good to cry out in tones of execration against the traders, the kidnappers, the hireling overseers, and brutal drivers, so long as nothing is said to fasten the guilt on those who move in a higher circle.

The fact that slavery was introduced into the American colonies, while they were under the control of the British Crown, is a sufficient reason why Englishmen should feel a lively interest in its abolition; and now that the genius of mechanical invention has brought the two countries so near together, and both having one language and one literature, the influence of British public opinion is very great on the people of the New World.

If the incidents set forth in the following pages should add anything new to the information already given to the Public through similar publications, and should thereby aid in bringing British influence to bear upon American slavery, the main object for which this work was written will have been accomplished.

W. WELLS BROWN
22, *Cecil Street, Strand, London.*

NARRATIVE OF THE LIFE AND ESCAPE OF WILLIAM WELLS BROWN

"Shall tongues be mute when deeds are wrought
Which well might shame extremest Hell?
Shall freemen lack th' indignant thought?
Shall Mercy's bosom cease to swell?
Shall Honour bleed?—shall Truth succumb?
Shall pen, and press, and *soul* be dumb?"
—*Whittier.*[1]

William Wells Brown, the subject of this narrative, was born a slave in Lexington, Kentucky, not far from the residence of the late Hon. Henry Clay.[2] His mother was the slave of Doctor John Young. His father was a slaveholder, and, besides being a near relation of his master, was connected with the Wicklief family, one of the oldest, wealthiest, and most aristocratic of the Kentucky planters. Dr. Young was the owner of forty or fifty slaves, whose chief employment was in cultivating tobacco, hemp, corn, and flax. The Doctor removed from Lexington, when William was five or six years old, to the state of Missouri, and commenced farming in a beautiful and fertile valley, within a mile of the Missouri river.

Here the slaves were put to work under a harsh and cruel overseer named Cook. A finer situation for a farm could not have been selected in the state. With climate favourable to agriculture, and soil rich, the products came in abundance. At an early age William was separated from his mother, she being worked in the field, and he as a servant in his master's medical department.[3] When about ten years of age, the young slave's feelings were much hurt at hearing the cries of his mother, while being flogged by the Negro driver for being a few minutes behind the other hands in reaching the field.⁴ He heard her cry, "Oh, pray! oh, pray! oh, pray!" These are the words which slaves generally utter when imploring mercy at the hands of their oppressors. The son heard it, though he was some way off. He heard the crack of the whip and the groans of his poor mother. The cold chill ran over him, and he wept aloud; but he was a slave like his mother, and could render her no assistance. He was taught by the most bitter experience, that nothing could be more heart-rending than to see a dear and beloved mother or sister tortured by unfeeling men, and to hear her cries, and not be able to render the least aid. When William was twelve years of age, his master left his farm and took up his residence near St. Louis. The Doctor having more hands than he wanted for his own use, William was let out to a Mr. Freeland, an innkeeper. Here the young slave found himself in the hands of a most cruel and heartless master. Freeland was one of the real chivalry of the South; besides being himself a slaveholder, he was a horse-racer, cock-fighter, gambler, and, to crown the whole, an inveterate drunkard. What else but bad treatment could be expected from such a character? After enduring the tyrannical and inhuman usage of this man for five or six months, William resolved to stand it no longer, and therefore ran away, like other slaves who leave their masters, owing to severe treatment; and not knowing where to flee, the young fugitive went into the forest, a few miles from St. Louis. He had been in the woods but a short time, when he heard the barking and howling of dogs, and was soon satisfied that he was pursued by the Negro dogs; and, aware of their ferocious nature, the fugitive climbed a tree, to save himself from being torn to pieces. The hounds were soon at the trunk of the tree, and remained there, howling and barking, until those in whose charge they were came up. The slave was ordered down, tied, and taken home. Immediately on his arrival there, he was, as he expected, tied up in the smoke-house, and whipped till Freeland was satisfied, and then smoked with tobacco stems. This the slaveholder called "Virginia play." After being well whipped and smoked, he was again set to work. William remained with this monster a few months longer, and was then let out to Elijah P. Lovejoy,⁵ who years after became the editor of an abolition newspaper, and was murdered at Alton, Illinois, by a mob of slaveholders from the adjoining state of Missouri. The system of letting out slaves is one among the worst of the evils of slavery. The man who hires a slave, looks upon him in the same light as does the man who hires a horse for a limited period; he feels no interest in him, only to get the worth of his money. Not so with the man who owns the slave; he regards him as so much property, of which care should be taken. After being let out to a steamer as an under-steward, William was hired by James Walker, a slave-trader. Here the subject of our memoir was made superintendent of the gangs of slaves that were taken to the New Orleans market. In this capacity, William had opportunities, far greater than most slaves, of acquiring knowledge of the different phases of the *"peculiar institution."* Walker was a Negro speculator, who was amassing a fortune by trading in the bones, blood, and nerves, of God's children. The thoughts of such a traffic causes us to exclaim with the poet,

> "—Is there not some chosen curse,
> Some hidden thunder in the stores of heaven,
> Red with uncommon wrath, to blast the man
> Who gains his fortune from the blood of souls?"[6]

Between fifty and sixty slaves were chained together, put on board a steam-boat bound for New Orleans, and started on the voyage. New and strange scenes began to inspire the young slave with the hope of escaping to a land of freedom. There was in the boat a large room on the lower deck in which the slaves were kept, men and women promiscuously, all chained two and two together, not even leaving the poor slaves the privilege of choosing their partners. A strict watch was kept over them, so that they had no chance of escape. Cases had occurred in which slaves had got off their chains and made their escape at the landing-places, while the boat stopped to take in wood. But with all their care they lost one woman who had been taken from her husband and children, and having no desire to live without them, in the agony of her soul jumped overboard and drowned herself. Her sorrows were greater than she could bear;

slavery and its cruel inflictions had broken her heart. She, like William, sighed for freedom, but not the freedom which even British soil confers and inspires, but freedom from torturing pangs, and overwhelming grief.

At the end of the week they arrived at New Orleans, the place of their destination. Here the slaves were placed in a Negro pen, where those who wished to purchase could call and examine them. The Negro pen is a small yard surrounded by buildings, from fifteen to twenty feet wide, with the exception of a large gate with iron bars. The slaves are kept in the buildings during the night, and turned into the pen during the day. After the best of the gang were sold off, the balance was taken to the Exchange coffee-house auction-rooms, and sold at public auction. After the sale of the last slave, William and Mr. Walker left New Orleans for St. Louis.

After they had been at St. Louis a few weeks another cargo of human flesh was made up. There were amongst the lot several old men and women, some of whom had grey locks. On their way down to New Orleans William had to prepare the old slaves for market. He was ordered to shave off the old men's whiskers, and to pluck out the grey hairs where they were not too numerous; where they were, he coloured them with a preparation of blacking with a blacking brush. After having gone through the blacking process, they looked ten or fifteen years younger. William, though not well skilled in the use of scissors and razor, performed the office of the barber tolerably. After the sale of this gang of Negroes they returned to St. Louis, and a second cargo was made up. In this lot was a woman who had a child at the breast, yet was compelled to travel through the interior of the country on foot with the other slaves. In a published memoir of his life,[7] William says, "The child cried during the most of the day, which displeased Mr. Walker, and he told the mother that if her child did not stop crying, he would stop its mouth. After a long and weary journey under a burning sun, we put up for the night at a country inn. The following morning, just as they were about to start, the child again commenced crying. Walker stepped up to her and told her to give the child to him. The mother tremblingly obeyed. He took the child by one arm, as any one would a cat by the leg, and walked into the house where they had been staying, and said to the lady, 'Madam, I will make you a present of this little nigger; it keeps making such a noise that I can't bear it.' 'Thank you, sir,' said the lady. The mother, as soon as she saw that her child was to be left, ran up to Mr. Walker, and falling on her knees, begged of him in an agony of despair, to let her have her child. She clung round his legs so closely, that for some time he could not kick her off; and she cried, 'O my child, my child. Master, do let me have my dear, dear child. Oh! do, do. I will stop its crying, and love you for ever if you will only let me have my child again.' But her prayers were not heeded, they passed on, and the mother was separated from her child for ever.

"After the woman's child had been given away. Mr. Walker rudely commanded her to retire into the ranks with the other slaves. Women who had children were not chained, but those who had none were. As soon as her child was taken she was chained to the gang."

Some time after this, Walker bought a woman who had a blind child; it being considered worthless, it was given to the trader by the former owner of the woman on the score of humanity, he saying that he wished to keep mother and child together. At first Walker declined taking the child, saying that it would be too much trouble, but the mother wishing to have her boy with her, begged him to take it, promising to carry it the whole distance in her arms. Consequently he took the child, and the gang started on their route to the nearest steamboat landing, which was above one hundred miles. As might have been expected, the woman was unable to carry the boy and keep up with the rest of the gang. They put up at night at a small town, and the next morning, when about to start. Walker took the little boy from its mother and sold it to the innkeeper for the small sum of *one dollar*. The poor woman was so frantic at the idea of being separated from her only child, that it seemed impossible to get her to leave it. Not until the chains were put upon her limbs, and she fastened to the other slaves, could they get her to leave the spot. By main force this slave

mother was compelled to go on and leave her child behind.
Some days after, a lady from one of the free states was travelling the same road and put up at the same inn: she saw the child
the morning after her arrival, and heard its history from one of
the slaves, which was confirmed by the innkeeper's wife. A few
days after, the following poem appeared in one of the newspapers, from the pen of the lady who had seen the blind child:—

"Come back to me, mother! why linger away
From thy poor little blind boy, the long weary day!
I mark every footstep, I list to each tone,
And wonder my mother should leave me alone!
There are voices of sorrow and voices of glee,
But there's no one to joy or to sorrow with me;
For each hath of pleasure and trouble his share,
And none for the poor little blind boy will care.

"My mother, come back to me! close to thy breast
Once more let thy poor little blind one be pressed;
Once more let me feel thy warm breath on my cheek,
And hear thee in accents of tenderness speak!
O mother! I've no one to love me—no heart
Can bear like thy own in my sorrows a part;
No hand is so gentle, no voice is so kind!
Oh! none like a mother can cherish the blind!

"Poor blind one! no mother thy wailing can hear.
No mother can hasten to banish thy fear;
For the slave-owner drives her, o'er mountain and wild,
And for one paltry dollar hath sold thee, poor child!
Ah! who can in language of mortals reveal
The anguish that none but a mother can feel,
When man in his vile lust of mammon hath trod
On her child, who is stricken and smitten of God?

"Blind, helpless, forsaken, with strangers alone,
She hears in her anguish his piteous moan,
As he eagerly listens—but listens in vain,

> To catch the loved tones of his mother again!
> The curse of the broken in spirit shall fall
> On the wretch who hath mingled this wormwood and gall,
> And his gain like a mildew shall blight and destroy,
> Who hath torn from his mother the little blind boy."[8]

The thought that man can so debase himself as to treat a fellow-creature as here represented, is enough to cause one to blush at the idea that such men are members of a civilised and Christian nation.

Nothing was more grievous to the sensitive feelings of William, than seeing the separation of families by the slave-trader: husbands taken from their wives, and mothers from their children, without the least appearance of feeling on the part of those who separated them. While at New Orleans, on one occasion, William saw a slave murdered. The circumstances were as follows:—In the evening, between seven and eight o'clock, a slave came running down the levee, followed by several men and boys. The whites were crying out, "Stop that nigger! stop that nigger!" while the poor panting slave, in almost breathless accents, was repeating, "I did not steal the meat—I did not steal the meat." The poor man at last took refuge in the river. The whites who were in pursuit of him, ran on board of one of the boats to see if they could discover him. They finally espied him under the bow of the steamboat "Trenton." They got a pike-pole, and tried to drive him from his hiding-place. When they struck at him he would dive under the water. The water was so cold, that it soon became evident that he must come out or be drowned.

While they were trying to drive him from under the boat or drown him, he in broken and imploring accents said, "I did not steal the meat; I did not steal the meat. My master lives up the river. I want to see my master. I did not steal the meat. Do let me go home to master." After punching and striking him over the head for some time, he at last sunk in the water, to rise no more alive.

On the end of the pike-pole with which they had been striking him was a hook, which caught in his clothing, and they hauled him up on the bow of the boat. Some said he was dead; others said he was "playing 'possum"; while others kicked him to make him get up; but it was of no use—he was dead.

As soon as they became satisfied of this they·commenced leaving one after another. One of the hands on the boat informed the captain that they had killed the man, and that the dead body was lying on the deck. The captain, whose name was Hart, came on deck, and said to those who were remaining, "You have killed this nigger: now take him off my boat." The dead body was dragged on shore and left there. William went on board of the boat where the gang of slaves were, and during the whole night his mind was occupied with what he had seen.⁹ Early in the morning he went on shore to see if the dead body remained there. He found it in the same position that it was left the night before. He watched to see what they would do with it. It was left there until between eight and nine o'clock, when a cart, which took up the trash from the streets, came along, and the body was thrown in, and in a few minutes more was covered over with dirt, which they were removing from the streets.

At the expiration of the period of his hiring with Walker, William returned to his master, rejoiced to have escaped an employment as much against his own feelings as it was repugnant to human nature. But this joy was of short duration. The Doctor wanted money, and resolved to sell William's sister and two brothers. The mother had been previously sold to a gentleman residing in the city of St. Louis. William's master now informed him that he intended to sell him, and, as he was his own nephew, he gave him the privilege of finding some one to purchase him, who would treat him better than if he was sold on the auction block. William tried to make some arrangement by which he could purchase his own freedom, but the old Doctor would hear nothing of the kind. If there is one thing more revolting in the trade of human flesh than another, it is the selling of one's own blood relations.

He accordingly set out for the city in search of a new master. When he arrived there, he proceeded to the gaol with the hope of seeing his sister, but was again disappointed. On the following morning he made another attempt, and was allowed to see her once, for the last time. When he entered the room where she was seated in one corner, alone and disconsolate, there were four other women in the room, belonging to the same man, who were bought, the gaoler said, for the master's own use.

William's sister was seated with her face towards the door when he entered, but her gaze was transfixed on nothingness, and she did not look up when he walked up to her; but as soon as she observed him she sprang up, threw her arms around his neck, leaned her head upon his breast, and without uttering a word, in silent, indescribable sorrow, burst into tears. She remained so for some minutes, but when she recovered herself sufficiently to speak, she urged him to take his mother immediately, and try to get to the land of freedom. She said there was no hope for herself, she must live and die a slave. After giving her some advice, and taking a ring from his finger, he bade her farewell for ever. Reader, did ever a fair sister of thine go down to the grave prematurely, if so, perchance, thou hast drank deeply from the cup of sorrow? But how infinitely better is it for a sister to "go into the silent land" [10] with her honour untarnished, but with bright hopes, than for her to be sold to sensual slaveholders.

William had been in the city now two days, and as he was to be absent for only a week, it was well that he should make the best use of his time if he intended to escape. In conversing with his mother, he found her unwilling to make the attempt to reach the land of liberty, but she advised him by all means to get there himself if he possibly could. She said, as all her children were in slavery, she did not wish to leave them; but he loved his mother so intensely, that he could not think of leaving without her. He consequently used all his simple eloquence to induce her to fly with him, and at last he prevailed. They consequently fixed upon the next night as the time for their departure. The time at length arrived, and they left the city just as the clock struck nine. Having found a boat, they crossed the river in it. Whose boat it was he did not know; neither did he care: when it had served his purpose, he turned it adrift, and when he saw it last, it was going at a good speed down the river. After

walking in the main road as fast as they could all night, when
the morning came they made for the woods, and remained
there during the day, but when night came again, they proceeded on their journey with nothing but the North Star to
guide them. They continued to travel by night, and to bury
themselves in the silent solitudes of the forest by day. Hunger
and fatigue could not stop them, for the prospect of freedom at
the end of the journey nerved them up. The very thought of
leaving slavery, with its democratic whips, republican chains,
and bloodhounds, caused the hearts of the weary fugitives to
leap with joy. After travelling ten nights and hiding in the
woods during the day for fear of being arrested and taken
back, they thought they might with safety go the rest of their
way by daylight. In nearly all the free states there are men who
make a business of catching runaway slaves and returning them
to their owners for the reward that may be offered;[11] some of
these were on the alert for William and his mother, for they
had already seen the runaways advertised in the St. Louis newspapers.

All at once they heard the click of a horse's hoof, and looking
back saw three men on horseback galloping towards them.
They soon came up, and demanded them to stop. The three
men dismounted, arrested them on a warrant, and showed
them a handbill, offering two hundred dollars for their appre-
hension and delivery to Dr. Young and Isaac Mansfield in St.
Louis.

While they were reading the handbill, William's mother
looked him in the face, and burst into tears. "A cold chill ran
over me," says he, "and such a sensation I never experienced
before, and I trust I never shall again." They took out a rope
and tied him, and they were taken back to the house of the individual who appeared to be the leader. They then had something given them to eat, and were separated. Each of them was
watched over by two men during the night. The religious characteristic of the American slaveholder soon manifested itself, as
before the family retired to rest they were all called together to
attend prayers; and the very man who, but a few hours before,
had arrested poor panting, fugitive slaves, now read a chapter

from the Bible and offered a prayer to God; as if that benignant and omnipotent One consecrated the infernal act he had just committed.

The next morning they were chained and handcuffed, and started back to St. Louis. A journey of three days brought the fugitives again to the place they had left twelve days previously with the hope that they would never return. They were put in prison to await the orders of their owners. When a slave attempts to escape and fails, he feels sure of either being severely punished, or sold to the Negro traders and taken to the far south, there to be worked up on a cotton, sugar, or rice plantation. This William and his mother dreaded. While they were in suspense as to what would be their fate, news came to them that the mother had been sold to a slave speculator. William was soon sold to a merchant residing in the city, and removed to his new owner's dwelling. In a few days the gang of slaves, of which William's mother was one, were taken on board a steamer to be carried to the New Orleans market. The young slave obtained permission from his new owner to go and take a last farewell of his mother. He went to the boat, and found her there, chained to another woman, and the whole number of slaves, amounting to some fifty or sixty, chained in the same manner. As the son approached his mother she moved not, neither did she weep; her emotions were too deep for tears. William approached her, threw his arms around her neck, kissed her, fell upon his knees begging her forgiveness, for he thought he was to blame for her sad condition, and if he had not persuaded her to accompany him she might not have been in chains then.

She remained for some time apparently unimpressionable, tearless, sighless, but in the innermost depths of her heart moved mighty passions. William says, "She finally raised her head, looked me in the face, and such a look none but an angel can give, and said, 'My dear son, you are not to blame for my being here. You have done nothing more nor less than your duty. Do not, I pray you, weep for me; I cannot last long upon a cotton plantation. I feel that my heavenly Master will soon call me home, and then I shall be out of the hands of the slaveholders.' I could hear no more—my heart struggled to free itself from the human form. In a moment she saw Mr. Mansfield, her master, coming toward that part of the boat, and she whispered in my ear. 'My child, we must soon part to meet no more on this side of the grave. You have ever said that you would not die a slave; that you would be a freeman. Now try to get your liberty! You will soon have no one to look after but yourself!' and just as she whispered the last sentence into my ear, Mansfield came up to me, and with an oath said, 'Leave here this instant; you have been the means of my losing one hundred dollars to get this wench back'—at the same time kicking me with a heavy pair of boots. As I left her she gave one shriek, saying, 'God be with you!' It was the last time that I saw her, and the last word I heard her utter.

"I walked on shore. The bell was tolling. The boat was about to start. I stood with a heavy heart, waiting to see her leave the wharf. As I thought of my mother, I could but feel that I had lost

> 'The glory of my life,
> My blessing and my pride!
> I half forgot the name of slave,
> When she was by my side."[12]

"The love of liberty that had been burning in my bosom had well-nigh gone out. I felt as though I was ready to die. The boat moved gently from the wharf, and while she glided down the river, I realised that my mother was indeed

> 'Gone—gone—sold and gone,
> To the rice swamp, dark and lone!'[13]

"After the boat was out of sight I returned home; but my thoughts were so absorbed in what I had witnessed, that I knew not what I was about. Night came, but it brought no sleep to my eyes." When once the love of freedom is born in the slave's mind, it always increases and brightens, and William having heard so much about Canada, where a number of his acquaintances had found a refuge and a home, he heartily desired to join them. Building castles in the air in the daytime; incessantly thinking of freedom, he would dream of the land of liberty, but on waking in the morning would weep to find it but a dream.

> "He would dream of Victoria's domain,
> And in a moment he seemed to be there;
> But the fear of being taken again,
> Soon hurried him back to despair."[14]

Having been for some time employed as a servant in an hotel, and being of a very active turn, William's new owner resolved to let him out on board a steamboat. Consequently the young slave was hired out to the steamer St. Louis, and soon after sold to Captain Enoch Price, the owner of that boat. Here he was destined to remain but a short period, as Mrs. Price wanted a carriage-driver, and had set her heart upon William for that purpose.

Scarcely three months had elapsed from the time that William became the property of Captain Price, ere that gentleman's family took a pleasure trip to New Orleans, and William accompanied them. From New Orleans the family proceeded to Louisville. The hope of escape again dawned upon the slave's mind, and the trials of the past were lost in hopes for the future. The love of liberty, which had been burning in his bosom for years, and which at times had been well nigh extinguished, was now resuscitated. Hopes nurtured in childhood, and strengthened as manhood dawned, now spread their sails to the gales of his imagination. At night, when all around was peaceful, and in the mystic presence of the everlasting starlight, he would walk the steamer's decks, meditating on his happy prospects, and summoning up gloomy reminiscences of the dear hearts he was leaving behind him. When not thinking of the future his mind would dwell on the past. The love of a dear mother, a dear and affectionate sister, and three brothers yet living, caused him to shed many tears. If he could only be assured of their being dead, he would have been comparatively happy; but he saw in imagination his mother in the cotton-field, followed by a monster task-master, and no one to speak a consoling word to her. He beheld his sister in the hands of the slave-driver, compelled to submit to his cruelty, or, what was unutterably worse, his lust; but still he was far away from them, and could not do anything for them if he remained in slavery; consequently he resolved, and consecrated the resolve with a prayer, that he would start on the first opportunity.[15]

That opportunity soon presented itself. When the boat got to the wharf where it had to stay for some time, at the first convenient moment Brown made towards the woods, where he remained until night-time. He dared not walk during the day, even in the state of Ohio; he had seen so much of the perfidy of white men, and resolved, if possible, not to get into their hands. After darkness covered the world, he emerged from his hiding-place; but he did not know east from west, or north from south; clouds hid the North Star from his view. In this desolate condition he remained for some hours, when the clouds rolled away, and his friend, with its shining face—the North Star—welcomed his sight. True as the needle to the pole he obeyed its attractive beauty, and walked on till daylight dawned.

It was winter-time; the day on which he started was the 1st of January, and, as it might be expected, it was intensely cold; he had no overcoat, no food, no friend, save the North Star, and the God which made it. How ardently must the love of freedom burn in the poor slave's bosom, when he will pass through so many difficulties, and even look death in the face, in winning his birth-right, freedom. But what crushed the poor slave's heart in his flight most was, not the want of food or clothing, but the thought that every white man was his deadly enemy. Even in the free states the prejudice against colour is so strong, that there appears to exist a deadly antagonism between the white and coloured races.

William in his flight carried a tinder-box with him, and when he got very cold he would gather together dry leaves and stubble and make a fire, or certainly he would have perished. He was determined to enter into no house, fearing that he might meet a betrayer.

It must have been a picture which would have inspired an artist, to see the fugitive roasting the ears of corn that he found or took from barns during the night, at solitary fires in the deep solitudes of woods.

The suffering of the fugitive was greatly increased by the cold, from the fact of his having just come from the warm climate of New Orleans. Slaves seldom have more than one name, and William was not an exception to this, and the fugitive began to think of an additional name. A heavy rain of three days, in which it froze as fast as it fell, and by which the poor fugitive was completely drenched, and still more chilled, added to the depression of his spirits already created by his weary journey. Nothing but the fire of hope burning within his breast could have sustained him under such overwhelming trials.

> "Behind he left the whip and chains.
> Before him were sweet Freedom's plains."[16]

Through cold and hunger, William was now ill, and he could go no further. The poor fugitive resolved to seek protection, and accordingly hid himself in the woods near the road, until some one should pass. Soon a traveller came along, but the slave dared not speak. A few moments more and a second passed, the fugitive attempted to speak, but fear deprived him of voice. A third made his appearance. He wore a broad-brimmed hat and a long coat, and was evidently walking only for exercise. William scanned him well, and though not much skilled in physiognomy, he concluded he was the man. William approached him, and asked him if he knew any one who would help him, as he was sick. The gentleman asked whether he was not a slave. The poor slave hesitated; but, on being told that he had nothing to fear, he answered, "Yes." The gentleman told him he was in a pro-slaving neighbourhood, but, if he would wait a little, he would go and get a covered waggon, and convey him to his house. After he had gone, the fugitive meditated whether he should stay or not, being apprehensive that the broad-brimmed gentleman had gone for some one to assist him: he however concluded to remain.

After waiting about an hour—an hour big with fate to him—
he saw the covered waggon making its appearance, and no one
on it but the person he before accosted. Trembling with hope
and fear, he entered the waggon, and was carried to the person's house. When he got there, he still halted between two
opinions, whether he should enter or take to his heels; but he
soon decided after seeing the glowing face of the wife. He saw
something in her that bid him welcome, something that told
him he would not be betrayed.

He soon found that he was under the shed of a Quaker, and
a Quaker of the George Fox stamp.[17] He had heard of Quakers
and their kindness; but was not prepared to meet with such
hospitality as now greeted him. He saw nothing but kind looks,
and heard nothing but tender words. He began to feel the pul-
sations of a new existence. White men always scorned him, but
now a white benevolent woman felt glad to wait on him; it was
a revolution in his experience. The table was loaded with good
things, but he could not eat. If he were allowed the privilege of
sitting in the kitchen, he thought he could do justice to the
viands. The surprise being over his appetite soon returned.

"I have frequently been asked," says William, "how I felt
upon finding myself regarded as a man by a white family: especially having just run away from one. I cannot say that I have
ever answered the question yet. The fact that I was, in all probability, a freeman, sounded in my ears like a charm. I am satisfied that none but a slave could place such an appreciation
upon liberty as I did at that time. I wanted to see my mother
and sister, that I might tell them that "I was free!" I wanted to
see my fellow-slaves in St. Louis, and let them know that the
chains were no longer upon my limbs. I wanted to see Captain
Price, and let him learn from my own lips that I was no more a
chattel, but a MAN. I was anxious, too, thus to inform Mrs.
Price that she must get another coachman, and I wanted to see
Eliza more than I did Mr. Price or Mrs. Price.[18] The fact that I
was a freeman—could walk, talk, eat, and sleep as a man, and
no one to stand over me with the blood-clotted cow-hide—all
this made me feel that I was not myself."

The kind Quaker, who so hospitably entertained William,

was called Wells Brown. He remained with him about a fortnight, during which time he was well fed and clothed. Before
leaving, the Quaker asked him what was his name besides
William. The fugitive told him he had no other. "Well," said
he, "thee must have another name. Since thee has got out of
slavery, thee has become a man, and men always have two
names."

William told him that as he was the first man to extend the
hand of friendship to him, he would give him the privilege of
naming him.

"If I name thee," said he, "I shall call thee Wells Brown, like
myself."

"But," said he, "I am not willing to lose my name of
William. It was taken from me once against my will, and I am
not willing to part with it on any terms." [19]

"Then," said the benevolent man, "I will call thee William
Wells Brown."

"So be it," said William Wells Brown, and he has been
known by this name ever since.

After giving the newly-christened freeman "a name," the
Quaker gave him something to aid him to get "a local habitation." So, after giving him some money, Brown[20] again started
for Canada. In four days he reached a public-house, and went
in to warm himself. He soon found that he was not out of the
reach of his enemies. While warming himself, he heard some
men in an adjoining bar-room talking about some runaway
slaves. He thought it was time to be off, and, suiting the action
to the thought, he was soon in the woods out of sight. When
night came, he returned to the road and walked on; and so, for
two days and two nights, till he was faint and ready to perish
of hunger.

In this condition he arrived in the town of Cleveland, Ohio,
on the banks of Lake Erie, where he determined to remain until
the spring of the year, and then to try and reach Canada. Here
he was compelled to work merely for his food. "Having lived
in that way," said he in a speech at a public meeting in Exeter
Hall,[21] "for some weeks, I obtained a job, for which I received
a shilling. This was not only the only shilling I had, but it was

the first I had received after obtaining my freedom, and that shilling made me feel, indeed, as if I had a considerable stock in hand. What to do with my shilling I did not know. I would not put it into the bankers' hands, because, if they would have received it, I would not trust them. I would not lend it out, because I was afraid I should not get it back again. I carried the shilling in my pocket for some time, and finally resolved to lay it out; and after considerable thinking upon the subject, I laid out 6d. for a spelling-book, and the other 6d.[22] for sugar candy or barley sugar. Well, now, you will all say that the one 6d. for the spelling-book was well laid out; and I am of opinion that the other was well laid out too; for the family in which I worked for my bread had two little boys, who attended the school every day, and I wanted to convert them into teachers; so I thought that nothing would act like a charm so much as a little barley sugar. The first day I got my book and stock in trade, I put the book into my bosom, and went to saw wood in the wood-house on a very cold day. One of the boys, a little after four o'clock, passed through the wood-house with a bag of books. I called to him, and I said to him, 'Johnny, do you see this?' taking a stick of barley sugar from my pocket and showing it to him. Says he, 'Yes; give me a taste of it.' Said I, 'I have got a spelling-book too,' and I showed that to him. 'Now,' said I, 'if you come to me in my room, and teach me my A, B, C, I will give you a whole stick.' 'Very well,' said he, 'I will; but let me taste it.' 'No; I can't.' 'Let me have it now.' Well, I thought I had better give him a little taste, until the right time came; and I marked the barley sugar about a quarter of an inch down, and told him to bite that far and no farther. He made a grab, and bit half the stick, and ran off laughing. I put the other piece in my pocket, and after a little while the other boy, little David, came through the wood-house with his books. I said nothing about the barley sugar, or my wish to get education. I knew the other lad would communicate the news to him. In a little while he returned, and said, 'Bill, John says you have got some barley sugar.' 'Well.' I said, 'what of that?' 'He said you gave him some; give me a little taste.' 'Well, if you come to-night and help me to learn my letters, I will give you a whole stick.' 'Yes;

but let me taste it.' 'Ah! but you want to bite it.' 'No, I don't, but just let me taste it.' Well, I thought I had better show it to him. 'Now,' said he, 'let me touch my tongue against it.' I thought then that I had better give him a taste, but I would not trust him so far as I trusted John; so I called him to me, and got his head under my arm, and took him by the chin, and told him to hold out his tongue; and as he did so, I drew the barley sugar over very lightly. He said, 'That's very nice; just draw it over again.' 'I could stand here and let you draw it across my tongue all day.' The night came on; the two boys came out of their room up into the attic where I was lodging, and there they commenced teaching me the letters of the alphabet. We all laid down upon the floor, covered with the same blanket; and first one would teach me a letter, and then the other, and I would pass the barley sugar from one side to the other. I kept those two boys on my sixpenny worth of barley sugar for about three weeks. Of course I did not let them know how much I had. I first dealt it out to them a quarter of a stick at a time. I worked along in that way, and before I left that place where I was working for my bread, I got so that I could spell. I had a book that had the word *baker* in it, and the boys used to think that when they got so far as that, they were getting on pretty well. I had often passed by the school-house, and stood and listened at the window to hear them spell, and I knew that when they could spell *baker* they thought something of themselves; and I was glad when I got that far. Before I left that place I could read. Finally, from that I went on until I could write. How do you suppose I first commenced writing? for you will understand that up to the present time I never spent a day in school in my life, for I had no money to pay for schooling, so that I had to get my learning first from one and then from another. I carried a piece of chalk in my pocket, and whenever I met a boy I would stop him and take out my chalk and get at a board fence and then commence. First I made some flourishes with no meaning, and called a boy up, and said, 'Do you see that? Can you beat that writing?' Said he, 'That's not writing.' Well, I wanted to get so as to write my own name. I had got out of slavery with only one name. While escaping, I received the hospitality of a very good man, who had spared part of his name to me, and finally my name got pretty long, and I wanted to be able to write it. 'Now, what do you call that?' said the boy, looking at my flourishes. I said. 'Is not that *William Wells Brown?*' 'Give me the chalk,' says he, and he wrote out in large letters *'William Wells Brown,'* and I marked up the fence for nearly a quarter of a mile, trying to copy, till I got so that I could write my name. Then I went on with my chalking, and, in fact, all board fences within half a mile of where I lived were marked over with some kind of figures I had made, in trying to learn how to write. I next obtained an arithmetic, and then a grammar, and I stand here tonight, without having had a day's schooling in my life." Such were some of the efforts made by a fugitive slave to obtain for himself an education. Soon after his escape, Brown was married to a free coloured woman, by whom he has had three daughters, one of whom died in infancy.[23] Having tasted the sweets of freedom himself, his great desire was to extend its blessing to his race, and in the language of the poet he would ask himself,

> "Is true freedom but to break
> Fetters for our own dear sake
> And with leathern hearts forget
> That we owe mankind a debt?
>
> "No! true freedom is to share
> All the chains our brothers wear,
> And with heart and hand to be
> Earnest to make others free."[24]

While acting as a servant to one of the steamers on Lake Erie, Brown often took fugitives from Cleveland and other ports to Buffalo, or Detroit, from either of which places they could cross to Canada in an hour. During the season of 1842, this fugitive slave conveyed no less than *sixty-nine* runaway slaves across Lake Erie, and placed them safe on the soil of Canada. The following interesting account of Brown's first going into business for himself, which we transcribe from his "Three Years in Europe,"²⁵ will show the energy of the man. He says, "In the autumn of 1835, having been cheated out of the previous summer's earnings by the captain of the steamer in which I had been employed running away with the money, I was, like the rest of the men, left without any means of support during the winter, and therefore had to seek employment in the neighbouring towns. I went to the town of Monroe in the state of Michigan, and while going through the principal streets looking for work, I passed the door of the only barber in the town, whose shop appeared to be filled with persons waiting to be shaved. As there was but one man at work, and as I had, while employed in the steamer, occasionally shaved a gentleman who could not perform that office himself, it occurred to me that I might get employment here as a journeyman barber. I therefore made immediate application for work, but the barber told me he did not need a hand. But I was not to be put off so easily, and after making several offers to work cheap, I frankly told him, that if he would not employ me, I would get a room near him, and set up an opposition establishment. This threat, however, made no impression on the barber: and as I was leaving, one of the men, who were waiting to be shaved, said, 'If you want a room in which to commence business, I have one on the opposite side of the street.' This man followed me out; we went over, and I looked at the room. He strongly urged me to set up, at the same time promising to give me his influence. I took the room, purchased an old table, two chairs, got a pole with a red stripe painted around it, and the next day opened, with a sign over the door, 'Fashionable Hair-dresser from New York, Emperor of the West.' I need not add that my enterprise was very annoying to the 'shop over the way,' especially my sign, which happened to be the most extensive part of the concern. Of course I had to tell all who came in, that my neighbour on the opposite side did not keep clean towels, that his razors were dull, and, above all, he never had been to New York to see the fashions. Neither had I. In a few weeks I had the entire business of the town, to the great discomfiture of the other barber.

At this time, money matters in the Western States were in a sad condition. Any person who could raise a small amount of money was permitted to establish a bank, and allowed to issue notes for four times the sum raised. This being the case, many persons borrowed money merely long enough to exhibit to the bank inspectors, and the borrowed money was returned, and the bank left without a dollar in its vaults, if, indeed, it had a vault about its premises. The result was, that banks were started all over the Western States, and the country flooded with worthless paper. These were known as the 'Wild Cat Banks.' Silver coin being very scarce, and the banks not being allowed to issue notes for a smaller amount than one dollar, several persons put out notes of from 6 to 75 cents in value; these were called 'Shinplasters.' The Shinplaster was in the shape of a promissory note, made payable on demand. I have often seen persons with large rolls of these bills, the whole not amounting to more than five dollars. Some weeks after I had commenced business on my 'own hook,' I was one evening very much crowded with customers; and while they were talking over the events of the day, one of them said to me, 'Emperor, you seem to be doing a thriving business. You should do as other business men, issue your Shinplasters.' This of course, as it was intended, created a laugh; but with me it was no laughing matter, for from that moment I began to think seriously of becoming a banker. I accordingly went a few days after to a printer, and he, wishing to get the job of printing, urged me to put out my notes, and showed me some specimens of engravings that he had just received from Detroit. My head being already filled with the idea of the bank, I needed but little persuasion to set the thing finally afloat. Before I left the printer the notes were partly in type, and I studying how I should keep the public from counterfeiting them. The next day, my Shinplasters were handed to me, the whole amount being twenty dollars; and, after being duly signed, were ready for circulation. The first night I had my money, my head was so turned and dizzy, that I could not sleep. In fact, I slept but little for weeks after the issuing of my bills. This fact satisfied me, that people of wealth pass many sleepless hours. At first my notes did not take well; they were too new, and viewed with a suspicious eye. But through the assistance of my customers, and a good deal of exertion on my part, my bills were soon in circulation; and nearly all the money received in return for my notes was spent in fitting up and decorating my shop. Few bankers get through this world without their difficulties, and I was not to be an exception. A short time after my money had been out, a party of young men, either wishing to pull down my vanity, or to try the soundness of my bank, determined to give it 'a run.' After collecting together a number of my bills, they came one at a time to demand other money for them; and I, not being aware of what was going on, was taken by surprise. One day as I was sitting at my table, stropping some new razors I had just purchased with the avails of my Shinplasters, one of the men entered and said, 'Emperor, you will oblige me if you will give me some other money for these notes of yours.' I immediately cashed the notes with the most worthless of the Wild Cat money that I had on hand, but which was a lawful tender. The young man had scarcely left, when a second appeared with a similar amount, and demanded payment. These were cashed, and soon a third came with his roll of notes. I paid these with an air of triumph, although I had but half a dollar left. I began now to think seriously what I should do, or how to act, provided another demand should be made. While I was thus engaged in thought, I saw the fourth man crossing the street, with a handful of notes, evidently my Shinplasters. I instantaneously shut the door, and looking out of the window said, 'I have closed business for to-day: come to-morrow and I will see you.' In looking across the street, I saw my rival standing at his shopdoor, grinning and clapping his hands at my apparent downfall. I was completely 'done *Brown*' for the day. However, I was not to be 'used up' in this way; so I escaped by the back door, and went in search of my friend, who had first suggested to me the idea of issuing my notes. I found him, told him of the difficulty I was in, and wished him to point out a way by which I might extricate myself. He laughed heartily at my sad position, and then said, 'You must act as all bankers do in this part of the country.' I inquired how they did; and he said, 'when your notes are brought to you, you must redeem them, and then send them out and get other money for them; and, with the latter, you can keep cashing your own Shinplasters.' This was, indeed, a new idea for me. I immediately commenced putting in circulation the notes which I had just redeemed, and my efforts were crowned with such success, that, together with the aid of my friend, who, like a philanthropist and Western Christian as he was, before I slept that night, my Shinplasters were again in circulation, and my bank once more on a sound basis."

In proportion as his mind expanded under the more favourable circumstances in which Brown was placed, he became anxious, not merely for the redemption of his race from personal slavery, but for the moral and religious elevation of those who were free. Finding that habits of intoxication were too prevalent among his coloured brethren, he, in conjunction with others, commenced a temperance reformation in their body. Such was the success of their efforts that, in three years, in the city of Buffalo alone, a society of upwards of 500 members was raised out of a coloured population of less than 700. Of that society Mr. Brown was thrice elected president. The intellectual powers of our author, coupled with his intimate acquaintance with the workings of the slave system, early recommended him to the Abolitionists, as a man eminently qualified to arouse the attention of the people of the Northern States to the great national sin of America. In 1843, he was engaged by the Western New York Anti-Slavery Society as a lecturing agent. From 1844 to 1847, he laboured in the Anti-Slavery cause in connection with the American Anti-Slavery Society;[26] and from that period up to the time of his departure for Europe, in 1849, he was an agent of the Massachusetts Anti-Slavery Society. The records of these societies furnish abundant evidence of the success of his labours. From the Massachusetts Anti-Slavery Society he early received the following testimonial. "Since Mr. Brown became an agent of this society, he has lectured in very many of the towns of this commonwealth, and gained for himself, the respect and esteem of all whom he met. Himself a fugitive slave, he can experimentally describe the situation of those in bonds as bound with them; and he powerfully illustrates the diabolism of that system which keeps in chains and darkness a host of minds, which, if free and enlightened, would shine among men like stars in the firmament." Another member of that society speaks thus of him:—"I need not attempt any description of the ability and efficiency which characterised the speeches of William Wells Brown throughout the meeting. To you who know him so well, it is enough to say that his lectures were worthy of himself. He has left an impression on the minds of the people, that few could have done. Cold indeed must be the hearts that could resist the appeals of so noble a specimen of humanity, in behalf of a crushed and despised race."

In 1847, Mr. Brown wrote a narrative of his life and escape from slavery, which rapidly ran through several editions. A copy of this he forwarded to his old master, from whom he had escaped, and soon after a friend of Mr. Brown's received the following letter:

"*St. Louis, Jan. 10th, 1848*

"Sir,—I received a pamphlet, or a narrative, so called on the title-page, of the Life of William W. Brown, a fugitive slave, purporting to have been written by himself; and in his book I see a letter from you to the said William W. Brown. This said Brown is named William; he is a slave belonging to me, and ran away from me the first day of January, 1834.

"I purchased him of Mr. S. Willi, the last of September, 1833. I paid six hundred and fifty dollars for him. If I had wanted to speculate on him, I could have sold him for three times as much as I paid for him. I was offered two thousand dollars for him in New Orleans at one time, and fifteen hundred dollars for him at another time, in Louisville, Kentucky. But I would not sell him. I was told that he was going to run away, but I did not believe the man, for I had so much confidence in William. I want you to see him, and see if what I say is not the truth. I do not want him as a slave, but I think that his friends, who sustain him and give him the right hand of fellowship, or he himself, could afford to pay my agent in Boston three hundred and twenty five

dollars, and I will give him free papers, so that he may go wherever he wishes to. Then he can visit St. Louis, or any other place
he may wish.

"This amount is just half what I paid for him. Now, if this
offer suits Mr. Brown, and the Anti-Slavery Society of Boston, or
Massachusetts, let me know, and I will give you the name of my
agent in Boston, and forward the papers, to be given to William
W. Brown as soon as the money is paid.

"Yours respectfully,
"Enoch Price."

"To Edmund Quincy, Esq."[27]

While Mr. Brown would most gladly have accepted manu-
mission papers, relieving him from all future claim of the slaveholder, and thereby making his freedom more secure, he yet felt
that he could not conscientiously purchase his liberty, because,
by so doing, he would be putting money into the pockets of the
manstealer which did not justly belong to him. He therefore refused the offer of Mr. Price. Notwithstanding the celebrity he
had acquired in the North, as a man of genius and talent, and
the general respect his high character had gained him, the slave
spirit of America denied him the rights of a citizen. By the constitution of the United States he was every moment liable to be
arrested, and returned to the slavery from which he had fled.
His only protection from such a fate was the anomaly of the ascendancy of the public opinion over the law of the country.

It has been for years thought desirable and advantageous to
the cause of Negro emancipation in America, to have some tal-
ented man of colour always in Great Britain, who should be a
living refutation of the doctrine of the inferiority of the African
race; and it was moreover felt that none could so powerfully advocate the cause of "those in bonds" as one who had actually
been "bound with them." Mr. Brown having received repeated
invitations from distinguished English Abolitionists to visit
Great Britain, and being chosen a delegate to the Paris Peace
Congress of 1849 by the American Peace Society, and also by a
convention of the coloured people of Boston, he resolved to ac-

quiesce in the wishes of his numerous friends, and accordingly sailed from the United States on the 18th of July, 1849.

On leaving America he bore with him the following testimony from the Board of Managers of the Massachusetts Anti-Slavery Society:—

"In consequence of the departure for England of their esteemed friend and faithful co-labourer in the cause of the American slave, William W. Brown, the Board of Management of the Massachusetts Anti-Slavery Society would commend him to the confidence, respect, esteem, and hospitality of the friends of emancipation wherever he may travel:—

"1. Because he is a fugitive slave from the American house of bondage, and on the soil which gave him birth can find no spot on which he can stand in safety from his pursuers, protected by law.

"2. Because he is a man, and not a chattel; and while as the latter, he may at any time be sold at public vendue under the American star-spangled banner, we rejoice to know that he will be recognised and protected as the former under the flag of England.

"3. Because, for several years past, he has nobly consecrated his time and talents, at great personal hazard, and under the most adverse circumstances, to the uncompromising advocacy of the cause of his enslaved countrymen.

"4. Because he visits England for the purpose of increasing, consolidating, and directing British humanity and piety against that horrible system of slavery in America, by which three millions of human beings, by creation the children of God, are ranked with four-footed beasts, and treated as marketable commodities.

"5. Because he has long been in their employment as a lecturing agent in Massachusetts, and has laboured with great acceptance and success; and from the acquaintance thus formed, they are enabled to certify that he has invariably conducted himself with great circumspection, and won for himself the sympathy, respect, and friendship of a very large circle of acquaintance."

The Coloured convention unanimously passed the following resolution:

"*Resolved*—That we bid our brother, William Wells Brown, God speed in his mission to Europe, and commend him to the hospitality and encouragement of all true friends of humanity."

In a letter to an American journal,[28] announcing his arrival at Liverpool, he speaks as follows:—

"No person of my complexion can visit this country without being struck with the marked difference between the English and the Americans. The prejudice which I have experienced on all and every occasion in the United States, and to some degree on board the *Canada*, vanished as soon as I set foot on the soil of Britain. In America I had been bought and sold as a slave, in the Southern States. In the so-called Free States I had been treated as one born to occupy an inferior position; in steamers, compelled to take my fare on the deck; in hotels, to take my meals in the kitchen; in coaches, to ride on the outside; in railways, to ride in the 'Negro car'; and in churches, to sit in the 'Negro pew.' But no sooner was I on British soil than I was recognised as a man and an equal. The very dogs in the streets appeared conscious of my manhood. Such is the difference, and such is the change that is brought about by a trip of nine days in an Atlantic steamer. * * * For the first time in my life, I can say 'I am truly free.' My old master may make his appearance here, with the constitution of the United States in his pocket, the fugitive slave law in one hand and the chains in the other, and claim me as his property; but all will avail him nothing. I can here stand and look the tyrant in the face, and tell him that I am his equal! England is, indeed, the 'land of the free, and the home of the brave.' "

The reception of Mr. Brown at the Peace Congress in Paris was most flattering. He admirably maintained his reputation as a public speaker. His brief address upon that "war spirit of America which holds in bondage nearly four millions of his brethren," produced a profound sensation. At its conclusion the speaker was warmly greeted by Victor Hugo, the Abbé Duguerry, Emile de Girardin, Richard Cobden, and every man of note in the assembly.[29] At the soirée given by M. de Toc-

CLOTEL; OR, THE PRESIDENT'S DAUGHTER

querelle, the Minister for Foreign Affairs, and the other fêtes given to the members of the Congress, Mr. Brown was received with marked attention.

Having finished his Peace Mission in France, he returned to England, where he was received with a hearty welcome by some of the most influential abolitionists of this country. Most of the fugitive slaves, and in fact nearly all of the coloured men who have visited Great Britain from the United States, have come upon begging missions, either for some society or for themselves. Mr. Brown has been almost the only exception. With that independence of feeling, which those who are acquainted with him know to be one of his chief characteristics, he determined to maintain himself and family by his own exertions—by his literary labours, and the honourable profession of a public lecturer. From nearly all the cities and large provincial towns he received invitations to lecture or address public meetings. The mayors, or other citizens of note, presided over many of these meetings. At Newcastle-upon-Tyne[30] a soirée was given him, and an address presented by the citizens. A large and influential meeting was held at Bolton, Lancashire,[31] which was addressed by Mr. Brown, and at its close the ladies presented to him the following address:—

"An address, presented to Mr. William Wells Brown, the fugitive slave from America, by the ladies of Bolton, March 22nd, 1850:—

"Dear friend and brother,—We cannot permit you to depart from among us without giving expression to the feelings which we entertain towards yourself personally, and to the sympathy which you have awakened in our breasts for the three millions of our sisters and brothers who still suffer and groan in the prison-house of American bondage. You came among us an entire stranger; we received you for the sake of your mission; and having heard the story of your personal wrongs, and gazed with horror on the atrocities of slavery as seen through the medium of your touching descriptions, we are resolved, henceforward, in reliance on divine assistance, to render what aid we can to the cause which you have so eloquently pleaded in our presence.

"We have no words to express our detestation of the crimes which, in the name of liberty, are committed in the country which gave you birth. Language fails to tell our deep abhorrence of the impiety of those who, in the still more sacred name of religion, rob immortal beings not only of an earthly citizenship, but do much to prevent them from obtaining a heavenly one; and, as mothers and daughters, we embrace this opportunity of giving utterance to our utmost indignation at the cruelties perpetrated upon our sex, by a people professedly acknowledging the equality of all mankind. Carry with you, on your return to the land of your nativity, this our solemn protest against the wicked institution which, like a dark and baleful cloud, hangs over it; and ask the unfeeling enslavers, as best you can, to open the prison doors to them that are bound, and let the oppressed go free.

"Allow us to assure you that your brief sojourn in our town has been to ourselves, and to vast multitudes, of a character long to be remembered; and when you are far removed from us, and toiling, as we hope you may be long spared to do, in this righteous enterprise, it may be some solace to your mind to know that your name is cherished with affectionate regard, and that the blessing of the Most High is earnestly supplicated in behalf of yourself, your family, and the cause to which you have consecrated your distinguished talents."

A most respectable and enthusiastic public meeting was held at Sheffield,[32] to welcome Mr. Brown, and the next day he was invited to inspect several of the large establishments there. While going through the manufactory of Messrs. Broadhead and Atkin, silver and electroplaters, &c., in Love-street, and whilst he was being shown through the works, a subscription was hastily set on foot on his behalf, by the workmen and women of the establishment, which was presented to Mr. Brown in the counting-house by a deputation of the subscribers. The spokesman (the designer to Messrs. Broadhead and Atkin) addressing Mr. Brown on behalf of the workpeople, begged his acceptance of the present as a token of esteem, as well as an expression of their sympathy in the cause he advocates, viz, that of the American slave. Mr. Brown briefly thanked the parties for their spontaneous free will offering, accompanied as it was by a generous expression of sympathy for his afflicted brethren and sisters in bondage.

Mr. Brown has been in England nearly four years, and since his arrival he has travelled above twenty thousand miles through Great Britain, addressed one hundred and thirty public meetings, lectured in twenty-three mechanics and literary institutions, and given his services to many of the benevolent and religious societies on the occasion of their anniversary meetings. After a lecture, which he delivered before the Whittington Club,[33] he received from the managers of that institution the following testimonial:

> *"Whittington Club and Metropolitan Athenaeum,*
> *"189, Strand, June 21, 1850*

"My dear sir,

I have much pleasure in conveying to you the best thanks of the Managing Committee of this institution for the excellent lecture you gave here last evening, and also in presenting you in their names with an honorary membership of the club. It is hoped that you will often avail yourself of its privileges by coming amongst us. You will then see, by the cordial welcome of the members, that they protest against the odious distinctions made between man and man, and the abominable traffic of which you have been the victim.

"For my own part, I shall be happy to be serviceable to you in any way, and at all times be glad to place the advantages of the institution at your disposal.

> "I am, my dear sir,
> "Yours truly,
> "WILLIAM STRUDWICKE
> "Secretary."

"Mr. W. Wells Brown."

On the 1st of August, 1851, a meeting of the most novel character was held at the Hall of Commerce, London, the chief actors being American fugitive slaves. That meeting was most ably presided over by Mr. Brown, and the speeches made on the occasion by fugitive slaves were of the most interesting and creditable description. Although a residence in Canada is infinitely preferable to slavery in America, yet the climate of that country is uncongenial to the constitutions of the Negroes, and their lack of education is an almost insuperable barrier to their social progress. The latter evil Mr. Brown attempted to remedy by the establishment of Manual Labour Schools in Canada for fugitive slaves. A public meeting, attended by between 3,000 and 4,000 persons, was held on the 6th of January 1851, in the City Hall, Glasgow, which was presided over by Alexander Hastie, Esq., M.P., at which resolutions were unanimously passed, approving of Mr. Brown's scheme; which scheme, however, never received that amount of support which would have enabled him to bring it into practice; and the plan at present only remains as an evidence of its author's ingenuity and desire for the elevation of his oppressed and injured race. Mr. Brown subsequently made, through the columns of the *Times*,[34] a proposition for the emigration of American fugitive slaves, under fair and honourable terms, from Canada to the West Indies, where there is a great lack of that labour which they are so capable of undertaking. These efforts all show the willingness of this fugitive slave to aid those of his race. Last year Mr. Brown published his "Three Years in Europe; or, Places I have seen and People I have met." And his literary abilities may be partly judged of from the following commendations of that ably written work:—

"The extraordinary excitement produced by 'Uncle Tom's Cabin'[35] will, we hope, prepare the public of Great Britain and America for this lively book of travels by a real fugitive slave. Though he never had a day's schooling in his life, he has produced a literary work not unworthy of a highly educated gentleman. Our readers will find in these letters much instruction, not a little entertainment, and the beatings of a manly heart, on behalf of a down-trodden race, with which they will not fail to sympathise."

                                                        —*The Eclectic*.

*   *   *

"When he writes on the wrongs of his race, or the events of his own career, he is always interesting or amusing."

—*The Athenaeum.*

"The appearance of this book is too remarkable a literary event to pass without a notice. At the moment when attention in this country is directed to the state of the coloured people in America, the book appears with additional advantage; if nothing else were attained by its publication, it is well to have another proof of the capability of the Negro intellect. Altogether Mr. Brown has written a pleasing and amusing volume. Contrasted with the caricature and bombast of his white countrymen, Mr. Willis's description of 'People he has met,'[36] a comparison suggested by the similarity of the title, it is both in intellect and in style a superior performance, and we are glad to bear this testimony to the literary merit of a work by a Negro author."

—*The Literary Gazette.*

"That a man who was a slave for the first twenty years of his life, and who has never had a day's schooling, should produce such a book as this, cannot but astonish those who speak disparagingly of the African race."

—*The Weekly News and Chronicle.*

"This remarkable book of a remarkable man cannot fail to add to the practical protests already entered in Britain against the absolute bondage of 3,000,000 of our fellow creatures. The impression of a self-educated son of slavery here set forth, must hasten the period when the senseless and impious denial of common claims to a common humanity, on the score of colour, shall be scouted with scorn in every civilised and Christian country. And when this shall be attained, among the means of destruction of the hideous abomination, his compatriots will remember with respect and gratitude the doings and sayings of William Wells Brown. The volume consists of a sufficient variety of scenes, persons, arguments, inferences, speculations, and opinions, to satisfy and amuse the most *exigeant*[37] of those who read *pour se desennuyer*[38] while those who look deeper into things, and view with anxious hope the progress of nations and of mankind, will feel that the good cause of humanity and freedom, of Christianity, enlightenment, and brotherhood, cannot fail to be served by such a book as this."

—*Morning Advertiser*.

"He writes with ease and ability, and his intelligent observations upon the great question to which he has devoted, and is devoting his life, will be read with interest, and will command influence and respect."

—*Daily News*.

Mr. Brown is most assiduous in his studies even at the present time. The following extract from his writings will show how he spends most of his leisure hours:—[39]

"It was eight o'clock before I reached my lodgings. Although fatigued by the day's exertions, I again resumed the reading of Roscoe's 'Leo X.,'[40] and had nearly finished seventy-three pages, when the clock on St. Martin's Church[41] apprised me that it was two. He who escapes from slavery at the age of twenty years without any education, as did the writer of this letter, must read when others are asleep, if he would catch up with the rest of the world. 'To be wise,' says Pope, 'is but to know how little can be known.'[42] The true searcher after truth and knowledge is always like a child; although gaining strength from year to year, he still 'learns to labour and to wait.'[43] The field of labour is ever expanding before him, reminding him that he has yet more to learn; teaching him that he is nothing more than a child in knowledge, and inviting him onward with a thousand varied charms. The son may take possession of the father's goods at his death, but he cannot inherit with the property the father's cultivated mind. He may put on the father's old coat, but that is all: the immortal mind of the first wearer has gone to the tomb. Property may be bequeathed but knowledge cannot. Then let him who would be useful in his generation be up and doing. Like the Chinese student who learned perseverance from the woman whom he saw trying to rub a crowbar into a needle, so should we take the experience of the past to lighten our feet through the paths of the future."

The following testimonial to Mr. Brown's abilities, from an American journal of which Frederick Douglass[44] is editor, shows that his talents are highly appreciated in that country:—

"We have the pleasure to lay before our readers another interesting letter from W. Wells Brown. We rejoice to find our friend still persevering in the pursuit of knowledge, and still more do we rejoice to find such marked evidence of his rapid progress as his several letters afford. But a few years ago he was a despised, degraded, whip-scarred slave, knowing nothing of letters; and now we find him writing accounts of his travels in a distant land, of which a man reared under the most favourable educational advantages might be proud."

We should have said that it was Mr. Brown's intention to have returned to the United States to his family ere this. But the passage of the infamous "Fugitive Slave Law" prevented his returning. Mr. Brown's wife died in Buffalo N. Y. in Jan. 1851. He has two daughters who are now in this country, being trained for teachers.[45] Of course we need not add that for their education they are entirely dependent on their father's exertions. During last year, the Rev. Edward Hore, of Ramsgate, through a willingness to assist Mr. Brown in returning to the United States, wrote to his former owner, and offered him £50, if he would relinquish all claim to him, and furnish the fugitive with papers of emancipation, but the following note from the slaveowner speaks for itself:—

"St. Louis, Feb. 16th, 1852

"Rev. Sir.—I received your note, dated Jan 6th, concerning a runaway slave of mine now known by the name of William Wells Brown. You state that I offered to take three hundred and twenty five dollars for him, and give him free papers, in 1848. I did so then, but since that time the laws of the United States are materially changed. The Fugitive Slave Bill has passed since then. I can

now take him anywhere in the United States, and I have everything arranged for his arrest if he lands at any port in the United
States. But I will give him papers of emancipation, properly
authenticated by our statutes, for the sum of five hundred dollars
(or £100) that will make him as free as any white person. If this
suits your views, you can let me know, and I will have the papers
made out and forwarded to Boston, to Joseph Gruley, of the firm
of Charles Wilkins and Co., 33, Long Wharf. The money must
be paid before the papers are handed over to your agent.

> "Respectfully your obedient servant.
> "ENOCH PRICE"[46]

"To the Rev. Edward Hore."

CLOTEL;

OR,

THE PRESIDENT'S DAUGHTER

CHAPTER I
THE NEGRO SALE

"Why stands she near the auction stand,
    That girl so young and fair?
What brings her to this dismal place,
    Why stands she weeping there?"[1]

With the growing population of slaves in the Southern States of America, there is a fearful increase of half whites, most of whose fathers are slaveowners and their mothers slaves. Society does not frown upon the man who sits with his mulatto child upon his knee, whilst its mother stands a slave behind his chair. The late Henry Clay, some years since, predicted that the abolition of Negro slavery would be brought about by the amalgamation of the races.[2] John Randolph,[3] a distinguished slaveholder of Virginia, and a prominent statesman, said in a speech in the legislature of his native state, that "the blood of the first American statesmen coursed through the veins of the slave of the South." In all the cities and towns of the slave states, the real Negro, or clear black, does not amount to more than one in every four of the slave population. This fact is, of itself, the best evidence of the degraded and immoral condition of the relation of master and slave in the United States of America.

In all the slave states, the law says:[4]—"Slaves shall be deemed, sold [held], taken, reputed, and adjudged in law to be chattels[5] personal in the hands of their owners and possessors, and their executors, administrators and assigns, to all intents, constructions, and purposes whatsoever. A slave is one who is in the power of a master to whom he belongs. The master may sell him, dispose of his person, his industry, and his labour. He can do nothing, possess nothing, nor acquire anything, but what must belong to his master. The slave is entirely subject to the will of his master, who may correct and chastise him, though not with unusual rigour, or so as to maim and mutilate him, or expose him to the danger of loss of life, or to cause his death. The slave, to remain a slave, must be sensible that there is no appeal from his master." Where the slave is placed by law entirely under the control of the man who claims him, body and soul, as property, what else could be expected than the most depraved social condition? The marriage relation, the oldest and most sacred institution given to man by his Creator, is unknown and unrecognised in the slave laws of the United States. Would that we could say, that the moral and religious teaching in the slave states were better than the laws; but, alas! we cannot. A few years since, some slaveholders became a little uneasy in their minds about the rightfulness of permitting slaves to take to themselves husbands and wives, while they still had others living, and applied to their religious teachers for advice; and the following will show how this grave and important subject was treated:—

"Is a servant, whose husband or wife has been sold by his or her master into a distant country, to be permitted to marry again?"

The query was referred to a committee, who made the following report; which, after discussion, was adopted:—

"That, in view of the circumstances in which servants in this country are placed, the committee are unanimous in the opinion, that it is better to permit servants thus circumstanced to take another husband or wife."

Such was the answer from a committee of the "Shiloh Baptist Association"; and instead of receiving light, those who asked the question were plunged into deeper darkness!

A similar question was put to the "Savannah River Association," and the answer, as the following will show, did not materially differ from the one we have already given:—

"Whether, in a case of involuntary separation, of such a character as to preclude all prospect of future intercourse, the parties ought to be allowed to marry again."

Answer—

"That such separation among persons situated as our slaves are, is civilly a separation by death; and they believe that, in the sight of God, it would be so viewed. To forbid second marriages in such cases would be to expose the parties, nor only to stronger hardships and strong temptation, but to church-censure for acting in obedience to their masters, who cannot be expected to acquiesce in a regulation at variance with justice to the slaves, and to the spirit of that command which regulates marriage among Christians. The slaves are not free agents; and a dissolution by death is not more entirely without their consent, and beyond their control, than by such separation."

Although marriage, as the above indicates, is a matter which the slaveholders do not think is of any importance, or of any binding force with their slaves; yet it would be doing that degraded class an injustice, not to acknowledge that many of them do regard it as a sacred obligation, and show a willingness to obey the commands of God on this subject. Marriage is, indeed, the first and most important institution of human existence— the foundation of all civilisation and culture—the root of church and state. It is the most intimate covenant of heart formed among mankind; and for many persons the only relation in which they feel the true sentiments of humanity. It gives scope for every human virtue, since each of these is developed from the love and confidence which here predominate. It unites all which ennobles and beautifies life,—sympathy, kindness of will and deed, gratitude, devotion, and every delicate, intimate feeling. As the only asylum for true education, it is the first and last sanctuary of human culture. As husband and wife, through each other become conscious of complete humanity, and every human feeling, and every human virtue; so children, at their first awakening in the fond covenant of love between parents, both of whom are tenderly concerned for the same object, find an image of complete humanity leagued in free love. The spirit of love which prevails between them acts with creative power upon the young mind, and awakens every germ of goodness within it.

This invisible and incalculable influence of parental life acts more upon the child than all the efforts of education, whether by means of instruction, precept, or exhortation. If this be a true picture of the vast influence for good of the institution of marriage, what must be the moral degradation of that people to whom marriage is denied? Not content with depriving them of all the higher and holier enjoyments of this relation, by degrading and darkening their souls, the slaveholder denies to his victim even that slight alleviation of his misery, which would result from the marriage relation being protected by law and public opinion. Such is the influence of slavery in the United States, that the ministers of religion, even in the so-called free states, are the mere echoes, instead of the correctors, of public sentiment.[6]

We have thought it advisable to show that the present system of chattel slavery in America undermines the entire social condition of man, so as to prepare the reader for the following narrative of slave life, in that otherwise happy and prosperous country.

In all the large towns in the Southern States, there is a class of slaves who are permitted to hire their time of their owners, and for which they pay a high price. These are mulatto women, or quadroons,[7] as they are familiarly known, and are distinguished for their fascinating beauty. The handsomest usually pays the highest price for her time. Many of these women are the favourites of persons who furnish them with the means of paying their owners, and not a few are dressed in the most extravagant manner. Reader, when you take into consideration the fact, that amongst the slave population no safeguard is thrown around virtue, and no inducement held out to slave women to be chaste, you will not be surprised when we tell you that immorality and vice pervade the cities of the Southern States in a manner unknown in the cities and towns of the Northern States. Indeed most of the slave women have no higher aspiration than that of becoming the finely-dressed mistress of some white man.[8] And at Negro balls and parties, this class of women usually cut the greatest figure.

At the close of the year——the following advertisement appeared in a newspaper published in Richmond, the capital of the state of Virginia:—"Notice: Thirty-eight Negroes will be offered for sale on Monday, November 10th, at twelve o'clock, being the entire stock of the late John Graves, Esq. The Negroes are in good condition, some of them very prime; among them are several mechanics, able-bodied field hands, ploughboys, and women with children at the breast, and some of them very prolific in their generating qualities, affording a rare opportunity to any one who wishes to raise a strong and healthy lot of servants for their own use. Also several mulatto girls of rare personal qualities: two of them very superior. Any gentleman or lady wishing to purchase, can take any of the above slaves on trial for a week, for which no charge will be made."⁹ Amongst the above slaves to be sold were Currer and her two daughters, Clotel and Althesa; the latter were the girls spoken of in the advertisement as "very superior." Currer was a bright mulatto, and of prepossessing appearance, though then nearly forty years of age. She had hired her time for more than twenty years, during which time she had lived in Richmond. In her younger days Currer had been the housekeeper of a young slaveholder: but of later years had been a laundress or washerwoman, and was considered to be a woman of great taste in getting up linen. The gentleman for whom she had kept house was Thomas Jefferson, by whom she had two daughters. Jefferson being called to Washington to fill a government appointment,¹⁰ Currer was left behind, and thus she took herself to the business of washing, by which means she paid her master, Mr. Graves, and supported herself and two children. At the time of the decease of her master, Currer's daughters, Clotel and Althesa, were aged respectively sixteen and fourteen years, and both, like most of their own sex in America, were well grown. Currer early resolved to bring her daughters up as ladies, as she termed it, and therefore imposed little or no work upon them. As her daughters grew older, Currer had to pay a stipulated price for them; yet her notoriety as a laundress of the first class enabled her to put an extra price upon her charges, and thus she and her daughters lived in comparative luxury. To bring up Clotel and Althesa to attract attention, and especially at balls and parties, was the great aim of Currer. Although the term

"Negro ball" is applied to most of these gatherings, yet a majority of the attendants are often whites. Nearly all the Negro parties in the cities and towns of the Southern States are made up of quadroon and mulatto girls, and white men. These are democratic gatherings, where gentlemen, shopkeepers, and their clerks, all appear upon terms of perfect equality. And there is a degree of gentility and decorum in these companies that is not surpassed by similar gatherings of white people in the Slave States. It was at one of these parties that Horatio Green, the son of a wealthy gentleman of Richmond, was first introduced to Clotel. The young man had just returned from college, and was in his twenty-second year. Clotel was sixteen, and was admitted by all to be the most beautiful girl, coloured or white, in the city. So attentive was the young man to the quadroon during the evening that it was noticed by all, and became a matter of general conversation; while Currer appeared delighted beyond measure at her daughter's conquest. From that evening, young Green became the favourite visitor at Currer's house. He soon promised to purchase Clotel, as speedily as it could be effected, and make her mistress of her own dwelling; and Currer looked forward with pride to the time when she should see her daughter emancipated and free. It was a beautiful moonlight night in August, when all who reside in tropical climes are eagerly gasping for a breath of fresh air, that Horatio Green was seated in the small garden behind Currer's cottage, with the object of his affections by his side. And it was here that Horatio drew from his pocket the newspaper, wet from the press, and read the advertisement for the sale of the slaves to which we have alluded; Currer and her two daughters being of the number. At the close of the evening's visit, and as the young man was leaving, he said to the girl, "You shall soon be free and your own mistress."

As might have been expected, the day of sale brought an unusual large number together to compete for the property to be sold. Farmers who make a business of raising slaves for the market were there; slave-traders and speculators were also numerously represented; and in the midst of this throng was one who felt a deeper interest in the result of the sale than any other of the bystanders; this was young Green. True to his promise, he was there with a blank bank check in his pocket, awaiting with impatience to enter the list as a bidder for the beautiful slave. The less valuable slaves were first placed upon the auction block, one after another, and sold to the highest bidder. Husbands and wives were separated with a degree of indifference that is unknown in any other relation of life, except that of slavery. Brothers and sisters were torn from each other; and mothers saw their children leave them for the last time on this earth.

It was late in the day, when the greatest number of persons were thought to be present, that Currer and her daughters were brought forward to the place of sale. Currer was first ordered to ascend the auction stand, which she did with a trembling step. The slave mother was sold to a trader. Althesa, the youngest, and who was scarcely less beautiful than her sister, was sold to the same trader for one thousand dollars. Clotel was the last, and, as was expected, commanded a higher price than any that had been offered for sale that day. The appearance of Clotel on the auction block created a deep sensation amongst the crowd. There she stood, with a complexion as white as most of those who were waiting with a wish to become her purchasers; her features as finely defined as any of her sex of pure Anglo-Saxon; her long black wavy hair done up in the neatest manner: her form tall and graceful, and her whole appearance indicating one superior to her position. The auctioneer commenced by saying, that "Miss Clotel had been reserved for the last, because she was the most valuable. How much, gentlemen? Real Albino, fit for a fancy girl for any one. She enjoys good health, and has a sweet temper. How much do you say?"

"Five hundred dollars."

"Only five hundred for such a girl as this? Gentlemen, she is worth a deal more than that sum; you certainly don't know the value of the article you are bidding upon. Here, gentlemen, I hold in my hand a paper certifying that she has a good moral character."

"Seven hundred."

"Ah: gentlemen, that is something like. This paper also states that she is very intelligent."

"Eight hundred."

"She is a devoted Christian, and perfectly trustworthy."

"Nine hundred."

"Nine fifty."

"Ten."

"Eleven."

"Twelve hundred." Here the sale came to a dead stand. The auctioneer stopped, looked around, and began in a rough manner to relate some anecdotes relative to the sale of slaves, which, he said, had come under his own observation. At this juncture the scene was indeed strange. Laughing, joking, swearing, smoking, spitting, and talking kept up a continual hum and noise amongst the crowd; while the slave-girl stood with tears in her eyes, at one time looking towards her mother and sister, and at another towards the young man whom she hoped would become her purchaser.

"The chastity of this girl is pure; she has never been from under her mother's care; she is a virtuous creature."

"Thirteen."

"Fourteen."

"Fifteen."

"Fifteen hundred dollars," cried the auctioneer, and the maiden was struck for that sum. This was a Southern auction, at which the bones, muscles, sinews, blood, and nerves of a young lady of sixteen were sold for five hundred dollars; her moral character for two hundred; her improved intellect for one hundred; her Christianity for three hundred; and her chastity and virtue for four hundred dollars more.[11] And this, too, in a city thronged with churches, whose tall spires look like so many signals pointing to heaven, and whose ministers preach that slavery is a God-ordained institution!

What words can tell the inhumanity, the atrocity, and the immorality of that doctrine which, from exalted office, commends such a crime to the favour of enlightened and Christian people? What indignation from all the world is not due to the government and people who put forth all their strength and power to keep in existence such an institution? Nature abhors it; the age repels it; and Christianity needs all her meekness to forgive it.

Clotel was sold for fifteen hundred dollars, but her purchaser was Horatio Green. Thus closed a Negro sale, at which two daughters of Thomas Jefferson, the writer of the Declaration of American Independence, and one of the presidents of the great republic, were disposed of to the highest bidder!

> "O God! my every heart-string cries,
> Dost thou these scenes behold
> In this our boasted Christian land,
> And must the truth be told?
>
> "Blush, Christian, blush! for e'en the dark,
> Untutored heathen see
> Thy inconsistency; and, lo!
> They scorn thy God, and thee!"[12]

CHAPTER II
GOING TO THE SOUTH

"My country, shall thy honoured name,
  Be as a bye-word through the world?
Rouse! for, as if to blast thy fame,
  This keen reproach is at thee hurled;
The banner that above the waves,
  Is floating o'er three million slaves."[1]

Dick Walker,[2] the slave speculator, who had purchased Currer and Althesa, put them in prison until his gang was made up, and then, with his forty slaves, started for the New Orleans market. As many of the slaves had been brought up in Richmond, and had relations residing there, the slave trader determined to leave the city early in the morning, so as not to witness any of those scenes so common where slaves are separated from their relatives and friends, when about departing for the Southern market. This plan was successful; for not even Clotel, who had been every day at the prison to see her mother and sister, knew of their departure. A march of eight days through the interior of the state, and they arrived on the banks of the Ohio river, where they were all put on board a steamer, and then speedily sailed for the place of their destination.

Walker had already advertised in the New Orleans papers, that he would be there at a stated time with "a prime lot of able-bodied slaves ready for field service; together with a few extra ones, between the ages of fifteen and twenty-five." But, like most who make a business of buying and selling slaves for gain, he often bought some who were far advanced in years, and would always try to sell them for five or ten years younger than they actually were. Few persons can arrive at anything like the age of a Negro, by mere observation, unless they are well acquainted with the race. Therefore the slave-trader very frequently carried out this deception with perfect impunity. After the steamer had left the wharf, and was fairly on the bosom of the Father of Waters,³ Walker called his servant Pompey to him, and instructed him as to "getting the Negroes ready for market."⁴ Amongst the forty Negroes were several whose appearance indicated that they had seen some years, and had gone through some services. Their grey hair and whiskers at once pronounced them to be above the ages set down in the trader's advertisement. Pompey had long been with the trader, and knew his business; and if he did not take delight in discharging his duty, he did it with a degree of alacrity, so that he might receive the approbation of his master. "Pomp," as Walker usually called him, was of real Negro blood, and would often say, when alluding to himself, "Dis nigger is no countefit; he is de genewine artekil." Pompey was of low stature, round face, and, like most of his race, had a set of teeth, which for whiteness and beauty could not be surpassed; his eyes large, lips thick, and hair short and woolly. Pompey had been with Walker so long, and had seen so much of the buying and selling of slaves, that he appeared perfectly indifferent to the heart-rending scenes which daily occurred in his presence. It was on the second day of the steamer's voyage that Pompey selected five of the old slaves, took them in a room by themselves, and commenced preparing them for the market. "Well," said Pompey, addressing himself to the company, "I is de gentman dat is to get you ready, so dat you will bring marser a good price in de Orleans market. How old is you?" addressing himself to a man who, from appearance, was not less than forty.

"If I live to see next corn-planting time I will either be forty-five or fifty-five, I don't know which."⁵

"Dat may be," replied Pompey; "But now you is only thirty years old; dat is what marser says you is to be."

"I know I is more den dat," responded the man.

"I knows nothing about dat," said Pompey; "but when you get in de market, an anybody axe you how old you is, an you tell 'em forty-five, marser will tie you up an gib you de whip like smoke. But if you tell 'em dat you is only thirty, den he wont."

"Well den, I guess I will only be thirty when dey axe me," replied the chattel.

"What your name?" inquired Pompey.

"Geemes," answered the man.

"Oh, Uncle Jim, is it?"

"Yes."

"Den you must have off dem dare whiskers of yours, an when you get to Orleans you must grease dat face an make it look shiney." This was all said by Pompey in a manner which clearly showed that he knew what he was about.

"How old is you?" asked Pompey of a tall, strong-looking man.

"I was twenty-nine last potato-digging time," said the man.

"What's your name?"

"My name is Tobias, but dey call me 'Toby.' "

"Well, Toby, or Mr. Tobias, if dat will suit you better, you is now twenty-three years old, an no more. Dus you hear dat?"

"Yes," responded Toby.

Pompey gave each to understand how old he was to be when asked by persons who wished to purchase, and then reported to his master that the "old boys" were all right. At eight o'clock on the evening of the third day, the lights of another steamer were seen in the distance, and apparently coming up very fast. This was a signal for a general commotion on the Patriot, and everything indicated that a steamboat race was at hand. Nothing can exceed the excitement attendant upon a steamboat on the Mississippi river. By the time the boats had reached Memphis, they were side by side, and each exerting itself to keep the ascendancy in point of speed. The night was clear, the moon shining brightly, and the boats so near to each other that the passengers were calling out from one boat to the other. On board the Patriot, the firemen were using oil, lard, butter, and even bacon, with the wood, for the purpose of raising the steam to its highest pitch. The blaze, mingled with the black smoke, showed plainly that the other boat was burning more than wood. The two boats soon locked, so that the hands of the boats were passing from vessel to vessel, and the wildest excitement prevailed throughout amongst both passengers and crew. At this moment the engineer of the Patriot was seen to fasten down the safety-valve, so that no steam should escape. This was, indeed, a dangerous resort. A few of the boat hands who saw what had taken place, left that end of the boat for more secure quarters.

The Patriot stopped to take in passengers, and still no steam was permitted to escape. At the starting of the boat cold water was forced into the boilers by the machinery, and, as might have been expected, one of the boilers immediately exploded. One dense fog of steam filled every part of the vessel, while shrieks, groans, and cries were heard on every hand. The saloons and cabins soon had the appearance of a hospital. By this time the boat had landed, and the Columbia, the other boat, had come alongside to render assistance to the disabled steamer. The killed and scalded (nineteen in number) were put on shore, and the Patriot, taken in tow by the Columbia, was soon again on its way.

It was now twelve o'clock at night, and instead of the passengers being asleep the majority were gambling in the saloons. Thousands of dollars change hands during a passage from Louisville or St. Louis to New Orleans on a Mississippi steamer, and many men, and even ladies, are completely ruined.

"Go call my boy, steward," said Mr. Smith, as he took his cards one by one from the table. In a few moments a fine looking, bright-eyed mulatto boy, apparently about fifteen years of age, was standing by his master's side at the table. "I will see you, and five hundred dollars better," said Smith, as his servant Jerry approached the table.

"What price do you set on that boy?" asked Johnson, as he took a roll of bills from his pocket.

"He will bring a thousand dollars, any day, in the New Orleans market," replied Smith.

"Then you bet the whole of the boy, do you?"[6]

"Yes."

"I call you, then," said Johnson, at the same time spreading his cards out upon the table.

"You have beat me," said Smith, as soon as he saw the cards. Jerry, who was standing on top of the table, with the bank notes and silver dollars round his feet, was now ordered to descend from the table.

"You will not forget that you belong to me," said Johnson, as the young slave was stepping from the table to a chair.

"No, sir," replied the chattel.

"Now go back to your bed, and be up in time to-morrow morning to brush my clothes and clean my boots, do you hear?"

"Yes, sir," responded Jerry, as he wiped the tears from his eyes.

Smith took from his pocket the bill of sale and handed it to Johnson; at the same time saying. "I claim the right of redeeming that boy, Mr. Johnson. My father gave him to me when I came of age, and I promised not to part with him."

"Most certainly, sir, the boy shall be yours, whenever you hand me over a cool thousand," replied Johnson.

The next morning, as the passengers were assembling in the breakfast saloons and upon the guards of the vessel, and the servants were seen running about waiting upon or looking for their masters, poor Jerry was entering his new master's stateroom with his boots.

"Who do you belong to?" said a gentleman to an old black man, who came along leading a fine dog that he had been feeding.

"When I went to sleep last night, I belonged to Governor Lucas; but I understand dat he is bin gambling all night, so I don't know who owns me dis morning." Such is the uncertainty of a slave's position. He goes to bed at night the property of the man with whom he has lived for years, and gets up in the morning the slave of some one whom he has never seen before! To behold five or six tables in a steamboat's cabin, with half-a-dozen men playing at cards, and money, pistols, bowie-knives, &c. all in confusion on the tables, is what may be seen at almost any time on the Mississippi river.

On the fourth day, while at Natchez,[7] taking in freight and passengers, Walker, who had been on shore to see some of his old customers, returned, accompanied by a tall, thin-faced man, dressed in black, with a white neckcloth, which immediately proclaimed him to be a clergyman. "I want a good, trusty woman for house service," said the stranger, as they entered the cabin where Walker's slaves were kept.

"Here she is, and no mistake," replied the trader.

"Stand up, Currer, my gal; here's a gentleman who wishes to see if you will suit him."

Althesa clung to her mother's side, as the latter rose from her seat.

"She is a rare cook, a good washer, and will suit you to a T, I am sure."

"If you buy me, I hope you will buy my daughter too," said the woman, in rather an excited manner.

"I only want one for my own use, and would not need another," said the man in black, as he and the trader left the room. Walker and the parson went into the saloon, talked over the matter, the bill of sale was made out, the money paid over, and the clergyman left, with the understanding that the woman should be delivered to him at his house. It seemed as if poor Althesa would have wept herself to death, for the first two days after her mother had been torn from her side by the hand of the ruthless trafficker in human flesh. On the arrival of the boat at Baton Rouge, an additional number of passengers were taken on board; and, amongst them, several persons who had been attending the races. Gambling and drinking were now the order of the day. Just as the ladies and gentlemen were assembling at the supper-table, the report of a pistol was heard in the direction of the Social Hall, which caused great uneasiness to the ladies, and took the gentlemen to that part of the cabin. However, nothing serious had occurred. A man at one of the tables where they were gambling had been seen attempting to conceal a card in his sleeve, and one of the party seized his pistol and fired; but fortunately the barrel of the pistol was knocked up, just as it was about to be discharged, and the ball passed through the upper deck, instead of the man's head, as intended. Order was soon restored: all went on well the remainder of the

night, and the next day, at ten o'clock, the boat arrived at New
Orleans, and the passengers went to the hotels and the slaves to
the market!

> "Our eyes are yet on Afric's shores,
> Her thousand wrongs we still deplore;
> We see the grim slave trader there;
> We hear his fettered victim's prayer;
> And hasten to the sufferer's aid.
> Forgetful of *our own 'slave trade.'*

> "The Ocean 'Pirate's' fiend-like form
> Shall sink beneath the vengeance-storm;
> His heart of steel shall quake before
> The battle-din and havoc roar:
> *The knave shall die*, the Law hath said,
> While it protects our own *'slave trade.'*

> "What earthly eye presumes to scan
> The wily Proteus-heart of man?—
> What potent hand will e'er unroll
> The mantled treachery of his soul!—
> O where is he who hath surveyed
> The horrors of *our own 'slave trade?'*

> "There is an eye that wakes in light,
> There is a hand of peerless might;
> Which, soon or late, shall yet assail
> And rend dissimulation's veil:
> Which *will* unfold the masquerade
> Which justifies *our own 'slave trade.'*"

CHAPTER III
THE NEGRO CHASE

We shall now return to Natchez, where we left Currer in the hands of the Methodist parson. For many years, Natchez has enjoyed a notoriety for the inhumanity and barbarity of its inhabitants, and the cruel deeds perpetrated there, which have not been equalled in any other city in the Southern States. The following advertisements, which we take from a newspaper published in the vicinity, will show how they catch their Negroes who believe in the doctrine that "all men are created free."[1]

"NEGRO DOGS.—The undersigned, having bought the entire pack of Negro dogs (of the Hay and Allen stock), *he now proposes to catch runaway Negroes*. His charges will be three dollars a day for hunting, and fifteen dollars for catching a runaway. He resides three and one half miles north of Livingston, near the lower Jones' Bluff Road.

"WILLIAM GAMBREL."[2]

"Nov. 6, 1845."

"NOTICE.—The subscriber, living on Carroway Lake, on Hoe's Bayou, in Carroll parish, sixteen miles on the road leading from Bayou Mason to Lake Providence, is ready with a pack of dogs to hunt runaway Negroes at any time. These dogs are well trained, and are known throughout the parish. Letters addressed to me at Providence will secure immediate attention. My terms are five dollars per day for hunting the trails, whether the Negro is caught or not. Where a twelve hours' trail is shown, and the Negro not taken, no charge is made.

For taking a Negro, twenty-five dollars, and no charge made
for hunting.

"JAMES W. HALL."

"Nov. 26, 1847."

These dogs will attack a Negro at their master's bidding and
cling to him as the bull-dog will cling to a beast. Many are the
speculations, as to whether the Negro will be secured alive or
dead, when these dogs once get on his track. A slave hunt took
place near Natchez, a few days after Currer's arrival, which
was calculated to give her no favourable opinion of the people.
Two slaves had run off owing to severe punishment. The dogs
were put upon their trail. The slaves went into the swamps,
with the hope that the dogs when put on their scent would be
unable to follow them through the water. The dogs soon took
to the swamp, which lies between the highlands, which was
now covered with water, waist deep: here these faithful animals, *swimming* nearly all the time, followed the zigzag course,
the tortuous twistings and windings of these two fugitives,
who, it was afterwards discovered, were lost; sometimes scent-
ing the tree wherein they had found a temporary refuge from
the mud and water; at other places where the deep mud had
pulled off a shoe, and they had not taken time to put it on
again. For two hours and a half, for four or five miles, did men
and dogs wade through this busy, dismal swamp, surrounded
with grimvisaged alligators, who seemed to look on with jeal-
ous eye at this encroachment of their hereditary domain; now
losing the trail—then slowly and dubiously taking it off again,
until they triumphantly threaded it out, bringing them back to
the river, where it was found that the Negroes had crossed their
own trail, near the place of starting. In the meantime a heavy
shower had taken place, putting out the trail. The Negroes
were now at least four miles ahead.

It is well known to hunters that it requires the keenest scent
and best blood to overcome such obstacles, and yet these persevering and sagacious animals conquered every difficulty. The
slaves now made a straight course for the Baton Rouge and
Bayou Sara road, about four miles distant.

Feeling hungry now, after their morning walk, and perhaps thirsty, too, they went about half a mile off the road, and ate a good, hearty, substantial breakfast. Negroes must eat, as well as other people, but the dogs will tell on them. Here, for a moment, the dogs are at fault, but soon unravel the mystery, and bring them back to the road again; and now what before was wonderful, becomes almost a miracle. Here, in this common highway— the thoroughfare for the whole country around—through mud and through mire, meeting waggons and teams, and different solitary wayfarers, and, what above all is most astonishing, actually running through a gang of Negroes, their favourite game, who were working on the road, they pursue the track of the two Negroes; they even ran for eight miles to the very edge of the plain—the slaves near them for the last mile. At first they would fain believe it some hunter chasing deer. Nearer and nearer the whimpering pack presses on; the delusion begins to dispel; all at once the truth flashes upon them like a glare of light; their hair stands on end; 'tis Tabor with his dogs. The scent becomes warmer and warmer. What was an irregular cry, now deepens into one ceaseless roar, as the relentless pack rolls on after its human prey. It puts one in mind of Actæon[3] and his dogs. They grow desperate and leave the road, in the vain hope of shaking them off. Vain hope, indeed! The momentary cessation only adds new zest to the chase. The cry grows louder and louder; the yelp grows short and quick, sure indication that the game is at hand. It is a perfect rush upon the part of the hunters, while the Negroes call upon their weary and jaded limbs to do their best, but they falter and stagger beneath them. The breath of the hounds is almost upon their very heels, and yet they have a vain hope of escaping these sagacious animals. They can run no longer; the dogs are upon them; they hastily attempt to climb a tree, and as the last one is nearly out of reach, the catch-dog seizes him by the leg, and brings him to the ground; he sings out lustily and the dogs are called off. After this man was secured, the one in the tree was ordered to come down; this, however, he refused to do, but a gun being pointed at him, soon caused him to change his mind. On reaching the ground, the fugitive made one more bound, and the chase again commenced. But it was of no use to run and he soon yielded. While being tied, he committed an unpardonable offence: he resisted, and for that he must be made an example on their arrival home. A mob was collected together, and a Lynch court was held, to determine what was best to be done with the Negro who had had the impudence to raise his hand against a white man. The Lynch court decided that the Negro should be burnt at the stake. A Natchez newspaper, the *Free Trader*, giving an account of it says,

"The body was taken and chained to a tree immediately on the banks of the Mississippi, on what is called Union Point. Faggots were then collected and piled around him, to which he appeared quite indifferent. When the work was completed, he was asked what he had to say. He then warned all to take example by him, and asked the prayers of all around; he then called for a drink of water, which was handed to him; he drank it, and said, 'Now set fire—I am ready to go in peace!' The torches were lighted, and placed in the pile, which soon ignited. He watched unmoved the curling flame that grew, until it began to entwine itself around and feed upon his body; then he sent forth cries of agony painful to the ear, begging some one to blow his brains out; at the same time surging with almost superhuman strength, until the staple with which the chain was fastened to the tree (not being well secured) drew out, and he leaped from the burning pile. At that moment the sharp ringing of several rifles was heard: the body of the Negro fell a corpse on the ground. He was picked up by some two or three, and again thrown into the fire, and consumed, not a vestige remaining to show that such a being ever existed."[4]

Nearly 4,000 slaves were collected from the plantations in the neighborhood to witness this scene. Numerous speeches were made by the magistrates and ministers of religion to the large concourse of slaves, warning them, and telling them that the same fate awaited them, if they should prove rebellious to their owners. There are hundreds of Negroes who run away and live in the woods. Some take refuge in the swamps, because they are less frequented by human beings. A Natchez newspaper gave the following account of the hiding-place of a slave who had been captured:—

"A runaway's den was discovered on Sunday, near the Washington Spring, in a little patch of woods, where it had been for several months so artfully concealed under ground, that it was detected only by accident, though in sight of two or three houses, and near the road and fields where there has been constant daily passing. The entrance was concealed by a pile of pine straw, representing a hog-bed, which being removed, discovered a trap-door and steps that led to a room about six feet square, comfortably ceiled with plank, containing a small fire-place, the flue of which was ingeniously conducted above ground and concealed by the straw. The inmates took the alarm, and made their escape; *but Mr. Adams and his excellent dogs being put upon the trail, soon run down and secured one of them*, which proved to be a Negro-fellow who had been out about a year. He stated that the other occupant was a woman, who had been a runaway a still longer time. In the den was found a quantity of meal, bacon, corn, potatoes, &c. and various cooking utensils and wearing apparel."

— *VICKSBURGH SENTINEL*, Dec. 6th, 1838.

Currer was one of those who witnessed the execution of the slave at the stake, and it gave her no very exalted opinion of the people of the cotton growing district.

CHAPTER IV
THE QUADROON'S HOME

"How sweetly on the hill-side sleeps
The sunlight with its quickening rays!
The verdant trees that crown the steeps,
Grow greener in its quivering blaze."

About three miles from Richmond is a pleasant plain, with here and there a beautiful cottage surrounded by trees so as scarcely to be seen.[1] Among them was one far retired from the public roads, and almost hidden among the trees. It was a perfect model of rural beauty. The piazzas that surrounded it were covered with clematis and passion flower. The pride of China mixed its oriental looking foliage with the majestic magnolia, and the air was redolent with the fragrance of flowers, peeping out of every nook and nodding upon you with a most unexpected welcome. The tasteful hand of art had not learned to imitate the lavish beauty and harmonious disorder of nature, but they lived together in loving amity, and spoke in accordant tones. The gateway rose in a gothic arch, with graceful tracery in iron work, surmounted by a cross, round which fluttered and played the mountain fringe, that lightest and most fragile of vines. This cottage was hired by Horatio Green for Clotel, and the quadroon girl soon found herself in her new home.

The tenderness of Clotel's conscience, together with the care her mother had with her and the high value she placed upon virtue, required an outward marriage; though she well knew that a union with her proscribed race was unrecognised by law, and therefore the ceremony would give her no legal hold on Horatio's constancy. But her high poetic nature regarded reality rather than the semblance of things; and when he playfully asked how she could keep him if he wished to run away, she replied, "If the mutual love we have for each other, and the dictates of your own conscience do not cause you to remain my husband, and your affections fall from me, I would not, if I could, hold you by a single fetter." It was indeed a marriage sanctioned by heaven, although unrecognised on earth. There the young couple lived secluded from the world, and passed their time as happily as circumstances would permit. It was Clotel's wish that Horatio should purchase her mother and sister, but the young man pleaded that he was unable, owing to the fact that he had not come into possession of his share of property, yet he promised that when he did, he would seek them out and purchase them. Their first-born was named Mary, and her complexion was still lighter than her mother. Indeed she was not darker than other white children. As the child grew older, it more and more resembled its mother. The iris of her large dark eye had the melting mezzotinto, which remains the last vestige of African ancestry, and gives that plaintive expression, so often observed, and so appropriate to that docile and injured race. Clotel was still happier after the birth of her dear child: for Horatio, as might have been expected, was often absent day and night with his friends in the city, and the edicts of society had built up a wall of separation between the quadroon and them. Happy as Clotel was in Horatio's love, and surrounded by an outward environment of beauty, so well adapted to her poetic spirit, she felt these incidents with inexpressible pain. For herself she cared but little; for she had found a sheltered home in Horatio's heart, which the world might ridicule, but had no power to profane. But when she looked at her beloved Mary, and reflected upon the unavoidable and dangerous position which the tyranny of society had awarded her, her soul was filled with anguish. The rare loveliness of the child increased daily, and was evidently ripening into most marvellous beauty. The father seemed to rejoice in it with unmingled pride; but in the deep tenderness of the mother's eye, there was an indwelling sadness that spoke of anxious thoughts and fearful foreboding. Clotel now urged Horatio to remove to France or England, where both her [sic] and her child would be free, and where colour was not a crime. This request excited but little opposition, and was so attractive to his imagination, that he might have overcome all intervening obstacles, had not "a change come over the spirit of his dreams."[1] He still loved Clotel; but he was now becoming engaged in political and other affairs which kept him oftener and longer from the young mother; and ambition to become a statesman was slowly gaining the ascendancy over him.

Among those on whom Horatio's political success most depended was a very popular and wealthy man, who had an only daughter. His visits to the house were at first purely of a political nature; but the young lady was pleasing, and he fancied he discovered in her a sort of timid preference for himself. This excited his vanity, and awakened thoughts of the great worldly advantages connected with a union. Reminiscences of his first love kept these vague ideas in check for several months; for with it was associated the idea of restraint. Moreover, Gertrude, though inferior in beauty, was yet a pretty contrast to her rival. Her light hair fell in silken ringlets down her shoulders, her blue eyes were gentle though inexpressive, and her healthy cheeks were like opening rosebuds. He had already become accustomed to the dangerous experiment of resisting his own inward convictions; and this new impulse to ambition, combined with the strong temptation of variety in love, met the ardent young man weakened in moral principle, and unfettered by laws of the land. The change wrought upon him was soon noticed by Clotel.

CHAPTER V

THE SLAVE MARKET

"What! mothers from their children riven!
What! God's own image bought and sold!
Americans to market driven,
And barter'd as the brute for gold."
—*Whittier.*[1]

Not far from Canal-street, in the city of New Orleans, stands a large two story flat building surrounded by a stone wall twelve feet high, the top of which is covered with bits of glass, and so constructed as to prevent even the possibility of any one's passing over it without sustaining great injury. Many of the rooms resemble cells in a prison. In a small room near the "office" are to be seen any number of iron collars, hobbles, handcuffs, thumbscrews, cowhides, whips, chains, gags, and yokes. A back yard inclosed by a high wall looks something like the playground attached to one of our large New England schools, and in which are rows of benches and swings. Attached to the back premises is a good-sized kitchen, where two old Negresses are at work, stewing, boiling, and baking, and occasionally wiping the sweat from their furrowed and swarthy brows.

The slave-trader Walker, on his arrival in New Orleans, took up his quarters at this slave pen with his gang of human cattle: and the morning after, at ten o'clock, they were exhibited for sale. There, first of all, was the beautiful Althesa, whose pale countenance and dejected look told how many sad hours she had passed since parting with her mother at Natchez. There was a poor woman who had been separated from her husband and five children. Another woman, whose looks and manner were expressive of deep anguish, sat by her side. There, too, was "Uncle Geemes," with his whiskers off, his face shaved clean, and the grey hair plucked out, and ready to be sold for ten years younger than he was. Toby was also there, with his face shaved and greased, ready for inspection. The examination commenced, and was carried on in a manner calculated to shock the feelings of any one not devoid of the milk of human kindness. "What are you wiping your eyes for?" inquired a fat, red-faced man, with a white hat set on one side of his head, and a cigar in his mouth, of a woman who sat on one of the stools.

"I s'pose I have been crying."

"Why do you cry?"

"Because I have left my man behind."

"Oh, if I buy you I will furnish you with a better man than you left. I have lots of young bucks on my farm."

"I don't want, and will never have, any other man," replied the woman.

"What's your name?" asked a man in a straw hat of a tall Negro man, who stood with his arms folded across his breast, and leaning against the wall.

"My name is Aaron, sir."

"How old are you?"

"Twenty-five."

"Where were you raised?"

"In old Virginny, sir."

"How many men have owned you?"

"Four."

"Do you enjoy good health?"

"Yes, sir."

"How long did you live with your first owner?"

"Twenty years."

"Did you ever run away?"

"No, sir."

"Did you ever strike your master?"

"No, sir."

"Were you ever whipped much?"

"No, sir, I s'pose I did not deserve it."

"How long did you live with your second master?"

"Ten years, sir."

"Have you a good appetite?"

"Yes, sir."

"Can you eat your allowance?"

"Yes, sir, when I can get it."

"What were you employed at in Virginia?"

"I worked in de terbacar feel."

"In the tobacco field?"

"Yes, sir."

"How old did you say you were?"

"I will be twenty-five if I live to see next sweet potater-digging time."

"I am a cotton planter, and if I buy you, you will have to work in the cotton field. My men pick one hundred and fifty pounds a day, and the women one hundred and forty, and those who fail to pick their task receive five stripes from the cat² for each pound that is wanting. Now, do you think you could keep up with the rest of the hands?"

"I don't know, sir, I 'spec I'd have to."

"How long did you live with your third master?"

"Three years, sir."

"Why, this makes you thirty-three. I thought you told me you was only twenty-five?"

Aaron now looked first at the planter, then at the trader, and seemed perfectly bewildered. He had forgotten the lesson given him by Pompey as to his age, and the planter's circuitous talk (doubtless to find out the slave's real age) had the Negro off his guard.

"I must see your back, so as to know how much you have been whipped, before I think of buying," said the planter.

Pompey, who had been standing by during the examination, thought that his services were now required, and stepping forward with a degree of officiousness, said to Aaron, "Don't you hear de gentman tell you he want to zamon your limbs. Come, unharness yeself, old boy, an don't be standing dar."

Aaron was soon examined and pronounced "sound"; yet the conflicting statement about the age was not satisfactory.

Fortunate for Althesa she was spared the pain of undergoing such an examination. Mr. Crawford, a teller in one of the banks, had just been married, and wanted a maid-servant for his wife; and passing through the market in the early part of the day, was pleased with the young slave's appearance and purchased her, and in his dwelling the quadroon found a much better home than often falls to the lot of a slave sold in the New Orleans market. The heartrending and cruel traffic in slaves which has been so often described, is not confined to any particular class of persons. No one forfeits his or her character or standing in society, by buying or selling slaves; or even raising slaves for the market. The precise number of slaves carried from the slave-raising to the slave-consuming states, we have no means of knowing.[3] But it must be very great, as more than forty thousand were sold and taken out of the state of Virginia in one year. Known to God only is the amount of human agony and suffering which sends its cry from the slave markets and Negro pens, unheard and unheeded by man, up to his ear; mothers weeping for their children, breaking the night-silence with the shrieks of their breaking hearts. From some you will hear the burst of bitter lamentation, while from others the loud hysteric laugh, denoting still deeper agony. Most of them leave the market for cotton or rice plantations.

> "Where the slave-whip ceaseless swings,
> Where the noisome insect stings,
> Where the fever demon strews
> Poison with the falling dews,
> Where the sickly sunbeams glare
> Through the hot and misty air."[4]

CHAPTER VI
THE RELIGIOUS TEACHER

"What! preach and enslave men?
Give thanks—and rob thy own afflicted poor?
Talk of thy glorious liberty, and then
Bolt hard the captive's door?"

—*Whittier.*[1]

The Rev. John Peck[2] was a native of the state of Connecticut, where he was educated for the ministry, in the Methodist persuasion. His father was a strict follower of John Wesley,[3] and spared no pains in his son's education, with the hope that he would one day be as renowned as the great leader of his sect. John had scarcely finished his education at New Haven, when he was invited by an uncle, then on a visit to his father, to spend a few months at Natchez in the state of Mississippi. Young Peck accepted his uncle's invitation, and accompanied him to the South. Few young men, and especially clergymen, going fresh from a college to the South, but are looked upon as geniuses in a small way, and who are not invited to all the parties in the neighbourhood. Mr. Peck was not an exception to this rule. The society into which he was thrown on his arrival at Natchez was too brilliant for him not to be captivated by it; and, as might have been expected, he succeeded in captivating a plantation with seventy slaves, if not the heart of the lady to whom it belonged. Added to this, he became a popular preacher, had a large congregation with a snug salary. Like other planters, Mr. Peck confided the care of his farm to Ned Huckelby, an overseer of high reputation in his way. The Popular Farm, as it was called, was situated in a beautiful valley nine miles from Natchez, and near the river Mississippi. The once unshorn face of nature had given way, and now the farm blossomed with a splendid harvest, the neat cottage stood in a grove where Lombardy poplars lift their tufted tops almost to prop the skies; the willow, locust, and horse-chestnut spread their branches, and flowers never cease to blossom. This was the parson's country house, where the family spent only two months during the year.

The town residence was a fine villa, seated upon the brow of a hill at the edge of the city. It was in the kitchen of this house that Currer found her new home. Mr. Peck was, every inch of him, a democrat, and early resolved that his "people," as he called his slaves, should be well fed and not overworked, and therefore laid down the law and gospel to the overseer as well as the slaves.

"It is my wish," said he to Mr. Carlton, an old school-fellow, who was spending a few days with him, "it is my wish that a new system be adopted on the plantations in this estate. I believe that the sons of Ham[4] should have the gospel, and I intend that my Negroes shall. The gospel is calculated to make mankind better, and none should be without it."

"What say you," replied Carlton, "about the right of man to his liberty?"

"Now, Carlton, you have begun again to harp about man's rights; I really wish you could see this matter as I do. I have searched in vain for any authority for man's natural rights; if he had any, they existed before the fall. That is, Adam and Eve may have had some rights which God gave them, and which modern philosophy, in its pretended reverence for the name of God, prefers to call natural rights. I can imagine they had the right to eat of the fruit of the trees of the garden; they were restricted even in this by the prohibition of one. As far as I know without positive assertion, their liberty of action was confined to the garden. These were not 'inalienable rights,' however, for they forfeited both them and life with the first act of disobedience. Had they, after this, any rights? We cannot imagine them; they were condemned beings; they could have no rights, but by Christ's gift as king. These are the only rights man can have as an independent isolated being, if we choose to consider him in this impossible position, in which so many theorists have placed him. If he had no rights, he could suffer no wrongs. Rights and wrongs are therefore necessarily the creatures of society, such as man would establish himself in his gregarious state. They are, in this state, both artificial and voluntary. Though man has no rights, as thus considered, undoubtedly he has the power, by such arbitrary rules of right and wrong as his necessity enforces."

"I regret I cannot see eye to eye with you," said Carlton. "I am a disciple of Rousseau,[5] and have for years made the rights of man my study; and I must confess to you that I can see no difference between white men and black men as it regards liberty."

"Now, my dear Carlton, would you really have the Negroes enjoy the same rights with ourselves?"

"I would, most certainly. Look at our great Declaration of Independence; look even at the constitution of our own Connecticut, and see what is said in these about liberty."

"I regard all this talk about rights as mere humbug. The Bible is older than the Declaration of Independence, and there I take my stand. The Bible furnishes to us the armour of proof, weapons of heavenly temper and mould, whereby we can maintain our ground against all attacks. But this is true only when we obey its directions, as well as employ its sanctions. Our rights are there established, but it is always in connection with our duties. If we neglect the one we cannot make good the other. Our domestic institutions can be maintained against the world, if we but allow Christianity to throw its broad shield over them. But if we so act as to array the Bible against our social economy, they must fall. Nothing ever yet stood long against Christianity. Those who say that religious instruction is inconsistent with our peculiar civil polity, are the worst enemies of that polity. They would drive religious men from its defence. Sooner or later, if these views prevail, they will separate the religious portion of our community from the rest, and thus divided we shall become an easy prey. Why, is it not better that Christian men should hold slaves than unbelievers? We know how to value the bread of life, and will not keep it from our slaves."

"Well, every one to his own way of thinking," said Carlton, as he changed his position. "I confess," added he, "that I am

no great admirer of either the Bible or slavery. My heart is my
guide: my conscience is my Bible. I wish for nothing further to
satisfy me of my duty to man. If I act rightly to mankind, I
shall fear nothing."

Carlton had drunk too deeply of the bitter waters of infidelity, and had spent too many hours over the writings of
Rousseau, Voltaire, and Thomas Paine,[6] to place that appreciation upon the Bible and its teachings that it demands. During
this conversation there was another person in the room, seated
by the window, who, although at work upon a fine piece of
lace, paid every attention to what was said. This was Georgiana, the only daughter of the parson. She had just returned
from Connecticut, where she had finished her education. She
had had the opportunity of contrasting the spirit of Christianity and liberty in New England with that of slavery in her native state, and had learned to feel deeply for the injured Negro.
Georgiana was in her nineteenth year, and had been much ben-
efited by a residence of five years at the North. Her form was
tall and graceful: her features regular and well defined; and her
complexion was illuminated by the freshness of youth, beauty,
and health. The daughter differed from both the father and his
visitor upon the subject which they had been discussing, and as
soon as an opportunity offered, she gave it as her opinion, that
the Bible was both the bulwark of Christianity and liberty.
With a smile she said, "Of course, papa will overlook my dif-
fering from him, for although I am a native of the South, I am
by education and sympathy a Northerner." Mr. Peck laughed
and appeared pleased, rather than otherwise, at the manner in
which his daughter had expressed herself.

From this Georgiana took courage and said, "We must try
the character of slavery, and our duty in regard to it, as we
should try any other question of character and duty. To judge
justly of the character of anything, we must know what it does.
That which is good does good, and that which is evil does evil.
And as to duty, God's designs indicate his claims. That which
accomplishes the manifest design of God is right; that which
counteracts it, wrong. Whatever, in its proper tendency and
general effect, produces, secures, or extends human welfare, is

according to the will of God, and is good; and our duty is to favour and promote, according to our power, that which God favours and promotes by the general law of his providence. On the other hand, whatever in its proper tendency and general effect destroys, abridges, or renders insecure, human welfare, is opposed to God's will, and is evil. And as whatever accords with the will of God, in any manifestation of it should be done and persisted in, so whatever opposes that will should not be done, and if done, should be abandoned. Can that then be right, be well doing—can that obey God's behest, which makes a man a slave? which dooms him and all his posterity, in limitless generations, to bondage, to unrequited toil through life? 'Thou shalt love thy neighbor as thyself.' This single passage of Scripture should cause us to have respect to the rights of the slave. True Christian love is of an enlarged, disinterested nature. It loves all who love the Lord Jesus Christ in sincerity, without regard to colour or condition."

"Georgiana, my dear, you are an abolitionist; your talk is fanaticism," said Mr. Peck in rather a sharp tone; but the subdued look of the girl, and the presence of Carlton, caused the father to soften his language. Mr. Peck having lost his wife by consumption, and Georgiana being his only child, he loved her too dearly to say more, even if he felt displeased. A silence followed this exhortation from the young Christian. But her remarks had done a noble work. The father's heart was touched; and the sceptic, for the first time, was viewing Christianity in its true light.

"I think I must go out to your farm," said Carlton, as if to break the silence.

"I shall be pleased to have you go," returned Mr. Peck. "I am sorry I can't go myself, but Huckelby will show you every attention; and I feel confident that when you return to Connecticut, you will do me the justice to say, that I am one who looks after my people, in a moral, social, and religious point of view."

"Well, what do you say to my spending next Sunday there?"

"Why, I think that a good move; you will then meet with Snyder, our missionary."

"Oh, you have missionaries in these parts, have you?"

"Yes," replied Mr. Peck: "Snyder is from New York, and is our missionary to the poor, and preaches to our 'people' on Sunday; you will no doubt like him; he is a capital fellow."

"Then I shall go," said Carlton, "but only wish I had company." This last remark was intended for Miss Peck, for whom he had the highest admiration.

It was on a warm Sunday morning, in the month of May, that Miles Carlton found himself seated beneath a fine old apple tree, whose thick leaves entirely shaded the ground for some distance round. Under similar trees and near by, were gathered together all the "people" belonging to the plantation. Hontz Snyder was a man of about forty years of age, exceedingly low in stature, but of a large frame. He had been brought up in the Mohawk Valley, in the state of New York, and claimed relationship with the oldest Dutch families in that vicinity. He had once been a sailor, and had all the roughness of character that a sea-faring man might expect to possess; together with the half-Yankee, half-German peculiarities of the people of the Mohawk Valley. It was nearly eleven o'clock when a one-horse waggon drove up in haste, and the low squatty preacher got out and took his place at the foot of one of the trees, where a sort of rough board table was placed, and took his books from his pocket and commenced.

"As it is rather late," said he, "we will leave the singing and praying for the last, and take our text, and commence immediately. I shall base my remarks on the following passage of Scripture, and hope to have that attention which is due to the cause of God:—'All things whatsoever ye would that men should do unto you, do ye even so unto them'; that is, do by all mankind just as you would desire they should do by you, if you were in their place and they in yours.[7]

"Now, to suit this rule to your particular circumstances, suppose you were masters and mistresses, and had servants under you, would you not desire that your servants should do their business faithfully and honestly, as well when your back was turned as while you were looking over them? Would you not expect that they should take notice of what you said to them?

that they should behave themselves with respect towards you and yours, and be as careful of everything belonging to you as you would be yourselves? You are servants: do, therefore, as you would wish to be done by, and you will be both good servants to your masters and good servants to God, who requires this of you, and will reward you well for it, if you do it for the sake of conscience, in obedience to his commands.

"You are not to be eye-servants. Now, eye-servants are such as will work hard, and seem mighty diligent, while they think anybody is taking notice of them; but, when their masters' and mistresses' back are turned they are idle, and neglect their business. I am afraid there are a great many such eye-servants among you, and that you do not consider how great a sin it is to be so, and how severely God will punish you for it. You may easily deceive your owners, and make them have an opinion of you that you do not deserve, and get the praise of men by it; but remember that you cannot deceive Almighty God, who sees your wickedness and deceit, and will punish you accordingly. For the rule is, that you must obey your masters in all things, and do the work they set you about with fear and trembling, in singleness of heart as unto Christ; not with eye-service, as men-pleasers, but as the servants of Christ, doing the will of God from the heart; with good-will doing service as to the Lord, and not as to men.

"*Take care that you do not fret or murmur, grumble or re-pine at your condition; for this will not only make your life un-easy, but will greatly offend Almighty God.* Consider that it is not yourselves, it is not the people that you belong to, it is not the men who have brought you to it, but *it is the will of God who hath by his providence made you servants, because, no doubt, he knew that condition would be best for you in this world, and help you the better towards heaven if you would but do your duty in it.* So that any discontent at your not being free, or rich, or great, as you see some others, is quarrelling with your heavenly Master, and finding fault with God himself, who hath made you what you are, and hath promised you as large a share in the kingdom of heaven as the greatest man alive, if you will but behave yourself aright, and do the business he hath set you about in this world honestly and cheerfully. Riches and power have proved the ruin of many an unhappy soul, by drawing away the heart and affections from God, and fixing them on mean and sinful enjoyments; so that, when God, who knows our hearts better than we know them our-selves, sees that they would be hurtful to us, and therefore keeps them from us, it is the greatest mercy and kindness he could show us.

"You may perhaps fancy that, if you had riches and freedom, you could do your duty to God and man with greater pleasure than you can now. But pray consider that, if you can but save your souls through the mercy of God, you will have spent your time to the best of purposes in this world; and he that at last can get to heaven has performed a noble journey, let the road be ever so rugged and difficult. Besides, you really have a great advantage over most white people, who have not only the care of their daily labour upon their hands, but the care of looking forward and providing necessaries for to-morrow and next day, and of clothing and bringing up their children, and of getting food and raiment for as many of you as belong to their families, which often puts them to great difficulties, and distracts their minds so as to break their rest, and take off their thoughts from the affairs of another world. Whereas you are quite eased from all these cares, and have nothing but your daily labour to look after, and, when that is done, take your needful rest. Neither is it necessary for you to think of laying up anything against old age, as white people are obliged to do; for the laws of the coun-try have provided that you shall not be turned off when you are past labour, but shall be maintained, while you live, by those you belong to, whether you are able to work or not.

"There is only one circumstance which may appear grievous, that I shall now take notice of, and that is correction.

"Now, when correction is given you, you either deserve it, or you do not deserve it. But whether you really deserve it or not, it is your duty, and Almighty God requires that you bear it pa-tiently. You may perhaps think that this is hard doctrine; but, if you consider it right, you must needs think otherwise of it. Sup-pose, then, that you deserve correction, you cannot but say that it is just and right you should meet with it. Suppose you do not, or at least you do not deserve so much, or so severe a correction, for the fault you have committed, you perhaps have escaped a great many more, and are at last paid for all. Or suppose you are quite innocent of what is laid to your charge, and suffer wrongfully in that particular thing, is it not possible you may have done some other bad thing which was never discovered, and that Almighty God who saw you doing it would not let you escape without punishment one time or another? And ought you not, in such a case, to give glory to him, and be thankful that he would rather punish you in this life for your wickedness than destroy your souls for it in the next life? But suppose even this was not the case (a case hardly to be imagined), and that you have by no means, known or unknown, deserved the correction you suffered, there is this great comfort in it, that, if you bear it patiently, and leave your cause in the hands of God, he will reward you for it in heaven, and the punishment you suffer unjustly here shall turn to your exceeding great glory hereafter.

"Lastly, you should serve your masters faithfully, because of their goodness to you. See to what trouble they have been on your account. Your fathers were poor ignorant and barbarous creatures in Africa, and the whites fitted out ships at great trouble and expense and brought you from that benighted land to Christian America, where you can sit under your own vine and fig tree and no one molest or make you afraid. Oh, my dear black brothers and sisters, you are indeed a fortunate and a blessed people. Your masters have many troubles that you know nothing about. If the banks break, your masters are sure to lose something. If the crops turn out poor, they lose by it. If one of you die, your master loses what he paid for you, while you lose nothing. Now let me exhort you once more to be faithful."

Often during the delivery of the sermon did Synder cast an anxious look in the direction where Carlton was seated; no doubt to see if he had found favour with the stranger. Huckelby, the overseer, was also there, seated near Carlton. With all Synder's gesticulations, sonorous voice, and occasionally bringing his fist down upon the table with the force of a sledge hammer, he could not succeed in keeping the Negroes all interested: four or five were fast asleep, leaning against the trees; as many more were nodding, while not a few were stealthily cracking and eating hazelnuts.[8] "Uncle Simon, you may strike up a hymn," said the preacher as he closed his Bible. A moment more, and the whole company (Carlton excepted) had joined in the well known hymn, commencing with

> "When I can read my title clear
> To mansions in the sky."[9]

After the singing, Sandy closed with prayer, and the following questions and answers read, and the meeting was brought to a close.

"*Q*. What command has God given to servants concerning obedience to their masters?—*A*. 'Servants, obey in all things your masters according to the flesh, not with eye-service as menpleasers, but in singleness of heart, fearing God.'

"*Q*. What does God mean by masters according to the flesh?—*A*. 'Masters in this world.'

"*Q*. What are servants to count their masters worthy of?—*A*. 'All honour.'

"*Q*. How are they to do the service of their masters?—*A*. '*With good will*, doing service as unto the Lord, and not unto men.'

"*Q*. How are they to try to please their masters?—*A*. 'Please him well in all things, not answering again.'

"*Q*. Is a servant who is an eye-servant to his earthly master an eye-servant to his heavenly master?—*A*. 'Yes.'

"*Q*. Is it right in a servant, when commanded to do any thing, to be sullen and slow, and answer his master again?—*A*. 'No.'

"*Q*. If the servant professes to be a Christian, ought he not to be *as a Christian servant*, an example to all other servants of love and obedience to his master?—*A*. 'Yes.'

"*Q*. And, should his master be a Christian also, ought he not on that account specially to love and obey him?—*A*. 'Yes.'

"*Q*. But suppose the master is hard to please, and threatens

and punishes more than he ought, what is the servant to do?—
A. 'Do his best to please him.'

"Q. When the servant suffers *wrongfully* at the hands of his master, and, to please God, takes it patiently, will God reward him for it?—A. 'Yes.'

"Q. Is it right for the servant to *run away*, or is it right *to harbour* a runaway?—A. 'No.'

"Q. If a servant runs away, what should be done with him?—A. 'He should be caught and brought back.'

"Q. When he is brought back, what should be done with him?—A. 'Whip him well.'

"Q. Why may not the whites be slaves as well as the blacks?—A. 'Because the Lord intended the Negroes for slaves.'

"Q. Are they better calculated for servants than the whites?—A. 'Yes, their hands are large, the skin thick and tough, and they can stand the sun better than the whites.'

"Q. Why should servants not complain when they are whipped?—A. 'Because the Lord has commanded that they should be whipped.'

"Q. Where has He commanded it?—A. 'He says, He that knoweth his master's will, and doeth it not, shall be beaten with many stripes.'

"Q. Then is the master to blame for whipping his servant?—A. 'Oh, no! he is only doing his duty as a Christian.'"

Snyder left the ground in company with Carlton and Huckelby, and the three dined together in the overseer's dwelling.

"Well," said Joe, after the three white men were out of hearing, "Marser Snyder bin try hesef to-day."[10]

"Yes," replied Ned; "he want to show de strange gentman how good he can preach."

"Dat's a new sermon he gib us to-day," said Sandy.

"Dees white fokes is de very dibble," said Dick; "and all dey whole study is to try to fool de black people."

"Didn't you like de sermon?" asked Uncle Simon. "No," answered four or five voices.

"He rared and pitched enough," continued Uncle Simon.

Now Uncle Simon was himself a preacher, or at least he

thought so, and was rather pleased than otherwise, when he heard others spoken of in a disparaging manner. "Uncle Simon can beat dat sermon all to pieces," said Ned, as he was filling his mouth with hazelnuts.

"I got no notion of dees white fokes, no how," returned Aunt Dafney. "Dey all de time tellin' dat de Lord made us for to work for dem, and I don't believe a word of it."

"Marser Peck give dat sermon to Snyder. I know," said Uncle Simon.

"He jest de one for dat," replied Sandy.

"I think de people dat made de Bible was great fools," said Ned.

"Why?" Uncle Simon.

" 'Cause dey made such a great big book and put nuttin' in it, but servants obey yer masters."

"Oh," replied Uncle Simon, "thars more in de Bible den dat, only Snyder never reads any other part to us; I use to hear it read in Maryland, and thar was more den what Snyder lets us hear."

In the overseer's house there was another scene going on, and far different from what we have here described.

CHAPTER VII
THE POOR WHITES, SOUTH

"No seeming of logic can ever convince the American people, that thousands of our slave-holding brethren are not excellent, humane, and even Christian men, fearing God, and keeping His commandments."

—*Rev. Dr. Joel Parker.*[1]

"You like these parts better than New York," said Carlton to Snyder, as they were sitting down to dinner in the overseer's dwelling.

"I can't say that I do," was the reply; "I came here ten years ago as missionary, and Mr. Peck wanted me to stay, and I have remained. I travel among the poor whites during the week, and preach for the niggers on Sunday."

"Are there many poor whites in this district?"

"Not here, but about thirty miles from here, in the Sand Hill district; they are as ignorant as horses. Why it was no longer than last week I was up there, and really you would not believe it, that people were so poor off. In New England, and, I may say, in all the free states, they have free schools, and everybody gets educated. Not so here. In Connecticut there is only one out of every five hundred above twenty-one years that can neither read nor write. Here there is one out of every eight that can neither read nor write. There is not a single newspaper taken in five of the counties in this state. Last week I was at Sand Hill for the first time, and I called at a farmhouse. The man was out. It was a low log-hut, and yet it was the best house in that locality. The woman and nine children were there, and the geese, ducks, chickens, pigs, and children were all running about the floor. The woman seemed scared at me when I entered the house. I inquired if I could get a little dinner, and my horse fed. She said, yes, if I would only be good enough to feed him myself, as her 'gal,' as she called her daughter, would be afraid of the horse. When I returned into the house again from the stable, she kept her eyes upon me all the time. At last she said, 'I s'pose you aint never bin in these parts afore?' 'No,' said I. 'Is you gwine to stay here long?' 'Not very long,' I replied. 'On business, I s'pose.' 'Yes,' said I, 'I am hunting up the lost sheep of the house of Israel.' 'Oh,' exclaimed she, 'hunting for lost sheep is you? Well, you have a hard time to find 'em here. My husband lost an old ram last week, and he aint found him yet, and he's hunted every day.'² 'I am not looking for four-legged sheep,' said I, 'I am hunting for sinners.' 'Ah'; she said, 'then you are a preacher.' 'Yes,' said I. 'You are the first of that sort that's bin in these diggins for many a day.' Turning to her eldest daughter, she said in an excited tone, 'Clar out the pigs and ducks, and sweep up the floor; this is a preacher.' And it was some time before any of the children would come near me; one remained under the bed (which, by the by, was in the same room), all the while I was there. 'Well,' continued the woman, 'I was a tellin' my man only yesterday that I would like once more to go to meetin' before I died, and he said as he should like to do the same. But as you have come, it will save us the trouble of going out of the district.' "

"Then you found some of the lost sheep," said Carlton.

"Yes," replied Snyder. "I did not find anything else up there. The state makes no provision for educating the poor: they are unable to do it themselves, and they grow up in a state of ignorance and degradation. The men hunt and the women have to go in the fields and labour."

"What is the cause of it?" inquired Carlton.

"Slavery," answered Snyder, "slavery,—and nothing else. Look at the city of Boston; it pays more taxes for the support of the government than this entire state. The people of Boston do more business than the whole population of Mississippi put together. I was told some very amusing things while at Sand Hill. A farmer there told me a story about an old woman, who was very pious herself. She had a husband and three sons, who were sad characters, and she had often prayed for their conversion but to no effect. At last, one day while working in the cornfield, one of her sons was bitten by a rattlesnake. He had scarce reached home before he felt the poison, and in his agony called loudly on his Maker.

"The pious old woman, when she heard this, forgetful of her son's misery, and everything else but the glorious hope of his repentence, fell on her knees, and prayed as follows,—'Oh! Lord, I thank thee, that thou hast at last opened Jimmy's eyes to the error of his ways: and I pray that, in thy Divine mercy, thou wilt send a rattlesnake to bite the old man, and another to bite Tom, and another to bite Harry, for I am certain that nothing but a rattlesnake, or something of the kind, will ever turn them from their sinful ways, they are so hard-headed.' When returning home, and before I got out of the Sand Hill district, I saw a funeral, and thought I would fasten my horse to a post and attend. The coffin was carried in a common horse cart, and followed by fifteen or twenty persons very shabbily dressed, and attended by a man whom I took to be the religious man of the place. After the coffin had been placed near the grave, he spoke as follows,—

"'Friends and neighbours! you have congregated to see this lump of mortality put into a hole in the ground. You all know the deceased—a worthless, drunken, good-for-nothing vagabond. He lived in disgrace and infamy, and died in wretchedness. You all despised him—you all know his brother Joe, who lives on the hill? He's not a bit better though he has scrap'd together a little property by cheating his neighbours. His end will be like that of this loathsome creature, whom you will please put into the hole as soon as possible. I won't ask you to drop a tear, but brother Bohow will please raise a hymn while we fill up the grave.'"

"I am rather surprised to hear that any portion of the whites in this state are in so low a condition."

"Yet it is true," returned Snyder.

"These are very onpleasant facts to be related to ye, Mr. Carlton," said Huckelby; "but I can bear witness to what Mr. Snyder has tole ye." Huckelby was from Maryland, where many of the poor whites are in as sad a condition as the Sand Hillers of Mississippi. He was a tall man, of iron constitution, and could neither read nor write, but was considered one of the best overseers in the country. When about to break a slave in, to do a heavy task, he would make him work by his side all day; and if the new hand kept up with him, he was set down as an able bodied man. Huckelby had neither moral, religious, or political principles, and often boasted that conscience was a matter that never "cost" him a thought. "Mr. Snyder aint told ye half about the folks in these parts," continued he; "we who comes from more enlightened parts don't know how to put up with 'em down here. I find the people here knows mighty little indeed; in fact, I may say they are univarsaly onedicated. I goes out among none on 'em, 'cause they aint such as I have been used to 'sociate with. When I gits a little richer, so that I can stop work, I tend to go back to Maryland, and spend the rest of my days."

"I wonder the Negroes don't attempt to get their freedom by physical force."

"It aint no use for 'em to try that, for if they do, we puts 'em through by daylight," replied Huckelby.

"There are some desperate fellows among the slaves," said Snyder.

"Indeed," remarked Carlton.

"Oh, yes," replied the preacher. "A case has just taken place near here, where a neighbour of ours, Mr. J. Higgerson, attempted to correct a Negro man in his employ, who resisted, drew a knife, and stabbed him (Mr. H.) in several places. Mr. J. C. Hobbs (a Tennessean) ran to his assistance. Mr. Hobbs stooped to pick up a stick to strike the Negro, and, while in that position, the Negro rushed upon him, and caused his immediate death. The Negro then fled to the woods, but was pursued with dogs, and soon overtaken. He had stopped in a swamp to fight the dogs, when the party who were pursuing him came upon him, and commanded him to give up, which he refused to do. He then made several efforts to stab them. Mr. Roberson, one of the party, gave him several blows on the head with a rifle gun; but this, instead of subduing, only increased his desperate revenge. Mr. R. then discharged his gun at the Negro, and missing him, the ball struck Mr. Boon in the face, and felled him to the ground. The Negro, seeing Mr. Boon prostrated, attempted to rush up and stab him, but was prevented by the timely interference of some one of the party. He was then shot three times with a revolving pistol, and once with a rifle, and after having his throat cut, he still kept the knife firmly grasped in his hand, and tried to cut their legs when they approached to put an end to his life. This chastisement was given because the Negro grumbled, and found fault with his master for flogging his wife."

"Well, this is a bad state of affairs indeed, and especially the condition of the poor whites," said Carlton.

"You see," replied Snyder, "no white man is respectable in these slave states who works for a living.³ No community can be prosperous, where honest labour is not honoured. No society can be rightly constituted, where the intellect is not fed. Whatever institution reflects discredit on industry, whatever institution forbids the general culture of the understanding, is palpably hostile to individual rights, and to social well-being. Slavery is the incubus that hangs over the Southern States."

"Yes," interrupted Huckelby; "them's just my sentiments now, and no mistake. I think that, for the honour of our country, this slavery business should stop. I don't own any, no how, and I would not be an overseer if I weren't paid for it."

CHAPTER VIII
THE SEPARATION

"In many ways does the full heart reveal
The presence of the love it would conceal;
But in far more the estranged heart lets know
The absence of the love, which yet it fain would show."[1]

At length the news of the approaching marriage of Horatio met the ear of Clotel.[2] Her head grew dizzy, and her heart fainted within her; but, with a strong effort at composure, she inquired all the particulars, and her pure mind at once took its resolution. Horatio came that evening, and though she would fain have met him as usual, her heart was too full not to throw a deep sadness over her looks and tones. She had never complained of his decreasing tenderness, or of her own lonely hours; but he felt that the mute appeal of her heart-broken looks was more terrible than words. He kissed the hand she offered, and with a countenance almost as sad as her own, led her to a window in the recess shadowed by a luxuriant passion flower. It was the same seat where they had spent the first evening in this beautiful cottage, consecrated to their first loves. The same calm, clear moonlight looked in through the trellis. The vine then planted had now a luxuriant growth; and many a time had Horatio fondly twined its sacred blossoms with the glossy ringlets of her raven hair. The rush of memory almost overpowered poor Clotel; and Horatio felt too much oppressed and ashamed to break the long deep silence. At length, in words scarcely audible, Clotel said: "Tell me, dear Horatio, are you to be married next week?"

He dropped her hand as if a rifle ball had struck him; and it was not until after long hesitation, that he began to make some reply about the necessity of circumstances. Mildly but earnestly the poor girl begged him to spare apologies. It was enough that he no longer loved her, and that they must bid farewell. Trusting to the yielding tenderness of her character, he ventured, in the most soothing accents, to suggest that as he still loved her better than all the world, she would ever be his real wife, and they might see each other frequently. He was not prepared for the storm of indignant emotion his words excited. True, she was his slave; her bones, and sinews had been purchased by his gold, yet she had the heart of a true woman, and hers was a passion too deep and absorbing to admit of partnership, and her spirit was too pure to form a selfish league with crime.

At length this painful interview came to an end. They stood together by the Gothic gate, where they had so often met and parted in the moonlight. Old remembrances melted their souls.

"Farewell, dearest Horatio," said Clotel. "Give me a parting kiss."

Her voice was choked for utterance, and the tears flowed freely, as she bent her lips toward him. He folded her convulsively in his arms, and imprinted a long impassioned kiss on that mouth, which had never spoken to him but in love and blessing. With efforts like a death-pang she at length raised her head from his heaving bosom, and turning from him with bitter sobs. "It is our last. To meet thus is henceforth crime. God bless you. I would not have you so miserable as I am. Farewell. A last farewell."

"The last?" exclaimed he, with a wild shriek. "Oh God, Clotel, do not say that"; and covering his face with his hands, he wept like a child. Recovering from his emotion, he found himself alone. The moon looked down upon him mild, but very sorrowfully; as the Madonna seems to gaze upon her worshipping children, bowed down with consciousness of sin. At that moment he would have given worlds to have disengaged himself from Gertrude, but he had gone so far, that blame, disgrace, and duels with angry relatives would now attend any effort to obtain his freedom. Oh, how the moonlight oppressed him with its friendly sadness! It was like the plaintive eye of his forsaken one, like the music of sorrow echoed from an unseen world. Long and earnestly he gazed at that cottage, where he had so long known earth's purest foretaste of heavenly bliss. Slowly he walked away; then turned again to look on that charmed spot, the nestling-place of his early affections. He caught a glimpse of Clotel, weeping beside a magnolia, which commanded a long view of the path leading to the public road. He would have sprung toward her but she darted from him, and entered the cottage. That graceful figure, weeping in the moonlight, haunted him for years. It stood before his closing eyes, and greeted him with the morning dawn. Poor Gertrude, had she known all, what a dreary lot would hers have been; but fortunately she could not miss the impassioned tenderness she never experienced; and Horatio was the more careful in his kindness, because he was deficient in love. After Clotel had been separated from her mother and sister, she turned her attention to the subject of Christianity, and received that consolation from her Bible that is never denied to the children of God. Although it was against the laws of Virginia, for a slave to be taught to read, Currer had employed an old free Negro, who lived near her, to teach her two daughters to read and write.[3] She felt that the step she had taken in resolving never to meet Horatio again would no doubt expose her to his wrath, and probably cause her to be sold, yet her heart was too guileless for her to commit a crime, and therefore she had ten times rather have been sold as a slave than do wrong. Some months after the marriage of Horatio and Gertrude their barouche rolled along a winding road that skirted the forest near Clotel's cottage, when the attention of Gertrude was suddenly attracted by two figures among the trees by the wayside; and touching Horatio's arm, she exclaimed, "Do look at that beautiful child." He turned and saw Clotel and Mary. His lips quivered, and his face became deadly pale. His young wife looked at him intently, but said nothing. In returning home, he took another road; but his wife seeing this, expressed a wish to go back the way they had come. He objected, and suspicion was awakened in her heart, and she soon after learned that the mother of that lovely child bore the name of Clotel, a name which she had often heard Horatio murmur in uneasy slumbers. From gossiping tongues she soon learned more than she wished to know. She wept, but not as poor Clotel had done; for she never had loved, and been beloved like her, and her nature was more proud: henceforth a change came over her feelings and her manners, and Horatio had no further occasion to assume a tenderness in return for hers. Changed as he was by ambition, he felt the wintry chill of her polite propriety, and sometimes, in agony of heart, compared it with the gushing love of her who was indeed his wife. But these and all his emotions were a sealed book to Clotel, of which she could only guess the contents. With remittances for her and her child's support, there sometimes came earnest pleadings that she would consent to see him again; but these she never answered, though her heart yearned to do so. She pitied his young bride, and would not be tempted to bring sorrow into her household by any fault of hers. Her earnest prayer was, that she might not know of her existence. She had not looked on Horatio since she watched him under the shadow of the magnolia, until his barouche passed her in her rambles some months after. She saw the deadly paleness of his countenance, and had he dared to look back, he would have seen her tottering with faintness. Mary brought water from a rivulet, and sprinkled her face. When she revived, she clasped the beloved child to her heart with a vehemence that made her scream. Soothingly she kissed away her fears, and gazed into her beautiful eyes with a deep, deep sadness of expression, which poor Mary never forgot. Wild were the thoughts that passed round her aching heart, and almost maddened her poor brain; thoughts which had almost driven her to suicide the night of that last farewell. For her child's sake she had conquered the fierce temptation then; and for her sake, she struggled with it now. But the gloomy atmosphere of their once happy home overclouded the morning of Mary's life. Clotel perceived this, and it gave her unutterable pain.

"'Tis ever thus with woman's love,
     True till life's storms have passed;
And, like the vine around the tree,
     It braves them to the last."

CHAPTER IX
THE MAN OF HONOUR

"My tongue could never learn sweet soothing words,
But now thy beauty is propos'd, my fee,
My proud heart sues, and prompts my tongue to speak."
—*Shakespeare.*[1]

James Crawford, the purchaser of Althesa, was from the green mountains of Vermont, and his feelings were opposed to the holding of slaves. But his young wife persuaded him into the idea that it was no worse to own a slave than to hire one and pay the money to another. Hence it was that he had been induced to purchase Althesa. Henry Morton, a young physician from the same state, and who had just commenced the practice of his profession in New Orleans, was boarding with Crawford when Althesa was brought home.[2] The young physician had been in New Orleans but a few weeks, and had seen very little of slavery. In his own mountain home he had been taught that the slaves of the Southern states were Negroes, if not from the coast of Africa, the descendants of those who had been imported. He was unprepared to behold with composure a beautiful young white girl of fifteen in the degraded position of a chattel slave. The blood chilled in his young heart as he heard Crawford tell how, by bantering with the trader, he had bought her for two hundred dollars less than he first asked. His very looks showed that the slave girl had the deepest sympathy of his heart. Althesa had been brought up by her mother to look after the domestic concerns of her cottage in Virginia, and knew well the duties imposed upon her. Mrs. Crawford was much pleased with her new servant, and often made mention of her in [the] presence of Morton. The young man's sympathy ripened into love, which was reciprocated by the friendless and injured child of sorrow. There was but one course left; that was, to purchase the young girl and make her his wife, which he did six months after her arrival in Crawford's family. The young physician and his wife immediately took lodgings in another part of the city; a private teacher was called in, and the young wife taught some of those accomplishments which are necessary for one's taking a position in society. Dr. Morton soon obtained a large practice in his profession, and with it increased in wealth—but with all his wealth he never would own a slave. Mrs. Morton was now in a position to seek out and redeem her mother, whom she had not heard of since they parted at Natchez. An agent was immediately despatched to hunt out the mother and to see if she could be purchased. The agent had no trouble in finding out Mr. Peck: but all overtures were unavailable; he would not sell Currer. His excuse was, that she was such a good housekeeper that he could not spare her. Poor Althesa felt sad when she found that her mother could not be bought. However, she felt a consciousness of having done her duty in the matter, yet waited with the hope that the day might come when she should have her mother by her side.

CHAPTER X
THE YOUNG CHRISTIAN

"Here we see *God dealing in slaves;* giving them to his own
favourite child [Abraham], a man of superlative worth, and as a
reward for his eminent goodness."
—*Rev. Theodore Clapp, of New Orleans.*[1]

On Carlton's return the next day from the farm, he was overwhelmed with questions from Mr. Peck, as to what he thought
of the plantation, the condition of the Negroes, Huckelby and
Snyder; and especially how he liked the sermon of the latter.
Mr. Peck was a kind of a patriarch in his own way. To begin
with, he was a man of some talent. He not only had a good education, but was a man of great eloquence, and had a wonderful command of language. He too either had, or thought he
had, poetical genius; and was often sending contributions to
the *Natchez Free Trader,* and other periodicals. In the way of
raising contributions for foreign missions, he took the lead of
all others in his neighbourhood. Everything he did, he did for
the "glory of God," as he said: he quoted Scripture for almost
everything he did. Being in good circumstances, he was able to
give to almost all benevolent causes to which he took a fancy.
He was a most loving father, and his daughter exercised considerable influence over him, and owing to her piety and judgment, that influence had a beneficial effect. Carlton, though a
school-fellow of the parson's, was nevertheless nearly ten years
his junior; and though not an avowed infidel, was, however, a
free-thinker, and one who took no note of to-morrow. And for
this reason Georgiana took peculiar interest in the young man,
for Carlton was but little above thirty and unmarried. The
young Christian felt that she would not be living up to that
faith that she professed and believed in, if she did not exert herself to the utmost to save the thoughtless man from his down-
ward career; and in this she succeeded to her most sanguine

expectations. She not only converted him, but in placing the Scriptures before him in their true light, she redeemed those sacred writings from the charge of supporting the system of slavery, which her father had cast upon them in the discussion some days before.

Georgiana's first object, however, was to awaken in Carlton's breast a love for the Lord Jesus Christ. The young man had often sat under the sound of the gospel with perfect indifference. He had heard men talk who had grown grey bending over the Scriptures, and their conversation had passed by him unheeded; but when a young girl, much younger than himself, reasoned with him in that innocent and persuasive manner that woman is wont to use when she has entered with her whole soul upon an object, it was too much for his stout heart, and he yielded. Her next aim was to vindicate the Bible from sustaining the monstrous institution of slavery.[2] She said, "God has created of one blood all the nations of men, to dwell on all the face of the earth.[3] To claim, hold, and treat a human being as property is felony against God and man. The Christian religion is opposed to slaveholding in its spirit and its principles; it classes menstealers among murderers; and it is the duty of all who wish to meet God in peace, to discharge that duty in spreading these principles. Let us not deceive ourselves into the idea that slavery is right, because it is profitable to us. Slaveholding is the highest possible violation of the eighth commandment. To take from a man his earnings, is theft; but to take the earner is a compound, life-long theft; and we who profess to follow in the footsteps of our Redeemer, should do our utmost to extirpate slavery from the land. For my own part, I shall do all I can. When the Redeemer was about to ascend to the bosom of the Father, and resume the glory which he had with him before the world was, he promised his disciples that the power of the Holy Ghost should come upon them, and that they should be witnesses for him to the uttermost parts of the earth. What was the effect upon their minds? 'They all continued with one accord in prayer and supplication with the women.' Stimulated by the confident expectation that Jesus would fulfil his gracious promise, they poured out their hearts in fervent supplications, probably for strength to do the work which he had appointed them unto, for they felt that without him they could do nothing, and they consecrated themselves on the altar of God, to the great and glorious enterprise of preaching the unsearchable riches of Christ to a lost and perishing world. Have we less precious promises in the Scriptures of truth? May we not claim of our God the blessing promised unto those who consider the poor: the Lord will preserve them and keep them alive, and they shall be blessed upon the earth? Does not the language, 'Inasmuch as ye did it unto one of the least of these my brethren, ye did it unto me,' belong to all who are rightly engaged in endeavouring to unloose the bondman's fetters? Shall we not then do as the apostles did? Shall we not, in view of the two millions of heathen in our very midst, in view of the souls that are going down in an almost unbroken phalanx to utter perdition, continue in prayer and supplication, that God will grant us the supplies of his Spirit to prepare us for that work which he has given us to do? Shall not the wail of the mother as she surrenders her only child to the grasp of the ruthless kidnapper, or the trader in human blood, animate our devotions? Shall not the manifold crimes and horrors of slavery excite more ardent outpourings at the throne of grace to grant repentance to our guilty country, and permit us to aid in preparing the way for the glorious second advent of the Messiah, by preaching deliverance to the captives, and the opening of the prison doors to those who are bound?"

Georgiana had succeeded in riveting the attention of Carlton during her conversation, and as she was finishing her last sentence, she observed the silent tear stealing down the cheek of the newly born child of God. At this juncture her father entered, and Carlton left the room.

"Dear papa," said Georgiana, "will you grant me one favour; or, rather, make me a promise?"

"I can't tell, my dear, till I know what it is," replied Mr. Peck. "If it is a reasonable request, I will comply with your wish," continued he.

"I hope, my dear," answered she, "that papa would not think me capable of making an unreasonable request."

"Well, well," returned he; "tell me what it is."

"I hope," said she, "that in your future conversation with Mr. Carlton, on the subject of slavery, you will not speak of the Bible as sustaining it."

"Why, Georgiana, my dear, you are mad, aint you?" exclaimed he, in an excited tone.

The poor girl remained silent; the father saw in a moment that he had spoken too sharply; and taking her hand in his he said. "Now, my child, why do you make that request?"

"Because," returned she, "I think he is on the stool of repentance, if he has not already been received among the elect. He, you know, was bordering upon infidelity, and if the Bible sanctions slavery, then he will naturally enough say that it is not from God; for the argument from internal evidence is not only refuted, but actually turned against the Bible. If the Bible sanctions slavery, then it misrepresents the character of God. Nothing would be more dangerous to the soul of a young convert than to satisfy him that the Scriptures favoured such a system of sin."

"Don't you suppose that I understand the Scriptures better than you? I have been in the world longer."

"Yes," said she, "you have been in the world longer, and amongst slaveholders so long that you do not regard it in the same light that those do who have not become so familiar with its every-day scenes as you. I once heard you say, that you were opposed to the institution, when you first came to the South."

"Yes," answered he, "I did not know so much about it then."

"With great deference to you, papa," replied Georgiana, "I don't think that the Bible sanctions slavery. The Old Testament contains this explicit condemnation of it, 'He that stealeth a man, and selleth him, or if he be found in his hand, he shall surely be put to death'; and 'Woe unto him that buildeth his house by unrighteousness, and his chambers by wrong; that useth his neighbour's service without wages, and giveth him not for his work'; when also the New Testament exhibits such words of rebuke as these, 'Behold the hire of the labourers who have reaped down your fields, which is of you kept back by fraud, crieth; and the cries of them who have reaped are entered into the ears of the Lord of Sabaoth.' 'The law is not made for a righteous man, but for the lawless and disobedient, for the ungodly and for sinners, for unholy and profane, for murderers of fathers and murderers of mothers, for manslayers, for whore-mongers, for them that defile themselves with mankind, for *menstealers*, for liars, for perjured persons.' A more scathing denunciation of the sin in question is surely to be found on record in no other book. I am afraid," continued the daughter, "that the acts of the professed friends of Christianity in the South do more to spread infidelity than the writings of all the atheists which have ever been published. The infidel watches the religious world. He surveys the church, and, lo! thousands and tens of thousands of her accredited members actually hold slaves. Members 'in good and regular standing,' fellowshipped throughout Christendom except by a few anti-slavery churches generally despised as ultra and radical, reduce their fellow men to the condition of chattels, and by force keep them in that state of degradation. Bishops, ministers, elders, and deacons are engaged in this awful business, and do not consider their conduct as at all inconsistent with the precepts of either the Old or New Testaments. Moreover, those ministers and churches who do not themselves hold slaves, very generally defend the conduct of those who do, and accord to them a fair Christian character, and in the way of business frequently take mortgages and levy executions on the bodies of their fellow men, and in some cases of their fellow Christians.

"Now is it a wonder that infidels, beholding the practice and listening to the theory of professing Christians, should conclude that the Bible inculcates a morality not inconsistent with chattelising human beings? And must not this conclusion be strengthened, when they hear ministers of talent and learning declare that the Bible does sanction slaveholding, and that it ought not to be made a disciplinable offence in churches? And must not all doubt be dissipated, when one of the most learned professors in our theological seminaries asserts that the Bible 'recognises that the relation may still exist, *salva fide et salva ecclesia*' (without injury to the Christian faith or church) and

that only 'the *abuse* of it is the essential and fundamental
wrong?' Are not infidels bound to believe that these professors,
ministers, and churches understand their own Bible, and that,
consequently, notwithstanding solitary passages which appear
to condemn slaveholding, the Bible sanctions it? When nothing
can be further from the truth. And as for Christ, his whole life
was a living testimony against slavery and all that it inculcates.
When he designed to do us good, he took upon himself the
form of a servant. He took his station at the bottom of society.
He voluntarily identified himself with the poor and the despised. The warning voices of Jeremiah and Ezekiel were raised
in olden time, against sin. Let us not forget what followed.
'Therefore, thus saith the Lord—ye have not harkened unto me
in proclaiming liberty every one to his brother, and every one to
his neighbour—behold I proclaim a liberty for you, saith the
Lord, to the sword, to the pestilence, and to the famine.' Are
we not virtually as a nation adopting the same impious language, and are we not exposed to the same tremendous judg-
ments? Shall we not, in view of those things, use every laudable
means to awaken our beloved country from the slumbers of
death, and baptize all our efforts with tears and with prayers,
that God may bless them? Then, should our labour fail to accomplish the end for which we pray, we shall stand acquitted at
the bar of Jehovah, and although we may share in the national
calamities which await unrepented sins, yet that blessed ap-
proval will be ours—'Well done, good and faithful servants,
enter ye into the joy of your Lord.' "

"My dear Georgiana," said Mr. Peck, "I must be permitted
to entertain my own views on this subject, and to exercise my
own judgment."

"Believe me, dear papa," she replied. "I would not be understood as wishing to teach you, or to dictate to you in the least;
but only grant my request, not to allude to the Bible as sanc-
tioning slavery, when speaking with Mr. Carlton."

"Well," returned he, "I will comply with your wish."

The young Christian had indeed accomplished a noble work:
and whether it was admitted by the father, or not, she was his
superior and his teacher. Georgiana had viewed the right to

enjoy perfect liberty as one of those inherent and inalienable rights which pertain to the whole human race, and of which they can never be divested, except by an act of gross injustice. And no one was more able than herself to impress those views upon the hearts of all with whom she came in contact. Modest and self-possessed, with a voice of great sweetness, and a most winning manner, she could, with the greatest ease to herself, engage their attention.

CHAPTER XI

THE PARSON POET

"Unbind, unbind my galling chain,
And set, oh! set me free:
No longer say that I'll disdain
The gift of liberty."

Through the persuasion of Mr. Peck, and fascinated with the charms of Georgiana, Carlton had prolonged his stay two months with his old school-fellow. During the latter part of the time he had been almost as one of the family. If Miss Peck was invited out, Mr. Carlton was, as a matter of course. She seldom rode out, unless with him. If Mr. Peck was absent, he took the head of the table; and, to the delight of the young lady, he had on several occasions taken part in the family worship.

"I am glad," said Mr. Peck, one evening while at the tea table, "I am glad, Mr. Carlton, that my neighbour Jones has invited you to visit him at his farm. He is a good neighbour, but a very ungodly man; I want that you should see his people, and then, when you return to the North, you can tell how much better a Christian's slaves are situated than one who does nothing for the cause of Christ."

"I hope, Mr. Carlton," said Georgiana, "that you will spend the Sabbath with him, and have a religious interview with the Negroes."

"Yes," replied the parson, "that's well thought of, Georgy."

"Well, I think I will go up on Thursday next, and stay till Monday," said Carlton; "and I shall act upon your suggestion, Miss Peck," continued he; "and try to get a religious interview with the blacks. By-the-by," remarked Carlton, "I saw an advertisement in the *Free Trader* to-day that rather puzzled me. Ah, here it is now; and," drawing the paper from his pocket, "I will read it, and then you can tell me what it means:

" 'To PLANTERS AND OTHERS.—*Wanted fifty Negroes.* Any person having *sick Negroes,* considered *incurable* by their respective physicians, (their owners of course,) and wishing to dispose of them, Dr. Stillman will pay cash for Negroes affected with scrofula or king's evil, confirmed hypochondriacism, apoplexy, or diseases of the brain, kidneys, spleen, stomach and intestines, bladder and its appendages, diarrhoea, dysentery, &c. *The highest cash price will be paid as above.*'

"When I read this to-day I thought that the advertiser must be a man of eminent skill as a physician, and that he intended to cure the sick Negroes; but on second thought I find that some of the diseases enumerated are certainly incurable. What can he do with these sick Negroes?"

"You see," replied Mr. Peck, laughing, "that he is a doctor, and has use for them in his lectures. The doctor is connected with a small college. Look at his prospectus, where he invites students to attend, and that will explain the matter to you."

Carlton turned to another column, and read the following:

"Some advantages of a peculiar character are connected with this institution, which it may be proper to point out. No place in the United States offers as great opportunities for the acquisition of anatomical knowledge. Subjects being obtained from among the coloured population in sufficient numbers *for every purpose,* and proper dissections carried on *without offending any individuals in the community!*"

"These are for dissection, then?" inquired Carlton with a trembling voice.

"Yes," answered the parson.

"Of course they wait till they die before they can use them."

"They keep them on hand, and when they need one they bleed him to death," returned Mr. Peck.

"Yes, but that's murder."

"Oh, the doctors are licensed to commit murder, you know; and what's the difference, whether one dies owing to the loss of blood, or taking too many pills? For my own part, if I had to choose, I would rather submit to the former."

"I have often heard what I considered hard stories in abolition meetings in New York about slavery; but now I shall begin to think that many of them are true."[2]

"The longer you remain here the more you will be convinced of the iniquity of the institution," remarked Georgiana.

"Now, Georgy, my dear, don't give us another abolition lecture, if you please," said Mr. Peck. "Here, Carlton," continued the parson, "I have written a short poem for your sister's album, as you requested me; it is a domestic piece, as you will see."

"She will prize it the more for that," remarked Carlton; and taking the sheet of paper, he laughed as his eyes glanced over it.

"Read it out, Mr. Carlton," said Georgiana, "and let me hear what it is: I know papa gets off some very droll things at times." Carlton complied with the young lady's request, and read aloud the following rare specimen of poetical genius:[3]

"MY LITTLE NIG.

"I have a little nigger, the blackest thing alive,
  He'll be just four years old if he lives till forty-five;
  His smooth cheek hath a glossy hue, like a new polished boot,
  And his hair curls o'er his little head as black as any soot.
  His lips bulge from his countenance—his little ivories shine—
  His nose is what we call a little pug, but fashioned very fine:
  Although not quite a fairy, he is comely to behold,
  And I wouldn't sell him, 'pon my word, for a hundred all in gold.

"He gets up early in the morn, like all the other nigs,
  And runs off to the hog-lot, where he squabbles with the pigs—
  And when the sun gets out of bed, and mounts up in the sky,
  The warmest corner of the yard is where my nig doth lie.
  And there extended lazily, he contemplates and dreams,
  (I cannot qualify to this, but plain enough it seems;)
  Until 'tis time to take in grub, when you can't find him there,
  For, like a politician, he has gone to hunt his share.

"I haven't said a single word concerning my plantation,
  Though a prettier, I guess, cannot be found within the nation;
When he gets a little bigger, I'll take and to him show it,
  And then I'll say, 'My little nig, now just prepare to go it!'
I'll put a hoe into his hand—he'll soon know what it means,
  And every day for dinner, he shall have bacon and greens."

CHAPTER XII

A NIGHT IN THE PARSON'S KITCHEN

"And see the servants met,
Their daily labour's o'er;
And with the jest and song they set
The kitchen in a roar."

Mr. Peck kept around him four servants besides Currer, of whom we have made mention: of these, Sam was considered the first. If a dinner-party was in contemplation, or any company to be invited to the parson's, after all the arrangements had been talked over by the minister and his daughter, Sam was sure to be consulted upon the subject by "Miss Georgy," as Miss Peck was called by the servants. If furniture, crockery, or anything else was to be purchased, Sam felt that he had been slighted if his opinion had not been asked. As to the marketing, he did it all. At the servants' table in the kitchen, he sat at the head, and was master of ceremonies. A single look from him was enough to silence any conversation or noise in the kitchen, or any other part of the premises. There is, in the Southern States, a great amount of prejudice against colour amongst the Negroes themselves. The nearer the Negro or mulatto approaches to the white, the more he seems to feel his superiority over those of a darker hue. This is, no doubt, the result of the prejudice that exists on the part of the whites towards both mulattoes and blacks.[1] Sam was originally from Kentucky, and through the instrumentality of one of his young masters whom he had to take to school, he had learned to read so as to be well understood; and, owing to that fact, was considered a prodigy among the slaves, not only of his own master's, but those of the town who knew him. Sam had a great wish to follow in the footsteps of his master, and be a poet; and was, therefore, often heard singing doggrels of his own composition. But there was one great drawback to Sam, and that was his colour. He was one of the blackest of his race. This he evidently regarded as a great misfortune. However, he made up for this in his dress. Mr. Peck kept his house servants well dressed; and as for Sam, he was seldom seen except in a ruffled shirt. Indeed, the washerwoman feared him more than all others about the house.

Currer, as we have already stated, was chief of the kitchen department, and had a general supervision of the household affairs. Alfred the coachman, Peter, and Hetty made up the remainder of the house servants. Besides these, Mr. Peck owned eight slaves who were masons. These worked in the city. Being mechanics, they were let out to greater advantage than to keep them on the farm. However, every Sunday night, Peck's servants, including the bricklayers, usually assembled in the kitchen, when the events of the week were freely discussed and commented on. It was on a Sunday evening, in the month of June, that there was a party at Mr. Peck's, and, according to custom in the Southern States, the ladies had their maidservants with them. Tea had been served in "the house," and the servants, including the strangers, had taken their seats at the tea table in the kitchen. Sam, being a "single gentleman," was usually attentive to the "ladies" on this occasion. He seldom or ever let the day pass without spending at least an hour in combing and brushing up his "hair." Sam had an idea that fresh butter was better for his hair than any other kind of grease; and therefore, on churning days, half a pound of butter had always to be taken out before it was salted. When he wished to appear to great advantage, he would grease his face, to make it "shiny." On the evening of the party therefore, when all the servants were at the table, Sam cut a big figure. There he sat with his wool well combed and buttered, face nicely greased, and his ruffles extending five or six inches from his breast. The parson in his own drawing-room did not make a more imposing appearance than did his servant on this occasion.

"I jist bin had my fortune told last Sunday night," said Sam, as he helped one of the girls to some sweet hash.

"Indeed," cried half-a-dozen voices.

"Yes," continued he; "Aunt Winny told me I is to hab de prettiest yaller gal in town, and dat I is to be free."

All eyes were immediately turned toward Sally Johnson, who was seated near Sam.

"I speck I see somebody blush at dat remark," said Alfred.

"Pass dem pancakes and molasses up dis way, Mr. Alf, and none of your insinawaysion here," rejoined Sam.

"Dat reminds me," said Currer, "dat Dorcas Simpson is gwine to git married."

"Who to, I want to know?" inquired Peter.

"To one of Mr. Darby's field-hands," answered Currer.

"I should tink dat dat gal would not trow hersef away in dat manner," said Sally. "She good enough looking to get a house servant, and not to put up wid a fiel' nigger," continued she.

"Yes," said Sam, "dat's a wery insensible remark of yours, Miss Sally. I admire your judgment wery much, I assure you. Dah's plenty of suspectible and well-dressed house servants dat a gal of her looks can get, wid out taken up wid dem common darkies."

"Is de man black or a mulatto?" inquired one of the company.

"He's nearly white," replied Currer.

"Well den, dat's some exchuse for her," remarked Sam; "for I don't like to see dis malgemation of blacks and mulattoes, no how," continued Sam. "If I had my rights I would be a mulatto too, for my mother was almost as light-coloured as Miss Sally," said he.

Although Sam was one of the blackest men living, he nevertheless contended that his mother was a mulatto, and no one was more prejudiced against the blacks than he. A good deal of work, and the free use of fresh butter, had no doubt done wonders for his "hare" in causing it to grow long, and to this he would always appeal when he wished to convince others that he was part of an Anglo-Saxon.

"I always thought you was not clear black, Mr. Sam," said Agnes.

"You are right dahr, Miss Agnes. My hare tells what company I belong to," answered Sam. Here the whole company joined in the conversation about colour, which lasted for some

time, giving unmistakable evidence that caste is owing to ignorance. The evening's entertainment concluded by Sam's relating
a little of his own experience while with his first master in old
Kentucky.

Sam's former master was a doctor, and had a large practice
among his neighbours, doctoring both masters and slaves.
When Sam was about fifteen years of age, his old master set
him to grinding up the ointment, then to making pills. As the
young student grew older and became more practised in his
profession, his services were of more importance to the doctor.
The physician having a good business, and a large number of
his patients being slaves, the most of whom had to call on the
doctor when ill, he put Sam to bleeding, pulling teeth, and ad-
ministering medicine to the slaves. Sam soon acquired the name
amongst the slaves of the "Black Doctor." With this appella-
tion he was delighted, and no regular physician could possibly
have put on more airs than did the black doctor when his services were required. In bleeding, he must have more bandages,
and rub and smack the arm more than the doctor would have
thought of. We once saw Sam taking out a tooth for one of his
patients, and nothing appeared more amusing. He got the poor
fellow down on his back, and he got astraddle of the man's
chest, and getting the turnkeys on the wrong tooth, he shut
both eyes and pulled for his life. The poor man screamed as
loud as he could, but to no purpose. Sam had him fast. After a
great effort, out came the sound grinder, and the young doctor
saw his mistake; but consoled himself with the idea that as the
wrong tooth was out of the way, there was more room to get at
the right one. Bleeding and a dose of calomel was always considered indispensable by the "Old Boss"; and, as a matter of
course, Sam followed in his footsteps.

On one occasion the old doctor was ill himself, so as to be
unable to attend to his patients. A slave, with pass in hand,
called to receive medical advice, and the master told Sam to examine him and see what he wanted. This delighted him beyond
measure, for although he had been acting his part in the way of
giving out medicine as the master ordered it, he had never been
called upon by the latter to examine a patient, and this seemed

to convince him that, after all, he was no sham doctor. As might have been expected, he cut a rare figure in his first examination, placing himself directly opposite his patient, and folding his arms across his breast, and looking very knowingly, he began, "What's de matter wid you?"

"I is sick."

"Where is you sick?"

"Here," replied the man, putting his hand upon his stomach.

"Put out your tongue," continued the doctor. The man ran out his tongue at full length.

"Let me feel your pulse," at the same time taking his patient's hand in his, placing his fingers on his pulse, he said, "Ah, your case is a bad one; if I don't do something for you, and dat pretty quick, you i'll be a gone coon, and dat's sartin." At this the man appeared frightened and inquired what was the matter with him: in answer, Sam said, "I done told you dat your case is a bad one, and dat's enough."

On Sam's returning to his master's bedside, the latter said, "Well, Sam, what do you think is the matter with him?"

"His stomach is out of order, sir," he replied.

"What do you think had best be done for him?"

"I think I better bleed him and give him a dose of calomel," returned Sam. So to the latter's gratification the master let him have his own way. We need not further say, that the recital of Sam's experience as a physician gave him a high position amongst the servants that evening, and made him a decided favourite with the ladies, one of whom feigned illness, when the black doctor, to the delight of all, and certainly to himself, gave medical advice. Thus ended the evening amongst the servants in the parson's kitchen.

CHAPTER XIII
A SLAVE HUNTING PARSON

" 'Tis too much prov'd—that with devotion's visage,
And pious action, we do sugar o'er the devil himself."
—*Shakespeare.*[1]

"You will, no doubt, be well pleased with neighbour Jones," said Mr. Peck, as Carlton stepped into the chaise to pay his promised visit to the "ungodly man."

"Don't forget to have a religious interview with the Negroes," remarked Georgiana, as she gave the last nod to her young convert.

"I will do my best," returned Carlton, as the vehicle left the door.

As might have been expected, Carlton met with a cordial reception at the hands of the proprietor of the Grove Farm. The servants in the "Great House" were well dressed, and appeared as if they did not want for food. Jones knew that Carlton was from the North, and a non-slaveholder, and therefore did everything in his power to make a favourable impression on his mind. "My Negroes are well clothed, well fed, and not over worked," said the slaveholder to his visitor, after the latter had been with him nearly a week.

"As far as I can see your slaves appear to good advantage." replied Carlton. "But," continued he, "if it is a fair question, do you have preaching among your slaves on Sunday, Mr. Jones?"

"No, no," returned he, "I think that's all nonsense; my Negroes do their own preaching."

"So you do permit them to have meetings."

"Yes, when they wish. There's some very intelligent and clever chaps among them."

"As to-morrow is the Sabbath," said Carlton, "if you have no objection, I will attend meeting with them."

"Most certainly you shall, if you will do the preaching," returned the planter.

Here the young man was about to decline, but he remembered the parting words of Georgiana, and he took courage and said, "Oh, I have no objection to give the Negroes a short talk." It was then understood that Carlton was to have a religious interview with the blacks the next day, and the young man waited with a degree of impatience for the time.

In no part of the South are slaves in a more ignorant and degraded state than in the cotton, sugar, and rice districts.

If they are permitted to cease labour on the Sabbath, the time is spent in hunting, fishing, or lying beneath the shade of a tree, resting for the morrow. Religious instruction is unknown in the far South, except among such men as the Rev. C. C. Jones, John Peck, and some others who regard religious instruction, such as they impart to their slaves, as calculated to make them more trustworthy and valuable as property. Jones, aware that his slaves would make rather a bad show of intelligence if questioned by Carlton, resolved to have them ready for him, and therefore gave his driver orders with regard to their preparation. Consequently, after the day's labour was over, Dogget, the driver, assembled the Negroes together and said, "Now, boys and gals, your master is coming down to the quarters tomorrow with his visitor, who is going to give you a preach, and I want you should understand what he says to you. Now many of you who came of Old Virginia and Kentuck, know what preaching is, and others who have been raised in these parts do not. Preaching is to tell you that you are mighty wicked and bad at heart. This, I suppose, you all know. But if the gentleman should ask you who made you, tell him the Lord; if he ask if you wish to go to heaven, tell him yes. Remember that you are all Christians, all love the Lord, all want to go to heaven, all love your masters, and all love me. Now, boys and gals, I want you to show yourselves smart to-morrow: be on your p's and q's, and, Monday morning, I will give you all a glass of whiskey bright and early." Agreeable to arrangement the slaves were assembled together on Sunday morning under the large trees near the great house, and after going through another drilling from the driver, Jones and Carlton made their appearance. "You see," said Jones to the Negroes, as he approached them, "you see here's a gentleman that's come to talk to you about your souls, and I hope you 'ill all pay that attention that you ought." Jones then seated himself in one of the two chairs placed there for him and the stranger.

Carlton had already selected a chapter in the Bible to read to them, which he did, after first prefacing it with some remarks of his own. Not being accustomed to speak in public, he determined, after reading the Bible, to make it more of a conversational meeting than otherwise. He therefore began asking them questions. "Do you feel that you are a Christian?" asked he of a full-blooded Negro that sat near him.

"Yes, sir," was the response.

"You feel, then, that you shall go to heaven."

"Yes, sir."

"Of course you know who made you?"

The man put his hand to his head and began to scratch his wool; and, after a little hesitation, answered, "De overseer told us last night who made us, but indeed I forgot the gentmun's name."

This reply was almost too much for Carlton, and his gravity was not a little moved. However, he bit his tongue, and turned to another man, who appeared, from his looks, to be more intelligent. "Do you serve the Lord?" asked he.

"No, sir, I don't serve anybody but Mr. Jones; I neber belong to anybody else."

To hide his feelings at this juncture, Carlton turned and walked to another part of the grounds, to where the women were seated, and said to a mulatto woman who had rather an anxious countenance, "Did you ever hear of John the Baptist?"

"Oh yes, marser, John de Baptist; I know dat nigger bery well indeed; he libs in Old Kentuck, where I come from."[2]

Carlton's gravity here gave way, and he looked at the planter and laughed right out. The old woman knew a slave near her old master's farm in Kentucky, and was ignorant enough to suppose that he was the John the Baptist inquired about. Carlton occupied the remainder of the time in reading Scripture and talking to them.

"My niggers aint shown off very well to-day," said Jones, as he and his visitor left the grounds.

"No," replied Carlton.

"You did not get hold of the bright ones," continued the planter.

"So it seems," remarked Carlton.

The planter evidently felt that his neighbour, Parson Peck, would have a nut to crack over the account that Carlton would give of the ignorance of the slaves, and said and did all in his power to remove the bad impression already made; but to no purpose. The report made by Carlton, on his return, amused the parson very much. It appeared to him the best reason why professed Christians like himself should be slave-holders. Not so with Georgiana. She did not even smile when Carlton was telling his story, but seemed sore at heart that such ignorance should prevail in their midst. The question turned upon the heathen of other lands, and the parson began to expatiate upon his own efforts in foreign missions, when his daughter, with a child-like simplicity, said,

"Send Bibles to the heathen;
On every distant shore,
From light that's beaming o'er us,
Let streams increasing pour
But keep it from the millions
Down-trodden at our door.

"Send Bibles to the heathen,
Their famished spirits feed;
Oh! haste, and join your efforts,
The priceless gift to speed;
Then flog the trembling Negro
If he should learn to read."³

"I saw a curiosity while at Mr. Jones's that I shall not forget soon," said Carlton.

"What was it?" inquired the parson.

"A kennel of bloodhounds; and such dogs I never saw before. They were of a species between the bloodhound and the foxhound, and were ferocious, gaunt, and savage-looking animals. They were part of a stock imported from Cuba, he informed me. They were kept in an iron cage, and fed on Indian corn bread. This kind of food, he said, made them eager for their business. Sometimes they would give the dogs meat, but it was always after they had been chasing a Negro."

"Were those the dogs you had, papa, to hunt Harry?" asked Georgiana.

"No, my dear," was the short reply: and the parson seemed anxious to change the conversation to something else. When Mr. Peck had left the room, Carlton spoke more freely of what he had seen, and spoke more pointedly against slavery;⁴ for he well knew that Miss Peck sympathised with him in all he felt and said.

"You mentioned about your father hunting a slave," said Carlton, in an undertone.

"Yes," replied she; "papa went with some slave-catchers and a parcel of those nasty Negro-dogs, to hunt poor Harry. He belonged to papa and lived on the farm. His wife lives in town, and Harry had been to see her, and did not return quite as early as he should; and Huckelby was flogging him, and he got away and came here. I wanted papa to keep him in town, so that he could see his wife more frequently; but he said they could not spare him from the farm, and flogged him again, and sent him back. The poor fellow knew that the overseer would punish him over again, and instead of going back he went into the woods."

"Did they catch him?" asked Carlton.

"Yes," replied she. "In chasing him through the woods, he attempted to escape by swimming across a river, and the dogs were sent in after him, and soon caught him. But Harry had great courage and fought the dogs with a big club; and papa seeing the Negro would escape from the dogs, shot at him, as he says, only to wound him, that he might be caught; but the

CLOTEL; OR, THE PRESIDENT'S DAUGHTER   115

poor fellow was killed." Overcome by relating this incident, Georgiana burst into tears.

Although Mr. Peck fed and clothed his house servants well, and treated them with a degree of kindness, he was, nevertheless, a most cruel master. He encouraged his driver to work the field-hands from early dawn till late at night; and the good appearance of the house-servants, and the preaching of Snyder to the field Negroes, was to cause himself to be regarded as a Christian master. Being on a visit one day at the farm, and having with him several persons from the Free States, and wishing to make them believe that his slaves were happy, satisfied, and contented, the parson got out the whiskey and gave each one a dram, who in return had to drink the master's health, or give a toast of some kind. The company were not a little amused at some of the sentiments given, and Peck was delighted at every indication of contentment on the part of the blacks. At last it came to Jack's turn to drink, and the master expected something good from him, because he was considered the cleverest and most witty slave on the farm.

"Now," said the master, as he handed Jack the cup of whiskey; "now, Jack, give us something rich. You know," continued he, "we have raised the finest crop of cotton that's been seen in these parts for many a day. Now give us a toast on cotton; come, Jack, give us something to laugh at." The Negro felt not a little elated at being made the hero of the occasion, and taking the whiskey in his right hand, put his left to his head and began to scratch his wool, and said,

> "The big bee flies high,
> The little bee make the honey;
> The black folks makes the cotton,
> And the white folks gets the money."[5]

CHAPTER XIV
A FREE WOMAN
REDUCED TO SLAVERY

Althesa found in Henry Morton a kind and affectionate husband; and his efforts to purchase her mother, although unsuccessful, had doubly endeared him to her. Having from the commencement resolved not to hold slaves, or rather not to own any, they were compelled to hire servants for their own use. Five years had passed away, and their happiness was increased by two lovely daughters. Mrs. Morton was seated, one bright afternoon, busily engaged with her needle, and near her sat Salome, a servant that she had just taken into her employ. The woman was perfectly white; so much so, that Mrs. Morton had expressed her apprehensions to her husband, when the woman first came, that she was not born a slave.[1] The mistress watched the servant, as the latter sat sewing upon some coarse work, and saw the large silent tear in her eye. This caused an uneasiness to the mistress, and she said, "Salome, don't you like your situation here?"

"Oh yes, madam," answered the woman in a quick tone, and then tried to force a smile.

"Why is it that you often look sad, and with tears in your eyes?" The mistress saw that she had touched a tender chord, and continued, "I am your friend; tell me your sorrow, and, if I can, I will help you." As the last sentence was escaping the lips of the mistress, the slave woman put her check apron to her face and wept. Mrs. Morton saw plainly that there was cause for this expression of grief, and pressed the woman more closely. "Hear me, then," said the woman calming herself: "I will tell you why I sometimes weep. I was born in Germany, on the banks of the Rhine. Ten years ago my father came to this country, bringing with him my mother and myself. He was poor, and I, wishing to assist all I could, obtained a situation as nurse to a lady in this city. My father got employment as a labourer on the wharf, among the steamboats; but he was soon taken ill with the yellow fever, and died. My mother then got a situation for herself, while I remained with my first employer. When the hot season came on, my master, with his wife, left New Orleans until the hot season was over, and took me with them. They stopped at a town on the banks of the Mississippi river, and said they should remain there some weeks. One day they went out for a ride, and they had not been gone more than half an hour, when two men came into the room and told me that they had bought me, and that I was their slave. I was bound and taken to prison, and that night put on a steamboat and taken up the Yazoo river, and set to work on a farm. I was forced to take up with a Negro, and by him had three children. A year since my master's daughter was married, and I was given to her. She came with her husband to this city, and I have ever since been hired out."

"Unhappy woman," whispered Althesa, "why did you not tell me this before?"

"I was afraid," replied Salome, "for I was once severely flogged for telling a stranger that I was not born a slave."

On Mr. Morton's return home, his wife communicated to him the story which the slave woman had told her an hour before, and begged that something might be done to rescue her from the situation she was then in. In Louisiana as well as many others of the slave states, great obstacles are thrown in the way of persons who have been wrongfully reduced to slavery regaining their freedom. A person claiming to be free must prove his right to his liberty. This, it will be seen, throws the burden of proof upon the slave, who, in all probability, finds it out of his power to procure such evidence. And if any free person shall attempt to aid a freeman in regaining his freedom, he is compelled to enter into security in the sum of one thousand dollars, and if the person claiming to be free shall fail to establish such fact, the thousand dollars are forfeited to the state. This cruel and oppressive law has kept many a freeman from espousing the cause of persons unjustly held as slaves. Mr. Morton inquired and found that the woman's story was true, as regarded the time she had lived with her present owner; but the latter not only denied that she was free, but immediately removed her from Morton's. Three months after Salome had been removed from Morton's and let out to another family, she was one morning cleaning the door steps, when a lady passing by, looked at the slave and thought she recognised some one that she had seen before. The lady stopped and asked the woman if she was a slave.

"I am," said she."

"Were you born a slave?"

"No, I was born in Germany."

"What's the name of the ship in which you came to this country?" inquired the lady.

"I don't know," was the answer.

"Was it the *Amazon*?"

At the sound of this name, the slave woman was silent for a moment, and then the tears began to flow freely down her careworn cheeks.

"Would you know Mrs. Marshall, who was a passenger in the *Amazon*, if you should see her?" inquired the lady.

At this the woman gazed at the lady with a degree of intensity that can be imagined better than described, and then fell at the lady's feet. The lady was Mrs. Marshall. She had crossed the Atlantic in the same ship with this poor woman. Salome, like many of her countrymen, was a beautiful singer, and had often entertained Mrs. Marshall and the other lady passengers on board the *Amazon*. The poor woman was raised from the ground by Mrs. Marshall, and placed upon the door step that she had a moment before been cleaning. "I will do my utmost to rescue you from the horrid life of a slave," exclaimed the lady, as she took from her pocket her pencil, and wrote down the number of the house, and the street in which the German woman was working as a slave.

After a long and tedious trial of many days, it was decided that Salome Miller was by birth a free woman, and she was set at liberty. The good and generous Althesa had contributed some of the money toward bringing about the trial, and had done much to cheer on Mrs. Marshall in her benevolent object. Salome Miller is free, but where are her three children? They are still slaves, and in all human probability will die as such.

This, reader, is no fiction; if you think so, look over the files of the New Orleans newspapers of the years 1845–6, and you will there see reports of the trial.

CHAPTER XV
TO-DAY A MISTRESS,
TO-MORROW A SLAVE

"I promised thee a sister tale
Of man's perfidious cruelty;
Come, then, and hear what cruel wrong
Befel the dark ladie."

—*Coleridge.*[1]

Let us return for a moment to the home of Clotel. While she was passing lonely and dreary hours with none but her darling child, Horatio Green was trying to find relief in that insidious enemy of man, the intoxicating cup. Defeated in politics, forsaken in love by his wife, he seemed to have lost all principle of honour, and was ready to nerve himself up to any deed, no matter how unprincipled. Clotel's existence was now well known to Horatio's wife, and both her [*sic*] and her father demanded that the beautiful quadroon and her child should be sold and sent out of the state.[2] To this proposition he at first turned a deaf ear; but when he saw that his wife was about to return to her father's roof, he consented to leave the matter in the hands of his father-in-law. The result was, that Clotel was immediately sold to the slave-trader, Walker, who, a few years previous, had taken her mother and sister to the far South. But, as if to make her husband drink of the cup of humiliation to its very dregs, Mrs. Green resolved to take his child under her own roof for a servant. Mary was, therefore, put to the meanest work that could be found, and although only ten years of age, she was often compelled to perform labour, which, under ordinary circumstances, would have been thought too hard for one much older. One condition of the sale of Clotel to Walker was, that she should be taken out of the state, which was accordingly done. Most quadroon women who are taken to the lower countries to be sold are either purchased by gentlemen for their own use, or sold for waiting-maids; and Clotel, like her sister, was fortunate enough to be bought for the latter purpose. The town of Vicksburgh stands on the left bank of the Mississippi, and is noted for the severity with which slaves are treated. It was here that Clotel was sold to Mr. James French, a merchant.

Mrs. French was severe in the extreme to her servants. Well dressed, but scantily fed, and overworked were all who found a home with her. The quadroon had been in her new home but a short time ere she found that her situation was far different from what it was in Virginia. What social virtues are possible in a society of which injustice is the primary characteristic? in a society which is divided into two classes, masters and slaves? Every married woman in the far South looks upon her husband as unfaithful, and regards every quadroon servant as a rival. Clotel had been with her new mistress but a few days, when she was ordered to cut off her long hair. The Negro, constitutionally, is fond of dress and outward appearance. He that has short, woolly hair, combs it and oils it to death. He that has long hair, would sooner have his teeth drawn than lose it. However painful it was to the quadroon, she was soon seen with her hair cut as short as any of the full-blooded Negroes in the dwelling.

Even with her short hair, Clotel was handsome. Her life had been a secluded one, and though now nearly thirty years of age, she was still beautiful. At her short hair, the other servants laughed, "Miss Clo needn't strut round so big, she got short nappy har well as I," said Nell, with a broad grin that showed her teeth.

"She tinks she white, when she come here wid dat long har of hers," replied Mill.

"Yes," continued Nell; "missus make her take down her wool so she no put it up to-day."

The fairness of Clotel's complexion was regarded with envy as well by the other servants as by the mistress herself. This is one of the hard features of slavery. To-day the woman is mistress of her own cottage; to-morrow she is sold to one who aims to make her life as intolerable as possible. And be it remembered, that the house servant has the best situation which a slave can occupy. Some American writers have tried to make the world believe that the condition of the labouring classes of England is as bad as the slaves of the United States.[3]

The English labourer may be oppressed, he may be cheated, defrauded, swindled, and even starved; but it is not slavery under which he groans. He cannot be sold; in point of law he is equal to the prime minister. "It is easy to captivate the unthinking and the prejudiced, by eloquent declamation about the oppression of English operatives being worse than that of American slaves, and by exaggerating the wrongs on one side and hiding them on the other. But all informed and reflecting minds, knowing that bad as are the social evils of England, those of Slavery are immeasurably worse." But the degradation and harsh treatment that Clotel experienced in her new home was nothing compared with the grief she underwent at being separated from her dear child. Taken from her without scarcely a moment's warning, she knew not what had become of her. The deep and heartfelt grief of Clotel was soon perceived by her owners, and fearing that her refusal to take food would cause her death, they resolved to sell her. Mr. French found no difficulty in getting a purchaser for the quadroon woman, for such are usually the most marketable kind of property. Clotel was sold at private sale to a young man for a housekeeper; but even he had missed his aim.

CHAPTER XVI
DEATH OF THE PARSON

Carlton was above thirty years of age, standing on the last legs of a young man, and entering on the first of a bachelor. He had never dabbled in matters of love, and looked upon all women alike. Although he respected woman for her virtues, and often spoke of the goodness of heart of the sex, he had never dreamed of marriage. At first he looked upon Miss Peck as a pretty young woman, but after she became his religious teacher, he regarded her in that light, that every one will those whom they know to be their superiors. It was soon seen, however, that the young man not only respected and reverenced Georgiana for the incalculable service she had done him, in awakening him to a sense of duty to his soul, but he had learned to bow to the shrine of Cupid. He found, weeks after he had been in her company, that when he met her at table, or alone in the drawingroom, or on the piazza, he felt a shortness of breath, a palpitating of the heart, a kind of dizziness of the head; but he knew not its cause.

This was love in its first stage. Mr. Peck saw, or thought he saw, what would be the result of Carlton's visit, and held out every inducement in his power to prolong his stay. The hot season was just commencing, and the young Northerner was talking of his return home, when the parson was very suddenly taken ill. The disease was the cholera, and the physicians pronounced the case incurable. In less than five hours John Peck was a corpse. His love for Georgiana, and respect for her father, had induced Carlton to remain by the bedside of the dying man, although against the express orders of the physician. This act of kindness caused the young orphan henceforth to regard Carlton as her best friend. He now felt it his duty to remain with the young woman until some of her relations should be summoned from Connecticut. After the funeral, the family physician advised that Miss Peck should go to the farm, and spend the time at the country seat; and also advised Carlton to remain with her, which he did.

At the parson's death his Negroes showed little or no signs of grief. This was noticed by both Carlton and Miss Peck, and caused no little pain to the latter. "They are ungrateful," said Carlton, as he and Georgiana were seated on the piazza.

"What," asked she, "have they to be grateful for?"

"Your father was kind, was he not?"

"Yes, as kind as most men who own slaves; but the kindness meted out to blacks would be unkindness if given to whites. We would think so, should we not?"

"Yes," replied he.

"If we would not consider the best treatment which a slave receives good enough for us, we should not think he ought to be grateful for it.[1] Everybody knows that slavery in its best and mildest form is wrong. Whoever denies this, his lips libel his heart. Try him! Clank the chains in his ears, and tell him they are for him; give him an hour to prepare his wife and children for a life of slavery; bid him make haste, and get ready their necks for the yoke, and their wrists for the coffle chains; then look at his pale lips and trembling knees, and you have nature's testimony against slavery."[2]

"Let's take a walk," said Carlton, as if to turn the conversation. The moon was just appearing through the tops of the trees, and the animals and insects in an adjoining wood kept up a continued din of music. The croaking of bull-frogs, buzzing of insects, cooing of turtle-doves, and the sound from a thousand musical instruments, pitched on as many different keys, made the welkin ring. But even all this noise did not drown the singing of a party of the slaves, who were seated near a spring that was sending up its cooling waters.

"How prettily the Negroes sing," remarked Carlton, as they were wending their way towards the place from whence the sound of the voices came.

"Yes," replied Georgiana; "master Sam is there, I'll warrant you: he's always on hand when there's any singing or dancing. We must not let them see us, or they will stop singing."

"Who makes their songs for them?" inquired the young man.

"Oh, they make them up as they sing them; they are all impromptu songs."

By this time they were near enough to hear distinctly every word; and, true enough, Sam's voice was heard above all others. At the conclusion of each song they all joined in a hearty laugh, with an expression of "Dats de song for me;" "Dems dems."

"Stop," said Carlton, as Georgiana was rising from the log upon which she was seated; "stop, and let's hear this one." The piece was sung by Sam, the others joining in the chorus, and was as follows:

SAM

"Come, all my brethren, let us take a rest,
    While the moon shines so brightly and clear;
Old master is dead, and left us at last,
    And has gone at the Bar to appear.
Old master has died, and lying in his grave,
    And our blood will awhile cease to flow;
He will no more trample on the neck of the slave;
    For he's gone where the slaveholders go.

CHORUS.

"Hang up the shovel and the hoe—
Take down the fiddle and the bow—
Old master has gone to the slaveholder's rest;
He has gone where they all ought to go.

SAM.

"I heard the old doctor say the other night
    As he passed by the dining-room door—

'Perhaps the old man may live through the night,
    But I think he will die about four.'
Young mistress sent me, at the peril of my life,
    For the parson to come down and pray,
For says she, 'Your old master is now about to die,'
    And says I, 'God speed him on his way.'

"Hang up the shovel, &c.

"At four o'clock at morn the family was called
    Around the old man's dying bed;
And oh! but I laughed to myself when I heard
    That the old man's spirit had fled.
Mr. Carlton cried, and so did I pretend;
    Young mistress very nearly went mad;
And the old parson's groans did the heavens fairly rend;
    But I tell you I felt mighty glad.

"Hang up the shovel, &c.

"We'll no more be roused by the blowing of his horn,
    Our backs no longer he will score;
He no more will feed us on cotton-seeds and corn;
    For his reign of oppression now is o'er.
He no more will hang our children on the tree,
    To be ate by the carrion crow;
He no more will send our wives to Tennessee;
    For he's gone where the slaveholders go.

"Hang up the shovel and the hoe,
Take down the fiddle and the bow,
We'll dance and sing,
And make the forest ring,
With the fiddle and the old banjo."[3]

The song was not half finished before Carlton regretted that
he had caused the young lady to remain and hear what to her

must be anything but pleasant reflections upon her deceased parent. "I think we will walk," said he, at the same time extending his arm to Georgiana.

"No," said she; "let's hear them out. It is from these unguarded expressions of the feelings of the Negroes, that we should learn a lesson."

At its conclusion they walked towards the house in silence: as they were ascending the steps, the young man said, "They are happy, after all. The Negro, situated as yours are, is not aware that he is deprived of any just rights."

"Yes, yes," answered Georgiana: "you may place the slave where you please; you may dry up to your utmost the fountains of his feelings, the springs of his thought; you may yoke him to your labour, as an ox which liveth only to work, and worketh only to live; you may put him under any process which, without destroying his value as a slave, will debase and crush him as a rational being; you may do this, and *the idea that he was born to be free will survive it all*. It is allied to his hope of immorality; it is the ethereal part of his nature, which oppression cannot reach; it is a torch lit up in his soul by the hand of Deity, and never meant to be extinguished by the hand of man."

On reaching the drawing-room, they found Sam snuffing the candles, and looking as solemn and as dignified as if he had never sung a song or laughed in his life. "Will Miss Georgy have de supper got up now?" asked the Negro.

"Yes," she replied.

"Well," remarked Carlton, "that beats anything I ever met with. Do you think that was Sam we heard singing?"

"I am sure of it," was the answer.

"I could not have believed that that fellow was capable of so much deception," continued he.

"Our system of slavery is one of deception; and Sam, you see, has only been a good scholar. However, he is as honest a fellow as you will find among the slave population here. If we would have them more honest, we should give them their liberty, and then the inducement to be dishonest would be gone. I have resolved that these creatures shall all be free."

"Indeed!" exclaimed Carlton.

"Yes, I shall let them all go free, and set an example to those about me."

"I honour your judgment," said he. "But will the state permit them to remain?"

"If not, they can go where they can live in freedom. I will not be unjust because the state is."

CHAPTER XVII
RETALIATION

"I had a dream, a happy dream;
I thought that I was free:
That in my own bright land again
A home there was for me."

With the deepest humiliation Horatio Green saw the daughter of Clotel, his own child, brought into his dwelling as a servant. His wife felt that she had been deceived, and determined to punish her deceiver. At first Mary was put to work in the kitchen, where she met with little or no sympathy from the other slaves, owing to the fairness of her complexion. The child was white, what should be done to make her look like other Negroes, was the question Mrs. Green asked herself. At last she hit upon a plan: there was a garden at the back of the house over which Mrs. Green could look from her parlour window. Here the white slave-girl was put to work, without either bonnet or handkerchief upon her head. A hot sun poured its broiling rays on the naked face and neck of the girl, until she sank down in the corner of the garden, and was actually broiled to sleep. "Dat little nigger ain't working a bit, missus," said Dinah to Mrs. Green, as she entered the kitchen.

"She's lying in the sun, seasoning; she will work better by and by," replied the mistress.

"Dees white niggers always tink dey sef good as white folks," continued the cook.

"Yes, but we will teach them better; won't we, Dinah?"

"Yes, missus, I don't like dees mularter niggers, no how; dey always want to set dey sef up for something big." The cook was black, and was not without that prejudice which is to be found among the Negroes, as well as among the whites of the Southern States.[1] The sun had the desired effect, for in less than a fortnight Mary's fair complexion had disappeared, and she was but little whiter than any other mulatto children running about the yard. But the close resemblance between the father and child annoyed the mistress more than the mere whiteness of the child's complexion. Horatio made proposition after proposition to have the girl sent away, for every time he beheld her countenance it reminded him of the happy days he had spent with Clotel. But his wife had commenced, and determined to carry out her unfeeling and fiendish designs. This child was not only white, but she was the granddaughter of Thomas Jefferson, the man who, when speaking against slavery in the legislature of Virginia, said,

"The whole commerce between master and slave is a perpetual exercise of the most boisterous passions; *the most unremitting despotism on the one part and degrading submission on the other*. With what execration should the statesman be loaded who, permitting one half the citizens thus to trample on the rights of the other, transforms those into despots and these into enemies, destroys the morals of the one part, and the *amor patriae* of the other! For if the slave can have a country in this world, it must be any other in preference to that in which he is born to live and labour for another; in which he must lock up the faculties of his nature, contribute as far as depends on his individual endeavours to the evanishment of the human race, or entail his own miserable condition on the endless generations proceeding from him. And can the liberties of a nation be thought secure when we have removed their only firm basis, a conviction in the minds of the people that these liberties are the gift of God? that they are not to be violated but with his wrath? Indeed, I tremble for my country when I reflect that God is just; that his justice cannot sleep for ever; that, considering numbers, nature, and natural means only, a revolution of the wheel of fortune, an exchange of situation, is among possible events; that it may become probable by supernatural interference! The Almighty has no attribute which can take side with us in such a contest.

*   *   *

"What an incomprehensible machine is man! Who can endure toil, famine, stripes, imprisonment, and death itself, in vindication of his own liberty, and the next moment be deaf to all those motives, whose power supported him through his trial, and inflict on his fellow-men a bondage, *one hour of which is fraught with more misery than ages of that which he rose in rebellion to oppose!* But we must wait with patience the workings of an overruling Providence, and hope that that is preparing the deliverance of these our suffering brethren. When the measure of their tears shall be full—when their tears shall have involved heaven itself in darkness—doubtless a God of justice will awaken to their distress, and by diffusing light and liberality among their oppressors, or at length by his exterminating thunder, manifest his attention to things of this world, and that they are not left to the guidance of blind fatality."[2]

The same man, speaking of the probability that the slaves might some day attempt to gain their liberties by a revolution, said,

"I tremble for my country, when I recollect that God is just, and that His justice cannot sleep for ever. The Almighty has no attribute that can take sides with us in such a struggle."

But, sad to say, Jefferson is not the only American statesman who has spoken high-sounding words in favour of freedom, and then left his own children to die slaves.

CHAPTER XVIII
THE LIBERATOR

"We hold these truths to be self-evident, that all men are created free and equal; that they are endowed by their Creator with certain inalienable rights; among these are life, *liberty*, and the pursuit of happiness."

—*Declaration of American Independence.*

The death of the parson was the commencement of a new era in the history of his slaves. Only a little more than eighteen years of age, Georgiana could not expect to carry out her own wishes in regard to the slaves, although she was sole heir to her father's estate. There were distant relations whose opinions she had at least to respect. And both law and public opinion in the state were against any measure of emancipation that she might think of adopting; unless, perhaps, she might be permitted to send them to Liberia.[1] Her uncle in Connecticut had already been written to, to come down and aid in settling up the estate. He was a Northern man, but she knew him to be a tight-fisted yankee, whose whole counsel would go against liberating the Negroes.[2] Yet there was one way in which the thing could be done. She loved Carlton, and she well knew that he loved her; she read it in his countenance every time they met, yet the young man did not mention his wishes to her. There were many reasons why he should not. In the first place, her father was just deceased, and it seemed only right that he should wait a reasonable time. Again, Carlton was poor, and Georgiana was possessed of a large fortune; and his high spirit would not, for a moment, allow him to place himself in a position to be regarded as a fortune-hunter. The young girl hinted, as best she could, at the probable future; but all to no purpose. He took nothing to himself. True, she had read much of "woman's rights;" and had even attended a meeting, while at the North, which had been called to discuss the wrongs of woman;[3] but she could not nerve herself up to the point of putting the question to Carlton, although she felt sure that she should not be rejected. She waited, but in vain. At last, one evening, she came out of her room rather late, and was walking on the piazza for fresh air. She passed near Carlton's room, and heard the voice of Sam. The Negro had just come in to get the young man's boots, and had stopped, as he usually did, to have some talk. "I wish," said Sam, "dat Marser Carlton an Miss Georgy would get married; den, 'speck, we'd have good times."

"I don't think your mistress would have me," replied the young man.

"What make tink dat, Marser Carlton?"

"Your mistress would marry no one, Sam, unless she loved them."

"Den I wish she would lub you, cause I tink we have good times den. All our folks is de same 'pinion like me," returned the Negro, and then left the room with the boots in his hands.

During the conversation between the Anglo-Saxon and the African, one word had been dropped by the former that haunted the young lady the remainder of the night—"Your mistress would marry no one unless she loved them." That word awoke her in the morning, and caused her to decide upon this important subject. Love and duty triumphed over the woman's timid nature, and that day Georgiana informed Carlton that she was ready to become his wife. The young man, with grateful tears, accepted and kissed the hand that was offered to him. The marriage of Carlton and Miss Peck was hailed with delight by both the servants in the house and the Negroes on the farm. New rules were immediately announced for the working and general treatment of the slaves on the plantation. With this, Huckelby, the overseer, saw his reign coming to an end; and Snyder, the Dutch preacher, felt that his services would soon be dispensed with, for nothing was more repugnant to the feelings of Mrs. Carlton than the sermons preached by Snyder to the slaves. She regarded them as something intended to make them better satisfied with their condition, and more valuable as pieces of property, without preparing them for the world to come. Mrs. Carlton found in her husband a congenial spirit,

who entered into all her wishes and plans for bettering the condition of their slaves. Mrs. Carlton's views and sympathies
were all in favour of immediate emancipation; but then she
saw, or thought she saw, a difficulty in that. If the slaves were
liberated, they must be sent out of the state. This, of course,
would incur additional expense; and if they left the state, where
had they better go?

"Let's send them to Liberia," said Carlton.

"Why should they go to Africa, any more than to the Free
States or to Canada?" asked the wife.

"They would be in their native land," he answered.

"Is not this their native land? What right have we, more than
the Negro, to the soil here, or to style ourselves native Americans? Indeed it is as much their home as ours, and I have sometimes thought it was more theirs. The Negro has cleared up the
lands, built towns, and enriched the soil with his blood and
tears; and in return, he is to be sent to a country of which he
knows nothing. Who fought more bravely for American independence than the blacks? A Negro, by the name of Attucks[4]
was the first that fell in Boston at the commencement of the
revolutionary war; and, throughout the whole of the struggles
for liberty in this country, the Negroes have contributed their
share. In the last war with Great Britain, the country was
mainly indebted to the blacks in New Orleans for the achieve-
ment of the victory at that place,[5] and even General Jackson,
the commander in chief, called the Negroes together at the
close of the war, and addressed them in the following terms:—

"Soldiers!—When on the banks of the Mobile I called you to
take up arms, inviting you to partake the perils and glory of your
white fellow citizens, I expected much from you; for I was not
ignorant that you possess qualities most formidable to an invad-
ing enemy. I knew with what fortitude you could endure hunger
and thirst, and all the fatigues of a campaign. *I knew well how
you loved your native country*, and that you, as well as ourselves,
had to defend what *man* holds most dear—his parents, wife,
children, and property. *You have done more than I expected*. In
addition to the previous qualities I before knew you to possess, I

found among you a noble enthusiasm, which leads to the performance of great things.

" 'Soldiers! The President of the United States shall hear how
praiseworthy was your conduct in the hour of danger, and the
representatives of the American people will give you the praise
your exploits entitle you to. Your general anticipates them in ap-
pauding your noble ardour."⁶

"And what did these noble men receive in return for their
courage, their heroism? Chains and slavery. Their good deeds
have been consecrated only in their own memories. Who rallied with more alacrity in response to the summons of danger?
If in that hazardous hour, when our homes were menaced with
the horrors of war, we did not disdain to call upon the Negro
to assist in repelling invasion, why should we, now that the
danger is past, deny him a home in his native land?"

"I see," said Carlton, "you are right, but I fear you will have
difficulty in persuading others to adopt your views."

"We will set the example," replied she, "and then hope for
the best; for I feel that the people of the Southern States will
one day see their error. Liberty has always been our watch-
word, as far as profession is concerned. Nothing has been held
so cheap as our common humanity, on a national average. If
every man had his aliquot proportion of the injustice done in
this land, by law and violence, the present freemen of the
northern section would many of them commit suicide in self-
defence, and would court the liberties awarded by Ali Pasha of
Egypt to his subjects. Long ere this we should have tested, in
behalf of our bleeding and crushed American brothers of every
hue and complexion, every new constitution, custom, or practice, by which inhumanity was supposed to be upheld, the injustice and cruelty they contained, emblazoned before the great
tribunal of mankind for condemnation; and the good and available power they possessed, for the relief, deliverance and elevation of oppressed men, permitted to shine forth from under the
cloud, for the refreshment of the human race."

Although Mr. and Mrs. Carlton felt that immediate emancipation was the right of the slave and the duty of the master,

they resolved on a system of gradual emancipation, so as to give them time to accomplish their wish, and to prepare the Negro for freedom. Huckelby was one morning told that his services would no longer be required. The Negroes, ninety-eight in number, were called together and told that the whip would no longer be used, and that they would be allowed a certain sum for every bale of cotton produced. Sam, whose long experience in the cotton-field before he had been taken into the house, and whose general intelligence justly gave him the first place amongst the Negroes on the Poplar Farm, was placed at their head. They were also given to understand that the money earned by them would be placed to their credit; and when it amounted to a certain sum, they should all be free.

The joy with which this news was received by the slaves, showed their grateful appreciation of the boon their benefactors were bestowing upon them. The house servants were called and told that wages would be allowed them, and what they earned set to their credit, and they too should be free. The next were the bricklayers. There were eight of these, who had paid their master two dollars per day, and boarded and clothed themselves. An arrangement was entered into with them, by which the money they earned should be placed to their credit; and they too should be free, when a certain amount should be accumulated; and great was the change amongst all these people. The bricklayers had been to work but a short time, before their increased industry was noticed by many. They were no longer apparently the same people. A sedateness, a care, an economy, an industry, took possession of them, to which there seemed to be no bounds but in their physical strength. They were never tired of labouring, and seemed as though they could never effect enough. They became temperate, moral, religious, setting an example of innocent, unoffending lives to the world around them, which was seen and admired by all. Mr. Parker, a man who worked nearly forty slaves at the same business, was attracted by the manner in which these Negroes laboured. He called on Mr. Carlton, some weeks after they had been acting on the new system, and offered 2,000 dollars for the head workman, Jim. The offer was, of course, refused. A few days after the same gentleman called again, and made an offer of double the sum that he had on the former occasion. Mr. Parker, finding that no money would purchase either of the Negroes, said, "Now, Mr. Carlton, pray tell me what it is that makes your Negroes work so? What kind of people are they?"

"I suppose," observed Carlton, "that they are like other people, flesh and blood."

"Why, sir," continued Parker, "I have never seen such people; building as they are next door to my residence, I see and have my eye on them from morning till night. You are never there, for I have never met you, or seen you once at the building. Why, sir, I am an early riser, getting up before day; and do you think that I am not awoke every morning in my life by the noise of their trowels at work, and their singing and noise before day; and do you suppose, sir, that they stop or leave off work at sundown? No, sir, but they work as long as they can see to lay a brick, and then they carry up brick and mortar for an hour or two afterward, to be ahead of their work the next morning. And again, sir, do you think that they walk at their work? No, sir, they run all day. You see, sir, those immensely long ladders, five stories in height; do you suppose they walk up them? No, sir, they run up and down them like so many monkeys all day long. I never saw such people as these in my life. I don't know what to make of them. Were a white man with them and over them with a whip, then I should see and understand the cause of the running and incessant labour; but I cannot comprehend it; there is something in it, sir. Great man, sir, that Jim; great man; I should like to own him."

Carlton here informed Parker that their liberties depended upon their work; when the latter replied, "If niggers can work so for the promise of freedom, they ought to be made to work without it." This last remark was in the true spirit of the slaveholder, and reminds us of the fact that, some years since, the overseer of General Wade Hampton[7] offered the niggers under him a suit of clothes to the one that picked the most cotton in one day; and after that time that day's work was given as a task to the slaves on that plantation; and, after a while, was adopted by other planters.

The Negroes on the farm, under "Marser Sam," were also working in a manner that attracted the attention of the planters round about. They no longer feared Huckelby's whip, and no longer slept under the preaching of Snyder. On the Sabbath, Mr. and Mrs. Carlton read and explained the Scriptures to them; and the very great attention paid by the slaves showed plainly that they appreciated the gospel when given to them in its purity. The death of Currer, from yellow fever, was a great trial to Mrs. Carlton; for she had not only become much attached to her, but had heard with painful interest the story of her wrongs, and would, in all probability, have restored her to her daughter in New Orleans.

CHAPTER XIX

ESCAPE OF CLOTEL

"The fetters galled my weary soul—
A soul that seemed but thrown away;
I spurned the tyrant's base control,
Resolved at least the man to play."[1]

No country has produced so much heroism in so short a time, connected with escapes from peril and oppression, as has occurred in the United States among fugitive slaves, many of whom show great shrewdness in their endeavours to escape from this land of bondage. A slave was one day seen passing on the high road from a border town in the interior of the state of Virginia to the Ohio river.[2] The man had neither hat upon his head or coat upon his back. He was driving before him a very nice fat pig, and appeared to all who saw him to be a labourer employed on an adjoining farm. "No Negro is permitted to go at large in the Slave States without a written pass from his or her master, except on business in the neighbourhood."

"Where do you live, my boy?" asked a white man of the slave, as he passed a white house with green blinds.

"Jist up de road, sir," was the answer.

"That's a fine pig."

"Yes, sir, marser like dis choat berry much."

And the Negro drove on as if he was in great haste. In this way he and the pig travelled more than fifty miles before they reached the Ohio river. Once at the river they crossed over; the pig was sold; and nine days after the runaway slave passed over the Niagara river,[3] and, for the first time in his life, breathed the air of freedom. A few weeks later, and, on the same road, two slaves were seen passing; one was on horseback, the other was walking before him with his arms tightly bound, and a long rope leading from the man on foot to the one on horseback.

"Oh, ho, that's a runaway rascal, I suppose," said a farmer, who met them on the road.

"Yes, sir, he bin runaway, and I got him fast. Marser will tan his jacket for him nicely when he gets him."

"You are a trustworthy fellow, I imagine," continued the farmer.

"Oh yes, sir; marser puts a heap of confidence in dis nigger."

And the slaves travelled on. When the one on foot was fatigued they would change positions, the other being tied and driven on foot. This they called "ride and tie." After a journey of more than two hundred miles they reached the Ohio river, turned the horse loose, told him to go home, and proceeded on their way to Canada. However they were not to have it all their own way. There are men in the Free States, and especially in the states adjacent to the Slave States, who make their living by catching the runaway slave, and returning him for the reward that may be offered. As the two slaves above mentioned were travelling on towards the land of freedom, led by the North Star, they were set upon by four of these slave-catchers, and one of them unfortunately captured. The other escaped. The captured fugitive was put under the torture, and compelled to reveal the name of his owner and his place of residence. Filled with delight, the kidnappers started back with their victim. Overjoyed with the prospect of receiving a large reward, they gave themselves up on the third night to pleasure. They put up at an inn. The Negro was chained to the bed-post, in the same room with his captors. At dead of night, when all was still, the slave arose from the floor upon which he had been lying, looked around, and saw that the white men were fast asleep. The brandy punch had done its work. With palpitating heart and trembling limbs he viewed his position. The door was fast, but the warm weather had compelled them to leave the window open. If he could but get his chains off, he might escape through the window to the piazza, and reach the ground by one of the posts that supported the piazza. The sleeper's clothes hung upon chairs by the bedside; the slave thought of the padlock key, examined the pockets and found it. The chains were soon off, and the Negro stealthily making his way to the window: he stopped and said to himself, "These men are villains, they are enemies to all who like me are trying to be free. Then why not I teach them a lesson?" He then undressed himself, took the clothes of one of the men, dressed himself in them, and escaped through the window, and, a moment more, he was on the high road to Canada. Fifteen days later, and the writer of this gave him a passage across Lake Erie, and saw him safe in her Britannic Majesty's dominions.[4]

We have seen Clotel sold to Mr. French in Vicksburgh, her hair cut short, and everything done to make her realise her position as a servant. Then we have seen her re-sold, because her owners feared she would die through grief. As yet her new purchaser treated her with respectful gentleness, and sought to win her favour by flattery and presents, knowing that whatever he gave her he could take back again. But she dreaded every moment lest the scene should change, and trembled at the sound of every footfall. At every interview with her new master Clotel stoutly maintained that she had left a husband in Virginia, and would never think of taking another. The gold watch and chain, and other glittering presents which he purchased for her, were all laid aside by the quadroon, as if they were of no value to her. In the same house with her was another servant, a man, who had from time to time hired himself from his master. William was his name. He could feel for Clotel, for he, like her, had been separated from near and dear relatives, and often tried to console the poor woman. One day the quadroon observed to him that her hair was growing out again.

"Yes," replied William, "you look a good deal like a man with your short hair."

"Oh," rejoined she, "I have often been told that I would make a better looking man than a woman. If I had the money," continued she, "I would bid farewell to this place." In a moment more she feared that she had said too much, and smilingly remarked, "I am always talking nonsense."

William was a tall, full-bodied Negro, whose very countenance beamed with intelligence. Being a mechanic, he had, by his own industry, made more than what he paid his owner; this he laid aside, with the hope that some day he might get enough to purchase his freedom. He had in his chest one hundred and fifty dollars. His was a heart that felt for others, and he had again and again wiped the tears from his eyes as he heard the story of Clotel as related by herself. "If she can get free with a little money, why not give her what I have?" thought he, and then he resolved to do it. An hour after, he came into the quadroon's room, and laid the money in her lap, and said, "There, Miss Clotel, you said if you had the means you would leave this place; there is money enough to take you to England, where you will be free. You are much fairer than many of the white women of the South, and can easily pass for a free white lady."⁵

At first Clotel feared that it was a plan by which the Negro wished to try her fidelity to her owner; but she was soon convinced by his earnest manner, and the deep feeling with which he spoke, that he was honest. "I will take the money only on one condition," said she; "and that is, that I effect your escape as well as my own."

"How can that be done?" he inquired.

"I will assume the disguise of a gentleman and you that of a servant, and we will take passage on a steamboat and go to Cincinnati, and thence to Canada."⁶ Here William put in several objections to the plan. He feared detection, and he well knew that, when a slave is once caught when attempting to escape, if returned is sure to be worse treated than before. However, Clotel satisfied him that the plan could be carried out if he would only play his part.

The resolution was taken, the clothes for her disguise procured, and before night everything was in readiness for their departure. That night Mr. Cooper, their master, was to attend a party, and this was their opportunity. William went to the wharf to look out for a boat, and had scarcely reached the landing ere he heard the puffing of a steamer. He returned and reported the fact. Clotel had already packed her trunk, and had only to dress and all was ready. In less than an hour they were on board the boat. Under the assumed name of "Mr. Johnson," Clotel went to the clerk's office and took a private state room for herself, and paid her own and servant's fare. Besides being attired in a neat suit of black, she had a white silk handkerchief tied round her chin, as if she was an invalid. A pair of green glasses covered her eyes; and fearing that she would be talked to too much and thus render her liable to be detected, she assumed to be very ill. On the other hand, William was playing his part well in the servants' hall; he was talking loudly of his master's wealth. Nothing appeared as good on the boat as in his master's fine mansion. "I don't like dees steamboats no how," said William; "I hope when marser goes on a journey again he will take de carriage and de hosses." Mr. Johnson (for such was the name by which Clotel now went) remained in his room, to avoid, as far as possible, conversation with others. After a passage of seven days they arrived at Louisville, and put up at Gough's Hotel. Here they had to await the departure of another boat for the North. They were now in their most critical position. They were still in a slave state, and John C. Calhoun,[7] a distinguished slave-owner, was a guest at this hotel. They feared, also, that trouble would attend their attempt to leave this place for the North, as all persons taking Negroes with them have to give bail that such Negroes are not runaway slaves. The law upon this point is very stringent: all steamboats and other public conveyances are liable to a fine for every slave that escapes by them, besides paying the full value for the slave. After a delay of four hours, Mr. Johnson and servant took passage on the steamer Rodolph, for Pittsburgh. It is usual, before the departure of the boats, for an officer to examine every part of the vessel to see that no slave secrets himself on board.

"Where are you going?" asked the officer of William, as he was doing his duty on this occasion.

"I am going with marser," was the quick reply.

"Who is your master?"

"Mr. Johnson, sir, a gentleman in the cabin."

"You must take him to the office and satisfy that captain that all is right, or you can't go on this boat."

William informed his master what the officer had said. The

boat was on the eve of going, and no time could be lost, yet they knew not what to do. At last they went to the office, and Mr. Johnson, addressing the captain, said, "I am informed that my boy can't go with me unless I give security that he belongs to me."

"Yes," replied the captain, "that is the law."

"A very strange law indeed," rejoined Mr. Johnson, "that one can't take his property with him."

After a conversation of some minutes, and a plea on the part of Johnson that he did not wish to be delayed owing to his illness, they were permitted to take their passage without farther trouble, and the boat was soon on its way up the river. The fugitives had now passed the Rubicon,[8] and the next place at which they would land would be in a Free State. Clotel called William to her room, and said to him, "We are now free, you can go on your way to Canada, and I shall go to Virginia in search of my daughter." The announcement that she was going to risk her liberty in a Slave State was unwelcome news to William. With all the eloquence he could command, he tried to persuade Clotel that she could not escape detection, and was only throwing her freedom away. But she had counted the cost, and made up her mind for the worst. In return for the money he had furnished, she had secured for him his liberty, and their engagement was at an end.

After a quick passage the fugitives arrived at Cincinnati, and there separated. William proceeded on his way to Canada, and Clotel again resumed her own apparel, and prepared to start in search of her child. As might have been expected, the escape of those two valuable slaves created no little sensation in Vicksburgh. Advertisements and messages were sent in every direction in which the fugitives were thought to have gone. It was soon, however, known that they had left the town as master and servant; and many were the communications which appeared in the newspapers, in which the writers thought, or pretended, that they had seen the slaves in their disguise. One was to the effect that they had gone off in a chaise; one as master, and the other as servant. But the most probable was an account given by a correspondent of one of the Southern newspapers, who happened to be a passenger in the same steamer in which the slaves escaped, and which we here give:—

"One bright starlight night, in the month of December last, I found myself in the cabin of the steamer Rodolph, then lying in the port of Vicksburgh, and bound to Louisville. I had gone early on board, in order to select a good berth, and having got tired of reading the papers, amused myself with watching the appearance of the passengers as they dropped in, one after another, and I being a believer in physiognomy, formed my own opinion of their characters.

"The second bell rang, and as I yawningly returned my watch to my pocket, my attention was attracted by the appearance of a young man who entered the cabin supported by his servant, a strapping Negro.

"The man was bundled up in a capacious overcoat; his face was bandaged with a white handkerchief, and its expression entirely hid by a pair of enormous spectacles.

"There was something so mysterious and unusual about the young man as he sat restless in the corner, that curiosity led me to observe him more closely.

"He appeared anxious to avoid notice, and before the steamer had fairly left the wharf, requested, in a low, womanly voice, to be shown his berth, as he was an invalid, and must retire early: his name he gave as Mr. Johnson. His servant was called, and he was put quietly to bed. I paced the deck until Tybee light grew dim in the distance, and then went to my berth.

"I awoke in the morning with the sun shining in my face; we were then just passing St. Helena. It was a mild beautiful morning, and most of the passengers were on deck, enjoying the freshness of the air, and stimulating their appetites for breakfast. Mr. Johnson soon made his appearance, arrayed as on the night before, and took his seat quietly upon the guard of the boat.

"From the better opportunity afforded by daylight, I found that he was a slight build, apparently handsome young man, with black hair and eyes, and of a darkness of complexion that betokened

Spanish extraction. Any notice from others seemed painful to him; so to satisfy my curiosity, I questioned his servant, who was standing near, and gained the following information.

"His master was an invalid—he had suffered for a long time under a complication of diseases, that had baffled the skill of the best physicians in Mississippi; he was now suffering principally with the 'rheumatism,' and he was scarcely able to walk or help himself in any way. He came from Vicksburgh, and was now on his way to Philadelphia, at which place resided his uncle, a celebrated physician, and through whose means he hoped to be restored to perfect health.

"This information, communicated in a bold, off-hand manner, enlisted my sympathies for the sufferer, although it occurred to me that he walked rather too gingerly for a person afflicted with so many ailments."[9]

After thanking Clotel for the great service she had done him in bringing him out of slavery, William bade her farewell. The prejudice that exists in the Free States against coloured persons, on account of their colour, is attributable solely to the influence of slavery, and is but another form of slavery itself. And even the slave who escapes from the Southern plantations, is surprised when he reaches the North, at the amount and withering influence of this prejudice. William applied at the railway station for a ticket for the train going to Sandusky,[10] and was told that if he went by that train he would have to ride in the luggage-van.

"Why?" asked the astonished Negro.

"We don't send a Jim Crow carriage but once a day, and that went this morning."

The "Jim Crow"[11] carriage is the one in which the blacks have to ride. Slavery is a school in which its victims learn much shrewdness, and William had been an apt scholar. Without asking any more questions, the Negro took his seat in one of the first-class carriages. He was soon seen and ordered out. Afraid to remain in the town longer, he resolved to go by that train; and consequently seated himself on a goods' box in the luggage-van. The train started at its proper time, and all went on well. Just before arriving at the end of the journey, the conductor called on William for his ticket.

"I have none," was the reply.

"Well, then, you can pay your fare to me," said the officer.

"How much is it?" asked the black man.

"Two dollars."

"What do you charge those in the passenger-carriage?"

"Two dollars."

"And do you charge me the same as you do those who ride in the best carriages?" asked the Negro.

"Yes," was the answer.

"I shan't pay it," returned the man.

"You black scamp, do you think you can ride on this road without paying your fare?"

"No, I don't want to ride for nothing; I only want to pay what's right."

"Well, launch out two dollars, and that's right."

"No, I shan't; I will pay what I ought, and won't pay any more."

"Come, come, nigger, your fare and be done with it," said the conductor, in a manner that is never used except by Americans to blacks.

"I won't pay you two dollars, and that enough," said William.

"Well, as you have come all the way in the luggage-van, pay me a dollar and a half and you may go."

"I shan't do any such thing."

"Don't you mean to pay for riding?"

"Yes, but I won't pay a dollar and a half for riding up here in the freight-van. If you had let me come in the carriage where others ride, I would have paid you two dollars."

"Where were you raised? You seem to think yourself as good as white folks."

"I want nothing more than my rights."

"Well, give me a dollar, and I will let you off."

"No, sir, I shan't do it."

"What do you mean to do then—don't you wish to pay anything?"

"Yes, sir, I want to pay you the full price."

"What do you mean by full price?"

"What do you charge per hundred-weight for goods?" inquired the Negro with a degree of gravity that would have astonished Diogenes[12] himself.

"A quarter of a dollar per hundred," answered the conductor.

"I weigh just one hundred and fifty pounds," returned William, "and will pay you three eighths of a dollar."

"Do you expect that you will pay only thirty-seven cents for your ride?"

"This, sir, is your own price. I came in a luggage-van, and I'll pay for luggage."

After a vain effort to get the Negro to pay more, the conductor took the thirty-seven cents, and noted in his cash-book, "Received for one hundred and fifty pounds of luggage, thirty-seven cents." This, reader, is no fiction; it actually occurred in the railway above described.[13]

Thomas Corwin,[14] a member of the American Congress, is one of the blackest white men in the United States. He was once on his way to Congress, and took passage in one of the Ohio river steamers. As he came just at the dinner hour, he immediately went into the dining saloon, and took his seat at the table. A gentleman with his whole party of five ladies at once left the table. "Where is the captain?" cried the man in an angry tone. The captain soon appeared, and it was sometime before he could satisfy the old gent, that Governor Corwin was not a nigger. The newspapers often have notices of mistakes made by innkeepers and others who undertake to accommodate the public, one of which we give below.

On the 6th inst., the Hon. Daniel Webster[15] and family entered Edgartown,[16] on a visit for health and recreation. Arriving at the hotel, without alighting from the coach, the landlord was sent for to see if suitable accommodation could be had. That dignitary appearing, and surveying Mr. Webster, while the hon. senator addressed him, seemed woefully to mistake the dark features of the traveller as he sat back in the corner of the carriage, and to suppose him a *coloured man*, particularly as there were two coloured servants of Mr. W. outside. So he promptly declared that there was no room for him and his family, and he could not be accommodated there—at the same time suggesting that he might perhaps find accommodation at some of the huts "up back," to which he pointed. So deeply did the prejudice of looks possess him, that he appeared not to notice that the stranger introduced himself to him as Daniel Webster, or to be so ignorant as not to have heard of such a personage; and turning away, he expressed to the driver his astonishment that he should bring *black* people there for *him* to take in. It was not till he had been repeatedly assured and made to understand that the said Daniel Webster was a real live senator of the United States, that he perceived his awkward mistake and the distinguished honour which he and his house were so near missing.

In most of the Free States, the coloured people are disfranchised on account of their colour. The following scene, which we take from a newspaper in the state of Ohio, will give some idea of the extent to which this prejudice is carried.

"The whole of Thursday last was occupied by the Court of Common Pleas for this county in trying to find out whether one Thomas West was of the VOTING COLOUR, as some had very *constitutional doubts* as to whether his colour was orthodox, and whether his hair was of the official crisp! Was it not a dignified business? Four profound judges, four acute lawyers, twelve grave jurors, and I don't know how many venerable witnesses, making in all about thirty men, perhaps, all engaged in the profound, laborious, and illustrious business, of finding out whether a man who pays tax, works on the road, and is an industrious farmer, has been born according to the republican, Christian constitution of Ohio—so that he can vote! And they wisely, gravely, and 'JUDGMATICALLY' decided that he should not vote! What wisdom—what research it must have required to evolve this truth! It was left for the Court of Common Pleas for Columbian county, Ohio, in the United States of North America, to find out what Solomon[17] never dreamed of—the courts of all civilised, heathen, or Jewish countries, never contemplated.

Lest the wisdom of our courts should be circumvented by some such men as might be named, who are so near being born constitutionally that they might be taken for white by sight, I would suggest that our court be invested with SMELLING powers, and that if a man don't exhale the constitutional smell, he shall not vote! This would be an additional security to our liberties."

William found, after all, that liberty in the so-called Free States was more a name than a reality; that prejudice followed the coloured man into every place that he might enter. The temples erected for the worship of the living God are no exception. The finest Baptist church in the city of Boston has the following paragraph in the deed that conveys its seats to pewholders:

"And it is a further condition of these presents, that if the owner or owners of said pew shall determine hereafter to sell the same, it shall first be offered, in writing, to the standing committee of said society for the time being, at such price as might otherwise be obtained for it; and the said committee shall have the right, for ten days after such offer, to purchase said pew for said society, at that price, first deducting therefrom all taxes and assessments on said pew then remaining unpaid. And if the said committee shall not so complete such purchase within said ten days, then the pew may be sold by the owner or owners thereof (after payment of all such arrears) to any one respectable *white person*, but upon the same conditions as are contained in this instrument; and immediate notice of such sale shall be given in writing, by the vendor, to the treasurer of said society."

Such are the conditions upon which the Rowe Street Baptist Church, Boston, disposes of its seats. The writer of this is able to put that whole congregation, minister and all, to flight, by merely putting his coloured face in that church. We once visited a church in New York that had a place set apart for the sons of Ham. It was a dark, dismal looking place in one corner of the gallery, grated in front like a hen-coop, with a black border around it. It had two doors; over one was B. M.—black men; over the other B. W.—black women.

CHAPTER XX
A TRUE DEMOCRAT

"Who can, with patience, for a moment see
The medley mass of pride and misery,
Of whips and charters, manacles and rights,
Of slaving blacks and democratic whites,
And all the piebald policy that reigns
In free confusion o'er Columbia's plains?
To think that man, thou just and gentle God!
Should stand before thee with a tyrant's rod,
O'er creatures like himself, with souls from thee,
Yet dare to boast of perfect liberty!"
                                    —*Thomas Moore.*[1]

Educated in a free state, and marrying a wife who had been a victim to the institution of slavery, Henry Morton became strongly opposed to the system. His two daughters, at the age of twelve years, were sent to the North to finish their education, and to receive that refinement that young ladies cannot obtain in the Slave States. Although he did not publicly advocate the abolition of slavery, he often made himself obnoxious to private circles, owing to the denunciatory manner in which he condemned the "peculiar institution." Being one evening at a party, and hearing one of the company talking loudly of the glory and freedom of American institutions, he gave it as his opinion that, unless slavery was speedily abolished, it would be the ruin of the Union. "It is not our boast of freedom," said he, "that will cause us to be respected abroad. It is not our loud talk in favour of liberty that will cause us to be regarded as friends of human freedom; but our acts will be scrutinised by the people of other countries. We say much against European despotism; let us look to ourselves. That government is despotic where the rulers govern subjects by their own mere will—by decrees and laws emanating from their uncontrolled will, in the enactment and execution of which the ruled have no voice, and under which they have no right except at the will of the rulers. Despotism does not depend upon the number of the rulers, or the number of the subjects. It may have one ruler or many. Rome was a despotism under Nero;[2] so she was under the triumvirate. Athens was a despotism under Thirty Tyrants; under her Four Hundred Tyrants; under her Three Thousand Tyrants. It has been generally observed that despotism increases in severity with the number of despots; the responsibility is more divided, and the claims more numerous. The triumvirs each demanded his victims. The smaller the number of subjects in proportion to the tyrants, the more cruel the oppression, because the less danger from rebellion. In this government, the free white citizens are the rulers—the sovereigns, as we delight to be called. All others are subjects. There are, perhaps, some sixteen or seventeen millions of sovereigns, and four millions of subjects.

"The rulers and the ruled are of all colours, from the clear white of the Caucasian tribes to the swarthy Ethiopian.[3] The former, by courtesy, are all called white, the latter black. In this government the subject has no rights, social, political, or personal. He has no voice in the laws which govern him. He can hold no property. His very wife and children are not his. His labour is another's. He, and all that appertain to him, are the absolute property of his rulers. He is governed, bought, sold, punished, executed, by laws to which he never gave his assent, and by rulers whom he never chose. He is not a serf merely, with half the rights of men like the subjects of despotic Russia; but a native slave, stripped of every right which God and nature gave him, and which the high spirit of our revolution declared inalienable—which he himself could not surrender, and which man could not take from him. Is he not then the subject of despotic sway?

"The slaves of Athens and Rome were free in comparison. They had some rights—could acquire some property; could choose their own masters, and purchase their own freedom; and, when free, could rise in social and political life.[4] The

slaves of America, then, lie under the most absolute and grinding despotism that the world ever saw. But who are the
despots? The rulers of the country—the sovereign people!⁵ Not
merely the slaveholder who cracks the lash. He is but the instrument in the hands of despotism. That despotism is the government of the Slave States, and the United States, consisting of
all its rulers—all the free citizens. Do not look upon this as a
paradox, because you and I and the sixteen millions of rulers
are free. The rulers of every despotism are free. Nicholas of
Russia is free. The grand Sultan of Turkey is free. The butcher
of Austria is free. Augustus, Anthony, and Lepidus were free,
while they drenched Rome in blood.⁶ The Thirty Tyrants—the
Four Hundred—the Three Thousand, were free while they
bound their countrymen in chains. You, and I, and the sixteen
millions are free, while we fasten iron chains, and rivet manacles on four millions of our fellowmen—take their wives and
children from them—separate them—sell them, and doom
them to perpetual, eternal bondage. Are we not then despots—
despots such as history will brand and God abhor?

"We, as individuals, are fast losing our reputation for honest
dealing. Our nation is losing its character. The loss of a firm
national character, or the degradation of a nation's honour, is
the inevitable prelude to her destruction. Behold the once
proud fabric of a Roman empire—an empire carrying its arts
and arms into every part of the Eastern continent; the mon-
archs of mighty kingdoms dragged at the wheels of her tri-
umphal chariots; her eagle waving over the ruins of desolated
countries;—where is her splendour, her wealth, her power, her
glory? Extinguished for ever. Her mouldering temples, the
mournful vestiges of her former grandeur, afford a shelter to
her muttering monks. Where are her statesmen, her sages, her
philosophers, her orators, generals? Go to their solitary tombs
and inquire. She lost her national character, and her destruction
followed. The ramparts of her national pride were broken
down, and Vandalism⁷ desolated her classic fields. Then let the
people of our country take warning ere it is too late. But most
of us say to ourselves,

" 'Who questions the right of mankind to be free?
Yet, what are the rights of the *Negro* to me?
I'm well fed and clothed, I have plenty of pelf—
I'll care for the blacks when I turn black myself.'

"New Orleans is doubtless the most immoral place in the
United States. The theatres are open on the Sabbath. Bullfights, horse-racing, and other cruel amusements are carried on
in this city to an extent unknown in any other part of the
Union. The most stringent laws have been passed in that city
against Negroes, yet a few years since the State Legislature
passed a special act to enable a white man to marry a coloured
woman, on account of her being possessed of a large fortune.
And, very recently, the following paragraph appeared in the
city papers:—

" 'There has been quite a stir recently in this city, in consequence
of a marriage of a white man, named Buddington, a teller in the
Canal Bank, to the Negro daughter of one of the wealthiest mer-
chants. Buddington, before he could be married, was obliged to
swear that he had Negro blood in his veins, and to do this he
made an incision in his arm, and put some of her blood in the
cut. The ceremony was performed by a Catholic clergyman, and
the bridegroom has received with his wife a fortune of fifty or
sixty thousand dollars.'

"It seems that the fifty or sixty thousand dollars entirely covered the Negro woman's black skin, and the law prohibiting
marriage between blacks and whites was laid aside for the occasion."

Althesa felt proud, as well she might, at her husband's taking
such high ground in a slaveholding city like New Orleans.

CHAPTER XXI
THE CHRISTIAN'S DEATH

"O weep, ye friends of freedom weep!
Your harps to mournful measures sweep."[1]

On the last day of November, 1620, on the confines of the Grand Bank of Newfoundland, lo! we behold one little solitary tempest-tost and weather-beaten ship; it is all that can be seen on the length and breadth of the vast intervening solitudes, from the melancholy wilds of Labrador[2] and New England's iron-bound shores, to the western coasts of Ireland and the rock-defended Hebrides,[3] but one lonely ship greets the eye of angels or of men, on this great throughfare of nations in our age. Next in moral grandeur, was this ship, to the great discoverer's: Columbus found a continent; the May-flower[4] brought the seed-wheat of states and empire. That is the May-flower, with its servants of the living God, their wives and little ones, hastening to lay the foundations of nations in the occidental lands of the setting-sun. Hear the voice of prayer to God for his protection, and the glorious music of praise, as it breaks into the wild tempest of the mighty deep, upon the ear of God. Here in this ship are great and good men. Justice, mercy, humanity, respect for the rights of all; each man honoured, as he was useful to himself and others; labour respected, law-abiding men, constitution-making and respecting men; men, whom no tyrant could conquer, or hardship overcome, with the high commission sealed by a Spirit divine, to establish religious and political liberty for all. This ship had the embryo elements of all that is useful, great, and grand in Northern institutions; it was the great type of goodness and wisdom, illustrated in two and a quarter centuries gone by; it was the good genius of America.

But look far in the South-east, and you behold on the same day, in 1620, a low rakish ship hastening from the tropics, solitary and alone, to the New World.[5] What is she? She is freighted with the elements of unmixed evil. Hark! hear those rattling chains, hear that cry of despair and wail of anguish, as they die away in the unpitying distance. Listen to those shocking oaths, the crack of that flesh-cutting whip. Ah! it is the first cargo of slaves on their way to Jamestown, Virginia. Behold the May-flower anchored at Plymouth Rock, the slave-ship in James River. Each a parent, one of the prosperous, labour-honouring, law-sustaining institutions of the North; the other the mother of slavery, idleness, lynch-law, ignorance, unpaid labour, poverty, and duelling, despotism, the ceaseless swing of the whip, and the peculiar institutions of the South. These ships are the representation of good and evil in the New World, even to our day. When shall one of those parallel lines come to an end?

The origin of American slavery is not lost in the obscurity of by-gone ages. It is a plain historical fact, that it owes its birth to the African slave trade, now pronounced by every civilised community the greatest crime ever perpetrated against humanity.[6] Of all causes intended to benefit mankind, the abolition of chattel slavery must necessarily be placed amongst the first, and the Negro hails with joy every new advocate that appears in his cause. Commiseration for human suffering and human sacrifices awakened the capacious mind, and brought into action the enlarged benevolence, of Georgiana Carlton. With respect to her philosophy—it was of a noble cast. It was, that all men are by nature equal; that they are wisely and justly endowed by the Creator with certain rights, which are irrefragable; and that, however human pride and human avarice may depress and debase, still God is the author of good to man—and of evil, man is the artificer to himself and to his species. Unlike Plato and Socrates,[7] her mind was free from the gloom that surrounded theirs; her philosophy was founded in the school of Christianity; though a devoted member of her father's church, she was not a sectarian.

We learn from Scripture, and it is a little remarkable that it is the only exact definition of religion found in the sacred volume, that "pure religion and undefiled before God, even the Father, is this, to visit the fatherless and widows in their affliction, and to keep oneself unspotted from the world." "Look not every man on his own things, but every man also on the things of others." "Remember them that are in bonds as bound with them." "Whatsoever ye would that others should do to you, do ye even so to them."[8]

This was her view of Christianity, and to this end she laboured with all her energies to convince her slaveholding neighbours that the Negro could not only take care of himself, but that he also appreciated liberty, and was willing to work and redeem himself. Her most sanguine wishes were being realized when she suddenly fell into a decline. Her mother had died of consumption, and her physician pronounced this to be her disease. She was prepared for this sad intelligence, and received it with the utmost composure. Although she had confidence in her husband that he would carry out her wishes in freeing the Negroes after her death, Mrs. Carlton resolved upon their immediate liberation. Consequently the slaves were all summoned before the noble woman, and informed that they were no longer bondsmen. "From this hour," said she, "you are free, and all eyes will be fixed upon you. I dare not predict how far your example may affect the welfare of your brethren yet in bondage. If you are temperate, industrious, peaceable, and pious, you will show to the world that slaves can be emancipated without danger. Remember what a singular relation you sustain to society. The necessities of the case require not only that you should behave as well as the whites, but better than the whites; and for this reason: if you behave no better than they, your example will lose a great portion of its influence. Make the Lord Jesus Christ your refuge and exemplar. His is the only standard around which you can successfully rally. If ever there was a people who needed the consolations of religion to sustain them in their grievous afflictions, you are that people. You had better trust in the Lord than to put confidence in man. Happy is that people whose God is the Lord. Get as much education as possible for yourselves and your children. An ignorant people can never occupy any other than a degraded station in society; they can never be truly free until they are intelligent. In a few days you will start for the state of Ohio, where land will be purchased for some of you who have families, and where I hope you will all prosper. We have been urged to send you to Liberia, but we think it wrong to send you from your native land. We did not wish to encourage the Colonization Society,⁹ for it originated in hatred of the free coloured people. Its pretences are false, its doctrines odious, its means contemptible. Now, whatever may be your situation in life, 'Remember those in bonds as bound with them.' You must get ready as soon as you can for your journey to the North."

Seldom was there ever witnessed a more touching scene than this. There sat the liberator,—pale, feeble, emaciated, with death stamped upon her countenance, surrounded by the sons and daughters of Africa; some of whom had in former years been separated from all that they had held near and dear, and the most of whose backs had been torn and gashed by the Negro whip. Some were upon their knees at the feet of their benefactress; others were standing round her weeping. Many begged that they might be permitted to remain on the farm and work for wages, for some had wives and some husbands on other plantations in the neighbourhood, and would rather remain with them.¹⁰

But the laws of the state forbade any emancipated Negroes remaining, under penalty of again being sold into slavery. Hence the necessity of sending them out of the state. Mrs. Carlton was urged by her friends to send the emancipated Negroes to Africa. Extracts from the speeches of Henry Clay, and other distinguished Colonization Society men, were read to her to induce her to adopt this course. Some thought they should be sent away because the blacks are vicious; others because they would be missionaries to their brethren in Africa. "But," said she, "if we send away the Negroes because they are profligate and vicious, what sort of missionaries will they make? Why not send away the vicious among the whites for the same reason, and the same purpose?"

Death is a leveller, and neither age, sex, wealth, nor usefulness can avert when he is permitted to strike. The most beautiful flowers soon fade, and droop, and die; this is also the case with man; his days are uncertain as the passing breeze. This hour he glows in the blush of health and vigour, but the next he may be counted with the number no more known on earth.

Although in a low state of health, Mrs. Carlton had the pleasure of seeing all her slaves, except Sam and three others, start for a land of freedom. The morning they were to go on board the steamer, bound for Louisville, they all assembled on the large grass plot, in front of the drawing-room window, and wept while they bid their mistress farewell. When they were on the boat, about leaving the wharf, they were heard giving the charge to those on shore—"Sam, take care of Misus, take care of Marser, as you love us, and hope to meet us in de Hio (Ohio), and in heben; be sure and take good care of Misus and Marser."

In less than a week after her emancipated people had started for Ohio, Mrs. Carlton was cold in death. Mr. Carlton felt deeply, as all husbands must who love their wives, the loss of her who had been a lamp to his feet, and a light to his path. She had converted him from infidelity to Christianity; from the mere theory of liberty to practical freedom. He had looked upon the Negro as an ill-treated distant link of the human family; he now regarded them as a part of God's children. Oh, what a silence pervaded the house when the Christian had been removed. His indeed was a lonesome position.

> " 'Twas midnight, and he sat alone—
>   The husband of the dead,
> That day the dark dust had been thrown
>   Upon the buried head."

In the midst of the buoyancy of youth, this cherished one had drooped and died. Deep were the sounds of grief and mourning heard in that stately dwelling, when the stricken friends, whose office it had been to nurse and soothe the weary sufferer, beheld her pale and motionless in the sleep of death.

Oh what a chill creeps through the breaking heart when we look upon the insensible form, and feel that it no longer contains the spirit we so dearly loved! How difficult to realise that

the eye which always glowed with affection and intelligence—
that the ear which had so often listened to the sounds of sorrow
and gladness—that the voice whose accents had been to us like
sweet music, and the heart, the habitation of benevolence and
truth, are now powerless and insensate as the bier upon which
the form rests. Though faith be strong enough to penetrate the
cloud of gloom which hovers near, and to behold the freed
spirit safe, *for ever*, safe in its home in heaven, yet the thoughts
will linger sadly and cheerlessly upon the grave.

Peace to her ashes! she fought the fight, obtained the Christian's victory, and wears the crown. But if it were that departed
spirits are permitted to note the occurrences of this world, with
what a frown of disapprobation would hers view the effort
being made in the United States to retard the work of emancipation for which she laboured and so wished to see brought about.

In what light would she consider that hypocritical priesthood
who gave their aid and sanction to the infamous "Fugitive
Slave Law." If true greatness consists in doing good to mankind, then was Georgiana Carlton an ornament to human nature. Who can think of the broken hearts made whole, of sad
and dejected countenances now beaming with contentment of
joy, of the mother offering her free-born babe to heaven, and of
the father whose cup of joy seems overflowing in the presence
of his family, where none can molest or make him afraid. Oh,
that God may give more such persons to take the whip-scarred
Negro by the hand, and raise him to a level with our common
humanity! May the professed lovers of freedom in the new
world see that true liberty is freedom for all! and may every
American continually hear it sounding in his ear:—

> "Shall every flap of England's flag
>   Proclaim that all around are free,
> From 'farthest Ind' to each blue crag
>   That beetles o'er the Western Sea?
> And shall we scoff at Europe's kings,
>   When Freedom's fire is dim with us,
> And round our country's altar clings
>   The damning shade of Slavery's curse?"[11]

of the cardinal principles of Christianity and freedom is the equality and brotherhood of man."

Every day Mr. Linwood became more and more familiar with Jerome, and eventually they were on the most intimate terms.

Fifteen days from the time that Clotelle was introduced into her father's room, they left Ferney for Geneva. Many were the excursions Clotelle made under the shadows of Mont Blanc, and with her husband and father for companions; she was now in the enjoyment of pleasures hitherto unknown.

CHAPTER XXXV

THE FATHER'S RESOLVE

Aware that her father was still a slave-owner, Clotelle determined to use all her persuasive power to induce him to set them free, and in this effort she found a substantial supporter in her husband.

"I have always treated my slaves well," said Mr. Linwood to Jerome, as the latter expressed his abhorrence of the system; "and my neighbors, too, are generally good men; for slavery in Virginia is not like slavery in the other States," continued the proud son of the Old Dominion.

"Their right to be free, Mr. Linwood," said Jerome, "is taken from them, and they have no security for their comfort, but the humanity and generosity of men, who have been trained to regard them not as brethren, but as mere property. Humanity and generosity are, at best, but poor guaranties for the protection of those who cannot assert their rights, and over whom law throws no protection."

It was with pleasure that Clotelle obtained from her father a promise that he would liberate all his slaves on his return to Richmond. In a beautiful little villa, situated in a pleasant spot, fringed with hoary rocks and thick dark woods, within sight of the deep blue waters of Lake Leman, Mr. Linwood, his daughter, and her husband, took up their residence for a short time. For more than three weeks, this little party spent their time in visiting the birth-place of Rousseau, and the former abodes of Byron, Gibbon, Voltaire, De Stael, Shelley, and other literary characters.

We can scarcely contemplate a visit to a more historic and interesting place than Geneva and its vicinity. Here, Calvin, that great luminary in the Church, lived and ruled for years; here, Voltaire, the mighty genius, who laid the foundation of the French Revolution, and who boasted, "When I shake my wig, I powder the whole republic," governed in the higher walks of life.

Fame is generally the recompense, not of the living, but of the dead,—not always do they reap and gather in the harvest who sow the seed; the flame of its altar is too often kindled from the ashes of the great. A distinguished critic has beautifully said, "The sound which the stream of high thought, carried down to future ages, makes, as it flows—deep, distant, murmuring ever more, like the waters of the mighty ocean." No reputation can be called great that will not endure this test. The distinguished men who had lived in Geneva transfused their spirit, by their writings, into the spirit of other lovers of literature and everything that treated of great authors. Jerome and Clotelle lingered long in and about the haunts of Geneva and Lake Leman.

An autumn son sent down her bright rays, and bathed every object in her glorious light, as Clotelle, accompanied by her husband and father set out one fine morning on her return home to France. Throughout the whole route, Mr. Linwood saw by the deference paid to Jerome, whose black complexion excited astonishment in those who met him, that there was no hatred to the man in Europe, on account of his color; that what is called prejudice against color is the offspring of the institution of slavery; and he felt ashamed of his own countrymen, when he thought of the complexion as distinctions, made in the United States, and resolved to dedicate the remainder of his life to the eradication of this unrepublican and unchristian feeling from the land of his birth, on his return home.

After a stay of four weeks at Dunkirk, the home of the Fletchers,[1] Mr. Linwood set out for America, with the full determination of freeing his slaves, and settling them in one of the Northern States, and then to return to France to end his days in the society of his beloved daughter.

THE END.

Note.—The author of the foregoing tale was formerly a Kentucky slave. If it serves to relieve the monotony of camp-life to the soldiers of the Union, and therefore of Liberty, and at the same time kindles their zeal in the cause of universal emancipation, the object both of its author and publisher will be gained.

J. R.[1]

Appendix C

FROM *CLOTELLE; OR, THE COLORED HEROINE. A TALE OF THE SOUTHERN STATES* (1867)

CHAPTER XXXVI[1]
THE RETURN HOME

The first gun fired at the American Flag, on the 12th of April, eighteen sixty-one, at Fort Sumter,[2] reverberated all over Europe, and was hailed with joy by the crowned heads of the Old World, who hated republican institutions, and who thought they saw, in this act of treason, the downfall of the great American experiment. Most citizens, however, of the United States, who were then sojourning abroad, hastened home to take part in the struggle,—some to side with the rebels, others to take their stand with the friends of liberty. Among the latter, none came with swifter steps or more zeal than Jerome and Clotelle Fletcher.[3] They arrived in New Orleans a week after the capture of that city by the expedition under the command of Major-Gen. B. F. Butler.[4] But how changed was society since Clotelle had last set feet in the Crescent City![5] Twenty-two years had passed; her own chequered life had been through many shifting scenes; her old acquaintances in New Orleans had all disappeared; and with the exception of the black faces which she beheld at every turn, and which in her younger days were her associates, she felt herself in the midst of strangers; and these were arrayed against each other in mortal combat. Possessed with ample means, Mr. and Mrs. Fletcher set about the work of assisting those whom the rebellion had placed in a state of starvation and sickness.

With a heart overflowing with the milk of human kindness, and a tear for every sufferer, no matter of what color or sect, Clotelle was soon known as the "Angel of Mercy."[6]

The "General Order No. 63," issued on the 22d of August, 1862, by Gen. Butler, recognizing, and calling into the service of the Federal Government, the battalion of colored men known as the "Native Guard," at once gave full scope to Jerome's military enthusiasm; and he made haste to enlist in the organization.

The "Native Guard" did good service in New Orleans and vicinity, till ordered to take part in the seige of Port Hudson,[7] where they appeared under the name of the "First Louisiana," and under the immediate command of Lieut.-Col. Bassett.[8] The heroic attack of this regiment, made on the 27th of May, 1863, its unsurpassed "charge," its great loss, and its severe endurance on the field of battle, are incidents which have passed into history. The noble daring of the First Louisiana gained for the black soldiers in our army the praise of all Americans who value Republican institutions.

There was, however, one scene, the closing one in the first day's attack on Port Hudson, which, while it reflects undying credit upon the bravery of the negro, pays but a sorry tribute to the humanity of the white general who brought the scene into existence. The field was strewn with the dead, the dying, and the wounded; and as the jaded regiments were leaving the ground, after their unsuccessful attack, it was found that Capt. Payne, of the Third Louisiana, had been killed; and his body, which was easily distinguished by the uniform, was still on the battle-field. The colonel of the regiment, pointing to where the body lay, asked, "Are there four men here who will fetch the body of Capt. Payne from the field?" Four men stepped out, and at once started. But, as the body lay directly under the range of the rebel batteries, they were all swept down by the grape, canister, and shell which were let loose by the enemy.

The question was again repeated, "Are there four men who will go for the body?" The required number came forth, and started upon a run; but, ere they could reach the spot, they were cut down. "Are there four more who will try?" The third call was answered in the affirmative, and the men started upon the double-quick. They, however, fell before getting as far as the preceding four. Twelve men had been killed in the effort to obtain the body of the brave Payne, but to no purpose. Humanity forbade another trial, and yet it was made. "Are there four more men in the regiment who will volunteer to go for Capt. Payne's body?" shouted the officer. Four men sprang forward, as if fearful that they would miss the opportunity of these last: one was Jerome Fletcher, the hero of our story. They started upon the run; and, strange to tell, all of them reached the body, and had nearly borne it from the field, when two of the number were cut down. Of these, one was Jerome. His head was entirely torn off by a shell. The body of the deceased officer having been rescued, an end was put to the human sacrifice.

CHAPTER XXXVII

THE ANGEL OF MERCY

The sad intelligence of Jerome's death was brought to Clotelle while she was giving her personal attention to the sick and wounded that filled the hospitals of New Orleans. For a time she withdrew from the gaze of mankind, and gave herself up to grief. Few unions had been productive of more harmonious feelings than hers. And this blow, so unexpected and at a time when she was experiencing such a degree of excitement caused by the rebellion, made her, indeed, feel the affliction severely.

But the newspaper accounts of the intense suffering of Union prisoners in the rebel States aroused her, and caused her to leave her retirement. In the month of October, 1863, Clotelle resolved to visit Andersonville, Ga.,¹ for the purpose of alleviating the hardships of our sick and imprisoned soldiers, and at once put her resolution into effect by going immediately to that place. After crossing the lines, she passed as a rebel lady, to enable her the more successfully to carry out her object. On her arrival at Andersonville, Clotelle took up her abode with a private family, of Union proclivities, and commenced her work of mercy. She first visited the hospitals, the buildings of which were merest excuses for hospitals.

It was the beginning of November; and, even in that southern latitude, the cold made these miserable abodes uncomfortable nights and mornings. The dirty, unventilated rooms, with nothing but straw upon the cold, damp floor, for beds, upon which lay the ragged, emaciated Union prisoners, worn down to skin and bone with disease and starvation, with their sunken eyes and wild looks, made them appear hideous in the extreme. The repulsive scenes, that showed the suffering, neglect, and cruelty which these poor creatures had experienced, made her heart sink within her.

Having paid considerable attention to hospital life in Europe, and so recently from amongst the sick at New Orleans, Clotelle's experience, suggestions, and liberal expenditure of money, would have added greatly to the comfort of these helpless men, if the rebel authorities had been so disposed. But their hatred to Union prisoners was so apparent, that the interest which this angel of humanity took in the condition of the rebel sick could not shield her from the indignation of the secession officials for her good feeling for Union men. However, with a determination to do all in her power for the needy, she labored in season and out.

The brutal treatment and daily murders committed upon our soldiers in the Andersonville prisons caused Clotelle to secretly aid prisoners in their escape. In the latter work, she brought to her assistance the services of a negro man named Pete. This individual was employed about the prison, and, having the entire confidence of the commandant, was in a position to do much good without being suspected. Pete was an original character, of a jovial nature, and, when intending some serious adventure, would appear very solemn, and usually singing a doleful ditty, often the following, which was a favorite with him:—

"Come listen, all you darkies, come listen to my song:
It am about ole Massa, who use me bery wrong.
In de cole, frosty mornin', it ain't so bery nice,
Wid de water to de middle, to hoe among de rice;
    When I neber hab forgotten
    How I used to hoe de cotton,
    How I used to hoe de cotton,
        On de ole Virginny shore;
    But I'll neber hoe de cotton,
    Oh! neber hoe de cotton
        Any more.

"If I feel de drefful hunger, he tink it am a vice,
And he gib me for my dinner a little broken rice,—
A little broken rice and a bery little fat,
And he grumble like de debbil if I eat too much of dat;
    When I neber hab forgotten, etc.

"He tore me from my Dinah; I tought my heart would burst:
He made me lub anoder when my lub was wid de first;
He sole my picanninnies because he got dar price,
And shut me in de marsh-field to hoe among de rice;
    When I neber hab forgotten, etc.

"And all de day I hoe dar, in all de heat and rain;
And, as I hoe away dar, my heart go back again,—
Back to de little cabin dat stood among de corn,
And to de ole plantation where she and I war born!
    Oh! I wish I had forgotten, etc.

"Den Dinah am beside me, de chil'ren on my knee,
And dough I am a slave dar, it 'pears to me I'm free,
Till I wake up from my dreaming, and wife and chil'ren gone,
I hoe away and weep dar, and weep dar all alone!
    Oh! I wish I had forgotten, etc.

"But soon a day am comin', a day I long to see,
    When dis darky in de cole ground, foreber will be free,
    When wife and chil'ren wid me, I'll sing in Paradise,
    How He, de blessed Jesus, hab bought me wid a price;
            How de Lord hab not forgotten
            How well I hoed de cotton,
            How well I hoed de cotton
                On de ole Virginny shore;
            Dar I'll neber hoe de cotton,
            Oh! I'll neber hoe de cotton
                Any more."

When away from the whites, and among his own class, Pete
could often be heard in the following strains;—[2]

                "A storm am brewin' in de Souf,
                    A storm am brewin' now.
                Oh! hearken den, and shut your mouf,
                    And I will tell you how:
                And I will tell you how, ole boy,
                    De storm of fire will pour,
                And make de darkies dance for joy,
                    As dey neber danced afore;
                So shut your mouf as close as deafh,
                And all you niggas hole your breafh,
                    And I will tell you how.

                "De darkies at de Norf am ris,
                    And dey am comin' down—
                Am comin' down, I know dey is,
                    To do de white folks brown!
                Dey'll turn ole Massa out to grass,
                    And set de niggas free,
                And when dat day am come to pass
                    We'll all be dar to see!
                So shut your mouf as close as deafh,
                And all you niggas hole your breafh,
                    And do de white folks brown!

"Den all de week will be as gay
    As am de Chris'mas time;
We'll dance all night and all de day,
    And make de banjo chime—
And make de banjo chime, I tink,
    And pass de time away,
Wid 'nuf to eat and nuf to drink,
    And not a bit to pay!
So shut your mouf as close as deafh,
And all you niggas hole your breafh,
    And make de banjo chime."

How to escape from prison was ever the thoughts by day and
dreams by night of the incarcerated. Plans were concocted,
partly put into execution, and then proved failures. Some of
these caused increased suffering to the prisoners after their discovery; for, where the real parties could not be found, the
whole were ill-treated as a punishment to the guilty.[3] Tunnelling was generally the mode for escape; and tunnelling became the order of the day, or, rather, the work for the night. In
the latter part of November, 1863, the unusual gaiety of the
prisoners showed that some plan of exit from the prison was
soon to be exhibited.

CHAPTER XXXVIII

THE GREAT TUNNEL AND THE MISTAKE

For several weeks, some ten or fifteen of the most able-bodied
of the prisoners had been nightly at work; and the great tunnel,
the *largest* ever projected by men for their escape from prison,
was thought to be finished, with the exception of the tapping
outside of the prison wall. The digging of a tunnel is not an
easy job, and, consequently, is of slow progress. The Andersonville prisoners had to dig ten feet down into the earth, after cut-
ting through the floor, and then went a distance of fifty feet to
get beyond the wall. The digging was done in the following

way: As soon as the operator was below the surface, and had a place large enough to admit the body, he laid down upon his face, at full length, and with his knife, spoon, piece of earthenware, or old iron, dug away with all his energies, throwing the dirt behind him, which was gathered up by a confederate, carried off, and hid. This mode of operating was carried on night after night, and the flooring replaced during the day, to prevent suspicion. The want of fresh air in the tunnel, as it progressed to completion, often drove the men from their work, and caused a delay, which proved fatal to their successful escape.

The long-looked for day arrived. More than three hundred had prepared to leave this hated abode, by the tunnel. All they waited for was the tapping and the signal. The time came, the place of egress was tapped, and the leader had scarcely put his head out of the hole, ere he was fired upon by the sentinels, which soon alarmed and drew the entire guard to the spot. Great was the commotion throughout the prison, and all who were caught in the tunnel were severely punished.

This failure seemed to depress the spirits of the men more than any previous attempt. Heavy irons were placed upon the limbs of many of the prisoners, and their lot was made otherwise harder by the keepers. Clotelle, though often permitted to see the prisoners and contribute to their wants, and, though knowing much of their designs, knew nothing of the intended escape, and therefore was more bold in her intercessions in their behalf when failure came upon them.

The cruelty which followed this mishap, induced Clotelle to interest herself in another mode of escape for the men thus so heavily ironed.

Pete, the man of all work, whose sympathies were with the Union prisoners, was easily gained over to a promise of securing the keys of the prison and letting the men escape, especially when Clotelle offered him money to enable him to make good his own way to the North.

The night of the exodus came. It was favored with darkness; and it so happened that the officials were on a spree, owing to the arrival of Confederate officers with news of a rebel victory.

Before getting the keys, Pete supplied the sentinels on duty with enough whiskey, which he had stolen from the keepers' store-room, to make them all drunk. At the chosen moment, the keys were obtained by Pete, the doors and gates were opened, and ninety-three prisoners, including the tunnel workers, whose irons were taken off, made their escape, allowing the faithful negro to accompany them. Nothing was known of the exit of the men till breakfast hour on the next morning. On examination of the store-room, it was found, that, in addition to the whiskey Pete had taken a large supply of stores for the accommodation of the party. Added to this, a good number of arms with ammunition had been furnished the men by the African.

The rebels were not prepared to successfully pursue the fleeing prisoners, although armed men were sent in different directions. Nothing, however, was heard of them till they reached the Union lines. Long suspected of too freely aiding Union prisoners, Clotelle was now openly charged with a knowledge of the escape of these men, and was compelled to leave Andersonville.

CHAPTER XXXIX

CONCLUSION

The fiendish and heartless conduct of a large number of the people of the South towards Union men during the war, and especially the unlady-like demeanor of rebel women at New Orleans and other points, is a matter that has passed into history.[1] In few places were the women more abusive to those of Union proclivities than the female portion of the inhabitants of Greenville, Alabama.[2] While passing through this town, on her return from Andersonville to New Orleans, Clotelle had to encounter the fierce ill-treatment of these chivalrous daughters of the South. There were, during the rebellion, many brave and generous women, who, in the mountains and lowlands of Alabama, gave aid to Federals,—soldiers and civilians,—in their wanderings and escape from the cruelties of the traitors. One of these patriotic women was arrested while on a visit to Greenville for the purpose of procuring medicine and other necessaries for sick Union men then hid away in the woods. This large-hearted woman—Eunice Hastings—had her horse taken from her, robbed of the goods she had purchased, and, after experiencing almost death at the hands of the rebel women, was released and turned out penniless, and without the means of reaching her home in the country; when Clotelle, who had just arrived at the dilapidated and poorly kept hotel, met her, and, learning the particulars of her case, offered assistance to the injured woman, which brought down upon her own head the condemnation of the secesh[3] population of the place. However, Clotelle purchased a fine horse from the landlord, gave it to Miss Hastings, who, after securing some articles for which she had come to Greenville, left town under cover of night, and escaped further molestation. This act of kindness to a helpless sister at once stirred up the vilest feelings of the people.

"The worst of slaves is he whom passion rules."[4]

As has already been said, there was nothing in the appearance of Clotelle to indicate that a drop of African blood coursed through her veins, except, perhaps, the slight wave in the hair, and the scarcely perceptible brunettish tinge upon the countenance. She passed as a rebel lady; yet the inhabitants of Greenville could not permit sympathy with, and aid to, a Union woman to pass unnoticed, and therefore resolved on revenge.

"Revenge, at first though sweet,
Bitter ere long, back on itself recoils."[5]

Clotelle's person, trunks, and letters were all searched with the hope and expectation of finding evidences of a spy. Nothing of the kind being found, she was then rigorously interrogated as to her sympathies with the two contending armies. With no wish whatever to conceal her opinions, she openly avowed that she was a Union woman. This was enough. After being persecuted during the day, she was put in charge of a committee of rebel women for the night, with a promise of more violent treatment on the morrow. The loyalty of the negroes of the South, during the severest hours of the rebellion, reflects the greatest possible credit on the race. Through their assistance, hundreds of Union men were enabled to make their escape from prisons, and thousands kept from starvation when on their way to the Federal lines, or while keeping out of the way of rebel recruiting gangs. They seldom, if ever, hesitated to do the white Unionists a service, at the risk even of life, and, under the most trying circumstances, revealed a devotion and a spirit of self-sacrifice that were heroic. No one ever made an appeal to thom they did not answer. They were degraded and ignorant, which was attributable to the cruel laws and equally unchristian practices of the people of the South; but their hearts were always open, and the slightest demand upon their sympathies brought forth their tears. They never shunned a man or woman who sought food or shelter on their way to freedom. The goodness of heart and the guileless spirit of the blacks was not better understood by any one than Clotelle; and she felt a secret joy at seeing all the servants in the Greenville hotel negroes. She saw from their very looks that she had their undivided sympathies. One of the servants overheard the rebels in a conversation, in which it was determined to send Clotelle to the county town, for safe keeping in the jail, the following day; and this fact was communicated to the unfortunate woman. The slave woman who gave the information told her that she could escape if she desired.

Having already been robbed of every thing except the apparel upon her person and some money she had concealed about her, she at once signified to the black woman her wish to get out of the reach of her persecutors. The old worn-out clock in the narrow dining hall had struck one; a cold rain was patting upon the roof, and the women watchers, one after another, had fallen asleep; and even the snuff-dippers, whose dirty practice creates a nervousness that keeps them awake longer than any other class, had yielded to the demands of Morpheus,[6] when Aggy, the colored servant, stealthily entered the room, beckoned to Clotelle, and both left in silence.

Cautiously and softly the black woman led the way, followed by the "Angel of Mercy," till, after passing down through the cellar with the water covering the floor, they emerged into the back yard. Two horses had been provided. Clotelle mounted one, and a black man the other; the latter leading the way. Both dashed off at a rapid pace, through a drenching storm, with such a pall-like darkness that they could not see each other. After an hour's ride the negro halted, and informed Clotelle that he must leave her, and return with the horses, but that she was with friends. He then gave a whistle, and for a moment held his breath. Just as the faithful black was about to repeat the signal, he heard the response; and in a moment the lady alighted, and with dripping garments, limbs chilled to numbness, followed her new guide to a place of concealment, near the village of Taitsville.

"You is jes as wet as a drownded rat," said the mulatto woman, who met Clotelle as she entered the negro's cabin.

"Yes," replied the latter, "this is a stormy night for one to be out."

"Yes mam, dese is hard times for everybody dat 'bleves in de Union. I 'spose deys cotched your husband, an' put him in de army, ain't dey?"

"No: my husband died at Port Hudson, fighting for the Union," said Clotelle.

"Oh, mam, dats de place whar de black people fight de rebels so, wasn't it?" remarked Dinah, for such was her name.

"Yes, that was the place," replied the former. "I see that your husband has lost one of his hands: did he lose it in the war?"

"Oh no missus," said Dinah. "When dey was taken all de men, black an white, to put in de army, dey cotched my ole man too, and took him long wid 'em. So you see, he said he'd die afore he'd shoot at de Yanks. So you see, missus, Jimmy jes took and lay his left han' on a log, and chop it off wid de hatchet. Den, you see, dey let him go, an' he come home. You see, missus, my Jimmy is a free man: he was born free, an' he bought me, an' pay fifteen hundred dollars for me."

It was true that Jim had purchased his wife; nor had he forgotten the fact, as was shown a day or two after, while in conversation with her. The woman, like many of her sex, was an inveterate scold, and Jim had but one way to govern her tongue. "Shet your mouf, madam, an' hole your tongue," said Jim, after his wife had scolded and sputtered away for some minutes. "Shet your mouf dis minit, I say: you shan't stan' dar, an' talk ter me in dat way. I bought you, an' paid my money fer you, an' I ain't gwine ter let you sase me in dat way. Shet your mouf dis minit: ef you don't I'll sell you; 'fore God I will. Shet up, I say, or I'll sell you." This had the desired effect, and settled Dinah for the day.

After a week spent in this place of concealment, Jim conveyed Clotelle to Leaksville, Mississippi,[7] through the Federal lines, and from thence she proceeded to New Orleans.

The Rebellion was now drawing to a close. The valley of the Mississippi was in full possession of the Federal government. Sherman was on his raid, and Grant was hemming in Lee.[8] Everywhere the condition of the freedmen attracted the attention of the friends of humanity, and no one felt more keenly their wants than Clotelle; and to their education and welfare she resolved to devote the remainder of her life, and for this purpose went to the State of Mississippi, and opened a school for the freedmen; hired teachers, paying them out of her own purse. In the summer of 1866, the Poplar Farm[9] on which she had once lived as a slave, was confiscated and sold by Government authority, and was purchased by Clotelle, upon which she established a Freedmen's School, and where at this writing,—now June, 1867,—resides the "Angel of Mercy."

Explanatory Notes

PREFACE

1. *introduction of slaves in 1620*: Dutch traders brought the first
   cargo of twenty Africans (which included some women) to the
   British colony of Jamestown, Virginia, in 1619. According to historians James Oliver Horton and Lois E. Horton, "The early black
   laborers in Virginia, not yet slaves but less free than white indentured servants, were sometimes allowed their freedom after a set
   period of time, almost always serving a longer indenture than
   white servants. There is evidence that some black servants were already serving for life by the middle of the seventeenth century."
   James Oliver Horton and Lois E. Horton, *Hard Road to Freedom:
   The Story of African America* (New Brunswick, N.J.: Rutgers University Press, 2001), 28.

2. *Fugitive Slave Law*: The Fugitive Slave Law of 1850, part of the
   Compromise of 1850, was much stricter than any previous fugitive
   slave law. Protecting or helping fugitive slaves became a federal
   crime that could be punished by fines or imprisonment. This law
   made it easier for slaveholders to capture slaves who had escaped
   to the North.

3. *"honours the corruption... hide his head"*: Shakespeare, *Julius
   Caesar* IV. iii, 13–14. See Robert S. Levine, ed., *Clotel; or, The
   President's Daughter: A Narrative of Slave Life in the United States*
   (Boston: Bedford/St. Martin's, 2000), 46.

NARRATIVE OF THE LIFE AND ESCAPE OF
WILLIAM WELLS BROWN

1. *"Shall tongues be mute"*: From John Greenleaf Whittier (1807–1892), "Stanzas for the Times" (1835). See William Edward Farrison, *William Wells Brown: Author and Reformer* (Chicago: University of Chicago Press, 1969), 216. Whittier, a poet and abolitionist born in Massachusetts, was the son of Quaker parents.

2. *Henry Clay:* Clay (1777–1852), was a congressman, senator, and secretary of state from Virginia. He played a major role in promoting both the Missouri Compromise of 1820 and the Compromise of 1850.

3. *his master's medical department:* Brown remained interested in medicine. Later in life, after reading in medicine for years, he started practicing it in 1864 and began writing "M.D." after his name. He had no formal degree, but that was not unusual at the time. He practiced medicine for his last nineteen years. See William Edward Farrison, *William Wells Brown: Author and Reformer* (Chicago: University of Chicago Press, 1969), 399–402.

4. The scene of a slave child who witnesses but cannot intervene while one of his female relatives is physically abused by her master features prominently also in the first chapter of Frederick Douglass's *Narrative of the Life of Frederick Douglass, an American Slave, Written by Himself* (1845) as a traumatizing rite of passage into the horrors of slavery.

5. *Elijah P. Lovejoy:* At the time Brown worked for him, Reverend Elijah Parish Lovejoy (1802–1837) was editor of the *St. Louis Times.* See William L. Andrews, ed., *From Fugitive Slave to Free Man: The Autobiographies of William Wells Brown* (New York: Mentor, 1993), 34. The abolitionist newspaper Lovejoy later edited in Alton, Illinois, was the *Observer.* Lovejoy, the "martyr abolitionist," was murdered by a proslavery mob in Alton in 1831.

6. *"Is there not some chosen curse":* From Joseph Addison (1672–1719), *Cato* (1716) I.1, 21–24. See Robert S. Levine, ed., *Clotel; or, The President's Daughter: A Narrative of Slave Life in the United States* (Boston: Bedford/St. Martin's, 2000), 51.

7. *published memoir of his life:* Brown quotes from his own *Narrative of William W. Brown, A Fugitive Slave* (1847).

8. *"Come back to me, mother!":* This poem is by Margaret Bailey

(1807–1859). Brown had already included this poem in his second, enlarged edition of the *Narrative* (1848) and also in his volume *The Anti-Slavery Harp: A Collection of Songs for Anti-Slavery Meetings* (1848). Larry Gara has identified Margaret Bailey as the wife of Gamaliel Bailey. See Larry Gara, ed., *The Narrative of William Wells Brown, A Fugitive Slave* (Reading, Mass.: Addison Wesley Publishing Company, 1969), 52. Gamaliel Bailey (1807–1859), editor of the *National Era*, an abolitionist newspaper published in Washington, D.C., married Margaret Lucy Shands of Virginia in 1833.

9. *his mind was occupied with what he had seen*: Brown's reactions to the violence of slavery seem contained, understated, as if he wanted to involve his readers actively in his story by making them bear the burden of horror and indignation. His strategy worked with Edmund Quincy, who, in his prefatory letter to the first edition of the *Narrative*, observed: "What I have admired, and marvelled at, in your Narrative, is the simplicity and calmness with which you describe scenes and actions which might well 'move the very stones to rise and mutiny' against the National Institution that makes them possible." See William L. Andrews, ed. *From Fugitive Slave to Free Man*, 21. Edmund Quincy (1808–1877), reformer and author, was born in Boston. Of aristocratic origin, he became an abolitionist and was corresponding secretary of the Massachusetts Anti-Slavery Society, vice president of the American Anti-Slavery Society, and an editor of the *Anti-Slavery Standard*. He was also known as a writer of fiction and biography.

10. *"go into the silent land"*: From Henry Wadsworth Longfellow (1807–1882), "Song of the Silent Land" (1839), a translation of a poem by the German poet J. G. Von Salis-Seewis (1762–1834). See Robert S. Levine, ed., *Clotel*, 56.

11. Brown's condemnation of Northern racism and of the federal government's complicity in supporting slavery is very strong in the first edition of *Clotel*. It will be softened in the two book-form editions published in the United States during and after the Civil War.

12. *"The glory of my life"*: From Elizabeth Margaret Chandler (1807–1834), "The Bereaved Father," in *The Poetical Works of Elizabeth Margaret Chandler; with a Memoir of Her Life and Character*, by Benjamin Lundy (Philadelphia, 1836). See Robert S. Levine, ed., *Clotel*, 59.

13. *"Gone—gone—"*: From John Greenleaf Whittier, "The Farewell

of a Virginia Slave Mother to Her Daughters Sold into Southern Bondage" (1838). See Robert S. Levine, ed., *Clotel*, 59.

14. *"He would dream"*: Levine speculates that Brown, who wrote poetry, may be the author of these verses. See Robert S. Levine, ed., *Clotel*, 59.

15. William Edward Farrison, author of the definitive biography of Brown, notes that this passage gives "the false impression that Brown escaped from Price in Louisville instead of in Cincinnati." See William Edward Farrison, *William Wells Brown: Author and Reformer* (Chicago: University of Chicago Press, 1969), 216.

16. *"Behind he left the whip and chains"*: From anon., "The Flying Slave," a poem Brown included in *The Anti-Slavery Harp*. See Robert S. Levine, ed., *Clotel*, 61.

17. *George Fox*: Fox (1624–1691) was the British mystic who founded the Christian sect of the Quakers. Also known as the Society of Friends, Quakers believed in nonviolence and were against slavery.

18. In his *Narrative of William W. Brown, A Fugitive Slave, Written by Himself*, Brown recounts how his mistress, Mrs. Price, purchased Eliza in the hope that he would marry her. Brown comments: "The more I thought about the trap laid by Mrs. Price to make me satisfied with my new home, by getting me a wife, the more I determined never to marry any woman on earth until I should get my liberty." See William L. Andrews, ed. *From Fugitive Slave to Free Man*, 69. Strategically, Brown feigns interest in Eliza in order to seem more reconciled with his life as a slave and to dispel his owner's doubts about taking him on a trip to Cincinnati. Brown's plan worked, and in Cincinnati he made his escape. This is an instance of strategic lying which, though he thought it was amply justified by the grosser injustice of slavery, Brown does not include in *Clotel*'s prefatory autobiographical narrative, where he is interested in presenting himself to his readers as a straightforwardly reliable and trustworthy author. For an illuminating analysis of Brown's *Narrative*, see William L. Andrews, *To Tell a Free Story: The First Century of Afro-American Autobiography, 1760–1865* (Urbana, University of Illinois Press, 1986).

19. The name William had been given to him by his mother. Sandford, on the contrary, was the name that had been imposed on Brown, when he was a child, by his owner Dr. Young, who had just adopted a nephew named William. Brown discards the name Sandford immediately after his escape and goes back to his original name. William L. Andrews (*To Tell a Free Story*, 148) has

noted how in Brown's *Narrative* the change of name "signifies the transformation of the narrator from a man of deceitful appearances, signified by the false name he had to wear as a slave, into a radically changed man."

20. Brown uses names to signal his change of status. When describing his life as a slave, he refers to himself as William. After becoming free, he calls himself by his newly acquired last name, Brown. After he starts his public work as a temperance and abolitionist activist, he refers to himself as Mr. Brown.

21. *Exeter Hall:* Exeter Hall opened in London in 1831. It could seat three thousand and was regularly used for antislavery meetings. See Robert S. Levine, ed., *Clotel*, 63.

22. *6d.:* Six pence, or half a shilling.

23. *died in infancy:* Brown married Elizabeth Schooner, a free black, in 1834, just a few months after his escape from slavery. They had three daughters, one of whom died in infancy. The two daughters who survived were Clarissa and Josephine.

24. *"Is true freedom but to break":* From James Russell Lowell (1819–1891), "Stanzas on Freedom" (1844). See Robert S. Levine, ed., *Clotel*, 66.

25. *"Three Years in Europe":* Brown published his travel book *Three Years in Europe; or, Places I Have Seen and People I Have Met* in London in 1852.

26. *American Anti-Slavery Society:* A national abolitionist organization founded under the leadership of William Lloyd Garrison in 1833. It would be formally dissolved in 1877. The Western New York Anti-Slavery Society and the Massachusetts Anti-Slavery Society were among its many auxiliary societies. Garrison (1805–1879), a native of Massachusetts, was president of the American Anti-Slavery Society for more than twenty years, and he was also founder and editor of the abolitionist newspaper *Liberator* (1831–1865).

27. *Edmund Quincy, Esq.:* Brown sent the book to his last owner, Enoch Price. Price, in turn, wrote to Edmund Quincy, Esq. (see note 9), who had written a prefatory letter to Brown's *Narrative*.

28. *American journal:* The journal may be William Lloyd Garrison's *Liberator*, which printed pieces Brown wrote while in Great Britain.

29. *every man of note in the assembly:* Victor Marie Hugo (1802–1885) was a French poet, playwright, and novelist, author of such novels as *The Hunchback of Notre Dame* (1831) and *Les Misérables* (1862); the Abbé Duguerry was curé of the Church of

the Madeleine in Paris; Emile de Girardin (1806–1881) was a French journalist, politician, and writer; Richard Cobden (1804–1865) was a British economist and politician. Brown talks at greater length about these persons in his travelogue *Three Years in Europe* (1852).

30. *Newcastle-upon-Tyne:* A town on the river Tyne in the county of Tyne and Wear, in the northeast of England near the border with Scotland.

31. *Bolton, Lancashire:* A town in the northwest of England.

32. *Sheffield:* A town in the county of South Yorkshire, in the North of England.

33. *Whittington Club:* A prestigious club in London whose membership included Charles Dickens and several members of Parliament. Brown was made an honorary member of the club. See William Edward Farrison, *William Wells Brown*, 172.

34. *the Times:* This letter appeared in the London *Times* on July 4, 1851. See Robert S. Levine, ed., *Clotel*, 77.

35. *"Uncle Tom's Cabin":* Harriet Beecher Stowe (1811–1896) serialized *Uncle Tom's Cabin; or, Life among the Lowly* in Gamaliel Bailey's abolitionist newspaper *National Era* between June 1851 and April 1852. She published the novel in book form in March 1852. *Uncle Tom's Cabin* had an enormous success and became an international bestseller.

36. *"Mr. Willis's description":* The reviewer refers to Nathaniel Parker Willis (1806–1867), journalist, poet, editor, and dramatist native of Maine, who enjoyed great popularity in America. He published *People I Have Met* in 1850. He was the brother of Sarah Willis Parton, also known as "Fanny Fern" (1811–1872), journalist and novelist and one of the first women in the United States to have her own newspaper column.

37. *exigeant:* French for "particular, hard to please."

38. *pour se desennuyer:* French phrase for "to entertain themselves."

39. *extract from his writings:* Brown quotes from his volume *Three Years in Europe* (1852).

40. *Roscoe's "Leo X":* William Roscoe (1753–1831) was a British historian who published volumes on the Italian Renaissance, including the one Brown mentions: *The Life and Pontificate of Leo the Tenth* (1805). He was opposed to slavery and wrote *The Wrongs of Africa: A Poem* (1787).

41. *St. Martin's Church:* A church in London.

42. *"To be wise," says Pope:* From Alexander Pope (1688–1744), *An Essay on Man* (1734). See Robert S. Levine, ed., *Clotel*, 79.

43. *"learns to labour and to wait"*: From Henry Wadsworth Longfellow, "Resignation" (1848). See Robert S. Levine, ed., *Clotel*, 79.

44. *Frederick Douglass*: Douglass (1818–1895) was a fugitive slave who published a bestselling autobiography, *Narrative of the Life of Frederick Douglass, An American Slave, Written by Himself* (1845). He was the editor of the *North Star*, where the testimonial Brown refers to appeared on April 17, 1851. See Robert S. Levine, ed., *Clotel*, 79.

45. Brown separated from his wife, Elizabeth Schooner, in 1847 and took custody of their daughters, Clarissa and Josephine. They followed him to Europe, where they entered an established teacher-training institute, the Home and Colonial School in London. They became schoolmistresses and were appointed to teaching positions. Clarissa decided to remain in England, while Josephine followed her father back to the United States in 1855 but eventually returned to England in 1856. That same year she published a biography of her father, *Biography of an American Bondman, by His Daughter* (1856). In 1860 Brown married a black woman of Cambridgeport (Mass.), Annie Elizabeth Gray. They had two children: a boy, who died a few months after his birth, and a girl, who also died in her childhood (1862–1870). See William Edward Farrison, *William Wells Brown*. The daughter's name was Clotelle. As Brown notes in the dedication of the last edition of his novel, *Clotelle; or, The Colored Heroine* (1867), his wife "so much admired the character of Clotelle as to name [their] daughter after the heroine."

46. Brown's freedom was eventually purchased for $300 by British friends in 1854, thanks to negotiations made by Ellen Richardson of Newcastle-upon-Tyne, who belonged to the same family that had also collaborated in buying Frederick Douglass's freedom. See William Edward Farrison, *William Wells Brown*, 240.

CLOTEL; OR, THE PRESIDENT'S DAUGHTER

Chapter I: *The Negro Sale*

1. *"Why stands she near the auction stand"*: The opening stanza of anon., "The Slave Auction—A Fact," a poem included in Brown's *The Anti-Slavery Harp* (1848). See Robert S. Levine, ed., *Clotel; or, The President's Daughter: A Narrative of Slave Life in the United States* (Boston: Bedford/St. Martin's, 2000), 81.

2. *amalgamation of the races:* According to Robert S. Levine (*Clotel*, 81), Brown manipulates Henry Clay's argument: "Clay saw 'amalgamation' as the nightmarish but inevitable outcome of what the abolitionists wanted to impose on the United States. Clay advocated colonizing blacks to Africa precisely because he believed blacks were inferior to whites and that black-white unions were 'unnatural.' "

3. *John Randolph:* Randolph (1773–1833) was a statesman and orator from Virginia. He owned nearly four hundred slaves and thousands of acres of land. He was a defender of states' rights, but in his will he freed his slaves.

4. *the law says:* What follows is a shortened collage of excerpts from slave laws Brown had already cited in the appendix to his 1848 *Narrative* and which he had very probably derived from Theodore Dwight Weld's *The Bible against Slavery* (1837). Weld (1803–1895) was an abolitionist from Connecticut who authored also another text from which Brown drew documentary material he included in *Clotel*, entitled *Slavery As It Is: The Testimony of a Thousand Voices* (1839).

5. *chattels:* The term "chattel" defines an item of tangible movable or immovable property except real estate.

6. This long initial tirade against slavery was edited out of the following American editions of *Clotel*, where Brown also eliminates the prefatory autobiographical sketch as well as the last chapter documenting his sources, thereby making his book more assuredly fictional.

7. *quadroons:* Terms like "quadroon" or "octoroon," indicating a person who was considered to be one-fourth or one-eighth black, were part of a system of racial classification that is now obsolete.

8. This puzzlingly sweeping indictment of black women contrasts with the episodes of slave women's resistance to their master's sexual advances that Brown recounts in *Clotel*.

9. Farrison notes that this advertisement resembles one which appeared in the Charleston, South Carolina, *Mercury* for May 16, 1838, and which had been reprinted in Theodore Dwight Weld's *American Slavery As It Is* (1839). See William Edward Farrison, ed., *Clotel; or, The President's Daughter: A Narrative of Slave Life in the United States* (New York: Carol Publishing, 1989), 249.

10. *to fill a government appointment:* Since Thomas Jefferson resided in Washington from 1800 to 1809, the ages of his slave daughters seem to date the beginning of the action in *Clotel* around 1814, a

date which is inconsistent with other historical references found in the novel, including Nat Turner's revolt (1831) and Salome's trial (1844–1845). See William Edward Farrison, ed., *Clotel*, 249. This is the first of the many chronological inconsistencies that characterize *Clotel* and that Farrison points out in his biography of Brown. Brown seems to have been more interested in the efficacy of his plot than in the chronological accuracy of its sequence of events, a fact that proves the intended fictionality of his text and his awareness of the greater freedom available to novelists as opposed to historians.

11. This description of the sale of Clotel is very similar to the one in "A True Story of Slave Life," an earlier short story by Brown that had appeared in the *Anti-Slavery Advocate* in December 1852. See William Edward Farrison, *William Wells Brown: Author and Reformer* (Chicago: University of Chicago Press, 1969), 210.

12. "*O God! My every heart-string cries*": from anon., "The Slave Auction—A Fact," a poem included in Brown's *The Anti-Slavery Harp* (1848). See Robert S. Levine, ed., *Clotel*, 88.

Chapter II: *Going to the South*

1. "*My country, shall thy honoured name*": from R. C. Wateston, "Freedom's Banner," in Brown's *The Anti-Slavery Harp* (1848). See Robert S. Levine, ed., *Clotel; or, The President's Daughter: A Narrative of Slave Life in the United States* (Boston: Bedford/St. Martin's, 2000), 89.

2. *Dick Walker*: As described in the prefatory autobiographical "Narrative," the slave trader Brown himself worked for was named James Walker. By choosing the same last name for his fictional slave speculator, Brown once again emphasizes how his novel is founded in truth. In the American editions of *Clotel*, which will no longer include the autobiographical sketch of the author, Brown will change the trader's name to Dick Jennings.

3. *Father of Waters*: A reference to the Mississippi River.

4. "*getting the Negroes ready for market*": As he recounts in his opening autobiographical sketch, one of Brown's duties when he worked for Walker was to prepare the old slaves for market. In *Clotel* he expands on this real-life episode, showing his ability in fictionalizing autobiographical material.

5. "*I don't know which*": As part of the effort to undermine the personal identity of slaves, it was common to keep them ignorant of their birthdates. Frederick Douglass also comments on this aspect

of the psychological brutality of slavery at the very beginning of his autobiography (1845): "By far the larger part of the slaves know as little of their ages as horses know of theirs, and it is the wish of most masters within my knowledge to keep their slaves thus ignorant. I do not remember to have ever met a slave who could tell of his birthday. They seldom came nearer to it than planting-time, harvest-time, cherry-time, spring-time, or fall-time." See Houston A. Baker, Jr., ed., *Narrative of the Life of Frederick Douglass, An American Slave, Written by Himself* (New York: Penguin, 1986), 47. Like Douglass, in this passage of *Clotel* Brown emphasizes the resistance of the slaves and their use of the means at their disposal ("corn-planting time") to define their age.

6. *"bet the whole of the boy"*: This question implicitly contemplates the absurd possibility of betting only part of the boy. Brown takes to its extreme, paradoxical consequences the notion that human beings could be considered chattel property. This paradox anticipates the one at the heart of Mark Twain's *Puddn'head Wilson* (1894), i.e., the possibility of disposing of one half of a dog.

7. *Natchez*: A town on the Mississippi River in the southwestern part of the state of Mississippi.

Chapter III: *The Negro Chase*

1. *"all men are created free"*: Even when he does not explicitly mention Jefferson, Brown intersperses his novel with scathingly ironic references to the contrast between the ideals of the Declaration of Independence and the practice of American democracy.

2. Brown quoted this advertisement in the appendix to the second (1848) edition of his *Narrative*, where he said it had appeared in the Livingston County (Alabama) *Whig*.

3. *Actæon*: A Greek mythological figure, Actæon was a hunter who saw Artemis bathing naked. The goddess turned him into a stag that was then devoured by his own hounds.

4. Brown quoted a shorter account of this execution in the appendix to the 1848 edition of his *Narrative*, where he said it had appeared in the Natchez *Free Trader* on June 16, 1842. His different use of this account, which in *Clotel* is presented as the tragic ending of a longer story, shows how he transformed his documentary material into fiction.

Chapter IV: *The Quadroon's Home*

1. In this chapter Brown followed closely, and at times quoted verbatim, the first part of abolitionist Lydia Maria Child's short story "The Quadroons," which appeared in *The Liberty Bell* in 1842 and was republished in her volume *Fact and Fiction: A Collection of Stories* (1847). Child (1802–1880) was the author of an abolitionist work, *An Appeal in Favor of that Class of Americans Called Africans* (1833). Brown uses the rest of Child's short story in chapters VIII, XV, and XXIII. He acknowledged his debt to Child in the last chapter of *Clotel*, where he mentions her as one of his sources. Brown changed some details of Child's story, like the names of the characters (he renames the daughter Mary, avoiding the Spanish and Moorish exoticism of the name Child chose: Xarifa), the location (Richmond in Virginia, instead of Augusta, Georgia), as well as more important aspects of the characterization of the protagonists, which will be mentioned in subsequent explanatory notes.

2. *"a change come over the spirit of his dreams"*: From Lord Byron (1788–1824), "The Dream" (1816). Brown changes the quote from the first to the third person. See Robert S. Levine, ed., *Clotel; or, The President's Daughter: A Narrative of Slave Life in the United States* (Boston: Bedford/St. Martin's, 2000), 101.

Chapter V: *The Slave Market*

1. *"What! mothers from their children riven!"*: from John Greenleaf Whittier, "Expostulation" (1834). See Robert S. Levine, ed., *Clotel; or, The President's Daughter: A Narrative of Slave Life in the United States* (Boston: Bedford/St. Martin's, 2000), 103.

2. *"cat"*: Refers to a whip called cat-o'-nine-tails, which was usually made of nine knotted cords fastened to a handle.

3. The abolition of the international slave trade in 1808 stimulated and made very profitable the internal slave trade.

4. *"Where the slave-whip ceaseless swings"*: From John Greenleaf Whittier, "The Farewell of a Virginia Slave Mother to Her Daughters Sold into Southern Bondage" (1838). See Robert S. Levine, ed., *Clotel*, 104.

Chapter VI: *The Religious Teacher*

1. *"What! preach and enslave men?":* From John Greenleaf Whittier, "Clerical Oppressors" (1838). See Robert S. Levine, ed., *Clotel; or, The President's Daughter: A Narrative of Slave Life in the United States* (Boston: Bedford/St. Martin's, 2000), 106.

2. *The Rev. John Peck:* The character of Mr. Peck is based on the real-life Reverend Mr. Peck of Rochester, whose speech against inalienable natural rights Brown heard in 1846 at the convention of the New York State Liberty Party in Farmington, New York. See William Edward Farrison, *William Wells Brown: Author and Reformer* (Chicago: University of Chicago Press, 1969), 97–98.

3. *John Wesley:* Wesley (1703–1791) was a British theologian and the founder of Methodism. He was opposed to slavery and wrote *Thoughts upon Slavery* (1774).

4. *sons of Ham:* In Genesis, Ham is the second son of Noah. He surprised his father naked in a drunken stupor and derided him. When Noah learned about it, he cursed Ham's son Canaan and his descendants. Africans were believed to be descendants of Ham, and proslavery apologists invoked Noah's curse as a Biblical justification for African enslavement.

5. *Rousseau:* Jean-Jacques Rousseau (1712–1778) was a writer and philosopher of Swiss origin.

6. *Voltaire . . . Thomas Paine:* François Marie Arouet, known as Voltaire (1694–1778), was a French writer and philosopher. Thomas Paine (1737–1809) was a political writer of British origin who authored a pamphlet supporting the independence of the American colonies (*Common Sense*, 1776).

7. Snyder's sermon is based on two sermons by Reverend Thomas Bacon that had been published in London in 1749 and reprinted in the United States in 1813. See William Edward Farrison, ed., *Clotel; or, The President's Daughter: A Narrative of Slave Life in the United States* (New York: Carol Publishing, 1989), 250. Thomas Bacon (c. 1700–1768), was a slaveholding clergyman of the Church of England in Maryland. In the mid-1750s Bacon was involved in a criminal court case in Maryland. Rachel Beck, a mulatto, accused him of having committed adultery and fathering a child with her.

8. *hazelnuts:* Within the economy of Brown's novel, even sleeping or furtively cracking nuts during a proslavery sermon emerges as one of the many strategies of everyday resistance of the slave community.

9. *"When I can read"*: From Isaac Watts (1647–1748), *Hymns and Spiritual Songs* (1707). See Robert S. Levine, ed., *Clotel*, 114.

10. Here Brown provides an early glimpse of "the unguarded expressions of the Negro" on which he will comment explicitly in chapter XVI. When unheard by whites, slaves make fun of their masters' religious hypocrisy and reveal their own clear awareness of slavery as a system of exploitation. Brown's use of the vernacular in this scene emphasizes the critical wit of the slaves. As such, it is not so much a tool of comic characterization of blacks, but rather of whites' blatant, simple-minded proslavery propaganda.

Chapter VII: *The Poor Whites, South*

1. *Rev. Dr. Joel Parker*: Parker (1799–1873) was a Presbyterian clergyman and native of Vermont.

2. In contrast with the slaves' use of the vernacular in the previous chapter, here the use of nonstandard English characterizes these poor whites as unwittingly comic figures.

3. Brown set forth a similar argument about "how slavery makes labor disreputable" in the "Extracts from the American Slave Code" he appended to his 1848 *Narrative*. See William L. Andrews, ed. *From Fugitive Slave to Free Man: The Autobiographies of William Wells Brown* (New York: Mentor, 1993), 106. Brown's strategy to use a white character to express his critique of slavery and of its negative impact on whites as well as blacks will be adopted by following African American novelists.

Chapter VIII: *The Separation*

1. *"In many ways does the full heart reveal"*: From Samuel T. Coleridge's (1772–1834) "Eros aei lalethros etairos" ("Love, always a talkative companion," 1828). See Robert S. Levine, ed., *Clotel; or, The President's Daughter: A Narrative of Slave Life in the United States* (Boston: Bedford/St. Martin's, 2000), 120.

2. In this chapter Brown continues to follow closely, as he did in chapter IV, Lydia Maria Child's short story "The Quadroons," but he also makes some significant changes. He downplays the sentimentalism of Child's story, and instead emphasizes the condemnation of the institution of slavery in two ways: he interrupts the sentimental thrust of the scene by adding an explicit reference to the fact that "she [Clotel] was his [Horatio's] slave; her bones, and sinews had been purchased by his gold," and also has Clotel

use a strong, legalistic word ("crime") to refuse any further relation with a soon-to-be-married man.

3. *"After Clotel had been separated . . . to read and write"*: Brown adds these two sentences on Clotel's Christianity and literacy that were not present in Child's story, to give further depth to his protagonist and anticipate the spirit of resistance to slavery that she will also demonstrate in her escape and in her attempt to rescue her daughter.

Chapter IX: *The Man of Honour*

1. *"My tongue could never learn"*: Shakespeare, *Richard III*, I.ii, 183–185. See Robert S. Levine, ed., *Clotel; or, The President's Daughter: A Narrative of Slave Life in the United States* (Boston: Bedford/St. Martin's, 2000), 124.

2. The story of Clotel's sister, Althesa, and her husband, Henry Morton (see also chapters XV and XXIII), is an expanded version of the eighth view of Brown's *A Description of William Wells Brown's Original Panoramic Views* (1850). See William Edward Farrison, *William Wells Brown: Author and Reformer* (Chicago: University of Chicago Press, 1969), 174–175.

Chapter X: *The Young Christian*

1. *Rev. Theodore Clapp*: Clapp (1792–1866) was a Unitarian clergyman from Massachusetts who later moved to New Orleans, where he founded the New Orleans Unitarian Church of the Messiah in 1834. See Robert S. Levine, ed., *Clotel; or, The President's Daughter: A Narrative of Slave Life in the United States* (Boston: Bedford/St. Martin's, 2000), 126.

2. *vindicate the Bible*: In this chapter, Georgiana quotes several Biblical passages that abolitionists used to prove that the Bible did not defend slavery. Brown may have drawn on a book he quoted earlier in the novel (chapter I), Theodore Dwight Weld's *The Bible against Slavery* (1837).

3. *"God has created . . ."*: Georgiana quotes almost verbatim from the Bible: "God has made of one blood all nations of men for to dwell on all the face of the earth," Acts 17: 26. Abolitionists argued the common origin of all humankind, opposing the polygenic arguments of proslavery advocates. See, for instance, pastor Alexander McLeod's (1774–1833) *Negro Slavery Unjustifiable* (1802), in Mason Lowance, ed., *Against Slavery: An Abolitionist*

Reader (New York: Penguin, 2000), 73–74. It is interesting to note that the Biblical passage Georgiana quotes will provide the title for a later African American novel that was influenced by Brown's *Clotel*: Pauline E. Hopkins's *Of One Blood; or, The Hidden Self* (1902–1903).

Chapter XI: *The Parson Poet*

1. Both the advertisement and the prospectus had been reprinted in Theodore Dwight Weld's *American Slavery As It Is* (1839) from the Charleston *Mercury*. The *Mercury* specified that the college in question was the South Carolina Medical College in Charleston. See William Edward Farrison, ed., *Clotel: or, The President's Daughter: A Narrative of Slave Life in the United States* (New York: Carol Publishing, 1989), 250–251. Such medical practices were not uncommon. In the 1840s, a gynecologist born in South Carolina, James Marion Sims (1813–1883), conducted experiments on slave women for the surgical treatment of fistula cases. His autobiography, *The Story of My Life*, was published in 1884. Brown insists on the connections between racism and science also in the first American edition of his novel. In *Miralda*, Brown inserts a minor episode in which a woman is subjected to medical experiments to determine whether she "showed any signs of African descent" (December 22, 1860, 1). On medical experiments and racist arguments, see Sander L. Gilman, *Difference and Pathology: Stereotypes of Sexuality, Race, and Madness* (Ithaca: Cornell University Press, 1985).

2. Through Carlton, Brown dramatizes the process of understanding and interpretive retraining he hoped to inspire in his readers.

3. *rare specimen of poetical genius:* Brown ridicules the parson's poetic pretensions in ways that anticipate the comic tone that will characterize the following chapter, which focuses on the medical pretensions of the parson's slave Sam. The author thus undermines the supposed racial specificity of the stereotype of the self-important slave by juxtaposing it to the portrait of the self-important master.

Chapter XII: *A Night in the Parson's Kitchen*

1. Brown's repeated condemnations of intraracial color prejudice make clear that his choice of all-but-white characters (which is instrumental to showing the paradoxes of slavery embodied in the

living oxymoron of a "white negro") should not be misinterpreted as an assertion of white superiority. On the contrary, he asserts forcefully that "caste is owing to ignorance" (*Clotel*, 108).

Chapter XIII: *A Slave Hunting Parson*

1. " *'Tis too much prov'd* ": Shakespeare, *Hamlet* III.i, 51–53. See Robert S. Levine, ed., *Clotel; or, The President's Daughter: A Narrative of Slave Life in the United States* (Boston: Bedford/St. Martin's, 2000), 140.
2. As in most comic scenes in *Clotel*, Brown makes sure that his humor involves not only blacks but also whites. The ignorance of the slaves ridicules their master's attempt to show off with his Northern guest and also mirrors the ignorance of the slave-driver. Consistent with his condemnation of color prejudice among the slave population, he also makes sure to involve slaves of all shades in the comic scene.
3. *"Send Bibles to the heathen":* Georgiana's satirical lines exposing the religious hypocrisy of slaveholders anticipate the tone of Sam's song of resistance and emphasize Georgiana's understanding of the point of view of the slaves.
4. To underline the despotism of slavery, Brown shows how it limits the freedom of speech of whites as well. Like the slaves, Carlton has to take advantage of the master's absence to speak "more pointedly against slavery."
5. *"The big bee flies high":* Brown had included a couple of satirical poems similar in tone to Jack's toast in his volume *The Anti-Slavery Harp* (i.e., "A Song for Freedom" and "The Slave's Song").

Chapter XIV: *A Free Woman Reduced to Slavery*

1. *not born a slave:* Brown refers to a real-life case. The trial of Salome Miller, whose original name was Müller, was held in New Orleans in May 1844. Salome lost her suit but appealed to the state's supreme court and won her case in 1845. Articles about the case appeared in the *National Anti-Slavery Standard* for July 31, 1845, and January 1, 1846. See William Edward Farrison, *William Wells Brown: Author and Reformer* (Chicago: University of Chicago Press, 1969), 222. By emphasizing both the inefficacy of Althesa's legal efforts and the fact that Salome eventually regains her freedom only because, by sheer coincidence, she is recognized by a woman she had met on the boat that brought her from Europe to the United

States, Brown tells the story in a way aimed to condemn the absence of legal recourse against the injustices of slavery. His use of this historical episode shows once again his ability in fictionalizing documentary material.

Chapter XV: *To-Day a Mistress, To-Morrow a Slave*

1. *"I promised thee a sister tale"*; from Samuel T. Coleridge, "Introduction to the Tale of the Dark Ladie" (1799). See Robert S. Levine, ed., *Clotel; or, The President's Daughter: A Narrative of Slave Life in the United States* (Boston: Bedford/St. Martin's, 2000), 149. Lydia Maria Child quoted these verses at the beginning of her short story "The Quadroons."

2. In telling the story of Clotel and her daughter Mary after Horatio's marriage and his wife's discovery of his premarital relation, Brown departs from and expands Child's "The Quadroons." While Child focused mainly on the tragic individual fate of her sentimental heroines, Brown points to the systemic immorality of slavery and its crimes against the family (both black and white). In Child's story the protagonist dies a few months after being abandoned by her lover. The repenting lover takes care of his daughter and, after his death, his white widow generously carries on for a time her husband's wishes with regard to the child. In *Clotel*, on the contrary, Gertrude's jealousy and anger at her husband's deception transform her into an altered and revengeful person who basely mistreats Mary, while Horatio does not protect his daughter and also lets Clotel be sold to a slave trader. See also chapter XVII of *Clotel*, significantly entitled "Retaliation."

3. *as bad as the slaves of the United States*: The contention that the condition of European factory workers was worse than that of American slaves was frequently advanced by proslavery apologists. In the same year when *Clotel* was published, in the United States appeared a book entitled *The White Slaves of England. Compiled from Official Documents. With Twelve Spirited Illustrations* (Auburn, N.Y.: Derby and Miller, 1853). The author, John C. Cobden, outlines his argument as follows: "Sometimes slavery is founded upon the inferiority of one race to another; and then it appears in its most agreeable garb, for the system may be necessary to tame and civilize a race of savages. But the subjection of the majority of a nation to an involuntary, hopeless, exhausting, and demoralizing servitude, for the benefit of an idle and luxurious few of

the same nation, is slavery in its most appalling form. Such a system of slavery, we assert, exists in Great Britain" (13–14).

Chapter XVI: *Death of the Parson*

1. This is the first of the lessons in interpretation that Carlton (and Brown's readers) receives in this important chapter where the author provides the hermeneutic tools to understand his own strategy of representation of slavery.
2. This passage is a quote from Connecticut abolitionist Theodore Dwight Weld's *American Slavery As It Is* (1839). See William Edward Farrison, ed., *Clotel; or, The President's Daughter: A Narrative of Slave Life in the United States* (New York: Carol Publishing, 1989), 251.
3. In chapter XII, Sam uses the vernacular, while here his song is in standard English. This is an instance of the strategic bilingualism Brown confers on some of his folk characters. By using standard English, Brown may have also wanted to prevent superficially comic, minstrel readings of Sam's antislavery song.

Chapter XVII: *Retaliation*

1. *prejudice which is to be found among the Negroes:* In condemning it, Brown stresses how color prejudice within the black community is a reflection of the societal hierarchies that dominate the American nation at large. Dinah's enmity towards Clotel finds a deeper motivation in the first American edition of the novel, where Brown explains: "Dinah was the mother of thirteen children, all of whom had been taken from her when young; and this, no doubt, did much to harden her feelings, and make her hate all white persons" (*Miralda*, January 5, 1861, 1).
2. These quotes from Thomas Jefferson derive, respectively, from *Notes on the State of Virginia*, Query XVIII, and from his "Observations" of June 22, 1786. See William Edward Farrison, ed., *Clotel; or, The President's Daughter: A Narrative of Slave Life in the United States* (New York: Carol Publishing, 1989), 251.

Chapter XVIII: *The Liberator*

1. *Liberia:* the colony on the West African coast that the American Colonization Society (established in 1817) founded in 1821 with the purpose of removing free-born American blacks and emanci-

pated slaves to Africa. Many abolitionists, including Brown, opposed this colonization project (e.g., William Lloyd Garrison's 1832 *Thoughts on African Colonization*) and in this chapter Georgiana gives voice to some of their arguments.

2. Brown, who espoused the connections between abolitionism and women's rights, shows Georgiana's lack of power as a single woman. The means to acquire some control over her own property, and avoid having to obey her uncle's "counsel," is to marry a man who shares her goals.

3. *a meeting . . . to discuss the wrongs of woman:* Brown may be referring to the first American Women's Rights Convention that was held in Seneca Falls, N.Y., in 1848.

4. *Attucks:* Crispus Attucks escaped from slavery in 1750. On March 5, 1770, he participated and was killed in what became known as the "Boston Massacre," when British soldiers fired against a crowd of American colonists. He has been seen as the first casualty in the cause of American independence. See James Oliver Horton and Lois E. Horton, *Hard Road to Freedom: The Story of African America* (New Brunswick, N.J.: Rutgers University Press, 2001), 60–62.

5. Brown refers to the war of 1812–1814. The battle of New Orleans took place in 1815, after the treaty of peace had been signed. In New Orleans, General Andrew Jackson (1767–1845), who would later become the seventh president of the United States, recruited black troops to fight against the British. Winning this battle made Jackson a hero of the war and a national figure.

6. Brown quotes from the second proclamation Jackson issued during the war of 1812, in which he praised the courage of black troops. Levine notes that the proclamations were reprinted in 1851 in William Cooper Nell's *Services of Colored Americans in the Wars of 1776 and 1812.* See Robert S. Levine, ed., *Clotel; or, The President's Daughter: A Narrative of Slave Life in the United States* (Boston: Bedford/St. Martin's, 2000), 262–263. Nell (1816–1874), an African American historian and abolitionist from Boston, founded in 1858 the Crispus Attucks celebration, to honor the black patriot who died in the Boston Massacre. See *The Concise Oxford Companion to African American Literature*, eds. William L. Andrews, Frances Smith Foster, and Trudier Harris (New York: Oxford University Press, 2001), 310–311.

7. *General Wade Hampton:* Hampton, (1818–1902), Confederate general, governor of South Carolina, U.S. senator, came from a family of the planter aristocracy.

Chapter XIX: *Escape of Clotel*

1. *"The fetters galled my weary soul"*: From Elizur Wright, Jr. (1814–1885), "The Fugitive Slave to the Christian," in Brown's *The Anti-Slavery Harp* (1848). See Robert S. Levine, ed., *Clotel; or, The President's Daughter: A Narrative of Slave Life in the United States* (Boston: Bedford/St. Martin's, 2000), 165.

2. *Ohio river*: Because it separated the free states of Ohio and Pennsylvania from the slave states of Virginia and Kentucky, the Ohio River featured prominently in antislavery fiction as the boundary between slavery and freedom.

3. *Niagara river*: The Niagara River, which connects Lake Erie to Lake Ontario, is the border between the state of New York and Canada.

4. *her Britannic Majesty's dominions*: A reference to Canada.

5. William, like Sam before him (chapter XVI), represents another case of strategic bilingualism. When speaking privately to Clotel he uses standard English; during the escape, to increase his "authenticity" as the loyal servant of "Mr. Johnson," he speaks dialect; after reaching the free states he resumes standard English to argue with a white train conductor. Brown's novelistic depiction of his black characters' strategic use of language reinforces his emphasis on their profound knowledge of and resistance to prevalent racial and cultural hierarchies.

6. Clotel's plan is modelled after the real-life escape of William and Ellen Craft from slavery in Georgia in 1848. Brown lectured with the Crafts in the United States 1849 and later also in Britain. He was the first person to put in print their story in a letter ("Singular Escape") that appeared in the *Liberator* on January 12, 1849. The Crafts would publish their own autobiography, *Running a Thousand Miles for Freedom*, in 1860. See William Edward Farrison, *William Wells Brown: Author and Reformer* (Chicago: University of Chicago Press, 1969), 134–135.

7. *John C. Calhoun*: John Caldwell Calhoun (1782–1850) was a prominent politician (he served as secretary of war, vice president, senator, and secretary of state), political philosopher, and slaveholder from South Carolina who defended slavery and state rights. This episode involving Calhoun must be one of those that Brown acknowledged he "derived . . . from the lips of those who . . . have run away from the land of bondage" (*Clotel's* 208). Further blurring the boundary between fact and fiction, this episode (like Clotel's stagecoach ride in Chapter XXII) will later

be included also in Josephine Brown's description of the Crafts' escape in her biography of her father, *Biography of an American Bondman. By His Daughter* (1856), as well as in the Crafts' own autobiography, *Running a Thousand Miles for Freedom* (1860).

8. *Rubicon:* A small river in northern Italy. In 49 B.C., defying the Roman senate, Julius Caesar crossed it with his troops, a decision which led to civil war. In popular usage, "to cross the Rubicon" means to reach the point of no turning back.

9. Brown reports almost verbatim the account that an unidentified observer had written about the Crafts and that had been published in the Newark, New Jersey, *Daily Mercury* on January 19, 1849. See William Edward Farrison, ed., *Clotel; or, The President's Daughter: A Narrative of Slave Life in the United States* (New York: Carol Publishing, 1989), 252.

10. *Sandusky:* A town in Ohio, on the shores of Lake Erie.

11. *"Jim Crow":* A term that designates segregation. Originally, it was the name of a minstrel routine ("Jump Jim Crow") that, beginning 1828, Thomas Dartmouth ("Daddy") Rice performed in blackface and that became extremely popular.

12. *Diogenes:* A cynic philosopher in ancient Greece, fourth century B.C.

13. *no fiction:* In her 1856 biography of her father, Josephine Brown recounts, at times almost verbatim, a very similar episode Brown himself experienced in 1844 while travelling in Ohio.

14. *Thomas Corwin:* Corwin (1794–1865) was governor of Ohio, senator, and secretary of the Treasury.

15. *the Hon. Daniel Webster:* Webster (1782–1852) was a statesman born in New Hampshire. Though not in favor of slavery, he supported the Compromise of 1850. He was noted for his eloquent oratory.

16. *Edgartown:* A town on the island of Martha's Vineyard, Massachusetts.

17. *Solomon:* Son and successor of David, a mid-tenth-century B.C. king of Israel noted for his wisdom. Most of the information about him comes from the Bible.

Chapter XX: *A True Democrat*

1. *"Who can, with patience":* from Thomas Moore (1779–1852), "To the Lord Viscount Forbes. From the City of Washington," in *The Poetical Works* (1840–1841). See Robert S. Levine, ed., *Clotel; or, The President's Daughter: A Narrative of Slave Life in the United States* (Boston: Bedford/St. Martin's, 2000), 176.

2. *Nero:* Emperor of Rome from 58 to 68 A.D.

3. *Ethiopian:* A term used to refer to Africans. During the nineteenth century, "Ethiopianism" was a form of African American nationalism. It derived from a Biblical passage that could be read as a prophecy of deliverance: "Princes shall come out of Egypt; Ethiopia shall soon stretch out her hands unto God" (Psalms 68:31). For a discussion of Ethiopianism, see Wilson Jeremiah Moses, *The Golden Age of Black Nationalism, 1850–1925* (New York: Oxford University Press, 1978).

4. Levine (*Clotel*, 177) points out that African American writer David Walker (1785–1830) made a similar comparison between Roman and American slaves in his pamphlet *An Appeal to the Colored Citizens of the World* (1829).

5. Brown argued that "Slavery is a national institution" also in the appendix to his 1848 *Narrative*. See William L. Andrews, ed. *From Fugitive Slave to Free Man: The Autobiographies of William Wells Brown* (New York: Mentor, 1993), 88.

6. *rulers of every despotism:* Robert S. Levine (*Clotel* 148) identifies this list of despots as follows: Nicholas I (1796–1855) was czar of Russia from 1825 to 1855; Adb al-Majid (1823–1861) reigned as the Ottoman sultan from 1839 to 1861; Franz Joseph (1830–1916) was emperor of Austria from 1848 to 1916; Augustus (63 B.C.–14 A.D.) was the first Roman emperor; Marc Anthony and Marcus Aemilius Lepidus formed Rome's second triumvirate circa 43 B.C.

7. *Vandalism:* Vandals were Germanic barbaric hordes that invaded the Roman empire and sacked Rome in 455 A.D.

Chapter XXI: *The Christian's Death*

1. *"O weep, ye friends":* from D. H. Jacques, "Your Brother Is a Slave," in Brown's *The Anti-Slavery Harp.* See Robert S. Levine, ed., *Clotel; or, The President's Daughter: A Narrative of Slave Life in the United States* (Boston: Bedford/St. Martin's, 2000), 180.

2. *Labrador:* A peninsula on the Atlantic coast of Canada.

3. *Hebrides:* Islands west of Scotland.

4. *May-flower:* In 1620 the Puritan Pilgrim Fathers sailed aboard the *Mayflower* from Southampton, England, and settled in Plymouth, Massachusetts.

5. Dutch traders brought the first cargo of twenty Africans (including some women) to the English colony of Jamestown, Virginia in 1619.

These Africans were indentured servants, rather than slaves proper.

6. The United States Congress officially abolished the African slave trade and the importation of slaves in 1808.

7. *Plato and Socrates:* Plato (428 B.C.–348/347 B.C. and Socrates (470 B.C.–399 B.C.) were philosophers in ancient Greece.

8. James 1:27, Philippians 2:4, Hebrews 13:3, Matthew 7:12. See Robert S. Levine, ed., *Clotel,* 182.

9. *Colonization Society:* The American Colonization Society was founded in 1817 with the purpose of removing free-born American blacks and ex-slaves from the United States to Africa.

10. Georgiana's deathbed scene may recall Harriet Beecher Stowe's description of Little Eva's death in *Uncle Tom's Cabin* (1852), but its spirit is quite different. Unlike Little Eva, Georgiana succeeds in emancipating her slaves. As a result, in *Clotel* the slaves' devotion to their dying mistress does not simply heighten the pathos of the scene, but rather reenforces Brown's emphasis on their love for freedom.

11. *"Shall every flap of England's flag":* from John Greenleaf Whittier, "Expostulation" (1834). See Robert S. Levine, ed., *Clotel,* 185.

Chapter XXII: *A Ride in a Stage-Coach*

1. Farrison notes how Brown here skews his chronology once again. The only year when Martin Van Buren, William Henry Harrison, and Henry Clay were simultaneously considered by their parties as presidential candidated was 1839, and that date is inconsistent with information previously given about Clotel's and Mary's ages. See William Edward Farrison, ed., *Clotel; or, The President's Daughter: A Narrative of Slave Life in the United States* (New York: Carol Publishing, 1989), 252. Brown uses the presidential election to provide a fictional pretext for a discussion of politics and of other serious issues that interested him, including temperance. Throughout his life, Brown was an active supporter of the temperance cause.

2. *"Old Tip":* William Henry Harrison (1773–1841), ninth president of the United States, was born at the plantation of "Berkeley" in Virginia. In 1811 he won a battle against the Shawnee Native Americans at Tippecanoe (Indiana), which explains his nickname "Old Tip."

3. *Odd Fellows . . . mason . . . Son of Temperance:* Brown list various masonic organizations. Many of these lodges did not admit

African Americans to membership. See William Edward Farrison, *William Wells Brown: Author and Reformer* (Chicago: University of Chicago Press, 1969), 430.

4. *"Maine Law"*: Passed in 1851, the Maine Law banned the trade of liquor within that state.

5. *Lowell and Manchester . . . Birmingham*: Lowell in Massachusetts, and Manchester and Birmingham in England were factory towns.

6. *"three advertisements"*: Brown quoted from New Orleans newspapers several shorter advertisements of cock fights, turkey shootings, bullfights, and fights with bears and dogs in the appendix to his 1848 *Narrative*, to exemplify the brutal pastimes popular among Southerners who, because of slavery, had become inured violence.

7. Levine suggests that "Because the United States acquired California following the war with Mexico, Brown may have used this newspaper story to comment ironically on U.S. expansionism as incarnated by Andrew Jackson." See Robert S. Levine, ed., *Clotel; or, The President's Daughter: A Narrative of Slave Life in the United States* (Boston: Bedford/St. Martin's, 2000), 194. Jackson (1767–1845) was the seventh president of the United States.

8. Brown may have heard this story from William and Ellen Craft. A more detailed version of this episode of unwitting same-sex attraction (taking place on a train, rather than in a stagecoach) will be included also in Josephine Brown's description of the Crafts' escape in her biography of her father, *Biography of an American Bondman. By His Daughter* (1856), as well as in the Crafts' own autobiography, *Running a Thousand Miles for Freedom* (1860).

Chapter XXIII: *Truth Stranger than Fiction*

1. *"Is the poor privilege to turn the key"*: From Lord Byron (1788–1824), *Don Juan* (1819–1824), Canto X. See Robert S. Levine, ed., *Clotel; or, The President's Daughter: A Narrative of Slave Life in the United States* (Boston: Bedford/St. Martin's, 2000), 195.

2. *Yellow Fever*: Brown borrowed the description of this epidemic from a book just published in London: John R. Beard's *The Life of Toussaint L'Ouverture, the Negro Patriot of Hayti* (1853). See William Edward Farrison, ed., *Clotel; or, The President's Daughter: A Narrative of Slave Life in the United States* (New York: Carol Publishing, 1989), 252–253.

3. Brown continues (see chapters IX and XV) the story of Althesa

and Henry Morton, which he had told in a more concise version in the eighth view of *A Description of William Wells Brown's Original Panoramic Views* (1850). In contrast with the first version, in *Clotel* Brown follows the tragic fate of Althesa's daughters after they have been sold at the slave market. He emphasizes the sexual abuse fostered and institutionalized by slavery, but has both of his heroines die before being violated.

4. *Smithfield market:* A meat market in London.

5. As he has already done in chapters IV, VIII, and XV, Brown follows closely and expands the last part of Child's "The Quadroons," in connection no longer with the title protagonist Clotel (whose story becomes more combative and politically charged), but rather with the minor character of Althesa's younger daughter Jane. Brown continues to change Child's story in interesting ways. Whereas in "The Quadroons" Jane's lover was the son of an Englishman, Brown chooses instead a Frenchman, Volney Lapuc. The choice of this name is revealing of the attention that Brown, in writing his novel, devoted even to minute details. Constantin-Francois Chassebeuf de Boisgirais, better known as Volney (1757–1820), was a French writer and politician who, in his well-known book *Voyage en Egypte et en Syrie* (*Travels through Syria and Egypt,* 1787), had acknowledged the African origins of Egyptian art. He was seen by African Americans as a supporter of the cultural and artistic achievements of blacks, and as such he is mentioned also in a later African American novel like Pauline Hopkins's *Of One Blood* (1902–1903). Another important revision Brown makes to Child's story concerns the ending. In contrast with "The Quadroons," in *Clotel* Jane dies before being sexually abused, an authorial decision that shows Brown's unwillingness to advance the abolitionist cause at the expense of the fictional dignity of his female characters. For a radically innovative fictional portrayal of a black woman who survives rape, see Pauline Hopkins's *Contending Forces: A Romance Illustrative of Negro Life North and South* (1900).

6. This closing paragraph is absent from Child's "The Quadroons." It is important because Brown once again departs from the sentimental tone that dominates the closure of Child's story. Instead, he emphasizes the emblematic, though not necessarily representative, value of his all-but-white characters, moving from individual cases to a broader condemnation of slavery as an institution.

Chapter XXIV: *The Arrest*

1. *"The fearful storm"*: From Mrs. J. G. Carter, "Ye Sons of Free-dom," in Brown's *The Anti-Slavery Harp*. See Robert S. Levine, ed., *Clotel: or, The President's Daughter: A Narrative of Slave Life in the United States* (Boston: Bedford/St. Martin's, 2000), 200.

2. Brown borrowed the last two sentences from John R. Beard's *The Life of Toussaint L'Ouverture, the Negro Patriot of Hayti* (1853). See William Edward Farrison, ed., *Clotel; or, The President's Daughter: A Narrative of Slave Life in the United States* (New York: Carol Publishing, 1989), 253.

3. *"Nat Turner"*: Brown devoted an eloquent page in praise of Nat Turner also in the Appendix to his 1848 *Narrative*. In 1831, Turner led a slave insurrection in Southampton, Virginia. Brown presented him as "another Moses, whose duty it was to lead his people out of bondage," and as prophetic evidence "that the American slave will eventually get his freedom." See William L. Andrews, ed. *From Fugitive Slave to Free Man: The Autobiographies of William Wells Brown* (New York: Mentor, 1993), 85–86.

4. *Picquilo*: Brown modeled his depiction of Picquilo on the historical figure of Lamour de Rance, the Afro-Haitian revolutionary John R. Beard describes in *The Life of Toussaint L'Ouverture, the Negro Patriot of Hayti* (1853). See William Edward Farrison, ed., *Clotel*, 253.

Chapter XXV: *Death Is Freedom*

1. *"I asked but freedom"*: William J. Snelling's (1804–1848) anti-slavery poems were often printed in the *Liberator*. See Robert S. Levine, ed., *Clotel; or, The President's Daughter: A Narrative of Slave Life in the United States* (Boston: Bedford/St. Martin's, 2000), 216.

2. *Long Bridge*: A bridge over the Potomac River linking Washington, D.C., to Virginia.

3. *Mr. George W. Custis*: In his tale of the horrors of slavery, Brown evokes another slaveholding founding father of the American republic, George Washington, the first President of the United States. George Washington Parke Custis (1781–1857) was the son of John Parke Custis, the stepson of George Washington. Following the early death of his father, he grew up under Washington's charge at Mount Vernon, Virginia.

4. Brown points to the American hypocrisy of supporting revolutionary movements abroad while keeping blacks enslaved at home. Other abolitionists advanced this argument, including James Freeman Clarke (1810–1888) in *Slavery in the United States* (1843). See Mason Lowance, ed., *Against Slavery: An Abolitionist Reader* (New York: Penguin Books, 2000), 67.

5. *"Now, rest for the wretched!":* Brown quoted this poem, "The Leap from the Long Bridge" from Grace Greenwood's (1823–1904) collection *Poems* (1851). See William Edward Farrison, ed., *Clotel; or, The President's Daughter: A Narrative of Slave Life in the United States* (New York: Carol Publishing, 1989), 254. He changed the next to last stanza and added a final one that, by invoking once again George Washington, ironizes on the contrast between American democratic ideals and slaveholding practices. Brown's explicit satire deeply revises the more pathetic thrust of Greenwood's original poem.

Chapter XXVI: *The Escape*

1. *"No refuge is found":* from A. E. Atlee, "The Star Spangled Banner," *Liberator*, 13 September 1844. See Robert S. Levine, ed., *Clotel; or, The President's Daughter: A Narrative of Slave Life in the United States* (Boston: Bedford/St. Martin's, 2000), 210.

2. In this and the next two chapters the story of Mary is borrowed from Brown's *Three Years in Europe* (1852), Letter XXII. See William Edward Farrison, ed., *Clotel; or, The President's Daughter: A Narrative of Slave Life in the United States* (New York: Carol Publishing, 1989), 254.

3. *as white as most white persons:* In the three subsequent American editions of *Clotel* Brown will no longer describe George as all but white but rather as dark-skinned.

4. George echoes Frederick Douglass's speech "What to the Slave Is the Fourth of July?" (1852).

5. Robert S. Levine (*Clotel*, 213) points out that this is a paraphrase of Jesus's admonition in Matthew 23.37–38. Brown substitutes Washington for Jerusalem.

6. *"Star of the North!":* From John Pierpoint (1785–1866), "The Fugitive Slave's Apostrophe to the North Star," in *Airs of Palestine and Other Poems* (1840). See Robert S. Levine, ed., *Clotel*, 214.

7. This episode involving Quakers, who were also called "Society of Friends," can be read as a tribute to Quaker Wells Brown, who

helped Brown during his own escape. In gratitude, Brown dedicated to Wells Brown the first edition of his *Narrative* (1847).

Chapter XXVII: *The Mystery*

1. George's shame of his African descent contrasts with his previous portrayal as a proud slave freedom fighter. Aware of the possible prejudices of his British audience, Brown may have decided to make George pass in order to avoid discussing the issue of color discrimination in Europe. Similarly, George's faithfulness to Mary neutralizes the threat of black male sexuality.

2. Like his focus on the marriage plot, Brown's deferment of the happy ending, which underlines the long-term consequences of the familial disruption caused by slavery, will strongly influence other nineteenth-century African American novelists like Frances E. Harper (1825–1911) and Pauline E. Hopkins (1859–1930).

3. *adopted his master's name:* In his *Narrative*, on the contrary, Brown declared that he "always detested the idea of being called by the name of either of my masters." See William L. Andrews, ed. *From Fugitive Slave to Free Man: The Autobiographies of William Wells Brown* (New York: Mentor, 1993), 74.

4. *Dunkirk:* A French town on the North Sea near the border with Belgium.

5. *Roscoe's Leo X:* This is the same book Brown reads in the "Narrative" (*Clotel*, 37). As in the aforementioned case of Walker the slave-trader (chapter II), these details that connect Brown's autobiographical sketch with his novel serve to impress almost subliminally on the minds of his readers the fact that his fiction was founded in truth.

Chapter XXVIII: *The Happy Meeting*

1. *"Man's love is of man's life":* From Lord Byron (1788–1824), *Don Juan* (1819–1824), Canto I. See Robert S. Levine, ed., *Clotel; or, The President's Daughter: A Narrative of Slave Life in the United States* (Boston: Bedford/St. Martin's, 2000), 220.

2. *"sent out of the state":* In the American editions of Brown's novel, the heroine is also severely whipped for helping her lover escape from prison.

3. *Mobile:* A coast town in southern Alabama.

4. *Havre:* Le Havre is a town on the northern coast of France.

5. *"A woman's whole life":* From Washington Irving (1783–1859),

"The Broken Heart," in *The Sketch Book* (1819–1820). See Robert S. Levine, ed., *Clotel*, 224.

6. Brown closes the novel on a note that would be flattering for his British readers, while at the same time chastizing the United States for being less democratic than "old" Europe.

Chapter XXIX: *Conclusion*

1. Brown who, even in the opening autobiographical sketch, has always referred to himself in the third person, here uses the first. He addresses the reader directly, speaking as an author, documenting his sources, and arguing his right to make "free use" of them. He makes sure that his readers understand the aims of his novel by explaining once again his antislavery goals, and he incites them to become actively involved in the fight against slavery. This chapter, where Brown tries to bridge the boundary between fact and fiction, revealing some residual caution about his new role as novelist, will not be included in any of the subsequent American editions of *Clotel*.

2. Though contemporary reviewers and later scholars have often read *Clotel* in light of Stowe's bestselling *Uncle Tom's Cabin* (1852), Brown does not acknowledge Stowe's novel among his sources. Many African American critics and intellectuals, at the time as well as later, disassociated themselves from Stowe's portrayal of slave culture. Nevertheless, her book became a touchstone for abolitionist literature. This fact has led to many misinterpretations of the originality of early African American fiction, which is too often read as an attempt "to imitate the literary productions of Euro-Americans." See Frances Smith Foster, ed., *Minnie's Sacrifice, Sowing and Reaping, Trial and Triumph: Three Rediscovered Novels by Frances E. W. Harper* (Boston: Beacon Press, 1994), xxiii. Brown's specific case is particularly revealing of the reciprocal, intricate, and yet to be fully explored, artistic interconnections between black and white writers in the United States. As William Edward Farrison has pointed out, the twentieth view of Brown's *A Description of William Wells Brown's Original Panoramic Views* (1850) "portrayed a young woman with a child in her arms in flight from slavery in Kentucky crossing the Ohio River . . . by jumping from one cake of ice to another," an incident that had been reported in the antislavery press in 1848 and 1849. This is an episode that Stowe would retell one year later in *Uncle Tom's Cabin* as the story of Eliza's

escape. See William Edward Farrison, *William Wells Brown: Author and Reformer* (Chicago: University of Chicago Press, 1969), 176.

3. From Reverend Edward S. Matthews's "Statistical Account of the Connection of the Religious Bodies in America with Slavery" (1851). See William Edward Farrison, ed., *Clotel; or, The President's Daughter: A Narrative of Slave Life in the United States* (New York: Carol Publishing, 1989), 254.

4. *Year of Jubilee:* In the Old Testament, every fifty years, during the year of Jubilee dedicated to God, slaves would be freed.

5. *"earth indeed yield her increase":* Psalms 67:6–7. See Robert S. Levine, ed., *Clotel; or The President's Daughter: A Narrative of Slave Life in the United States* (Boston: Bedford/St. Martin's, 2000), 227.

APPENDIX A

FROM *MIRALDA; OR, THE BEAUTIFUL QUADROON.*

Chapter XXXIII: *The Happy Day*

1. The typescript of the last four chapters of *Miralda* was kindly provided by Prof. Christopher Mulvey (King Alfred's College, Winchester, England), editor of *Clotel by William Wells Brown: An Electronic Scholarly Edition* (Adam Matthews Publications Ltd., http://www.adam-matthew-publications.co.uk 2003).

2. *Cowper:* William Cowper (1731–1800) was one of the most widely read English poets of his day. He wrote verses also against the slave trade. The quotes that open each chapter in *Miralda* and in the 1853 edition of *Clotel* do not appear in the two American book-form editions of the novel.

3. *Jerome . . . Miralda:* In *Miralda*, Brown changes the names and the description of some of the protagonists. Isabella is the new name of the brave heroine who returns South to save her daughter but dies in the attempt, while the title heroine, now renamed Miralda, is her daughter, who eventually succeeds in escaping to France. The hero, whose name was George, is renamed Jerome. In contrast with the British edition of *Clotel*, where he was described as all-but-white, in *Miralda* Jerome is "of pure African

origin" and "perfectly black" (*Miralda*, January 19, 1861, 1). In the two subsequent American book-form editions, Brown will preserve all of these changes with the exception of the name of the title heroine, who will be named Clotelle.

4. *Rhine:* The Rhine River is a major waterway of the European continent. Rising in the Alps, it flows north, passing through Switzerland, Liechtenstein, Austria, France, Germany, and the Netherlands.

5. *Antwerp:* an important seaport city in northern Belgium, near the Dutch frontier.

6. *the Rhine surpasses them all:* Brown lists important rivers in the United States (Mississippi, Hudson), Italy (Tiber, Po, Mincio), England (Thames), France (Seine), Egypt (Nile), and the Middle East (Euphrates).

7. *"Childe Harold":* These two sentences and the following long quote from *Childe Harold's Pilgrimage* will not appear in the subsequent American book-form editions of *Clotel*. *Childe Harold's Pilgrimage* is a narrative poem by the English Romantic poet Lord Byron (1788–1824). The third canto, from which Brown quotes, was published in 1816. It describes the pilgrim's travels to Belgium, the Rhine, Switzerland, and the Alps.

8. *Coblentz:* Now known as Koblenz, a city in western Germany, at the juncture of the Rhine and the Moselle rivers.

9. *Brussels:* The capital of Belgium.

10. *In his native country . . . :* This and the next sentence will not be included in the subsequent American editions of *Clotel*, where Brown, for reasons that are explained in the introduction to this Penguin Classics volume, will soften both his critique of race prejudice in the North and also his contrastive celebration of the greater freedom African Americans enjoyed in Europe. At the time when *Miralda* was published, the king of Belgium was Leopold I, who reigned from 1831 to 1865.

11. *Cologne:* A large city in western Germany, a river port on the Rhine.

12. *Geneva:* A Swiss city which lies at the southwestern corner of Lake Geneva.

13. *Calvin:* John Calvin (1509–1564), French theologian, settled in Geneva, Switzerland. He was one of the most important Protestant Reformers of the sixteenth century.

14. This entire paragraph will not be included in the two subsequent American book-form editions of *Clotel*.

Chapter XXXIV: *Miralda Meets Her Father*

1. *Mrs. Hemans:* Brown may be quoting Mrs. Felicia Dorothea Hemans, née Browne (1793–1835), a well-known and prolific British poet whose work was very popular in the United States.
2. *Ferney:* The name of the property that French writer and philosopher Voltaire (1694–1778) bought in 1758 in Switzerland, near the border with France and where he spent the remainder of his life.
3. *Lake Lemon:* Brown misspells the French name ("Lac Léman") of Lake Geneva. The spelling error will be corrected in the subsequent American book-form editions of *Clotel*. Lake Geneva lies along the French-Swiss border.
4. *Henry Linwood:* In the first edition of *Clotel*, the name of the heroine's father was Horatio Green. His new name, Henry Linwood, will be kept also in the two subsequent American editions.
5. *"the tortures of that inward hell":* From Lord Byron, *The Giaour: A Fragment of a Turkish Tale* (1813). See Robert S. Levine, ed., *Clotel; or, The President's Daughter: A Narrative of Slave Life in the United States* (Boston: Bedford/St. Martin's, 2000), 311.
6. *Mrs. Miller:* Gertrude's mother, Mrs. Miller, was not mentioned in the first edition of *Clotel*. In *Miralda* and in the two subsequent American editions of the novel, Gertrude will be presented as a more sympathetic character, while the blame for mistreating her husband's mulatto daughter will fall mostly on Gertrude's cruel mother.
7. *"In the sight of God . . .":* This polemical sentence praising Europe in opposition to the United States will not be included in the subsequent American editions.
8. *Mont Blanc:* The highest peak in the Alps. It lies along the Italian-French border.

Chapter XXXV: *The Father's Resolve*

1. *Maria Weston Chapman:* Chapman (1806–1885), Massachusetts abolitionist and reformer, was an important figure in the Boston Female Anti-Slavery Society. She collaborated with abolitionist leader William Lloyd Garrison and for several years edited *The Liberty Bell*.
2. *Our own conditions . . . :* This and the next six paragraphs, which include Jerome's outspoken harangue against slavery and in defense of black rights, as well as Miralda's speech against race

prejudice, will not be included in the subsequent American editions, where Brown's commitment to the Civil War and to Reconstruction will lead him to soften the tone of his critique of the United States, since the country has finally become a home, however inhospitable.

3. *literary characters:* Brown lists major European intellectuals and writers. Jean-Jacques Rousseau (1712–1778) was a French philosopher and political theorist of Swiss descent; Lord Byron (1788–1824) was a major English Romantic poet; Edward Gibbon (1737–1794) was a celebrated English historian, author of *The History of the Decline and Fall of the Roman Empire* (1776–1788); Voltaire (1694–1778) was an important French writer and philosopher, best known as the author of *Candide* (1758); Madame de Stael (1766–1817) was a renowned French woman of letters who also maintained a salon for leading intellectuals of her time. Shelley probably indicates the English Romantic poet Percy Bysshe Shelley (1792–1822), but may refer to his wife, novelist Mary Wollstonecraft Shelley (1797–1851), author of *Frankenstein* (1818).

Chapter XXXVI: *Conclusion*

1. This chapter is not included in the two subsequent American editions.

2. *Halleck:* Brown may be quoting the Connecticut-born poet Fitz-Greene Halleck (1790–1867), a member of the Knickerbocker group. He was highly regarded as a poet in his time. His statue can be found in New York City's Central Park.

3. *Jerome Fletcher:* While in the British edition of *Clotel* the all-but-white hero George, once free, decides to adopt his master's last name, in *Miralda* and in the subsequent American editions Jerome will refuse to do so and will choose a different last name: Fletcher. Brown himself made a similar decision, as he describes in his autobiography: "I always detested the idea of being called by the name of either of my masters. And as for my father, I would rather have adopted the name of 'Friday,' and been known as the servant of some Robinson Crusoe, than to have taken his name." See William L. Andrews, ed. *From Fugitive Slave to Free Man: The Autobiographies of William Wells Brown* (New York: Mentor, 1993), 74–75.

4. *"a little lower than the angels":* Psalms 8:5.

5. *"have dominion over the fish . . ."* Genesis 1:26.

6. *Lyons:* A city in east central France.

7. *Paris:* The capital of France.

8. *Dunkirk:* A French town on the North Sea near the border with Belgium.

9. This short paragraph is the only part of this chapter that is retained in the subsequent American book-form editions, where it is placed at the end of chapter XXXIV.

10. In *Miralda,* as well as in the other two American editions, Brown's novel is not preceded by any ancillary autobiographical narrative, and the author also shows a less pronounced interest in providing documentary evidence. In the closing paragraph of *Miralda,* he does, however, insist on the truthfulness of his "tale." In the 1864 edition, a brief biographical sentence is included by the publisher, James Redpath, at the end of the novel. In 1867, Brown himself adds a short new preface (dated Cambridgeport, June, 1867) where he asserts: "Although romantic in many if its details, it [*Clotelle*] is, nevertheless, a truthful description of scenes which occurred in the places which are given. Both Clotelle and Jerome are real personages. Many of the incidents were witnessed by the author." In his closing reference to his own mixed family background (his father was a relative of his master), Brown's tone blends scathing irony with Christian faith in ways that foreground once again his rhetorical ability as a critic of the immorality of slavery.

APPENDIX B

FROM *CLOTELLE: A TALE OF THE SOUTHERN STATES* (1864)

Chapter XXXV: *The Father's Resolve*

1. *the Fletchers:* Brown is referring to Clotelle and Jerome. In this edition, Brown does not include the story of Jerome's choice of his last name, Fletcher, which he told in the last chapter of *Miralda.*

2. *J.R.:* the initials of James Redpath (1833–1891), the American abolitionist journalist and editor of Scottish origin who published this edition of *Clotel.* He was the author, among other works, of *The Roving Editor, or Talks with Slaves in the Southern States* (1859).

APPENDIX C

FROM *CLOTELLE; OR, THE COLORED HEROINE. A TALE OF THE SOUTHERN STATES* (1867)

Chapter XXXVI: *The Return Home*

1. Chapters XXXIII–XXXV of this edition are identical to those of the 1864 *Clotelle* and, therefore, have not been included in this appendix. Chapters XXXVI–XXXIX, however, are new and take the action of the novel up to the time of its publication.

2. *Fort Sumter:* On April 12, 1861, the Federal military installation of Fort Sumter in Charleston Harbor (North Carolina) was the site of the first Confederate aggression, which signalled the outbreak of the Civil War.

3. *Jerome and Clotelle Fletcher:* In these four new chapters, no mention is made of the fate of Clotelle's son by her deceased French husband.

4. *Major-Gen. B. F. Butler:* Benjamin Franklin Butler (1818–1893) was a Union army officer during the Civil War, and later became congressman and governor of Massachusetts. He refused to return fugitive slaves to the Confederacy, choosing instead to consider them "contraband of war," an interpretation later upheld also by the United States government. In 1862, Butler led Union forces in the victorious expedition against New Orleans.

5. *the Crescent City:* The location of New Orleans, Louisiana, along a bend in the Mississippi River accounts for its popular nickname of "Crescent City."

6. *"Angel of Mercy":* Brown previously used this phrase in his autobiography to describe a Ohio woman who, despite her husband's objections, fed him and helped him during his escape. Brown comments: "I was never before so glad to see a woman push a man aside! Ever since that act, I have been in favor of 'woman's rights!'" See William L. Andrews, ed. *From Fugitive Slave to Free Man: The Autobiographies of William Wells Brown* (New York: Mentor, 1993), 79.

7. *Port Hudson:* The site, in Louisiana, of an 1863 battle, one of the many bloody Civil War battles in which African American troops proved their military valor.

8. *Lieut. Col. Bassett:* Commander of the First Louisiana Native Guards, whose field officers were African American.

Chapter XXXVII: *The Angel of Mercy*

1. *Andersonville Ga.:* A village in Sumter County, in west-central Georgia, which was the site of a Confederate military prison in 1864–1865. The inadequate conditions at the prison led to the death of thousands of prisoners. After the end of the Civil War, the prison commander was tried and hanged.

2. *strains:* As was the case with Sam in the British edition of *Clotel,* Pete's resistance initially finds expression in songs. However, unlike Sam's, Pete's duplicity now emerges as patriotic, because in the context of the Civil War his struggle for liberation is paralleled by a similar commitment on the part of his country.

3. *How to escape . . . :* Brown's emphasis on the difficulties and the dangers faced by Union soldiers who attempted to escape, increases the reader's understanding of the even greater obstacles slaves encountered in their fight for freedom, as described in earlier chapters of the novel.

Chapter XXXIX: *Conclusion*

1. *The fiendish and heartless conduct . . . :* Brown underlines how during the Civil War the unchecked violence sanctioned by slavery turns against Union soldiers. Significantly, Brown here chooses an adjective ("fiendish") that in chapter XVII of the 1853 edition he had used to describe Gertrude's mistreatment of her husband's mulatto daughter.

2. *Greenville:* A city in south central Alabama.

3. *secesh:* Secessionist.

4. *"The worst of slaves is he whom passion rules":* From Thomas Franklin (1721–1784), *The Earl of Warwick* (1766), I.iii, 109. See Robert S. Levine, ed., *Clotel; or, The President's Daughter: A Narrative of Slave Life in the United States* (Boston: Bedford/St. Martin's, 2000), 324.

5. *"Revenge, at first though sweet":* From John Milton (1608–1674), *Paradise Lost* (1667), book IX. See Robert S. Levine, ed., *Clotel,* 324.

6. *Morpheus:* Greek dream god, son of Hypnos, god of sleep.

7. *Leakesville:* A town in southeastern Mississippi, near the border with Alabama.

8. *Sherman ... Grant ... Lee:* major military figures in the Civil War. Both William Tecumseh Sherman (1820–1891) and Ulysses S. Grant (1822–1885) were Union Generals. Grant would later become the eighteenth President of the United States. Robert Edward Lee (1807–1870) was a Confederate General. His surrender at Appomattox, in Virginia, on April 9, 1865, is commonly viewed as signalling the end of the Civil War.

9. *Poplar Farm:* In all three American editions of *Clotel*, the house where the title heroine works as a slave on her own father's property is described as surrounded by poplar trees. "Poplar Farm" appears also in Brown's last autobiographical volume, *My Southern Home: or, the South and Its People* (1880).

FOR THE BEST IN PAPERBACKS, LOOK FOR THE

In every corner of the world, on every subject under the sun, Penguin represents quality and variety—the very best in publishing today.

For complete information about books available from Penguin—including Penguin Classics, Penguin Compass, and Puffins—and how to order them, write to us at the appropriate address below. Please note that for copyright reasons the selection of books varies from country to country.

In the United States: Please write to *Penguin Group (USA), P.O. Box 12289 Dept. B, Newark, New Jersey 07101-5289* or call 1-800-788-6262.

In the United Kingdom: Please write to *Dept. EP, Penguin Books Ltd, Bath Road, Harmondsworth, West Drayton, Middlesex UB7 0DA.*

In Canada: Please write to *Penguin Books Canada Ltd, 10 Alcorn Avenue, Suite 300, Toronto, Ontario M4V 3B2.*

In Australia: Please write to *Penguin Books Australia Ltd, P.O. Box 257, Ringwood, Victoria 3134.*

In New Zealand: Please write to *Penguin Books (NZ) Ltd, Private Bag 102902, North Shore Mail Centre, Auckland 10.*

In India: Please write to *Penguin Books India Pvt Ltd, 11 Panchsheel Shopping Centre, Panchsheel Park, New Delhi 110 017.*

In the Netherlands: Please write to *Penguin Books Netherlands bv, Postbus 3507, NL-1001 AH Amsterdam.*

In Germany: Please write to *Penguin Books Deutschland GmbH, Metzlerstrasse 26, 60594 Frankfurt am Main.*

In Spain: Please write to *Penguin Books S. A., Bravo Murillo 19, 1° B, 28015 Madrid.*

In Italy: Please write to *Penguin Italia s.r.l., Via Benedetto Croce 2, 20094 Corsico, Milano.*

In France: Please write to *Penguin France, Le Carré Wilson, 62 rue Benjamin Baillaud, 31500 Toulouse.*

In Japan: Please write to *Penguin Books Japan Ltd, Kaneko Building, 2-3-25 Koraku, Bunkyo-Ku, Tokyo 112.*

In South Africa: Please write to *Penguin Books South Africa (Pty) Ltd, Private Bag X14, Parkview, 2122 Johannesburg.*